Star Song

Also Available from Shadowpaw Press

SHADOWPAWPRESS.COM

Paths to the Stars

Twenty-Two Fantastical Tales of Imagination

One Lucky Devil

The First World War Memoirs of Sampson J. Goodfellow

Spirit Singer

Award-winning YA fantasy

The Shards of Excalibur Series

Five-book award-nominated YA fantasy series

From the Street to the Stars

Andy Nebula: Interstellar Rock Star, Book 1

Shapers of Worlds

Science fiction & fantasy by authors featured on the Aurora Award-winning podcast *The Worldshapers*

Right to Know

Falcon's Egg

Far-future science fiction adventure

Star Song

Edward Willett

SHADOWPAW
PRESS

STAR SONG

Published by
Shadowpaw Press
Regina, Saskatchewan, Canada
www.shadowpawpress.com

First Printing July 2021

Print ISBN: 978-1-989398-03-6
Ebook ISBN: 978-1-989398-04-3

Cover art by Dan O'Driscoll
Interior design by Shadowpaw Press
Created with Vellum

Chapter One

Music shivered across the mirror-like surface of the secluded lake, tucked into a pocket canyon in the granite wall of the Featherwood Mountains. The trees that gave the mountains their name trailed pale-blue fronds in the water as though enraptured by the shimmering sound.

Kriss Lemarc lifted his hands from the fingerplates of the touchlyre, and the music faded away. He took a deep breath. *Not bad*, he thought. *Not bad at all*. The song was a new one, and it didn't have words yet. He'd ask Mella to help him with those that evening when he played it for her for the first time.

He put the instrument down beside him on the flat surface of the boulder on which he sat, then leaned back, stretching his legs. His skin, still wet from his latest swim, shone in the late-afternoon sunlight. He was naked, but that didn't matter out here: in all the years he'd been coming to the lake, since he was old enough for Mella to let him go off on his own for an afternoon, he'd never seen another soul.

The Black Rock villagers tended to stay close to their fields and houses.

Just as well, he thought. They didn't like him, and he didn't like them. The first time Mella had taken him down to the village with her as a small child, he'd clung to her skirt, frightened by the frown on almost every grown-up's face. Oh, they took Mella's money as she bought the things they couldn't grow or make for themselves, but only one or two of them smiled at her or at him. And later, he'd had to ask Mella what an "offworld bastard" was, words he'd heard muttered behind his back as they passed two men lounging outside a bar.

Mella had smiled sadly and told him not to worry about it. "It's just because you look different from their own children," she'd said. "Some people are like that."

Nothing had improved over the years. He avoided the village as much as he could, but sometimes he had to go down there. The villagers had grown only more hostile over the years. When he was little, his pale complexion and fair hair had made him stick out among the brown-skinned, black-haired Farrsians. Now he was taller than anyone in the village, too: he'd sprouted with puberty and towered over Mella, who had once seemed so tall to him.

Maybe things were better in Cascata, the capital city, site of Farr's World's only spaceport, where surely offworlders were more common, but out here in the boondocks, the native Farrsians never let him forget he wasn't one of them.

He sighed, wishing his thoughts hadn't gone down that particular well-trodden and unpleasant road. By way of changing the mental subject, he picked up the touchlyre again, not to play, but to admire. He ran his fingers over the three gently curving sides and the smooth, swelling back, remembering when Mella had given it to him.

Mella had been his guardian since his parents had died in an aircar accident when he was a baby. She'd never told him very much about them, and he'd never seen the touchlyre until what she said was his twelfth standard birthday (although he'd only been ten and a half Farrsian years old). In the cozy main room of their cottage, with a fire blazing in the hearth to ward off the chill of the cold air flowing down from the mountains, she'd opened a triangular case of red leather he'd never seen before—he still didn't know where she'd hidden it—revealing the touchlyre.

He'd stared at it with wide eyes. He'd never seen anything so beautiful. Made of black wood—stormwood, he thought, from one of the local trees—it had a roughly triangular body and a long neck. Six silver strings, glinting orange in the firelight, were strung from copper pegs, three to the side, near the top of the neck—but not at the very top: there, a plate of copper gleamed. Another plate of copper, this one oval, shone on the instrument's body, just to the right of the strings. There was no opening into the body like Kriss had seen in the guitars and zimrithers he'd admired in a shop window in the village, and no tuning keys.

"Where did it come from?" he'd asked Mella. "Who does it belong to?"

"Your father made it," she told him. "And it belongs to you." She touched the soft black wood of the body. "He carved and shaped it with his own hands," she said softly, "and all the time he worked on it, he talked about how much he looked forward to having a son or daughter to give it to. I'm just glad he left it with me for safekeeping before . . ."

Her voice trailed off. She looked back up at Kriss. "Just like he did you."

Before the aircar crashed that killed him and my mother, Kriss thought. With a lump in his throat, he, too, reached out and touched the wood. "How do you play it?"

"I'll show you," Mella said. She took it from its case and helped him position it, resting the broad base on his legs so that the slender neck rose to his left ear.

He touched the strangely keyless pegs. "How do you tune it?"

"It doesn't need tuning," Mella said. "It tunes itself."

"Cool," Kriss said. He'd flicked his fingers across the strings so that they gave a musical chime. "Do you play it like a guitar?"

"No," Mella said. "Your father called it a touchlyre. Put your fingers on the copper plates."

He put his left hand on the plate at the top of the neck, and his right hand on the plate on the body. Instantly, the strings shivered to life. He snatched his hands away, and they silenced.

Mella laughed at his startled face. "See?" she said. "A touchlyre. Try again."

He touched it again, and this time kept his fingers on the plates. The strings vibrated with a formless but pleasant sound.

"Now close your eyes," she said, "and play a song in your mind."

He blinked. "What song?"

"What's your favourite?"

"Um . . ." He closed his eyes again, trying to think, but his mind had gone blank. The first thing that finally came to mind was a silly Old-Earth children's song Mella used to sing to him when he was little. *Baa, baa, black sheep, have you any wool* ran through his mind . . .

. . . and the touchlyre played it. Perfectly and beautifully. His eyes snapped open, and he stared down at the strings. "Wow," he breathed.

"Wow," Mella agreed, her round, wrinkled face beaming. But then the smile vanished, and she leaned toward him, putting a hand on his knee. "But remember this, Kriss: this is very, very important. You must never let anyone else see this instrument or hear you play it."

He'd just been imagining himself giving concerts in front of cheering crowds in Cascata. The daydream vanished. "Why?" He looked down at the touchlyre. "It's just a musical instrument."

"It's not," Mella said. "It's more than that."

"What? How? What is it?"

Mella had just shaken her head. "I can't tell you. Not yet. I promised your parents. Not until you are older."

I'm older now, Kriss thought, sitting on the boulder and looking at the touchlyre. But apparently, he wasn't old enough. He'd just had his sixteenth standard birthday—very close to his fourteenth Farr's World birthday, though Mella had always celebrated the standard ones. ("You get more that way," she'd pointed out, so he'd never argued.) He'd asked her again, and she'd refused again. "Your eighteenth birthday," she said. "That's what I promised your father. On your eighteenth standard birthday, I'll tell you what the touchlyre is. Then, you'll be old enough to decide what to do with it."

Mella, he thought, *I love you, but sometimes I think you still think I'm a baby.*

The touchlyre looked as beautiful now as it had in the firelight the night she'd given it to him, orange light giving a warm glow to the dark wood, the silver strings, the copper plates . . .

Wait a second. Orange light? He sat up straight and looked west, out the mouth of the little canyon, where the lake emptied itself into a noisy stream, tumbling down rocks toward the foothills rolling into the hazy distance. The sun was almost to the horizon. He'd have to run to make it home in time for supper.

He scrambled up, pulled on his clothes and boots, shoved the wrappings from his earlier lunch of bread and cheese into his slingpack, stuffed the touchlyre into its red-leather case, slung the pack's strap over his right shoulder and the touchlyre case's strap over his left, and then plunged in among the featherwood trees.

There wasn't exactly a path between the lake and Mella's cottage—he'd always varied his approaches to the lake to make sure there wasn't one since he didn't want anyone else to find his secret spot—but he knew the woods well, and even running in the gathering twilight, he didn't make a misstep.

He smelled smoke before he saw the cottage through the trees, which had darkened from the light-fronded featherwoods to the darker, spikier stormwoods of the lower slopes, and grinned even as he panted for breath: Mella had promised Earthbeef tonight, and there was nothing Kriss loved more than a rare—

He burst into the farmyard and skidded to halt, unable for a moment to process what he was seeing.

The smoke came not from Mella's cookfire but from the

cottage itself, or what was left of it: nothing but tumbled, blackened bricks and a few charred beams, flames still licking around them. The heart of the cottage, where he had slept the night before, where he had slept and played and sung and laughed and cried his whole life, was a hellish pile of glowing embers.

"Mella!" he screamed, and ran toward the cottage, but the heat drove him back before he even reached what was left of its walls. He'd come at it from the back, and now he stumbled around to the front, to where the door should have been, and the garden, and the path that led down the hill toward Black Rock, ten kilometres distant.

The garden was still there, but it had been trampled, all their precious Earth vegetables and Mella's beloved flowers crushed into the black dirt, the marks of booted feet everywhere.

Something lay on the path, *a bundle of old clothes*, his mind told him first, *that's all*, but he knew, even as he thought that, that it was nothing of the sort, that it was . . .

. . . Mella.

He dropped to his knees in the dirt beside her. She lay face down, and he rolled her over. Her pale-blue eyes stared sightlessly up at him. He looked for blood, or burns, but there wasn't a mark on her.

There wasn't a mark on her, but she was dead.

Heart attack? Stroke? Had the fire broken out, and the fear and stress had . . .

No, he thought then, staring at the bootmarks in the dirt all around Mella's body, in the trampled garden, going right up to the door of the cottage . . .

Not just bootmarks. There were pieces of clothing, some

his, some Mella's, the broken pieces of a table that had been beside Mella's bed, shattered crockery, a spilled bag of flour, a wheel of cheese, other scraps of food . . .

Someone had come to the cottage. Someone had ransacked the cottage, and then someone had burned the cottage. Maybe they hadn't deliberately killed Mella, but they'd killed her just the same.

Someone? Sick fury rose in him. *Someone?* He knew who it had to be.

The villagers. The Black Rock villagers.

Again, he heard their voices in his mind, the muttered comments he'd heard his whole life, since that first time Mella had taken him with her into town. *"Offworld bastard . . ." "What did she bring him here for?" "Not one of us . . ."*

Once, he'd overheard two men wondering in whispers—but whispers that had carried to his young ears—just how much money Mella had tucked away. "Always able to buy whatever she needs," one of them murmured. "I figure she was left a bundle by the boy's parents. Hidden up there in that cottage of hers . . ."

He'd told Mella about that. She'd laughed it off. "Would I be living in a three-room cottage without indoor plumbing outside of Black Rock if I were rich? I'd be in Cascata—or on some other planet." She told him she'd said as much to some of the villagers when she'd overheard similar rumours . . . but just denying something like that wouldn't have made the rumours go away. In fact, it might have strengthened them.

Had strengthened them, because here was the proof.

Villagers had come to rob Mella. He was sure of it. Maybe the fire had been an accident. Maybe they'd knocked over a lantern or kicked something into the fireplace. Maybe they'd fled when the cottage started to burn. Maybe Mella had still been alive then.

Maybe. But whether they'd meant it or not, they'd killed her, as surely as if they'd come to the cottage to murder her.

And no . . . he was alone.

The enormity of it hit him then, penetrating his anger, overwhelming everything else. He buried his face in his hands and wept, body heaving with shuddering sobs of a type he'd never experienced before, seized with grief that nothing in his life had ever come close to matching.

But he couldn't cry forever. Eventually, he raised his head. Night had fallen, only the barest hint of light remaining in the western sky. The glowing embers at the heart of the burned-out cottage gave very little light, but it was enough for Kriss to do what he had to do.

The garden shed had been ransacked, too, but he found the shovel not far from its door, and as the stars wheeled above him and the glow of the embers grew dimmer and dimmer, he dug a grave in Mella's beloved garden and buried her there.

His muscles ached, and he was exhausted, but he knew he wouldn't sleep. He sat by the grave in the dark for a long time, staring into the forest. He wanted to say some words over the grave, but they wouldn't come. He'd never been to a funeral. He didn't know what was customary . . . and even if he had, doing what was customary on Farr's World would have felt like a betrayal after what the villagers had done to Mella.

But maybe there was something he could do.

He retrieved his touchlyre from where he had set it aside

while he was digging the grave. He took it from the case, and, sitting cross-legged on the ground, held it in playing position, thinking that perhaps he could play some of Mella's favourite songs, that he might find some comfort in that.

He touched the copper plates.

The touchlyre screamed, a discordant wailing that sent sleeping starklings screaming skyward from the stormwood trees, and he snatched his fingers back, shocked: he'd never heard the touchlyre make a sound like that before.

Except . . . somehow, it had been right. Somehow, the touchlyre had perfectly captured his emotional upheaval in that one, horrible screech. And so, with tears once more streaming down his face, he touched the plates again. He did not think of music, of a melody or chords or rhythm, but simply let all his grief and love and loneliness pour up into his soul, and from there into the touchlyre.

The initial discord repeated, but then shifted and softened into shimmering, sorrowful clouds of sound that pulled his pain from his body, letting it fall like rain all around the darkened clearing.

How long he played, he didn't know. His eyes were closed from the beginning. At some point, even as the music welled out of him, he fell asleep.

He woke cold and stiff on his back in the dirt, the touchlyre cradled in his arms. Groaning, he got up, used the still-standing outhouse, and then began rooting through the scattered contents of the cottage for anything that might be useful.

He found bread, and an unbroken bottle of oil, and a few tomatoes, and made his breakfast from that. The wheel of cheese went into his backpack, as did some sticks of summer sausage and a couple of loaves of crusty bread he had to brush the dirt from. In all, he gathered what he though was perhaps seven or eight days' worth of food. His canteen had been in his slingpack, and of course he had the blanket he'd been sitting on beside the lake, so there was that, at least. His slingpack also held, in an inside pocket, all the money he owned: a dozen coins of various denominations, totalling not quite a fed.

Scrounging the contents of the cottage scattered around the yard, he found a shirt he could salvage, another pair of pants, two pairs of socks, and one pair of underwear. He wished he had a weapon, but not even a kitchen knife had survived.

By mid-morning, he was set. He had all the supplies he could gather and carry. He had his touchlyre.

And he had a plan.

My parents were offworlders, he thought, looking down at Mella's grave. *You never told me anything more than that. You never told me where this touchlyre came from, only that my father made it, and to never let anyone else see it . . . but I know it uses technology from offworld, too.*

He looked up at the blue sky. Last night, that sky had blazed with stars. Somewhere out among those stars, he must have relatives . . . uncles, perhaps. Aunts. Grandparents. Cousins . . .

Somewhere out there, he had family.

Whatever made the touchlyre work had to come from somewhere specific. It was the key to his past, the key to finding out more about his parents, the key to finding whatever family he might still have among the widespread planets of the Commonwealth.

With that key, he would open the door to his future.

He turned his back on the still-smoking ruins of the cottage that was the only home he'd ever known, and on the fresh grave of the woman who had been the closest thing to a parent he had ever know, the woman who had raised him and fed him and sheltered him and loved him, and he walked down the path without looking back, toward his future.

Toward the stars.

Chapter Two

Eight days later, Kriss toiled up a hill in the hot sun along a narrow path he'd thought was a shortcut when he'd left the main road a few kilometres back, a path offering no shade since it wound through the stumps of a recently logged native forest. There were Earth-tree saplings among the stumps, but it would twenty years before *they'd* provide any shelter from the sun.

His slingpack was almost empty, other than his change of clothes (not exactly clean anymore, since he'd been alternating the clothes in the pack with the ones he'd been wearing), and the touchlyre wasn't particularly heavy, but all the same, he was ready to wish them both to the bottom of the ocean.

Actually, the bottom of the ocean was beginning to sound good to him, too: at least it would be cool.

Something stabbed his foot, and he groaned. And *now*, he had something in his shoe.

He limped over to a stump and sat down on it. He pulled

the boot off and turned it upside down. Nothing fell out. He thumped the heel against the stump. No luck. He thumped it again, harder, this time swearing for good measure. Whatever it was *still* refused to come out.

Frustrated beyond measure, he threw the boot into the grass on the other side of the footpath—and then forgot all about it as the stump and the ground began to shake.

The rumbling vibration quickly swelled to a full-throated, crackling roar. Kriss twisted around to look up the slope. His heart leaped into his throat and pulled him to his feet as a tiny, glittering needle, riding a pillar of white fire, soared into view. He craned his neck to follow its ascent, watching it dwindle to a white-hot speck and vanish. Then, without bothering to put his boot back on, he ran up the hill.

Sweat stinging his eyes, heart pounding, stockinged foot bruised, Kriss crested the ridge and stared down, at long last, at Cascata.

The descending slope was also covered with stumps, so there were no trees to block his view of the capital of Farr's World, which sprawled across a vast plain, huge, smoky, and more daunting than he had ever imagined.

At its centre, beyond the rough wooden buildings of the city's verge, the jumbled structures of brick and stone farther in, and a handful of glittering glass towers, four silvery, slender spires shimmered like mirages in the middle of a vast, fenced-in duracrete rectangle—the spaceport. Smoke blowing across the pavement and trailing into the sky bore mute, fading testimony to the thunderous departure of the starship he had seen streaking into the sky moments before.

Kriss took a deep breath, suddenly feeling very young and alone. His food was gone. All he had left was his canteen, his clothes, a paltry sum of money, and the touch-lyre. It didn't seem like much with which to challenge the universe.

Challenging the universe half-shod didn't seem like a good idea, either, so he went back down the hill, retrieved his boot, and with several more solid thumps against the boulder (and some more swearing) managed, at last, to loosen and dump out the foot-plaguing pebble. Then he turned the boot right-side-up again prior to slipping it back on—and paused, blindsided by the memory of Mella's wrinkled hands patiently working a heavy needle through the thick leather, while she jokingly complained about the way he seemed to outgrow each pair of boots almost before she could make them.

He ran a finger over the boot's fine stitching. Then he took a deep breath, roughly shoved the boot back onto his foot, and stamped on the heel. Mella, and his childhood, lay dead and buried eight days behind him, beneath the fresh black mound of earth beside the trampled garden and now-cold embers of the burned-out farmhouse.

He could not change the past, and the future he had mapped out for himself would not happen unless he *made* it happen. Sitting by the side of the road wasn't going to do it.

But before anything else, he had to report Mella's death to the police. *The villagers*, he thought for the thousandth or ten-thousandth time. *The villagers who attacked the cottage have to pay.*

He tried to brush some of the dust from his faded blue shirt and black pants—the "clean" change of clothes when he'd set out—with little success. Then he wiped grimy sweat from his forehead, took a deep breath, and climbed up the ridge once more.

Once he was down the slope, the footpath took him between split-rail fences, corn to his left, wheat to his right, and then joined a much wider road that swept in from the north—re-joined it, really, since if he hadn't taken his "shortcut," he would have ended up in this exact same place. It had changed, though: when he'd left it, it had been gravel. Here, it was paved.

He looked left and right as he stepped onto the road. He saw a handful of people on foot in both directions, though nobody was very close. A horse-drawn wagon trundled along the road to his right, approaching the outskirts of the city . . .

And then, suddenly, as he looked that direction, something bright-red roared past, so close Kriss jumped back, tripped, and fell hard on to his rear end. He barely noticed, almost bouncing back to his feet so he could stare after the disappearing vehicle. *A groundcar!* He'd heard of them from Mella, but he'd never seen one. When he'd asked why there weren't any around Black Rock, she'd explained that complex machinery, electronics, and other high-tech devices were enormously expensive on metal-poor Farr's World. Those that existed did not make their way to the hinterland.

Making sure to stay well away from the middle of the road, Kriss hurried in the groundcar's wake. What other wonders might await in Cascata?

He soon found out. As he entered the city, the road became more and more crowded, with more wagons, more groundcars (though moving at more sedate speeds), massive automated transports, and, most of all, more people—more people than he had ever seen. Fortunately, there were now sidewalks, so the risk of getting run over lessened—or, at least, it did after he almost stepped off the curb in front of a transport, jumping back at the last second. After that, he made a point of looking both ways at every intersection.

Between his offworld colouring and height and his rumpled, dusty clothes, he felt painfully conspicuous, but no one spared him a second glance. Within a few blocks, he began to relax and enjoy a sensation new to him: anonymity.

At its outer edges, apart from the vehicles, Cascata seemed just a larger, dirtier, and much more crowded version of Black Rock. But after he had walked long enough to have passed through Black Rock a dozen times, the buildings changed from wood and plaster to brick and stone, the homes and shops and warehouses far grander than anything in Black Rock. And always, in the distance, gleamed the glass towers of the city's centre—and beyond them, he knew, lay the starships.

The road he had followed into the city eventually dumped him into a flagstone-paved courtyard with a bustling produce market. Aware of the suspicious gazes of the shoppers and sellers, he hurried across it to a new, smooth-surfaced road that arrowed straight downtown between warehouses whose blank walls, punctuated by loading docks, plunged him into shadow, a relief from the unremitting heat of the sun. Also a relief: no one else was on the sidewalks to stare at him. The road seemed devoted to automated transports, blank, silver, box-shaped drive units pulling multi-wheeled flatbed trailers. One of them hummed toward him and past him as he started down the road; he heard clanging noises behind him, and turned to see that it had pulled up in front of one of the loading docks, where men were now stacking bright-yellow metal boxes onto the trailer.

He turned and continued toward the spaceport. The transport soon passed him going the other way, stopping again at another loading dock a little farther on. He crossed to the other side of the street to avoid it. Ahead, the road ended in a T-intersection with a much broader road, along which traffic passed in both directions. Beyond that stood a tall fence, and beyond that, a vast expanse of duracrete, baking in the sun . . .

Sore feet forgotten, he broke into a run, burst out onto the busy road, dodged traffic to cross it, clung to the wire-mesh fence on the far side of it—and drank in his first close-up view of starships.

Curved, mirrored flanks cast back sharp reflections of the city and narrowed to needle-sharp, glittering prows pointing at the sky.

At the stars.

At his future.

Kriss drank in the sight, silently vowing he would be aboard one of those vessels when it launched. He saw someone come around a landing strut of the nearest ship, a slender figure, a young boy or girl—he couldn't tell at that distance—and his heart ached with the desire to be *that* youth, to stand there, at the base of a starship, to gaze out at a strange new world he had never visited before . . .

Then something much closer drew his attention: two men, just crossing the field, dressed alike in beige uniforms. Very tall and very pale, they walked with a strange, fluid grace.

Offworlders!

One of them looked up and saw him staring, and elbowed the other, who glanced Kriss's way and laughed. Kriss flushed and turned away, the assurance he had felt a moment before gone like a pricked puffplant, the young figure standing at the base of the distant starship forgotten. He looked up at the impersonal government towers. He had yet to talk to the police, and the afternoon was half over. It would soon be night, a night he would spend alone and without shelter in a strange city.

One thing at a time. Maybe the police could help.

When at last he found the police tower, halfway around the spaceport, he ran up the imposing flight of steps—and stopped, staring at his dusty, dishevelled reflection in the mirrored surface of the door. He couldn't blame them if they just locked him up.

Then at least I'll have a place to spend the night, he thought.

He stepped forward, and the door slid aside, taking his reflection with it.

Chapter Three

Tevera Annacrosta Evangeline di'*Thaylia* stepped off the dark-blue non-skid surface of the personnel disembarkation ramp, which extended like a rude tongue from between the landing struts of the starship that gave her her surname, and walked out onto the sun-baked expanse of blackened duracrete that passed for a spaceport on the backwater planet known as Farr's World. Of all *Thaylia*'s regular stops, it was the least prepossessing. Even the cargo they would take on here was boring: a type of grain prized on a far wealthier world for the making of gourmet pasta.

The snow-capped peaks in the distance looked far more interesting than the "city" of Cascata. Tevera knew, because she'd looked it up, that they were called the Featherwood Mountains, but she had no idea why they had such an intriguing name and knew she would never visit them to find out. She wondered how they compared to the ones on Feldenspar, the only world she'd ever lived on, and wished she could find out . . . but Family members did not stray far from the ports where they landed. Her life lay in the ship behind her, not at the bottom of a gravity well. Planets, the Family taught, were traps for the unwary, full of dangers, and how could she argue with that when her own parents had . . .?

Her mind shied away from the memory, as it usually did. She had only been six, in the standard Earth years the ship used, when they had been killed, and yet every day, though ten years had passed, she felt their absence like a hole in her heart.

You're being maudlin, she told herself.

And anyway, Cascata wasn't *completely* without merit: tonight, she and her brother, Rigel, would pay a visit to Andru's, where there was good food and drink to be had, and the opportunity to talk with crewmembers of other ships. *Bethelda*, which had just launched, had been the only other Family ship in port, but the crew of the Union ships with which they still shared the field would have news and gossip to share, even if they would have to be more guarded with them about their own ship's travel plans and cargo.

Two beige-clad Union crewmen were even then crossing the field in the distance, heading to one of the gates into the city. Beyond them, she glimpsed, outside the fence, another figure, a boy, she thought. She heard distant laughter from the Union men, and the boy suddenly turned and left the fence. She frowned. Spacefarers all made fun of worldhuggers, Family as well as Union, but she'd found their jokes less funny since their forced sojourn on Feldenspar. She'd gotten to know quite a few worldhuggers then, wandering farther afield than would ever have been allowed if they had not been grounded for repairs. Their lives were different, but they were people, all the same. She hoped the boy at the fence hadn't been too offended by whatever the Union men had said.

"Hello, little sister," said a voice behind her, and she glanced over her shoulder to see Rigel descending the ramp. Like her, he wore a pale-blue one-piece crewsuit with the scarlet image of a ringed planet embroidered over the left breast, the sigil of *Thaylia*. Unlike her, he wore two silver pips on his collar, indicative of his rank . . . nothing exalted, but considerably more exalted than her, since she would not formally receive rank until her eighteenth birthday.

He grinned at her, and she smiled back, but his expression soured as he joined her and looked out across the blackened pavement. "Stars, what a depressing place."

"I was thinking the same thing," Tevera said.

"Nice of you to keep me company while I arrange for the loading of the cargo," Rigel said. "It won't be very exciting."

"Better than staying cooped up in my cabin."

Rigel glanced at her, mouth quirking. "A planet, better than *Thaylia*?"

She flushed. "You know what I mean." Rigel had some sense of her un-Family-like attraction to planets. She'd talked about her infatuation with Feldenspar a bit too openly right afterward, and he'd expressed some concern that she might have picked up romantic notions of worldhugger life. She'd laughed it off and quit talking to him—or anyone else—about her enjoyment of the planet, but he'd never forgotten, and occasionally, like now, reminded her of it.

There's nothing wrong with liking planets, Tevera thought. *We all came from Earth originally. We still use its days and years. It doesn't mean I'm planning to leave the Family, or I don't like the Family, or I don't love* Thaylia. *It just means I don't hate planets.*

She gave her brother a friendly punch in the arm. "You like getting away from the ship when we're in port, too," she said. "Remember Shepardalia? I caught you staggering back on board in the middle of the night, smelling like a distillery. And cheap perfume."

Rigel winced. "Don't remind me." He looked up at the sun. "The afternoon's getting on. Let's get moving."

He set off across the hot duracrete. Tevera followed him, but not without one more glance at those distant, inviting mountains.

KRISS STEPPED INTO A HUGE, austere vestibule, with towering white walls and a floor of black stone. A thin, middle-aged woman in a grey uniform sat at a long white counter, behind which were six black doors. She looked up from a datascreen as he approached, and her lips pursed in disapproval. "What do you want?"

"I . . ." He cleared his throat. "I have to report a . . . a murder."

Her expression soured even further, if that were possible. "Second door, third office on the right. Lieutenant Carlo Elcar." She looked back down at her screen, dismissing him.

"Thank you," Kriss said to the top of her head. He walked toward the unmarked door she had indicated. Lieutenant Elcar would be different. He would *care.*

The door slid silently open as he approached, revealing a

long, utterly straight corridor, with the same antiseptically white walls, punctuated by closely spaced black doors. The third on the right bore Lieutenant Elcar's name in neat white letters. Kriss raised his hand to knock, but the door slid open before he touched it and, feeling foolish, he stepped through.

A short, pudgy man in a grey uniform like that of the woman at the counter, except with silver braid on the collar and cuffs, sat behind a glass-topped black desk. It, the chair where he sat, and a backless stool of silvery metal on Kriss's side of the desk were the only furnishings in the small office. Not so much as a family photo marred the pristine white walls.

"Lieutenant Elcar?" Kriss said.

"That's what it says on the door," Elcar said, his broad, brown Farrsian face impassive. "Have a seat."

Kriss sat down on the cold, hard stool.

"Name?"

"Kriss Lemarc. My—"

"Age?"

"Sixteen, standard. Look, I'm here because—"

"Local units, please."

Kriss felt a flash of irritation. "Fourteen. But why does that—"

"Address?"

"Listen to me!" Kriss snapped. "My—"

"I will listen to you in due course," Elcar said. "But there are procedures that must be followed. Address, please?"

Kriss clenched his fist, down where the policeman couldn't see it. "Black Rock. It's a village near—"

"I know the place. Parents' names?"

"I don't know." He felt a pang. Something else Mella had

said she'd tell him when he was older, always refusing to answer his questions, no matter how much he pleaded or, sometimes, yelled. Something else he hoped to learn, if he ever escaped Farr's World. "They died when I was a baby."

"Legal guardian, then."

"Mella Thalos."

"And where is she?"

"Dead. Murdered. *That's why I'm here!*"

"I see." Elcar tapped the glossy black surface of his desk with a fingertip. Lights chased across it. "When and where did she die?"

"Eight days ago. In Black Rock."

The lieutenant looked up. "Eight days? Why didn't you report it sooner?"

"I couldn't walk any faster."

"Black Rock has a constable. Why didn't you tell him about this supposed murder?"

Supposed? "Because I think the villagers killed Mella! And he might have been in on it!" Kriss glared at the policeman. "You sound like you think *I* did it!"

"I'm not accusing anyone. I don't have enough information." Elcar tapped his desk again. Something blinked at him. Looking at it instead of Kriss, the lieutenant said, "Why do you think the villagers killed your guardian?"

Kriss took a deep breath, trying to tamp down his anger. Mella had been murdered, and nobody seemed to give a damn, except him. "Maybe I'd better start at the beginning."

"Maybe you'd better," Elcar agreed. He tapped the desk again, and it went blank. He looked up at Kriss. "There's something very strange here."

"I know. Me." Kriss ran a hand through his hair. *Blond*

hair, he thought. *Like no one else's in Black Rock.* "Look, I don't know anything about my parents except they died when I was a baby. Mella was a friend of theirs, so she looked after me. She never told me anything more about them. She told me she would when I was older, but . . ." He paused. The lieutenant sat quietly, hands folded. "Aren't you going to take notes?"

"Everything is being recorded. Go on."

Kriss glanced at the blank desk. "All right. Eight days ago. I hiked out to a lake not far from the farm and spent the day swimming, fishing, just being lazy." He didn't say anything about playing the touchlyre, Mella's warning about letting anyone else know about it still nestled uncomfortably in the back of his mind, a warning clearly tied to the mysterious identity of his parents. "I . . . lost track of time. Before I knew it, the sun was going down. I'd promised to be home by sunset, so I ran . . ."

He told the rest of the story: running home, carefree, through the forest, smelling smoke, discovering the ruins of the cottage, finding Mella dead in front of it near her trampled garden, the marks of booted feet all around. He described how he had buried her.

By the time he finished, he could barely squeeze out the words through the fresh grief squeezing his throat. His voice choked off. *If only I had been there. If only . . . if only . . .* He looked down at his hands. They trembled. He clenched them into fists.

After a pause, Elcar cleared his throat. "Would you like a drink of water?"

Kriss let his hands fall limp. He nodded mutely. The lieutenant leaned down behind the right side of his desk. He straightened a moment later and handed a small plastic glass full of icy water to Kriss, who drank from it gratefully.

He hadn't mentioned the touchlyre, but thinking of that terrible night had made him think anew of the strange music the touchlyre had produced that night—and every night since, because he had played it every night on his journey to the city, and every night, it had been the same. He could still play tunes the old way, focusing on a specific song he already knew or improvising melodies and chords in his mind, but if he simply let his thoughts and feelings flow into the instrument, it gave them back as a complex wash of sound that perfectly matched his mental and emotional state.

Something had changed, in it, or in him, he didn't know. But he was more certain than ever that the touchlyre did not come from Farr's World—and that it could lead him to his true home, somewhere out among the stars, and maybe, just maybe, a new family.

He told Elcar none of that, of course. "The next morning, I packed what I could salvage and headed here," he concluded.

"And you think the people of Black Rock were responsible?"

"Who else? They hated me for being an offworlder. They mistrusted Mella because, even though she was a Farrsian, she came from somewhere else, and she'd brought me with her. And some of them thought she had money my parents had given her. I think that's what whoever attacked the cottage was looking for."

"Do you know why so many Farrsians dislike offworlders?" Elcar said.

Kriss shook his head. "No."

"Because fifty years ago, the Commonwealth . . . off-worlders . . . betrayed us," the lieutenant said, his voice thin and bitter. "We were supposed to be the administrative centre for this sector. That's why we have such magnificent government buildings, why the spaceport is large enough to accommodate twenty ships." He slapped his hands palms-down on the desk and leaned forward. "But then someone found another world, not that far away, not as beautiful but just as habitable, and with one thing Farr's World lacks—an abundant supply of metals, rare earth elements, and other valuable natural resources. And just like that, our beautiful garden world became a backwater. The Commonwealth turned its back on us, and the colonists who had come here with high hopes—many of them still alive, some of them living in Black Rock—found themselves on a primitive world out of the mainstream of galactic society." Elcar pointed at the ceiling. "That's why there are fourteen empty floors in this building. That's why some of the other government towers are nothing but hollow shells. That's why only four starships stand out there on that vast landing apron, and why it's nothing but a sheet of duracrete that only the smallest ships can land on, with no cradles for the big freighters or cruise ships and only the most basic repair and servicing facilities. *That's* why some Farrsians feel anger every time an offworlder walks by."

"Ancient history is no excuse for theft and murder!"

"No," Elcar said. "It's not. And that's why I don't think the villagers did it."

"But you just said . . ."

"Any rumours of Mella having a hidden pile of cash would have begun the moment she moved to Black Rock. If anyone were going to act on the rumours, it would have happened long ago. And it would be out of character. Almost all the violent crime—even robbery, let alone assault or murder—we investigate is committed by offworlders." His eyes bore into Kriss's. "There is some mystery in your past, some mystery involving your parents' identity, some secret your guardian was guarding even as she guarded you. Perhaps that mystery, that secret, caught up with her."

Kriss was suddenly acutely aware of the touchlyre in its red-leather case on his back. Mella had always been so adamant he keep it a secret . . . what if it was the treasure someone had come to the cottage looking for?

"And as for murder," Elcar continued, "you said yourself Mella didn't have a mark on her, that she might have died of a stroke or heart attack, brought on by the stress of the attack. So, murder? Almost certainly not. Involuntary manslaughter, at most." Kriss felt hot anger welling up in him, and some of it must have shown on his face, because the lieutenant raised placating hands. "I'm not trying to downplay the crime, just establish what happened." He tapped his desk. Lights blinked beneath the surface once more. "Eight days won't have left many clues, but we'll send out an investigator first thing in the morning. She'll talk to the local constable, take a look at the ruins of the cottage. Maybe she can turn up something."

Kriss glared across the glass-topped desk at the lieutenant. *He doesn't really care. He sympathizes more with the villagers than with me.*

Suddenly, he couldn't stand to be there anymore. He stood abruptly. "May I go?"

Surprised, Elcar also rose. "Of course. You're not my prisoner. Where are you staying?"

"I don't know. I don't have any money. I suppose I'll look for a job."

"They're hard to find. You'd be better off going back to the villages—not Black Rock, of course, but another, closer to the city. You look strong and healthy. Some farmer would hire you."

"No." *The only way I'm leaving this city is straight up. The sooner, the better.* "I won't go back out there."

"The city can be a rough place for a boy on his own," Elcar warned.

"You just said Farrsians aren't violent."

Elcar's lips tightened. "Suit yourself. But contact us when you find a place to stay. We may need to get in touch with you."

Kriss nodded once. "Anything else?"

"No." The lieutenant sat down again and swiped a hand across the surface of the desk, as though shoving everything they'd just talked about—*shoving the death of Mella*—to one side. "You can go."

The door slid open. Kriss spun and strode out, down the hallway, through the vestibule, and out into the early night. Only a little light remained in the western sky, visible over the vast flat expanse of the spaceport, and black clouds were rising to block it out.

Lightning flickered in those clouds and dust danced in tiny whirlwinds around Kriss's feet as he crossed the road, now almost deserted. He gripped the mesh of the spaceport fence and leaned against it, his last tears for Mella dimming his view of the floodlit spaceships. At that moment, the dream they represented seemed just as blurred and indistinct.

He didn't know how long he had been standing there, lost in memories and grief, when lightning split the sky, thunder cracked, and tiny drops of ice-cold rain spattered his cheek and the dusty pavement. In seconds the sprinkle became a downpour, and Kriss wrapped his arms around himself and dashed across the road and into an alley, pressing his body against the still-warm stone of a low building next to the police tower. Its bulk gave him some protection from the wind, but the cold drops still found him, as if to remind him he couldn't sleep in the streets.

He shivered. However bleak Elcar said the prospects for a job were, it was either work for a living or not live. He looked down the alley, away from the spaceport. From somewhere down there, the wind carried shouts, raucous laughter, and a wild strain of music.

An inn, he thought. *Only inns are open this time of night. And inns always need dishwashers, right?*

At that moment, the thought of plunging his freezing hands into hot dishwater seemed downright seductive. He stepped away from the wall and let the icy wind at his back propel him into the heart of Cascata.

Chapter Four

The rain soaked Kriss to the skin before he had gone twenty steps. The inviting sounds came from around the next corner. Shivering, miserable, he stepped from the alley. A passing groundcar splashed him waist-high. A man's mocking laughter trailed from it.

I should have spent more time with the lieutenant, he thought, his teeth chattering. *All night, maybe.* At least the touchlyre's case was waterproof . . . though he doubted water would harm the instrument anyway.

He spotted the inn a short distance away, on the other side of the road. Laughter and warm yellow light spilled out into the rainy night as someone entered. Kriss broke into a splashing run, and a moment later pushed open the front door.

Thirty or forty people, all Farrsians, filled the cozy stone-walled common room, along with smoke from the huge fireplace in the far wall and a savoury smell of roasting meat, drifting in from the kitchen, somewhere off to the left. Kriss asked a passing waiter where he could find the innkeeper, and gratefully accepted the offer to wait by the fire. He threaded his way across the sawdust-strewn floor and stood as close as he could to the blaze, steaming.

After a while, he turned to give his back a chance to dry, too, and took a better look at the room. Nothing in it gave a hint that ships leaped to the stars from only a kilometre away. The smoke-blackened beams in the ceiling, the furniture of golden farssa wood, even the clientele—*especially* the clientele—could have belonged to the little inn in Black Rock.

"What d'you want?" said someone to his right. He turned, saw only the top of a bald head, and then lowered his gaze to the wrinkled face of a man a full half-metre shorter than him, squinting up at him suspiciously.

"Are you the innkeeper, sir?"

"I am. What of it?"

"I've just arrived in Cascata, and I'm looking for work. I wondered if—"

"Forget it."

"I'll do *anything*," Kriss said desperately. "Wash dishes, wait on tables, make beds—"

The innkeeper snorted. "Kid, there are a thousand like you rattling around this city. They come from the villages to make their fortunes. The smart ones go home." He peered up at Kriss's blond hair, plastered to his skull. "You're an offworlder. Why do *you* want to work in a Farrsian inn?"

"I grew up in Black Rock."

"Then go back there." The old man turned away. "I've got no work for you."

"Can you at least point me to another inn?" Kriss pleaded.

Sighing, the innkeeper faced him again. "Kid, I can point you to Salazar himself, if you want me to. But even he can't give you a job when there's none available."

Kriss looked at him blankly. "Salazar? Who's Salazar?"

"Anton Salazar? Controls half the town?" Kriss shrugged, and the innkeeper shook his head. "You really *are* new, aren't you? All right, I'll tell you where to find another inn. But it won't do you any good."

"I have to try."

"Suit yourself." He gave Kriss brief directions, then had a waiter usher him out.

Kriss set out into the wind and rain again, thoughts bleak, his hope leaching away as quickly as the residual warmth of the inn's fire. If all the innkeepers felt the same way . . .

Three hours later, he knew they did. He visited eight inns. Some were as rustic as the first. Some were as modern as the police station. It didn't matter. At two, they threw him out at first sight. At the remaining six, he heard a variation of the first innkeeper's theme. Cascata was glutted with cheap labour, young people who came to the city to escape the villages. Most of them went home. Some of them starved . . . or worse.

At the eighth inn, one of the old-fashioned ones, the owner, though she didn't offer him work, at least took pity on him and fed him soup and bread at a table near the fire. As he ate, he asked her, as he had asked all the others, what other inns he might try.

She named a string of them. He'd already been to them all.

"There aren't any others," she said, then paused, and frowned. "Well, except . . ."

Kriss paused with his soup spoon halfway to his mouth. "Except?"

"Andru's. But that's not a Farrsian inn. Andru is an offworlder. He caters to shipcrews—offers all kinds of outlandish food and drink, and a place to sleep off-ship. None of *them* ever stay in *our* inns," she added bitterly.

"An offworlder?" Kriss felt a stirring of renewed hope. "Why didn't anyone else mention him?"

The innkeeper raised her hands. "Now, wait a minute, lad. You may both be offworlders, but Andru is still a poor bet. He's a strange man, with a whipcrack temper."

"I have to try, unless there's somewhere else . . ."

"There isn't. Not for you. There are other places, south of the spaceport, but you'll stay away from them if you know what's good for you."

Kriss had already heard of those "other places," where the kids who were on the "or worse" side of the "starved . . . or worse" equation ended up, selling the only thing they had left to sell: themselves. He thanked the innkeeper and finished his meal. Then he set out into the cold, wet night one more time, following the directions she had given him.

Andru's was a couple of kilometres distant, close to the spaceport. Soaked and shivering again, splashing through puddles along the all-but-deserted streets, Kriss had far too much time to ponder what he would do if Andru turned him away, as predicted.

"I can always take up begging," he muttered. "Or . . ." He swallowed, thinking of those "other places" the woman had mentioned. He wouldn't go *there*. Not ever.

But he couldn't help wondering how many other kids had once made exactly the same promise to themselves—and broken it once they got cold and hungry enough.

The warmth he had soaked up with his soup and bread was only a pleasant but hard-to-recall memory when, at last, he stood in front of Andru's. To his surprise, since it supposedly catered to offworlders, it looked as rustic as the first—and the last—of those he had already visited: two stories, wood and plaster, with a steeply sloping slate roof and two tall, red-brick chimneys. Blue smoke rose and faded away into the wet black sky above the streetlights' glare.

Kriss mounted the weathered wooden porch and stepped through the big steel-bound door into the common room. At first sight, it, too, was pure Farrsian. Its polished farssa-wood floor glowed orange in the light of the fire crackling in an enormous stone hearth to his left. Rough beams spanned the ceiling, and a long bar of black stormwood, matching the tables and chairs, stretched across the opposite wall, a brass rail gleaming at its base.

But the room was lit not only by the fire, but also by glowing white spheres floating in mid-air, and behind the bar, red, blue, and yellow liquids bubbled and frothed in convoluted tubes of glass. As Kriss watched, the barkeeper, a grey-haired giant of a man, drew a tiny glass of smoking green fluid from the machinery and handed it to a thin, black-skinned woman.

A strange quiet also gripped the room; the dozen or so patrons sat talking in low voices. They were all offworlders.

Other than the quiet mutter of conversation, the only sounds were the crackling of the fire and the gurgling of the bar machinery.

Kriss felt like an intruder, but he steeled himself, wiped his feet, and walked across to the barkeeper, who was pouring something from a metal can into a funnel in the machinery. "I don't sell liquor to children," the big man said without looking around, his voice a low rumble.

Caught off guard, Kriss said nothing, and the barkeeper turned to face him. "Well?"

"Uh—I'm looking for Andru."

The barkeeper crushed the can with an easy squeeze of his hand. "You've found him." He tossed the crumpled container into a chute in the wall.

Kriss blinked and examined the man more closely. Even for an offworlder, Andru was tall, not to mention broad-shouldered and deep-chested. He returned Kriss's gaze with eyes as silver-grey as his hair, set in a furrowed, dark-tanned face, then leaned forward, splaying his massive, calloused fingers on the wet black wood of the bar. "State your business or get out," he growled. "I'm not here to be stared at."

Kriss drew a deep breath to prevent stammering, then explained what he wanted.

Andru was shaking his head before he finished. "I've got no jobs."

"But I'll do anything—"

"I said, I've got no jobs."

Kriss thought of the cold, rainswept streets, and those "other places" on the far side of town. "How much for a room?" he asked desperately.

"Ten feds."

"I have just under a fed. Can I at least sit up the night in your common room?"

By way of an answer, Andru held out his hand. Kriss took off the touchlyre's case and put it on the bar, then slipped off the slingpack strap. He thumped the pack on the bar next to the touchlyre. His first day in Cascata was going to finish off his resources. Then what?

At least I'll have one night off the streets, he thought. Opening the pack, he began digging for the small pouch that contained the coins. At some point along the way, it had fallen out of the interior pocket where he'd put it. He started pawing through his clothes, searching for it. When at last he found it and pulled it out, he glanced up to see Andru resting one hand on the touchlyre's case.

"What's this?"

"A musical instrument." Kriss held out the little pouch. "Here's your money."

Andru ignored it. "Can you play it?"

"Why?" Kriss asked, still extending the pouch.

Andru gestured at the small crowd. "Business is slow. Maybe I need entertainment."

Mella's warnings instantly ran through his mind again. *Never let anyone see you with that . . . never let anyone hear you play it . . .*

Mella is dead, he told himself coldly. *Her reasons died with her. And what will I do if I don't take this chance? Starve in the streets? Take Elcar's advice and become a farmhand? Or try those "other places"?*

He made up his mind, but he still felt guilty as he met Andru's grey eyes. "I can play it."

"We'll see." The innkeeper walked the length of the bar

to Kriss's right, toward a staircase leading up, but turned left short of the stairs to pass through a bead-hung archway. Kriss grabbed the pack in one hand and the touchlyre case in the other and followed, the beads slithering over him. At the end of the short corridor he found himself in, a second stairway doubled back, up to the second floor, much narrower than the one leading up from the common room. There were doors to both left and right; Andru opened the one on the left and motioned Kriss through.

Kriss stepped into a small room panelled in black stormwood, lit by a glowing half-sphere set in the ceiling. Rain spattered the tiny square window in the back wall. Andru closed the door, then walked around Kriss and sat down in a straight-backed chair behind a grey metal desk, bare except for a battered-looking computer interface, its screen pushed down flat. The only other furnishing was a round wooden stool shoved into the corner. "Play," Andru commanded.

"And if I play well?" Kriss asked. He set his slingpack and touchlyre case on the floor and grabbed the stool.

"Board and room and fifty percent of whatever the audience gives you."

Kriss didn't know if fifty percent was a fair offer and didn't really care. All he cared about was the room and board. He thumped the stool onto the floor in front of the desk. "Agreed."

He picked up the touchlyre case, set it on the desk, and opened it, taking his time. What should he play? What kind of music did offworlders like?

Andru leaned forward with interest as the gleaming instrument was revealed. Kriss placed it on his lap, the neck resting on his left shoulder, closed his eyes, and placed his hands on the copper plates. The strings stirred to life, and a faint, shivering chord filled the room.

I'll play "Red Meadows," he decided. One of the first folk songs Mella had taught him, it had a simple but beautiful melody.

Maybe *too* simple for offworlders? He hesitated.

Andru shifted in his chair, but Kriss barely noticed. Weary, warm again at last, eyes closed, all he really wanted to do was sleep, yet he had to play *something*. All his hopes might depend on it . . . all his hopes . . .

His mind drifted back to that moment beside the trail when he had seen the starship leap into the sky above the ridge overlooking Cascata, and his heart had swelled with awe and joy . . .

. . . and the strings spoke. Just as they had the night of Mella's death, as they had in his lonely camps on the journey here, they played without his consciously shaping their tune. Instead, they sang out his story, sang of the years of isolation and longing, of Mella's death and his long journey, and above all, of his longing for the stars, for knowledge of his past, for the family that might be waiting out there somewhere; and somehow, all the shattering events of the past few days intertwined with the longing and his vision of that star-bound ship to end the music with a joyful chord of hope he would not have believed possible.

Utterly exhausted but content, he opened his eyes as the final ringing of the strings died away. Andru sat with his head bowed, his gnarled knuckles white against the dark wood of the arm of his chair. Finally, he took a deep breath and looked up to meet Kriss's gaze. "You're hired," he said, his voice rough. "You'll begin playing tomorrow night." He stood abruptly, strode to the door, and jerked it open. "Zendra!"

Hurried footsteps approached, and a plump middle-aged Farrsian woman, greying hair drawn back in a tight bun, appeared in the doorway. She was about Mella's age, and Kriss felt a pang at the sight of her. "Yes, Andru?"

"Take Kriss to room six. He's been hired to entertain." He started to leave, then hesitated and turned back. He reached down and, almost reverently, touched the smooth black wood of the instrument. His gaze met Kriss's for a brief moment, then he wheeled and was gone, brushing past Zendra, who stepped aside to let him pass.

Stunned by the sudden shift in his fortunes, Kriss stared after him. Had he really seen tears in the innkeeper's eyes? "I'm imagining things," he muttered. "I need sleep."

"Follow me, and you can have some," Zendra said, stepping back into the doorway and startling him: he'd forgotten she was there. He got up and returned the instrument to its wrapping, then turned to face her, getting a friendly smile. "You look like a drowned rat," she commented as she led him out into the hallway and up the back stairs.

Barely even conscious, Kriss didn't answer. He tripped twice, unable to lift his feet high enough to clear the steps. Zendra steadied him with a firm hand as they emerged into a long hallway. Off to his left, he saw a landing that had to be at the top of the main staircase from the common room. Zendra led him to a room close to the head of those stairs and let him into it with an old-fashioned metal key. "I won't bother calling you for breakfast," she said with a smile, handing him the key.

"G'night," he mumbled. He closed the door as she left,

locked it, and then turned to the bed. Stripping off his wet clothing and letting it lie where it fell, he crawled beneath the covers, and into sleep.

TEVERA, sipping the fragrant herbal tea she favoured while her brother, Rigel, nursed a tall glass of ale so dark it was almost black, watched from the shadows of one of the corner tables as a soaking-wet boy, a bulging pack on his back, entered the common room and went to the bar. He looked about her age and, from his height and colouring, was definitely an offworlder. She kicked Rigel under the table and, when he raised startled eyes to her, nodded in the boy's direction. Her brother glanced that way. "I wonder what ship he's from?" Tevera said. "Looks young to be a Union spacer."

Rigel shrugged. "Some officer's kid, probably." He turned back to his ale. "Probably not supposed to be here."

Tevera took another sip of her tea and watched as the boy followed Andru through the beaded curtain into the back hallway, frowning a little as she tried to imagine what *that* could be about. Then the plate of snickerjams she'd ordered arrived, and she forgot about the boy—until Andru emerged again, a strange expression on his face, stepped up onto a chair, and called out, "Gentlefolk, your attention for a moment."

Tevera exchanged a startled glance with Rigel, who twisted around to better see the innkeeper.

"I am pleased to announce the engagement, beginning tomorrow, of a most talented and unusual musician," Andru said. "Please, tell your crewmates. Half-price drinks for anyone here tonight who brings a friend with them tomorrow. Just leave me your name before you go."

That brought a buzz of talk from the handful of patrons who had made their way to Andru's through the rain. Andru, a small smile on his face, stepped down from the chair and returned to the bar.

"Wily old devil," Rigel said. "The place'll be twice as full tomorrow night."

"Can we come back?" Tevera said. "That boy we saw must be the musician. I'd love to hear him play."

"I doubt he's as special as Andru claims," Rigel said. "Marketing, that's all that is."

"Please, Rigel?" Tevera said. She gave him her best little-sister look.

He laughed. "All right. I'll see who else wants to come. Half-price drinks for you and me. You can order hot chocolate!"

Tevera's eyes widened. Chocolate, made only on Earth, was hideously expensive. "If I can have chocolate," she said, "I don't care if he sings flat and has a voice like a rusty freightlifter."

Rigel laughed again. "I guess we'll find out."

Tevera picked up another snickerjam and took a big bite. "I guess we will," she mumbled as she chewed.

Chapter Five

Kriss opened his eyes and blinked at the bright rectangle of sunlight on the white plaster wall. *Mella will be calling me for breakfast soon*, he thought sleepily, then frowned. The sunlight had never before struck his bedroom wall in *quite* that place or in *quite* that shape . . .

An instant later, all the memories of fires, journeys, storms, and spaceships came rushing back, and he closed his eyes for a moment, wishing it had all been a bad dream—and then suddenly felt guilty, because that wasn't quite true. He didn't wish it had *all* been a dream. Oh, he wished Mella were still alive; but having a job in Cascata, almost within sight of the spaceport, and working in an inn that catered to offworlders—he *couldn't* wish that was a dream. But not wishing it made him feel disloyal to Mella's memory, just like revealing the touchlyre to Andru had the night before.

He lay there, trying (and failing) to sort out his feelings, until hunger finally drove him to his feet. The only other door in the room beside the one leading to the hall proved to open into a bathroom (whose shining modern fixtures took him several increasingly urgent minutes to figure out). Twenty minutes later, clean, dressed in fresh (well, reasonably fresh) clothes from his pack, and feeling well-rested for the first time in days, Kriss made his way downstairs, wondering how to get breakfast.

Or dinner; a clock above the fireplace informed him he had slept past noon. Only three men sat in the common room, talking together in low voices in one of the booths. They didn't even look up as he entered, but Zendra, wiping glasses behind the bar, did. "Hungry, are you?" she said before he could open his mouth. "Sit anywhere, and I'll see what I can find."

"Thank you." He looked around. The big windows on either side of the main door stood open. He picked a table near the one on the left. Air, cooled and cleaned by the night's rain, drifted in along with the clatter of wagons and whine of groundcars from the bustling street. He found it hard to believe it was the same cold, wet, wind-swept, deserted route he had trudged in the night.

Zendra returned through the swinging kitchen door at the far end of the bar, and crossed to his table, carrying a platter loaded with bread, meat, cheese, and a glass of frenta juice, so cold it was beaded with condensation. She placed the tray in front of him. "Sleep well?"

"Umph," Kriss replied around his first mouthful.

Zendra laughed. "Does me good to see you dig in like that. A compliment to the chef, you might say."

He swallowed and reached for the juice, taking a big

gulp of delicious icy tartness before asking, "Where's Andru?"

"I don't know. Out somewhere. Why?"

"I want to know what my duties are." Kriss put down the glass and cut another slice of meat.

"Oh, I can tell you that," Zendra said with an airy wave of her hand. "You're to entertain—that's it. And that's not until tonight. Until then, do whatever you like. The day is yours." She winked one dark brown eye, then turned away with a sigh. "Unlike some of us . . ."

Kriss emptied the plate in a more leisurely fashion than he'd begun, then got up, stretched, and went out onto the sunlit porch. He stood there surveying the street, thinking how nice it was not to have to carry his backpack, now locked safely away in his room. The day was his, Zendra had said, so where to first?

He grimaced. Unfortunately, there was only one answer: the police. He had to tell Lieutenant Elcar where he was staying. "Not that Elcar is going to *do* anything," he muttered, but even that couldn't dim his enjoyment of the new day. In fact, as he walked toward the spaceport under the rainbow-hued shop awnings that had blossomed like flowers in the sunshine, he thought Cascata looked ten times cleaner and brighter than it had the day before. *And cooler*, he thought. Yesterday's heat had been washed away by the storm.

Even the stark black-and-white vestibule of the police headquarters seemed cheerier. Kriss smiled at the pretty young woman who had replaced the bored grey-haired dragon-lady of the previous night and explained his errand. She smiled back, called up his file on her desktop interface, and entered the information he provided.

After that, Kriss stood on the steps of police headquarters and gazed around. Where to start exploring? Though he had been over much of this side of the city the night before, it was one thing to see it in a rainstorm, drenched and miserable, and another to see it warm and dry in the sunshine.

Another easy question, really: he couldn't take his eyes off the spaceport. He watched a crew of men loading a transport with big metal cargo containers from one of the starships, and decided the rest of the city could wait. Down the steps he went, and a couple of hundred metres around the perimeter to the nearest gate.

A green-uniformed man in a glass-walled booth stopped him. "Port pass, please."

Crap, Kriss thought. "Uh . . . I don't have one."

"Then you can't go in, can you?"

"But I just want to look around . . ."

"No pass, no entry. Now step aside; you're holding up everybody else."

Kriss glanced back. There was no one behind him. He looked up at the gate guard to tell him so, but the man had turned away.

Fuming, Kriss retreated, plopping down on the steps of an empty tower across from the gate. Resting his chin on his fists, he gazed moodily across the spaceport.

The slim, youthful figure he had seen the day before descended the ramp of the smallest starship and started across the field to the sprawling customs building. A girl, Kriss decided, probably about his age. He watched her with envy. What strange worlds had she visited while he was stuck in Black Rock? She'd been across the galaxy, and he couldn't even get onto the landing field.

He straightened. "I *will* get into space!" he declared, banging his fist on his knee for emphasis—then winced and rubbed the place.

For the rest of the afternoon, he wandered around the spaceport fence, but he had no better luck getting through any of the other three gates, including the one in the customs building that had been the offworld girl's destination. Finally, as the shadows lengthened and the light turned orange, he started back to Andru's. Maybe the innkeeper could tell him how to get a port pass. He *had* to see those starships up close . . .

The first flutterbees began tumbling in his stomach as he approached the inn in the gathering gloom. He had never even played in public before—how could he hope to entertain a roomful of people who had travelled across the galaxy? What if they laughed at him?

Finding the common room almost full didn't help his nerves. Zendra and a thin, hard-faced woman he hadn't met moved among the offworlders, serving food and drinks. *Why are there so many more people?* he wondered irritably. The loud talking and raucous laughter made it hard for him to hear his own voice when he asked Andru, "When do I, uh . . .?"

"Eat first," Andru said. *His* voice carried through the din with no apparent effort. "They'll listen better when most are drinking instead of eating."

Kriss nodded, mouth dry, and found a seat at the bar. The hard-faced woman served him without a word, but he could eat only a little and, once the plates were cleared away, couldn't have told anyone what had been on them.

All too soon, Andru came over. "It's time."

Kriss swallowed, then went upstairs to his room. He felt a little more confident as he took the touchlyre from its case, but the feel of the smooth wood also brought back Mella's repeated warnings to never let anyone see it. Showing it to Andru had been bad enough; now he intended to reveal it to a hundred strangers, and offworlders, at that. Feeling guilty again, he stepped into the hallway, pulling the door closed behind him.

Andru met him at the foot of the stairs, and led him through the beaded curtain into the crowded common room, to a chair on a low platform by the fire. Kriss sat down, feeling naked.

The innkeeper stepped up beside him. "Guests!" Heads turned, but the murmur of conversation continued. "Guests!" Andru said again, and this time the note in his voice caused the gathered offworlders to set down their drinks and fall silent.

The innkeeper's gaze travelled around the room for a long moment before he spoke again. "You have seen little entertainment in my inn over the years, for I have seen few entertainers suited to my guests' tastes. But tonight is different. My guests, I present Kriss Lemarc, minstrel of Farr's World."

A handful of people applauded politely, but most, after a glance at Kriss, simply resumed their interrupted conversations. "Begin," Andru told Kriss, and stepped down from the platform.

Kriss looked down at the instrument and touched the

plates with trembling fingers. Infected with his nervousness, the touchlyre gave a harsh squawk. Andru frowned, and the nearest offworlders, a man and a woman, looked up, startled. The man leaned over and said something to the woman, who laughed, then turned her attention back to her plate.

Kriss ran his tongue over dry lips. Could he summon again what he had summoned the night Mella had died, and again last night for Andru? It hadn't really felt like he had done anything at all, except . . .

. . . except *remember*. And *feel*.

He closed his eyes.

He pictured himself sitting on the grey rock ledge by the mirror-smooth lake where he had so often gone to play the instrument . . . the place he had been when Mella died. He remembered that day, and all that had come after . . .

. . . and heard the music, the *real* music, begin.

It strengthened and steadied as he built the memory detail by detail. He forgot Andru's, forgot he sat in front of a room full of offworlders. Instead, he once again sat naked in the sun, drying from his swim and playing the new song he'd composed. Realizing he was late, he leaped up. He headed home. He smelled smoke . . .

The horror of finding Mella dead, the setting out for Cascata, the long journey on foot from Black Rock: all of it replayed itself in his mind and, though he was hardly aware of it anymore, in the music, until once more he saw the starship leaping into the sky and his song ended with a dream, his dream, the dream of rediscovering the contentment of the little lake by Black Rock—only this time, discovering it with his true family, somewhere among the stars.

Slowly, Kriss surfaced from wherever the touchlyre had

taken him—and heard . . . nothing. The room was so quiet he snapped his eyes open and looked up, convinced everyone had walked out.

But no one had left. Instead, they sat improbably still and silent. A few stared at him but looked away when his eyes met theirs; others gazed downward, or at the fire. Many had their eyes closed. One silver-haired woman cried silently, hand to her mouth, shoulders heaving, fire-lit tears on her cheeks.

Kriss stared at them in amazement, then looked down at the silver strings of the touchlyre, shining red in the firelight, remembering Andru's reaction the night before. What did others hear when he played the touchlyre in this strange new way?

Someone set a large wooden bowl by his feet, and he looked up, startled, into the innkeeper's grey eyes. "No more," Andru said in a low voice. "But stay put until I signal you." He returned to the bar, leaving Kriss feeling drained and bewildered.

The weeping woman suddenly got up from her table, dropped a coin into the bowl, and then hurried almost blindly from the room. As if the clatter of the fed-piece were a signal, others came forward. Only once they returned to their tables did they begin to talk to one another again, though in subdued voices at first, so that the murmur of normal conversation only gradually returned.

When no one had come up for two or three minutes, Andru waved, and Kriss carried the bowl to the bar. The offworlders glanced up as he walked by; some smiled, then looked away almost shyly, as though uncertain how to react to him.

He gave the bowl to Andru, who overturned it, spilling thin plastic bills and ceramic coins across the wet, dark wood of the bar. He counted quickly. "One hundred and seven feds. That's fifty-three and a half apiece." He pushed Kriss's share over to him, then moved to the far end of the bar to serve someone.

Kriss stared at the money in awe. Over fifty feds! He'd never seen that much money in his life. "Maybe I'll buy my *own* spaceship!" he breathed, then gathered up the coins and bills and dropped them into his pocket, where they made a pleasantly large lump. He tucked the instrument under his arm and went up the main staircase two steps at a time. So, that was all there was to it: play the instrument a few minutes, pocket the feds, and the rest of the time, take it easy. Even if he never got off the planet, he had it made.

But he *would* get off the planet. In fact, he intended to start working on the problem right away. Strike while the iron was hot, as the old saying Mella had been fond of went. At the moment, some of the offworlders in Andru's looked like they'd do anything he asked—and it just so happened, he had something to ask.

He went upstairs, locked the instrument in his room, then headed back down to the common room.

SEATED at a corner table with Rigel and Corvus, a slightly dim but genial cousin of theirs, Tevera blissfully sipped her hot chocolate and watched as the boy with the strange musical instrument sat down on the chair on the platform by the fire. The three of them had come in just a few minutes before and had been lucky to nab this table, vacated by a trio of Union spacers whose interest in the evening's activities had clearly been limited to the half-price drinks and not the promised entertainment.

The boy—"Kriss Lemarc, Minstrel of Farr's World," Andru had named him, though he was so clearly an offworlder she thought that must be a joke—looked abysmally nervous as his eyes flicked around the room. She would have given him an encouraging smile if he'd given any indication that he'd seen her, but in their shadowed corner, they were probably all but invisible to him.

He touched the copper plates on his strange, black, three-sided instrument, and its strings coughed out a harsh, metallic, discordant squawk that made her wince. Rigel groaned. "We're in for it now."

"He's probably just tuning?" Tevera ventured.

"Doesn't seem to be working," Corvus said, and Rigel laughed.

Tevera found herself gripping her hot chocolate mug much more tightly than she needed to. The boy looked close to her age, and she could empathize only too well with his discomfort: she hated being the centre of attention at Family gatherings. She couldn't play an instrument, but she could sing, and had been put on the spot more than once to impress some visiting captain or other.

The boy closed his eyes. For a moment he sat perfectly still, his hands still resting on the instrument's copper plates . . .

. . . and then the music began, a wash of sound, layer upon layer of it, shimmering arpeggios, crashing chords and discords, wailing notes as though a single string were being tortured, melodies she could feel and taste, and through it all, emotions, images . . . longing and loss and discovery and, in the end, a kind of joy and hope that brought tears to her eyes and a lump to her throat.

The music ended. She didn't know how long it had lasted, but her hot chocolate had gone cold in the cup. She swallowed some of it anyway, her hands shaking. Rigel's mouth hung open. Corvus looked confused. "What . . . what just happened?" he said.

Tevera didn't know. She tried to remember what she had heard, the actual sound of the music Kriss Lemarc had played, but it was gone from her memory, like a dream. All that remained was the emotion, the sense of deep loss, breathtaking longing . . . and hope.

The room was silent. No one applauded, but several sniffed or swiped at their eyes with the back of their hand. And then, one by one, offworlders began going forward to drop coins into the boy's bowl, while he sat there, head down.

She had no coin, so she stayed where she was and watched until, at last, something like the normal din of the common room resumed. Andru picked up the bowl, and he and Kriss spent a moment counting and dividing up what was in it; then Kriss took the instrument and literally bounded up the stairs, his earlier nervousness obviously soothed by what had to be a substantial amount of cash for his playing.

She swallowed the rest of her drink. It might not be *hot* chocolate anymore, but it was still chocolate, it cost ten feds a cup, and there was no way she was going to waste it.

Corvus still had a few swallows of beer left, but Rigel

was in the process of draining his . . . whatever it was he was drinking. He had a taste for strange cocktails, and the smoking purple liquid filled with floating black beads he'd ordered tonight certainly fit the bill. "What did you think?" Tevera asked him as he set down his glass.

"Pretty good," he said. "Bit sweet for my taste." He burped. "And fizzy."

"Not the drink," Tevera said impatiently. "The music."

"Oh." Rigel glanced at the empty chair where Kriss had sat to play. "Interesting. I wonder how he got that effect?" He looked back at his sister. "Not something I'd come back for, though. Give me a good naked-singularity technobopper any day."

Tevera grimaced. Rigel's taste in music was as weird as his taste in cocktails. She had no idea what a naked-singularity technobopper was, and didn't much care to find out. "What about you, cousin Corvus?" she asked, turning her attention to their companion.

"Didn't much like it," he said. "Made my head hurt."

Rigel laughed. "Then finish your beer and let's get out of here."

"Just a bit longer," Tevera said. "I want to see if Kriss comes out again."

"Who . . .?" Rigel blinked at her. Then he grinned. "Oh, the musician. First names, is it? Are you smitten, little sister?"

Tevera felt her face flush and was glad the lighting was dim. "Of course not," she snapped. "I don't even know him. But I liked his music. I'd like to tell him so. He's young. He'll appreciate it."

"He's young," Rigel said solemnly. "And good-looking?"

"I didn't notice," Tevera said primly, which was, of course, a lie: Kriss *was* good-looking, though almost painfully lean. Whatever ship he'd come from, they weren't feeding him properly . . .

She realized what she was thinking and almost laughed at herself. *What are you, his mother?*

"We can wait a few minutes," Rigel said. "But just a few. If he doesn't come back out . . ."

"There he is now," Corvus said, and Tevera, who had been looking at Rigel, turned her head and saw Kriss descending the stairs again. He stopped and surveyed the crowd, eyes flicking around the common room. He looked straight at her. She smiled a little.

And then, to her delight and astonishment, he headed their way.

"Mind if I join you?" he asked as he reached them.

Tevera had a strong urge to giggle. She managed to hold it down to a quirk of her mouth. She glanced at Rigel, who looked amused. He shrugged.

She looked back at Kriss. "Be our guest," she said, and the boy pulled out the fourth chair at the table and sat down.

Tevera took a closer look at him as he did so. He definitely had offworld colouring, but his skin tanned to something close to Farrsian brown. He'd either suffered a radiation exposure on his ship or had been spending a lot more time in the sun than most spacers ever cared to. His clothes were definitely Farrsian—nothing a spacer would normally wear—but that was probably just part of his act. His shaggy blond hair, curling around his collar, desperately needed trimming. Whatever ship he was from clearly didn't have very high standards. Her own light-brown hair was cropped short to keep it under control in zero-G, and she wore her usual light-blue Family jumpsuit and polished black boots.

She realized he was staring openly at her, as if he'd never seen a girl before. She raised an eyebrow. "Do you approve?"

He started. "I'm sorry. I didn't mean to—"

"Oh, I don't mind." She really didn't; it was kind of flattering. She gave him a grin, although out of the corner of her eye, she could tell that Rigel's expression of amusement had cooled considerably. "As long as you answer the question. Do you approve?"

"Uh . . . yes?" Kriss glanced at Corvus, who gave him a wave, then, like Rigel before him, burped. Tevera resisted the urge to roll her eyes.

Then Kriss gave a tentative smile to Rigel. Her brother, whose face was now impassive, gave him the slightest of nods, no more than a centimetre.

Get stuffed, big brother, Tevera thought. To Kriss, she said cheerfully, "Well, I approve of your looks, too. And now that's out of the way . . . what ship are you from?"

"Ship?"

She laughed. "Yes, ship. You know, the tall things at the spaceport? One of them flew you here? *Thaylia* is the only Family ship in port, so you must belong to one of the Union ones . . . the *Diefenbaker*, maybe?" The *Diefenbaker* was a bit of a rustbucket, always in need of repair—which could explain both his slightly slovenly appearance and the tan: he could have been stuck on Farr's World for weeks. She'd tanned quite a bit herself when *Thaylia* had been grounded.

"Um . . ."

And then she saw the truth in his eyes, and felt the smile

drop from her face. She stared at him. "You're . . . *not* off a ship?"

He cleared his throat. "My parents were offworlders—but I grew up on Farr's World. I'm not a spacer . . . not yet."

Crap, Tevera thought. Family Rule forbade fraternization with worldhuggers, especially for minors, but exactly what "fraternization" entailed was not spelled out in detail. Whoever was in command in a given situation made the call. In this situation, that was Rigel, and if she knew her brother . . .

She shot a look at him. Yes, she knew him well. His face now might have been carved from an asteroid. He stood. "It's time we returned to *Thaylia*."

Crap, Tevera thought again. She stood. So did Corvus. "Peace be yours," she said formally to the boy . . . the *worldhugger* boy . . . and then followed her brother out of the room.

"Sorry, Rigel," she said, once they were in the dark street and heading back toward the spaceport. "I didn't know."

"Me, either," Corvus put in. "Who'd have guessed it?"

"Not blaming you, little sister," Rigel said. "It surprised me, too. I wonder what his story is?"

He shook his head and picked up the pace. Corvus matched it. Tevera trailed a few steps behind. *So do I*, she thought. *So do I.* She glanced back down the street in the direction of Andru's. *If he's a worldhugger . . . where did he get that instrument? There's no way* that *technology originated on Farr's World.*

The phantom fingers of the instrument's strange song still ran through her mind.

I guess I'll never know, she thought sadly, then broke into a trot to rejoin her brother and cousin.

KRISS STARED after the suddenly departing offworlders, bewildered. *What did I say wrong?*

They'd drawn his attention at once when he'd come back down into the common room: three offworlders in matching crewsuits, seated at the same corner table near the windows where he'd eaten lunch, two young men a few years older than him, and a girl close to his own age. Slim, with short-cropped hair and hazel eyes, she'd looked familiar, and suddenly he'd realized the truth: she was the girl he'd envied as she crossed the spaceport that afternoon!

The fifty feds in his pocket had erased a lot of that envy. He fully expected to be jauntily descending from a starship into an alien spaceport himself before too long. But his curiosity had remained, and they'd seemed as likely prospects as any, so he'd straightened his vest, smoothed his shirt front, run his fingers through his hair, and casually (he hoped) walked across the room to the trio's table. Everything had seemed to be going well until, suddenly, it wasn't. The instant they'd discovered he wasn't a spacer from one of the starships in port, they'd jumped up and stalked off.

He glanced around at the remaining crowd, but the strange experience had soured him on approaching any more offworlders. Instead, sorely puzzled, he returned to his room, took a shower, and went to bed.

In the middle of the night, he woke and shot upright, unsure if dream or reality had disturbed him. He listened. At first, he heard only the racing drumbeat of his heart, but as he took a deep breath and started to settle back, a door opened down the hall. Instantly his own door, which he had closed and locked, slammed shut across the space of four or five centimetres. Footsteps pounded away, and someone shouted.

He threw back the covers, ran naked to the door, and opened it a crack, peering out just in time to see an offworlder in a bathrobe picking himself up off the floor.

"Who was that?" he spluttered, glaring at Kriss's eyes, all he could see of him (Kriss hoped).

"Where did he go?" Kriss countered.

"Downstairs and outside—after knocking me over first! What's going on?"

"I wish I knew." Other doors opened up and down the hall as awakened guests looked out to see what was happening, but Kriss closed his own and locked it again. Someone had been trying to break into his room—someone *had* broken into his room. Only the other man coming unexpectedly into the hall had kept that someone from walking right in and . . . what?

He turned on the light and looked around. Almost at once, he saw the pile of bills and coins he had emptied from his pocket onto the table by the bed. He could have kicked himself. Everyone in the inn that night had known he'd made that money, and he'd just left it lying in the open. He had to find a safer place for it, or he'd be asking for another break-in.

Another thought made him pause. Andru would want to know what had happened . . . but not tonight, he hoped. "He would have been in here by now if he wanted to see me tonight," he murmured, then yawned, his wakefulness fading with the excitement. Still, he paused and looked at the door before returning to bed. "This is silly," he muttered, but took a chair and stuck it under the doorknob anyway.

Despite that precaution he slept fitfully, listening, every time he woke, for someone at the door.

Chapter Six

Kriss entered the common room early the next morning to discover Andru already seated at the corner table by the window. The innkeeper motioned him over and, as he took a seat, said, "Someone broke into your room last night."

His tone was even, but Kriss couldn't help feeling he was being accused. He nodded, and Andru looked out the window, not exactly frowning, but certainly not smiling, either. Zendra emerged from the kitchen and winked at Kriss as she set toast and porridge on the table. Then she strode briskly away to serve a yawning offworlder who had just come down the stairs.

Andru faced Kriss again. "Why?"

"All that money I made last night, I guess."

"There are easier ways to steal fifty feds." Andru picked up a piece of toast, and Kriss hungrily followed his example. He hadn't felt he could start eating until his employer did.

"The amount is not as great as you seem to think," Andru continued, buttering the bread.

Kriss chewed and swallowed and said nothing. After a moment's silence, Andru said, "I must report this to the police. You will come with me."

"Yes, sir."

That concluded the conversation. After several more minutes of wordless eating, the innkeeper rose. "Let's go."

Kriss gulped down his juice, grabbed the last slice of toast, and followed Andru's broad, grey-clad back down the street, still chewing.

He told himself not to worry. He would put his money somewhere safer, that was all. He had a job, a place to live, food to eat, and he was in Cascata, gateway to the galaxy. Why should an inept burglar trouble him? The police would track him down in no time.

Like they tracked down Mella's killer? he thought, and between what that did to his mood and Andru's dour appearance, more than one smile on the face of a shopkeeper out sweeping his sidewalk died as they passed on their way to the police tower.

Appropriately, the sour-tempered woman from his first visit once more guarded the gates. If she remembered Kriss, she gave no sign. "Yes, sirs?"

"I'm here to report a break-in," said Andru.

"Fifth door. Constable . . ." she glanced down. "Rico Barron. Second door on your left down the hall."

"Come," Andru said to Kriss, who followed him across the room, feeling a bit like a well-trained dog.

The white corridor beyond the fifth door was indistinguishable from the one that had taken him to Lieutenant Elcar, and Constable Barron's office was identical to his colleague's, except for a painting of a mountain lake behind the desk—near enough in appearance to Kriss's hidden lake to make him look twice—and a potted Farrsian bluefern in the corner.

Barron looked a lot like the homicide detective, too, Kriss noted, except Elcar had never smiled, whereas Barron rose, grinning, to shake hands with both of them. "Sit down, please," he said, indicating the backless metal stools on their side of the desk.

Feeling a sense of *déjà vu*, Kriss started to comply, but stopped awkwardly when he realized Andru was remaining stiffly upright.

"I am here to report a break-in," the innkeeper said.

"Indeed." The constable looked from Andru to Kriss, who had straightened again. He shrugged and tapped the glassy surface of his desk. Blue light glowed beneath it. "Name?"

"Andru."

"Surname?"

"None." Kriss glanced at Andru in surprise, but the constable took it in stride.

"Address?"

"Andru's. One nineteen, Boulevard C."

"Ah, yes, the inn. And the boy?"

"Kriss Lemarc. Same address."

Barran glanced down at the desktop and frowned. "You were here two days ago, Kriss."

"Have you found something?" Kriss said eagerly, as Andru shot him a sharp look.

Barron tapped once. "Lieutenant Elcar has filed his

report. The investigator reported the state of the farm site to be consistent with your account but could discover no useful clues so long after the events you reported: in addition to the fire, there has been heavy rain in the area. The Black Rock constable had no knowledge of the incident. The case has been declared unsolvable, and the investigation abandoned."

Kriss stiffened. "You can't do that!"

Barron raised placating hands. "It has nothing to do with me. And I'm afraid it's already done."

"But they killed Mella!"

"Calm down, lad. I'm sorry, but . . . look, our force is simply too small to waste effort on a hopeless case. And it *is* hopeless. We know there are outlaws living in the Featherwood Mountains, but we don't have the manpower to track them down. This sort of thing, unfortunately, happens occasionally. All we can do is warn other residents in the area to be careful." He sighed. "I know how unsatisfactory that must be for *you*, but there's nothing to be done about it. The case is closed."

Kriss rubbed angry tears from his eyes with the heels of his hands. "What is this all about?" Andru growled, more to Kriss than to the constable, although only Barron answered.

"You'll have to ask the boy, sir. Now, if you'll give me your complaint . . ."

The innkeeper gave Kriss a hard stare before turning and telling the story crisply. Barron looked to Kriss when he was done. "You confirm this?"

He nodded, though he'd hardly been listening.

"Verbally, please."

"Yes."

"I'll send an investigator. Anything else?"

"No." Andru turned to go. "Come," he said to Kriss.

Barron rose. He met Kriss's gaze. "I'm sorry, son."

Kriss turned his back on the constable without replying and followed Andru out.

On the front steps, the innkeeper glanced at him. "Later, you *will* tell me what that was all about, when I return from my business in the spaceport. I expect to be back at the inn by noon—see that you are, too." He strode away.

Kriss sat down heavily on the bottom step and watched Andru thread his way through the people and traffic on the crowded street. He had been right; the police would do nothing about Mella's murder. They'd closed the case.

But he hadn't. He *couldn't.* Losing Mella, and not knowing why . . . it added to the pain he had borne all his life, the hurt of not knowing who his parents were and how and why they had died, abandoning him on Farr's World. Mella had promised to tell him about them someday, but now she, too, had been cut out of his life.

He raised his head and looked at the glittering spires of the starships, pillars of light in the morning sunshine, tantalizingly near, yet as inaccessible as the stars themselves. His only hope for answers lay in space. Somewhere out there, he might yet have family—grandparents, uncles, cousins. Perhaps they could tell him about his parents. *Someone* had to know who they were, why they had come here, why they had died. He had to find out. How could he understand himself until he knew those whose love had formed him?

Somehow, he had to get on one of those ships.

And then he saw the offworld girl, Tevera, coming through the spaceport gate—alone.

ASKED to go on a run to a local bakery to pick up some fresh bread for Captain Nicora's table, Tevera had been happy to comply. Otherwise, she'd have been stuck studying astronavigation, and while the stars themselves knew she needed the study—she sometimes thought they moved themselves around when she wasn't looking to make it all more difficult—after two hours her brain had seized up, and she didn't think she was making much progress anyway.

The bakery lay down a road that ran out from the ring road about a quarter of the way along the perimeter fence to her left as she exited the gate, but she'd only gone a hundred metres or so when she heard some remarkably colourful language from an angry wagon driver and turned to look, catching Kriss Lemarc in the act of reaching out a hand to tap her on the shoulder.

He froze, staring at her.

She froze, staring at him.

He cleared his throat. "Um . . . hello?"

I should go back into the spaceport, she thought—but she did no such thing. Instead, surprising herself—though probably not as much as she surprised him—she took a quick look around to be sure no Family were watching, then grabbed Kriss's hand, pulling him with her as she dashed across the ring road—getting shouted at by a different wagon driver than the one whose cursing at Kriss had first attracted her attention—and into the shadows of a narrow alley between two tall brick buildings.

The minute they were hidden, she released his hand. "What do you want?" she demanded out loud of him, while her inner voice silently demanded of her, *What are you doing?*

He blinked. "I just want to talk to you—"

"Well, you can't!" *No,* you *can't,* the inner voice said. *Shut up,* she told it. As if that would work.

"What?"

"Not here!" *Not anywhere,* added the annoyingly not-shutting-up inner voice.

"Then where?" he snapped. "You act like I have kilvapox or something."

"It's not that," she said. "It's just . . . you're a worldhugger."

His face closed. "So why are you talking to me at all?"

Good question, said the inner voice, but she knew the answer, and it came out in a rush. "I heard you play last night." *The raw emotion, the longing, the joy . . .* she got goosebumps even then, remembering. "It was . . ."

Her voice trailed off. She didn't have the words. "I . . . I'd like to talk to you, too," she finally said instead. "But I can't, not in the open like this. So . . . tonight. We'll talk tonight, after you play, outside Andru's. I'll leave first, you follow a few minutes later. All right?"

Speechless, he nodded.

"Good." She left him there, hurried around the corner, and continued along the ring road toward the street that would take her to the captain's favoured bakery.

Her heart pounded every step of the way.

KRISS FOLLOWED Tevera to the corner and watched her striding purposefully down the sidewalk. She didn't look back and soon turned down a side street, her slim figure disappearing from his sight.

He turned the other way, shaking his head. None of that had made a bit of sense to him. But she *had* agreed to talk to him. His spirits lifted a little.

A big man with the dark skin of a Farrsian but far taller and bulkier than most stared at Kriss as he passed the spaceport gate on his way back to Andru's. Thinking the man must have been at the inn the night before, Kriss nodded and smiled, but the stranger didn't smile back. "Everyone's a critic," Kriss muttered, and forgot him.

Back at the inn, he asked Zendra how he could clean his travel-stained clothes, and she showed him a special fixture, in the little bathroom off his room, whose function had puzzled him until then. Fascinated by the way he could open the hinged door, push his filthy clothes in, press a button, and a few seconds later pull them out as clean as the day they were made, he almost wished he had more dirty clothes.

Hey, I've got a job, he thought. *I could actually buy some! Clean ones, I mean.*

After the noon meal, Andru summoned him to his office and pointed him to the same stool on which he'd auditioned. "You know what I want to hear," he rumbled.

Kriss told his story. Andru watched him steadily and impassively with his fathomless grey eyes. When he'd finished, the innkeeper folded his hands on the desk and said, "I see no reason why this should affect your employment here."

Kriss hadn't imagined it could, and felt as if he'd dodged a bullet he hadn't even seen coming.

"And I am sorry for your loss," Andru continued. "As for last night's attempted theft . . . from now on, I will put your money in my safe. I will, of course, keep an accurate account of it, and you may withdraw any amount you wish from the accumulated total at any time." He paused, frowning. "Perhaps I should put your instrument there, too."

"The touchlyre?" Kriss blinked. "You think that's what he was *really* after?"

"It's possible. As you surely know, that is no ordinary musical instrument. It is clearly of offworld origin."

Kriss felt cold. It made sense, too much sense. Andru was right; fifty feds seemed like a fortune to him, but to a thief? He had to have been after something else, and what else of value did Kriss have but the touchlyre?

Again he wondered, *Was that what the raiders were after at the cottage?*

No, he thought. *Nobody knew it existed but me and Mella.*

Here in Cascata, though, many people knew about it, thanks to his performance the night before. And those people would talk to other people . . .

All the same, he didn't like the idea of being separated from it. In fact, now he liked that idea even less. "No," he said. "I don't want it locked up. I'll keep it safe myself."

Andru shrugged. "As you will. You may go."

Kriss climbed slowly to his room, where he lay on his bed and stared at the ceiling. All his life he'd had questions without answers: questions about his past, his parents, the touchlyre. Now he could add questions about why the cottage had been attacked, why Mella had been killed, why someone had broken into his room . . . and why Tevera was afraid to talk to him.

Always questions, never answers.

Maybe he would never have answers to some of his questions. But he intended to look for them anyway, beginning that night. Because one thing he knew: some of the answers were locked in the stars . . .

. . . and Tevera just might be the key.

Chapter Seven

When Kriss carried the touchlyre into the common room that night, heads turned, and people nudged their neighbours and pointed. Andru, however, continued wiping the bar as though Kriss didn't exist.

He looked around the room for Tevera but didn't see her. He shoved aside a stab of disappointment. *It's early yet.* Then he frowned. *On the other hand, she'd better hurry if she wants to find a place to sit.* He couldn't see an empty table anywhere, but as he stood by the equally packed bar looking for one, a rather fat spacer drained his drink, slid off his stool, and lurched away, and Kriss grabbed his vacated spot before anyone else could. Zendra waved as she passed by on her way to the kitchen. A few minutes later she emerged with a tray bearing a bowl of stew, a hunk of bread, a plate of fruit, and a tall glass of . . . something. Something pink.

"You're really packing them in," she said as she set the platter in front of him.

He blinked. "All these people came just to hear me?"

She laughed. "I wouldn't go *that* far. But quite a few came because they heard about you from someone who was here last night."

"What about the rest?"

Someone shouted from across the room, and she winked. "The rest are just hungry!" She hurried away.

Kriss took a cautious sip of the pink drink. It tasted of sugar and cinnamon and fizzed with bubbles that tickled his nose. He couldn't decide if he liked it or not, so he set it aside and instead dug into his stew. It, he *definitely* liked—he was starving. Again. In the back of his mind, Mella's complaints about how fast he grew echoed once more. The thought brought a pang, but it also made his lips twitch into a half-smile.

As he ate, he listened to the hubbub behind him, hoping to pick out some comment about his previous performance, some clue to how his audience experienced his strange new way of playing the touchlyre. What did they hear? What did they feel?

What did Tevera feel?

He shivered a little, remembering the image of the ledge by the lake he had built up in his mind the night before. It had been so incredibly real . . . far more real than anything his imagination normally conjured. It had felt as if . . . as if the touchlyre had somehow reached into his mind to draw out the image and its associated emotions, then translated those emotions into sound . . . sound, and maybe something more.

It's not a vampire, he told himself, trying to shake his

sudden sense of unease. *It doesn't suck your blood or your soul. It's only a musical instrument.*

A musical instrument he knew nothing about. Many people in Black Rock played fiddle, guitar, horn, pipe, drum, or keyboard, but no one else had an instrument that played at a touch. No one else had an instrument that one day, out of the blue, began playing their innermost thoughts. Just how *did* the touchlyre work—and where had it come from? His father had made the outside, the wood and the strings and the copper plate. But what was hidden away inside that black case, with no opening in it anywhere?

"Clearly of offworld origin," Andru had said, and Kriss had had the same thought, that whatever technology made the touchlyre work, it couldn't have originated on Farr's World.

When Mella had given him the instrument and told him his father had made it, he'd immediately formed a fond image of his father carving the space-black wood by firelight, polishing it until it glowed, embedding some mysterious mechanism of his own invention beneath the copper plates, then tuning the silver strings. He liked to think of his father, strong and kind, playing the touchlyre for his mother, whom he pictured as a tall and beautiful woman with golden hair and a warm, gentle smile. Thinking of his father's fingers resting on the touchplates made him feel as close to his shadowy parents as he ever could.

He clung to that image still. Maybe his father hadn't invented the technology inside the touchlyre, but he had crafted the instrument itself, and Mella had said he'd dreamed of giving it to his child. He hated the fact that he was beginning to wonder if that was the truth. Truth could be very cold, and right now, he didn't feel like turning his back on his warm fantasy. Instead, he turned his back on the bar and surveyed the crowd. It had thinned slightly, as those more interested in food than entertainment left for other amusements. Among those who remained, he thought he recognized several offworlders from the night before.

He also saw the big, dark-skinned man he'd seen near the spaceport that morning. The man sat by the door, massive arms folded, staring at Kriss with expressionless eyes—eyes that followed him as he made his way to the platform after Andru silently touched him on the shoulder.

Tonight, the crowd quieted expectantly as he took his seat in the hard wooden chair. In the sudden hush, and with a rush of relief, he saw Tevera enter at last—alone, and dressed in nondescript Farrsian clothes of brown and black instead of the light-blue crewsuit she'd worn before. She sat in a dim corner at the very back of the room, head down so Kriss couldn't catch her eye. He quit trying when he saw Andru frowning at him, and instead looked down at the touchlyre, closed his eyes, and touched the plates.

TEVERA WAS NOT SUPPOSED to be out in the city alone at night. She most definitely was not supposed to be out in the city alone at night for the express purpose of meeting a boy. And she most *definitely* definitely was not supposed to be out in the city alone at night for the express purpose of meeting a *worldhugger* boy. And yet, here she was. The inner voice that had plagued her earlier was silent, probably too terrified by her effrontery to say anything.

It had commented plenty during the long afternoon, trying to talk her out of what she had promised to do. To be honest, she'd wavered more than once. But as night approached, the memory of the music—or whatever it really was—she'd experienced in Andru's the night before took stronger and stronger hold of her, and in the end, she'd put aside her crewsuit for something less conspicuous and left the ship by the simple expedient of telling the crewman on duty—good old cousin Corvus—that Rigel had asked her to run over to the portmaster's office to retrieve a jacket he'd left there earlier. Corvus should have checked in with Rigel, who was on nightwatch duty on the bridge, but instead, as she'd hoped, he'd just waved her through. After all, she wouldn't lie to *him*, would she?

But yes, she would, and yes, she had, and now here she was, tucked into a corner of Andru's again, alone this time, waiting to see if lightning, in the form of the extraordinary music from Kriss Lemarc's instrument, would strike twice, and committed to talking to him afterward, outside, alone, in the dark, if it did.

Which . . . it did.

Once more, the music flooded her with sorrow and loss, terror and discovery, joy and, more than anything else, *longing*. Longing to leave this world. Longing to travel among the stars. Longing for what she had been born to, a life unbound by gravity, untethered to any one world, a life of endless, infinite possibility . . .

The music ended. Her cheeks were wet, and her throat caught in a sob. She wiped her tears away with her sleeve. She pressed her lips together and raised her head to see Kriss looking straight at her. Their eyes met. She swallowed, then glanced at the door and back at him. He nodded, and she turned and went out into the darkness.

There was an alley across the street, and she went there to wait, pressing her back against a brick wall and raising her head to look up at the stars. Here, beneath kilometres of atmosphere, they twinkled unnaturally, a strange dance that unsettled many of the Family when they were in port, even more than the press of gravity and the endless open spaces. She had come to love that jewel-like sparkle when she'd lived on Feldenspar, but even she could not imagine being trapped beneath such a distorting layer of gravity-bound gases forever. Soon, *Thaylia* would lift, and she and the others of her Family would leave Farr's World behind, like fish leaping above the surface of a lake and somehow taking to the air to fly to another.

Her mouth quirked as she realized what a tortured simile she'd crafted, and her imagination slid back down into her body. She turned and looked at the warm light spilling from the windows of Andru's. Shadowy figures moved behind the glass.

Where is he? She glanced at her wrist chronometer and was alarmed by how late it was. How long *had* she listened to Kriss's music?

By now, her absence had to have been noticed at the ship. They'd be looking for her.

She glanced up. Clouds were starting to swallow the stars. She lowered her gaze to Andru's again. *Hurry up,* she mouthed silently. *Hurry up!*

THIS TIME, as the music began, Kriss tried to consciously shape it into melody and harmony as he once had—but the touchlyre wouldn't let him. Even more strongly than the night before, it reached into his mind with intangible fingers and pulled him deep into himself, searching out the dreams and hopes and loneliness buried in his soul and translating them into sound and . . . whatever else the touchlyre projected.

When the strings stilled at last, he opened his eyes and blinked away tears. The offworlders were silent. The big man by the door still watched him, eyes narrowed, but Kriss barely spared him a glance before turning his gaze to Tevera. She sat with head bowed a moment longer, then swiped her sleeve across her face and looked up. Their eyes met. She glanced at the door, then back at him. He gave her the briefest of nods. She stood and went out.

He longed to follow her, but he couldn't yet. He had to wait as listeners crowded forward to drop coins into his bowl. The same silver-haired woman as the night before was first, but far from the last: at least twenty made the pilgrimage, and it seemed to take forever.

Finally, after no one had come forward for five minutes that felt more like an hour, Kriss glanced at Andru, who nodded. He snatched up the bowl and took it over to where the innkeeper stood, at the end of the bar nearest the beaded curtain and the main staircase. While Andru counted the money, Kriss took the touchlyre up to his room and locked it in. When he returned, the innkeeper said, "One hundred ninety-four feds. Do you want any of your share now?"

"No," Kriss said, impatient to be gone. "Put it in the safe."

"As you wish." Andru gathered up the bills and change. "You did very well," he added unexpectedly as Kriss turned to go. "I thank you." He rustled through the beads, headed for his office.

Startled by the compliment, Kriss stared after him for a moment, then remembered Tevera. He hurried past the scowling giant by the door—*what's his problem, anyway?*—and into the cool darkness.

Chapter Eight

As he crossed the road, he glanced up, hoping to see the stars, but they had largely disappeared behind thickening streamers of low-hanging, ragged clouds, lit from below by the lights of the city, riding a rising wind just beginning to moan around the inn's chimney.

He looked up and down the street, then finally spotted Tevera directly across from him, at the mouth of an alley. She gestured to him frantically. He crossed the street, and she grabbed his arm and jerked him into the darkness between the buildings. "No one must see us together!" she whispered.

"But—"

"Farther in." She pulled him along. "There aren't any lights back here. We should be safe."

Kriss followed. After a few metres, the alley turned left, then right again. Around that corner was a rectangular space beneath an overhanging roof, housing a blank steel door. They stepped into that shadowed space, where the darkness was all but total. The rising howl of the wind, louder here, masked all other sounds of the city.

They stood in silence for a moment. *Well, someone has to speak first,* Kriss thought. "Tevera—"

"Where did you get that thing you play?" she demanded, her words coming in a rush at the same moment he said her name.

"It's not a *thing*," he said, stung. "It's called a touchlyre."

"Fine," she said. "Touchlyre. But where did you get it? How does it do . . . what it does?"

"What *does* it do?" Kriss countered.

"You mean, you don't know?" She sounded almost angry.

"I know what it feels like to me, but I don't know what you—"

"Shhh!" She gripped his arm suddenly and painfully. "Listen!"

He heard only the wind. "I don't—" he began, then broke off as something rustled around the corner leading to the street. They both held their breaths, but the sound didn't come again. "Just a skrat," Kriss finally ventured.

"I guess so." Tevera released his arm, and he rubbed the place she'd squeezed so tight. "How can you not know what your own instrument does?" she demanded, returning to the argument abruptly, but with less heat.

"I don't really hear it when I'm playing. I'm . . . concentrating." He paused, wishing he could see her face in the darkness. "So please, tell me. Why are people reacting to it so strongly?"

For a moment, she was silent. "I *can't* tell you," she said at last.

He grimaced in the dark. "You can't tell me much, can you?"

"This is different. I just . . . I haven't . . . I don't have the right words."

"At least tell me if you enjoyed it."

"Enjoyed? No, I wouldn't say that . . . not exactly."

"I don't understand!" The words came out half-strangled by frustration.

"Neither do I." Tevera paused again. "You still haven't told me where it came from."

"From my father."

"And where is he? And your mother?"

"They died when I was a baby. I was raised by a guardian, Mella. She gave me the touchlyre when I turned twelve, standard. Now she's dead, too. I don't have any family left, not on this planet."

"No family?"

Tevera sounded so genuinely shocked Kriss felt a surge of hope. He rushed on. "That's why I came to Cascata. My parents were offworlders—you can tell just by looking at me—so somewhere off-planet, I must have relatives. I'm going to join a shipcrew so I can go look for them."

"Oh, no," Tevera whispered.

"What's wrong?"

She didn't answer. "The touchlyre is from offworld, too, isn't it?"

"Mella said my father made it."

"The outside, maybe. But not whatever's inside. Farr's World doesn't have technology like that."

"So what?" he said. "It's just a musical instrument."

"'Just a musical instrument' wouldn't affect the world-hoppers in Andru's like that."

"Like *what*? Just what does it do that's so terrible?"

"I think . . ." She hesitated, then rushed on. "I think it somehow projects emotions. *Your* emotions."

"Any well-played instrument will—"

"That's not what I mean. That 'touchlyre' actually makes people feel what you feel—*exactly* what you feel. It's like . . ." Her voice dropped. "Like you're standing up there naked, naked all the way down to your soul."

Ghostly fingers reaching inside his mind . . .

No! It's just a musical instrument.

"You're crazy," he said, and instantly regretted it.

TEVERA FELT A SURGE OF FURY. She was AWOL from *Thaylia*, she'd lied to Corvus, there'd be hell to pay when she got home, she'd risked all that to ask this worldhugger how that "touchlyre" of his did what it did, and he wouldn't even believe her when she told him what she'd experienced?

Her fists clenched. "Crazy?" Her anger must have been clear in her voice because she sensed him taking an involuntary step back. She stepped forward deliberately. "Crazy? Why do you think I'm out here? For my health?"

"I—"

"When I heard you play last night, I felt your loneliness. Not just intellectually, but in my heart, as if . . . as if the feelings were my own." And just like that, the anger fled, draining away like water down a suction tube, replaced by that memory, of last night's performance, and this night's, too. Her fists relaxed, and she looked down. "I've felt loneliness, too, among my people," she almost whispered. She'd never admitted it to anyone on *Thaylia*, especially not to Rigel, but since their parents had died . . . "I thought you might be someone who would understand."

She sensed movement, and then Kriss's hand touched her shoulder. She stiffened, coming suddenly back to herself, to the reality of her situation, and of her life. *This was a mistake*, she thought. She took a sharp step back, out of his reach, and when she spoke again, her voice was so tightly controlled that even in her own ears it sounded like it might have belonged to the ship's AI. "I was wrong to agree to talk to you. I have to return to my ship now."

"Wait a minute!" Kriss said. "You've asked your questions. What about mine?"

Leave now, she thought, but once more, the memory of the touchlyre's song softened her resolve. "All right," she said after a moment. "I suppose that's only fair. But be quick. What do you want to ask?"

"I told you what I want. You're a crewmember on a starship. That's what I want to be. How do I make it happen?"

That was the question she'd been afraid he would ask. "You don't," she said flatly. There was no way to let him down gently. "You can't."

"*What?*" His voice sounded as if she'd slapped him.

"You can never become a starship crewmember." She emphasized each word.

"Why not?"

Because you're a worldhugger. "Because you're neither Family nor Union."

"Family? Union? What are they?"

How could anyone be so clueless? "I'm not a public information terminal," she snapped. "Look it up. I've answered your question. I'm going back to my ship. Peace be yours."

She turned to leave.

"You can't go!" He grabbed her right shoulder from behind—not just touching this time but gripping, hard. Reflex took over. She grabbed his wrist with her left hand, pinning it to her shoulder, then bent her right arm and spun toward him with her elbow while she stepped back with her right foot. The motion twisted his arm and forced him toward the ground with a startled grunt. She could have kneed him in the chest or mouth then, felled him with a sharp blow to the back of his neck, or killed him, for that matter, but instead, she unflexed the bent arm and simply pushed him hard with her open palm. He fell to his hands and knees, and she stepped back. "*Don't touch me.*" Her voice sounded frightening in her own ears, equal parts ice and fire.

She took another step back, hands ready, as she heard him struggle to his feet, in case he rushed her. But he just stood there, breathing hard. "You can't drop something like that on me and then walk away!"

"Can't I?" But she felt guilty for what she'd just done. She knew how he longed for the stars . . . had experienced his longing as her own, when he played. She had just dashed the starship of dreams against the unyielding asteroid of truth. All he wanted was to understand why.

She took a deep breath and let her hands fall. "All right. I'll tell you what most people already know or guess. But that's all."

"Thanks a lot," he muttered.

She ignored the sarcasm. "I belong to the Family ship *Thaylia*. The Family is actually many families, each of which has its own ship, all bound by long-standing rules and traditions—one of which is that no one who is not born into or adopted by one of the families can ever serve on a Family ship." She paused to be sure he was following her.

"Go on," he said.

"The Union is the Interstellar Union of Spaceship Crews," she continued. "It's very powerful, both politically and financially. The Union requires all starships not of the Family to be crewed by Union members—no exceptions. And the Union is as closed as the Family. New members are recruited only from the Core worlds, and from a vanishingly small group of candidates, all of whom already have connections to the Union through family members, powerful political connections, or wealth. Here, on Farr's World . . . you cannot join. No one can."

And then, though she hated to do it, she smashed his dreams against truth one more time. "You are not a member of the Family. You cannot join the Union. And therefore, you can never join the crew of a ship."

After a moment's silence, he whispered, "But . . . there *has* to be a way."

She heard the pleading in his voice and felt for him . . . had literally felt his longing as if it were her own when he played . . . but it changed nothing.

"You said something about being adopted into the Family . . .?" he said after a moment.

"It hasn't happened in my lifetime," she said, as gently as she could.

"But it *has* happened."

She sighed. *Hopeless.* "Not for decades. A Family member has to give up his or her place in the Family to the one being adopted. No one of the Family could ever do that."

Another pause. "You're Family," he said in a low, desperate voice. "Can't you . . .?"

She took a step back, shocked almost beyond words. "Give up my place? Never!"

"No, I didn't mean that! I meant . . . the Family must have records . . . you could check them, see if you can find out anything about my parents. Maybe *they* were Union . . . or even Family!"

This was a mistake. The phrase was running over and over through her head now. *This was a mistake. This was a mistake!* "I've done all I can for you, and more than I should have!" she cried. "I shouldn't even be talking to you!"

She turned and fled.

This time, he let her go.

AS TEVERA TURNED THE CORNER, abandoning him, Kriss leaned back against the wall, stunned by the sudden crushing of his dream. No way to get into space . . . no way at all?

The future stretched out in front of him, bleak and hopeless, a future trapped on Farr's World. He'd have to leave Cascata. He couldn't live here, so near to the spaceport, watching ships descend and take off for space. It would tear him apart.

As though in sympathy, the wind shrieked . . .

And then he jerked his head back down. *That wasn't the wind!*

He darted around the corner—and crashed into Tevera and the man who held her, all three of them tumbling to the ground in a squirming, tangled heap. Tevera scrambled up first and dashed back around the kink in the alley, but when Kriss tried to follow her, her attacker grabbed his ankle and brought him crashing to the cobblestones, their sharp edges tearing his knees and palms.

He struggled up, but something hit him in the small of the back, and he thudded down against the hard stones again. He gasped for breath that wouldn't come, head spinning.

His attacker dug a hard knee into the small of his back. "We're going back to Andru's, boy," a harsh voice growled. "You've got something I want." The man gripped Kriss's shoulder with vise-like fingers and hauled him to his feet, and in the faint light Kriss recognized the big offworlder who had been seated by the door . . . and must have followed him out.

"Money's . . . in . . . safe . . ." he choked out, pretending to misunderstand.

"Don't play stupid!" His assailant threw him against the wall and held him there, arm twisted painfully behind his back, face pressed to the rough stone. "I've already wasted too much time on this job. You were lucky last night, but your luck's run out."

"Not quite," said a new voice, calm and deep. A cloaked figure stood at the entrance to the alley.

Kriss's attacker swore and threw Kriss to the side. Kriss fell to his hands and knees again, and his attacker lunged at the newcomer. Kriss scrambled up and staggered in the direction Tevera had taken. A brilliant flash lit the alley, and a chunk of the brick wall close by his head exploded. Hot slivers of stone stung his face as he rounded the corner where the alley zig-zagged left-right. Ten metres past the alcove where he'd talked with Tevera, the alley zig-zigged again, this time right-left. He burst out into a comparatively brightly lit street. Tevera clung to a nearby lamp post as though it were the only thing keeping her upright. He staggered toward her. "Run!" he gasped.

KRISS AT HER SIDE, Tevera fled down another alley and across two more streets. Stopping at last in the dark doorway of a deserted building, they both sank to the crumbling steps. "Are you all right?" she started to ask, but he asked it at the same moment, so that it came out in unison.

Kriss laughed shakily. "I think so."

There was more light there than there had been in the alley. Tevera saw something dark on Kriss's cheek, and without thinking, reached out and touched it. When she drew her hand back, her fingertips glistened. "You're bleeding!"

"Someone shot at me . . . just missed."

She'd seen the flash, hadn't known what it was. "Someone? The same man who grabbed me?"

"Or the other guy."

Tevera blinked. "What other guy?"

"Someone else showed up. The first guy tossed me aside and went after him. I ran."

"Someone else? Who?"

"I don't know." Kriss shook his head. "I don't know who *either* of them was!"

Tevera took a deep, still-shuddery breath. "I ran right into that man when I turned the corner. He grabbed me . . ."

Kriss flexed his right arm, the one she'd twisted to put him on the ground. "I'm surprised you didn't get away," he said ruefully.

Tevera remembered her struggle. He'd known what he was doing, and he'd been strong. So strong . . . "I tried. I couldn't." She took another shaky breath. "So I screamed."

"Good thing you did." Kriss struggled to his feet and held out his hand. "Come on."

She hesitated . . . but only for a moment. She let him take her hand and pull her to her feet. "Where?"

"Andru's. I have to tell him—"

Andru's? Tevera jerked her hand free. "No!"

He stared at her. "Why?"

"He'll tell the Family!"

"What will they do, spank you?" Kriss asked in renewed exasperation.

He doesn't know about Andru, she thought. But it wasn't up to her to tell him. And his words had stung. She drew herself upright. "That's right, why should you care? Go ahead—report it. Not that it will do any good. Andru will tell the Family, and then he'll tell the police—and that will be the end of it. Farrsian police are useless." Anger swelled in her. "But at least it will teach me to obey regulations in the future and have nothing to do with worldhuggers like you!"

"If you don't want me to tell Andru, I won't. But you've got to do something for me, too."

Anger became fury. "Is this blackmail? I won't look into Family records for you!"

"I never should have asked."

"No, you shouldn't."

Kriss took a breath. When he spoke again, he sounded almost desperate. "Look, what about this: see what your computer can tell you about my parents—public records only, nothing Family-specific. My name's Kriss Lemarc, and my parents died soon after I was born, about sixteen standard years ago. I don't know for sure if that was on Farr's World or somewhere else." He'd always thought it had happened here, but had Mella actually said that? Where *had* they lived before she took him to Black Rock? "How many Lemarcs can have died or vanished at the same time?" he hurried on. "If I can't join a shipcrew, my only hope is to find out which world my parents were from and buy passage there."

"Passenger tickets cost thousands of feds!" Didn't he know *anything*?

"I know," he said. "I know! But . . . it's the only hope I have left. Will you help me?"

Again, Tevera remembered the sorrow and loss and longing and hope in his music. She hesitated.

"I promise—not a word to Andru."

A simple computer search . . . there were no regulations against that. Weakening, she said, "All right. I'll see what I can find out."

"Good." Kriss looked nervously over his shoulder. "Let's get out of here."

That, she could agree with. She let him take her hand again and, his fingers warm in hers, they ran.

Chapter Nine

Well clear of both the alley where they had been attacked and of Andru's, Kriss and Tevera separated. "You promise you'll search the computer," he said to her as he released her hand.

"Yes," she said. "And you promise you won't tell Andru I was with you tonight."

"I promise."

"It may be a while before I can leave the spaceport again," Tevera warned him.

"I'm not going anywhere," Kriss said, with more than a little bitterness.

Tevera nodded and headed for the spaceport, soon vanishing in the shadows.

Kriss made his way cautiously back to Andru's, lingering down the street for a long time until he was certain his attacker wasn't waiting outside. When he went in, Andru nodded to him without a word as he passed the bar. He climbed the stairs to his room, where he lay sleepless for a long time, staring up into the darkness.

So what if Tevera says it's impossible? he thought. *She's wrong. She has to be. There has to be some way for me to get into space. There has to be!*

Tomorrow, he decided, he'd ask Andru.

But at the thought of the innkeeper, he felt guilty. The man who had attacked him in the alley had also broken into Andru's, and Kriss knew how much Andru would have liked to get his hands on him. *But a promise is a promise. I promised Tevera I won't tell anyone about us meeting if she tries to find out what she can about my parents.*

He threw himself onto his right side, uncomfortably aware that he was using, in a way, even blackmailing, the offworlder girl. *But she wouldn't have helped me otherwise!* he told his conscience.

Somehow, that didn't make him feel any better.

THE NEXT MORNING, after breakfast, he knocked diffidently on Andru's office door. "Enter," Andru said, and Kriss pushed the door open and looked in. The innkeeper sat at his computer interface, eyes flicking over the display. "What is it?" he said without looking up.

"May I talk to you, sir?"

"In a moment. Sit down."

Kriss sat on the familiar stool and waited. After a few uncomfortable minutes, Andru touched the control pad and looked up. "Yes?"

"I want to ask you something about—uh, starship crews."

His employer raised an eyebrow but nodded.

"Someone told me last night that only Union or Family members can get berths on starships. Is that true?"

"Yes."

Kriss slumped. "Then I should have stayed in Black Rock," he muttered.

"Anything else?" The innkeeper looked down at his screen again.

On impulse, Kriss said, "Yes. Can you tell me about the Family?"

Andru's head snapped up, eyes glaring. "Get out!" Kriss sat frozen with shock, and Andru rose, fists clenched, and started around the desk. "*Get out!*"

Kriss scrambled up, the stool clattering to the floor, backed to the door, and fumbled his way through it into the corridor. The door slammed behind him. Heart thudding, he leaned against the panelled wall and took a couple of deep breaths. What had brought *that* on?

He remembered the words of the innkeeper who had first told him about Andru. "He's a strange man, with a whipcrack temper." For the first time, he'd seen evidence that was true.

He spent the rest of the day at loose ends. He didn't want to see the spaceport, not after what he'd learned. He *did* want to see Tevera, but plainly that was impossible. Instead, he wandered the streets, kicking at bits of trash and brooding. When he returned to Andru's that night, he doubted he could play anything worth listening to, and he really didn't care. He picked at his supper, slouching in his chair and glaring at the crowd in the common room with a dull mixture of anger and self-pity. *Every one of them is either Union or Family. They can go anywhere in the galaxy. Some of them probably don't even like it. They'd love to settle down on a nice quiet planet like this, while I want to leave and can't. It's not fair!*

When he took his place by the fire, his music began harshly, with angry discords that drew frowns from the listeners and a black look from Andru. But almost instantly, with frightening speed and intensity, he felt the instrument's ghostly fingers in his mind, brushing aside depression and anger and touching the dream at the core of his soul, the dream that, despite everything, lived on.

When the music died, he raised his eyes to a room so silent the crackle of the fire seemed an intrusion, and Tevera's strange words about projected emotions came back to him. Could it be true? Certainly, the offworlders seemed to share something of what he felt. He saw a young man not much older than him surreptitiously wiping his eyes.

But he didn't see Tevera or the man who had attacked them; and if their mysterious rescuer was on hand, he had no way of knowing.

When he took the money bowl to the bar, he handed it to Andru a little hesitantly, but the innkeeper gave no hint of his morning rage. He simply divided the credits and said, "Good job."

It's as if nothing happened, Kriss thought as he climbed to his room later. *It's as if it were my first night here.*

THAT DAY SET a pattern for the next two weeks: nothing happened. No sign of Tevera, their attacker, or their rescuer.

No suggestion from anyone that he might ever find his way into space. Every night he played, and every night it seemed the touchlyre dug a little deeper into his soul, and his music moved his listeners a little more. His store of feds grew, but it would take him ten years to save enough to buy passage off the planet at this rate.

During the days, Kriss systematically explored the city, from the backwards suburbs to the glittering but half-empty centre. He even ventured to the sordid, run-down section on the other side of the spaceport from Andru's, a place where shadows lurked even in daytime between tall brick buildings with boarded-up windows and triple-locked doors.

Cascata, so strange and wonderful when he first saw it, began to pall as the days passed. At night, lying in his bed, Kriss spun an elaborate fantasy in which his parents proved to be important people in the Family, and Tevera escorted him triumphantly to her ship. But it remained fantasy; he began to think Tevera had broken their agreement. He even toyed with the idea of telling Andru about his meeting with the girl and the attack on them outside Andru's inn, in the spiteful hope the news would get back to Tevera's ship, and she would be punished.

Then, just when he had made up his mind that he wouldn't see her again, she returned.

THINGS HAD GONE PRETTY MUCH as Tevera expected upon her return to *Thaylia*. Corvus, still on duty, gave her a sorrowful look as she came in. "You're in trouble. And so am I."

"I'm sorry," she said.

"Where did you go?"

That, she wouldn't tell him. Or Rigel, when he confronted her later. "I just needed to get off the ship," she said. "That's all."

"Alone. In Cascata. At night." Rigel's voice was tight with anger. "Stars and moons, Tevera, you could have been . . ." He didn't finish the sentence. He didn't have to.

"I can take care of myself," she said. She spread her hands. "Look, here I am, safe and sound."

"And here you'll stay," he snapped. "Confined to ship for the next two weeks."

She didn't argue. That still gave her time to get a message back to Kriss before they were scheduled to lift. And being confined to the ship would also give her plenty of opportunities to conduct the computer search she'd promised.

Not that she thought she'd find anything . . .

. . . but as it turned out, she was wrong.

The moment her suspension was lifted, she asked for permission to listen to a local musical group in a very respectable eating establishment just across the street from one of the spaceport gates . . . making sure to ask for it on an evening when she knew her brother would also be out so that she didn't have to ask for it from him. "Three hours," the night officer said. "One minute later, and you won't get off the ship again until we lift."

"Three hours," she promised, and headed out into the night.

Chapter Ten

The music ended, the phantom fingers of the touchlyre slipped from his mind, and Kriss looked up at the silent crowd . . . and saw Tevera at the back of the common room, wearing the same clothes she'd worn the night of the attack. She jerked her head toward the door and went out.

He followed when he could, searching the street carefully before crossing to the same alley in which they'd met before. Though he saw no one, stepping into the dark passage where he'd been attacked made him feel unpleasantly vulnerable. "Tevera?" he whispered as he rounded the corner into darkness.

"Here," she said, and he felt her light touch on his arm.

"I'd about given up on you."

Her touch vanished. "I promised I would help you. No one in the Family breaks a promise."

He bit off a hot retort. He hadn't waited two weeks to see

her again just so he could start an argument. "What did you find out?"

She took a deep breath. "Only one couple named Lemarc disappeared in the time period you outlined—at least, only one was recorded in the Commonwealth Library."

"My parents!" Kriss's pulse raced.

"Maybe." He heard rustling, and a moment later, a tiny light clicked on in Tevera's right hand, lighting a sheet of paper in her left and also dimly illuminating her face. "I'll just read this to you. It's a transcript of a news report. I made a hard copy so I could erase the file from my data storage." She held the light close to the paper. "'Jon and Memory Lemarc, extraterrestrial archaeologists, were officially declared missing today by the Commonwealth Space Force when their scheduled monthly report became two weeks overdue.

"'The Lemarcs, who were funded by an anonymous wealthy patron, kept the location of their research secret, making a search impossible. Although their patron may know where they were working, the Space Force has been unable to identify him.

"'Anyone having any information about the Lemarcs' whereabouts is asked to contact their local or planetary police or the Commonwealth Space Force directly.'" She stopped.

Kriss let out a breath he hadn't realized he'd been holding. "There's nothing else?"

"That's all I can tell you," Tevera said. "I tried to access any personal files they might have left in the Library, but everything was privacy-locked."

"What about this mysterious patron?"

Tevera sighed. "Kriss, I really tried, but no luck. What I read you is all I know."

"My parents died on Farr's World. Could they have been doing research here?"

Tevera folded the printout and slipped it into her pocket, but left the light on, setting it on a window ledge close at hand. "The only ancient remains here are fish fossils. We're the first civilization on this planet. The ancient alien spacefarers your parents would have been studying never came here."

"They probably didn't have much use for it." Kriss tried the names Tevera had given him on his tongue. "Jon and Memory Lemarc. Jon and Memory . . ." He glanced at Tevera, barely visible in the glow from the little light. "Did you find out where they're from?"

She hesitated a moment. "Earth," she said finally.

"Earth!" Kriss swallowed. Passage to Earth would cost not just thousands but *tens* of thousands of feds, and even then, he couldn't be sure of getting to the planet's surface. Much like what Tevera had told him about joining the Union, you had to have connections.

Except . . .

Hope leaped in his heart. "But then . . . I'm an Earth citizen!"

Tevera shook her head. "It's not that simple. How can you prove it? You have no real evidence Jon and Memory Lemarc were your parents. Earth authorities are used to people trying to scam their way onto the home planet. They'll never believe you."

She's right. He leaned heavily against the metal door of

the building behind him. *Another dead end.* "So now what? I can't join a crew, I can't afford to buy passage, and even if I could, they wouldn't let me land!" He felt like a hand was closing on his throat, choking him. "Do I have to spend the rest of my life *here*?"

TEVERA HEARD the frustration in Kriss's voice . . . and again, remembered what she had felt in his music, his longing for the stars, for a home, for a family. She stepped closer. "Don't give up!" she said urgently. "You can still get off this planet. Buy a short passage somewhere else—Estercarth, or Dunnigan's Doom, anywhere. Your instrument is your ticket. People will pay to hear you play wherever you go!"

"But it's not just the travel! I want to see what's out there, but I . . ." The words choked off. "I don't want to see it alone," he finished in a whisper.

She reached out to him then, took his hand as he had taken hers before they'd separated the last time. "I wish I could help. But there's nothing else I can do."

His hand tightened on hers, and then he took her other hand, too. They stood facing each other. Her body tingled at his touch. "At least I know who my parents were," he said softly. "Thank you for that."

"Thank you for your music," she said. She hesitated. *He's a worldhugger*, she reminded herself. But she carried on anyway. "The way you feel . . . alone, I mean . . . I understand."

"How can you? You have your ship, your Family . . ."

"My parents . . . our parents, Rigel's and mine . . . died when I was six and he was ten. An accident. Like the one that killed yours."

"I'm sorry," Kriss murmured. "I didn't know . . ."

"How could you?" She squeezed his hands. "Three years ago, an onboard explosion damaged *Thaylia*. We limped to the nearest inhabited planet, Feldenspar, even more low-tech than Farr's World. Without proper facilities, it took us a long time to repair the ship: we had to message another Family ship to bring us the equipment we needed. We lived on that planet for almost a year.

"Most of the Family stayed close to the ship, with only brief forays into the surrounding countryside. But I went everywhere, saw everything I could—mountains, seas, prairies, forests; cities, farms, and villages." She'd been looking at their clasped hands; now she raised her eyes to his face. "I saw a lot of beauty, Kriss. For the first time, I realized there is something to be said for 'worldhugging,' that there can be other ways of living just as worthwhile as ours. Ever since, I've seen planets differently, as more than just places where we unload and pick up cargo and make money off gullible worldhuggers." She squeezed his hands tighter. "No one else on *Thaylia* feels the way I do. Not even Rigel. *Especially* not Rigel. Our parents died on a planet. I think he's hated them ever since." She shook her head. "Most of the Family would be shocked to hear what I just told you. I've seen a hundred different worlds—but even though I'm surrounded by my Family all the time, I've seen them alone."

And then . . . whether he started it, or she did, or they moved at the same moment, suddenly they were holding each other, arms around each other, and his body was warm against hers, her head resting on his chest, his cheek resting in her hair. Her heart was pounding, but it was a pleasurable pounding.

Oh, no, she though. *No, this isn't . . .*

His cheek moved from the top of her head. She lifted her gaze to him, to find his lips very close, and his eyes, bright even in the dim light of the little hand-lamp, and again, she couldn't have said if he started it or she did, but their lips met, and their arms tightened, and for a timeless instant only the two of them existed in all the universe . . .

But it couldn't last. It *mustn't* last. Tevera gasped, put her hands to Kriss's chest, and pushed him away. He stepped back and blinked at her, an expression of almost comical confusion on his face, as if he wasn't at all sure what had just happened.

She wasn't at all sure what had just happened, either. But she knew it shouldn't have. Knew it could never happen again . . .

. . . and already, the thought was breaking her heart. "I have to go," she said, voice unsteady. "Before someone finds us together."

His eyes stared at her, glittering in the light. His mouth was so close . . .

Swallowing hard, she reached out and switched off the hand-lamp, grabbed it from the windowsill, and started back toward the street.

Kriss followed close behind, without speaking.

"Tevera!" The harsh voice that rang from the porch of Andru's as Tevera reached the mouth of the alley demanded instant obedience. "Stay where you are!"

Rigel!

KRISS, dazed and confused by what had just happened, bumped into Tevera's back as she stopped dead at the sound of that shout. He peered across the street and saw one of the young men who had been with her the first night in Andru's appear out of the shadows and stalk toward them threateningly.

Kriss moved in front of Tevera, fists ready, but Tevera stopped him with a hand on his arm. "Don't, Kriss," she said. "He's my brother. Rigel."

Rigel stopped a couple of metres away and glared at his sister. "Return to *Thaylia*, Tevera. You are confined to the ship for the remainder of our stay on this planet. And there'll be more disciplinary action after we lift. Twice now you've lied to the night officer to leave the ship without permission."

"I had permission tonight," Tevera said.

"Not to come here," Rigel snapped. "Not to see this worldhugger."

"Rigel . . ."

"Back to the ship. Now!"

FOR A MOMENT, Tevera glared at her brother. She wanted to defy him, wanted to refuse his order to return to the ship . . .

. . . but she couldn't. He was not only her brother but her superior officer. To openly defy him was unthinkable. The Family was, first and foremost, a starship crew. Discipline was all-important. In an emergency, you had to know that people would obey orders.

This isn't an emergency, she thought. And it wasn't, to her. But it seemed clear from the look on her brother's face that to him, it was.

Confined to port. For the remainder of her time on this planet.

Kriss . . .

She gave the Farrsian boy a last, agonized look. "I'm sorry, Kriss," she said. "I . . ."

"Go," Rigel said. "Now. To your quarters."

"I have to go," she said to Kriss, then turned and walked away.

She did not run. She wouldn't give Rigel that satisfaction. Her steady footsteps echoed off the buildings around her as she walked toward the lights of the spaceport. The kiss and embrace she and Kriss had shared was a bright, glowing memory, but it had meant nothing. It *could* mean nothing.

She could never see Kriss Lemarc again.

His voice suddenly rang out behind her, a desperate shout. "Tevera! Come back!"

She took a deep, shuddering breath. She kept walking.

She didn't look back.

KRISS TOOK A STEP AFTER TEVERA, but Rigel blocked him. "You are perhaps unaware of our regulation prohibiting close contact between the Family and planet-dwellers," he said in a voice like ice. "But be warned now: we begin by punishing our own, but if necessary, we can deal with you, too." He took a step closer. "And as Tevera's brother, I swear —do not try to see her again, or we *will* deal with you!"

Furious, Kriss hardly heard the threat. "Tevera! Come back!" he shouted into the night.

Not even an echo answered. Kriss tried to sidestep Rigel, but Tevera's brother suddenly grabbed his arm, twisted it behind him, and shoved him hard against the nearest building. He held him there, one hand keeping Kriss's forearm pressed painfully to the small of his back, the other hand tight against Kriss's head, pushing his cheek into the crumbling brick. "I think," Rigel said, "we will give her a few minutes."

Kriss tried to struggle, but Rigel was older, bigger, and stronger. Kriss would have cursed him, but Rigel had his face shoved so tight to the wall he couldn't speak. He could barely breathe. He could do nothing but wait, seething with anger.

An interminable time later, Rigel suddenly pulled him from the wall and pushed him back in the direction of Andru's, so hard he stumbled and fell to his hands and knees. When he scrambled up and spun to face the Family crewman, Rigel was already walking away.

For a moment, Kriss almost chased after him, wanting to tackle him, shove him against the cobblestones, pin him as he had been pinned . . . but even in his anger, a voice of reason prevailed. The Family crew had been well-trained in self-defence, and Kriss hadn't. Tevera had already shown him that. Rigel would be expecting him to do something like that, and no doubt would have him on the ground in an instant . . . this time, maybe with a broken bone or two.

And so, instead, he stood impotently in the street and watched Rigel walk away, taking all his hopes and dreams with him.

Chapter Eleven

Once Rigel had disappeared into the darkness, Kriss turned the opposite direction. For an hour, he aimlessly walked the streets, blaming himself. He should never have gotten Tevera involved! *Now I'll never see her again—and she'll never forgive me!*

He could still feel the warmth of her body against his, the sweet touch of her lips on his. He could hardly bear the ache in his heart. When at last he returned to Andru's and went upstairs to his bed, the room closed around him like a trap from which he could never escape. He had lost his only contact with the universe beyond Farr's World.

It took him a long time to fall asleep.

The thunder of a rocket jolted him awake. He jerked upright, heart pounding, then recognized the noise, threw off the covers, ran to the window and banged open the shutters, sickly certain that *Thaylia* was leaving.

But no, the roar didn't fade, it grew louder. A *fifth* starship was coming to Farr's World.

His first impulse was to dress and rush to the port, but his excitement died as the night's events swept down to roost like black starklings. "Why bother?" he muttered. He slammed the shutters shut and crawled back into the sweat-dampened, wrinkled bed, where sleep mercifully reclaimed him.

Shortly after noon, he finally got up and went downstairs, not rested, but unable to stay in bed any longer. He sat at his usual table and stared glumly out the window at the sun-drenched street. An ancient groundcar rattled past, its choking exhaust fouling the fresh breeze.

"I wondered if we would see you today," Zendra said cheerfully behind him. "You're too late for breakfast, but I can still get you lunch."

He didn't even look at her. "I'm not hungry."

She circled the table to stand between him and the window; he looked down at his hands, listless on the dark wood. "Don't you feel well?"

"No." True, though not in the way she meant.

"I thought so. I told Andru there must be something wrong with you when you didn't come dashing downstairs the moment that ship landed this morning." She paused. "You did hear it, didn't you?"

"Yes."

"Well, you should see it, too! It's a tiny thing, barely half as tall as even that Family trader, and gold as a wedding ring." Leaning toward him, she lowered her voice. "Rumour is, it belongs to Carl Vorlick."

"Who?" The question emerged before Kriss remembered he wasn't interested.

"Carl Vorlick. Vorlick Interstellar? United Galaxy Spaceways? Pleasure Planets, Inc.?"

Kriss shrugged. "Never heard of him."

Zendra laughed. "Then Black Rock must be even more isolated than I thought. He's one of the richest men in the Commonwealth—always in the news."

"So, what's he doing on a nothing planet like this?"

"Oddly enough, he didn't tell me. Probably here to see our own local tycoon, Salazar. They're two of a kind, from what I hear. Buying and selling, that's all they care about, never mind who loses their job or home. In fact, Salazar was in here a few days ago trying to buy Andru's."

"What?" That startled Kriss out of his lethargy. "Why?"

"Who knows? He already owns a bunch of so-called 'inns' south of the port." Her voice dripped disapproval. "You can get anything you want over there, they say. Anything at all. But maybe Salazar wants a place over here. A *respectable* place."

Kriss remembered his one sojourn into the area south of the port, and what he had seen there. "Why don't the police do something about those places?"

Zendra snorted. "Salazar owns the police, too—or at least enough of them to do what he wants."

"And Vorlick is just like that?"

"Worse. Salazar buys and sells factories and businesses and corporations—and the lives of the people involved with them—here on Farr's World and in a couple of other nearby systems. Vorlick buys and sells whole planets, all over the Commonwealth." Her tone turned businesslike. "But this is no time for gossip. If you don't feel well, soup is the thing for you. Think you could get some down?"

He nodded absent-mindedly, his thoughts on what she had just told him. "Andru didn't sell, did he?" If Andru sold the inn, he'd lose his job *and* his last tenuous link with the stars.

"Andru wouldn't sell to Salazar if the alternative were being roasted alive on our own spit," Zendra said. She straightened. "Right. Soup and hot stimtea. That'll pick you up." She hurried off.

Kriss shook his head. Nothing could pick him up.

But supper the night before had been a long time ago, and despite himself, his mouth watered when the soup was set in front of him, steaming and spicy, with fresh-baked bread on the side. He polished it off and even drained the cup of stimtea, a strong green drink he normally avoided. When he was done, he felt a little better, though the bitterness of the tea lingered in his mouth. He decided he would go take a look at the new ship, after all.

He hardly dared to admit, even to himself, that he also hoped to glimpse Tevera.

The moment he came out onto the road circling the spaceport, he saw the new ship glittering in the sunlight, nearer the perimeter fence than any of the others. Sleek, needle-prowed, and golden-hulled, it put its scarred and tubby grey neighbours to shame.

A ramp extended from a small hatch near the base, and four people stood near one of the landing supports, talking. One of them, a short man whose bald head and silver-braided uniform both shone brightly in the midday sun, was the portmaster, Kriss knew from his previous explorations. Beside him stood another Farrsian, a woman, probably his assistant.

One of the remaining two, tall and fair-skinned, was obviously an offworlder, even though he wore Farrsian clothes, but the fourth was even shorter and darker than the portmaster. From the night-blue glimmer of his strangely cut business suit, Kriss thought he must be an offworlder, too, though he didn't otherwise look it. The tall offworlder struck him as familiar for some reason, but he had his back turned, and the intervening traffic prevented Kriss from getting a good look at him. As he watched, all four moved up the ramp into the starship.

Kriss looked both ways along the road, thinking he would cross and get a better look—and spotted the big man who had attacked him and Tevera two weeks before, standing near the fence, eyes on the golden ship. Heart racing, Kriss ducked behind a parked groundcar and knelt there. A passing woman looked at him suspiciously, but to his relief didn't stop or say anything. When he finally poked his head up again, the big man was gone.

Kriss headed for police headquarters. Enough was enough, and the reason for keeping the attack of the night before secret had vanished when Tevera's brother had seen her with Kriss. Even if her Family found out it hadn't been their first meeting, she could hardly be in worse trouble. In fact, by now, she'd probably told them herself.

He walked with his head down, thinking hard. Why was his attacker so interested in the golden ship? Had he sent for reinforcements? Did he work for this "Carl Vorlick" that Zendra seemed to think he ought to know about?

He glanced up to get his bearings—and froze as the big offworlder stepped through the door of the police tower, only a few metres away. He saw Kriss and smiled. Or, at least, showed his teeth.

After one heart-stopping moment, Kriss turned and ran, darting into the nearest alley and zigging and zagging his way through back streets until he finally had to stop, gulping huge lungfuls of dank, garbage-fouled air. He listened but heard no running footsteps in pursuit; and slowly, he made his troubled way back to Andru's.

Why hadn't the man chased him? The only answer he could come up with wasn't very comforting—that his attacker had a surer way to get what he wanted than grabbing him in full daylight.

Now, he *couldn't* go to the police. The man had come out of police headquarters! Nor did he see how he could talk to Andru, not after the way the innkeeper had exploded when he'd asked about the Family. Andru seemed to hate them—he might throw Kriss out of the inn altogether if he found out he'd been involved with the crew of *Thaylia*, and if that happened, he'd be at the mercy of all his enemies . . .

. . . whoever they were.

Wait, he told himself as he climbed to his room. *Just wait and see. If that golden ship is connected to this whole mess, then something else is going to happen very soon. Maybe then I'll be able to sort out what I should do.*

THAT NIGHT, carrying the touchlyre in its case, he descended to the common room to find it packed to the rafters with offworlders and, to his astonishment, even a few Farrsians. Smoke sweet and foul from a dozen different weeds from as many planets filled the air, mingling with the savoury smells from the kitchen and the sharp scents of the offworld drinks. The clink and rattle of glasses and dishes formed a counterpoint to the murmur of voices, some speaking languages from planets hundreds of light-years from Farr's World ... or so Kriss guessed, since he couldn't understand them. Kriss drank it all in with every sense, thinking bitterly that the sights, smells, and sounds of Andru's might be as close as he would ever come to the myriad worlds of the Commonwealth.

"Feeling better?" Zendra asked as she brought his supper to him at the bar.

He nodded, even though he wasn't.

"Good! I hoped you would be, so I brought you something a little more substantial than soup." She lowered her voice. "Keep your eyes open. Remember our chat about Carl Vorlick? One of his crewmen told me he might show up here tonight." She put her finger to her lips, winked, then spun in a swirl of skirts and returned to the kitchen.

Kriss turned and slowly scanned the room. Many of the faces were familiar, but every night there were a few new ones. None of them looked particularly wealthy, but then, he doubted this Vorlick would advertise his riches, especially not in a city like Cascata.

He shrugged and attacked the roast darbuk Zendra had brought. Just as he finished eating, Andru motioned to him. He gulped down the last of his iced frenta juice, took the touchlyre from its case, which Andru sequestered behind the bar for him, then headed for the platform. He positioned the touchlyre on his lap and then, as Andru introduced him, placed his fingers on the copper plates. The strings hummed to life. He closed his eyes as he felt the touchlyre reach into his mind once more.

This time, the instrument exposed more than just his dream of travelling into space. This time, it bared all the feelings he had tried to hide even from himself—pain, guilt, the beginning of despair; fear, confusion, and bewilderment. Tevera had said hearing him play the instrument was like seeing him standing in front of the crowd naked to his very soul, and for the first time, that was the way it felt to him, too, as if his innermost being were being stripped bare for everyone to see—including himself.

I'm not playing the touchlyre, he thought in one passing moment when, for an instant, he was dimly aware of himself. *The touchlyre is playing me.* Then it plunged him back into the music.

When he surfaced at last, as if from a deep, dark pool, his whole body shook. For a long moment, he sat with eyes closed and head bowed, trying to compose himself before facing the audience. When at last he looked up, he saw his pain mirrored in every face; then offworlders and Farrsians alike crowded forward to drop feds into his bowl.

It should have cheered him to think they understood what he felt . . . but instead, he began to understand Tevera's near-anger when she'd first told him her sense that the touchlyre projected, not just sounds that conjured up emotions in his listeners, but the actual emotions themselves. If that were true, he was manipulating these people, using them as he had tried to use Tevera; and abruptly, he got up and took the money bowl to the bar, roughly shoving the touchlyre back into its case while Andru counted the feds.

As he secured the latches, he sensed someone behind

him and turned to find himself face to face with the man he had seen on the landing ramp of the golden ship wearing a night-blue suit, though now he was dressed in unremitting black from head to toe.

Shorter than Kriss, short even for a Farrsian, the man emanated a sense of power and control that belied his lack of height. He smiled, showing even white teeth in a dark, fine-lined face, but the smile did not warm his eyes, which were a striking ice-blue that betrayed his offworld genetics as surely as Kriss's height and blond hair betrayed his. "Kriss Lemarc?" High-pitched and soft, his voice nevertheless carried an undertone like sharpened steel.

Kriss nodded uneasily.

"May I speak with you in private?"

Kriss felt he should not talk to this dangerous man in private *or* in public, but . . . "Is that your ship that came in this morning?"

The man nodded.

"You're Carl Vorlick?"

The man shrugged and spread his hands. "Guilty as charged."

"Then I'll talk." He tried to sound self-assured. "Where?"

"What could be more private than the streets of Cascata at night?"

"Out front, in ten minutes?"

Vorlick inclined his head. "Ten minutes." He turned and crossed the crowded room, sidestepping people like a cat avoiding puddles in the street.

Andru's face bore no expression when Kriss turned back

to him. "Two hundred fifty-seven feds," he said. "Do you want any of it now?"

"No, put it away." On impulse, he shoved the touchlyre case across the bar. "And put this with it. I don't want to leave it in my room tonight."

Andru accepted it without surprise. "As you wish."

"Thank you." Dry-mouthed, Kriss turned toward the door and the stranger beyond it.

Chapter Twelve

A thick mist shrouded the street outside Andru's, glowing faintly with the diffused radiance of hidden streetlights. Within seconds, it soaked through Kriss's clothes. He shivered.

A black shape materialized within the swirling fog. "A short ten minutes," said the soft voice. With its owner invisible, it sounded cold and emotionless, almost computer-like. "Shall we go?"

With some difficulty, Kriss found his own voice. "Where?"

"Only a little way, into a side street." Faint amusement touched the cold tones. "Sound carries in a fog. I don't want to be overheard."

"All right." Kriss followed Vorlick uneasily across the street. Disturbingly, the man led him into the same alley where he and Tevera had met and talked.

And kissed.

Kriss trailed his icy fingers against the wet stone on his

right to keep from walking into the wall in the misty darkness. Only the clicking of his companion's boots on the cobblestones indicated he wasn't alone.

The footsteps stopped, and so did Kriss. They had not gone as far as the alcove around the corner. He stood silently, waiting for the stranger to speak, wondering who else might be lurking in the darkness. *I was an idiot to come out here!*

"As you no doubt have heard," Vorlick said without preamble, 'I am one of the wealthiest individuals in the Commonwealth. I tell you that not as a boast, but so that you know my promises are good."

"What promises?"

Vorlick ignored the interruption. "My interests are far-ranging and include certain properties in Cascata. Recently one of my employees here informed me that a boy had appeared from nowhere, bearing a peculiar alien instrument."

That startled Kriss. "Alien?"

"Of a certainty. Or perhaps half-alien is a better term. The outside appears to have been crafted by a human to encase the alien mechanism within."

Alien? Kriss was still trying to get his mind around that. *I knew the technology inside had to be from offworld, but* alien?

"Among other pursuits, I collect and trade in ancient alien artifacts," Vorlick continued. "When I heard of your instrument, I decided to investigate it myself. None of my people here have the knowledge to properly evaluate it. I keep track of all archaeological expeditions to known alien sites. I may be able to link it to one of them, if you can answer a few questions for me ...?"

Kriss hesitated. "I guess." *Mella told me to never let*

anyone know about the instrument, he thought. *But it's way too late for that. And if this Vorlick character can tell me where the instrument came from, it could help me learn more about my parents.*

"How did it come to you?" Vorlick said.

"My guardian gave it to me when I was ten."

"And how old are you now?"

"Sixteen, standard. Fourteen, Farrsian."

"And where did your guardian obtain the instrument?"

"It belonged to my parents," Kriss said. "They died when I was a baby."

"My condolences," Vorlick said, without an erg of warmth in his voice. "What were their names?"

Kriss hesitated again. He sensed an unsettling undercurrent to the conversation, as though the offworlder knew more than he was telling. Yet, he could see no reason to keep the information Tevera had given him secret. And if it helped him learn more about his family . . . "Jon and Memory. Jon and Memory Lemarc."

Silence, then, for a long moment. He wished he could see Vorlick's face.

"I heard you play," Vorlick said, abruptly changing course. "Remarkable. Your fingers never touched the strings, only those copper plates—yet the strings sounded. Intriguing enough, but what *most* remarkable was that the instrument seemed to project your emotions along with the sound. We all felt them as if they were our own. Even me. You made hardened spacefarers weep."

Kriss remembered the almost frightening intensity with which the touchlyre had taken hold of him that evening.

Alien? he thought again. The idea made him uneasy. He said nothing.

"What do you call it?" Vorlick said then. "The instrument."

"Touchlyre," Kriss said. He felt faintly embarrassed; the name seemed almost childish now, talking to this offworlder.

"Touchlyre." Vorlick seemed to savour the word. "An interesting name."

There was another long pause. All Kriss could hear was his own breathing and heartbeat, and the slow drip of water: when Vorlick wasn't speaking, nothing betrayed his presence. It was like conversing with a ghost.

"You want to leave Farr's World, don't you?"

The sudden question startled Kriss, but he answered truthfully. "Yes."

"Your performance made that clear." Vorlick paused again. "Your 'touchlyre' could be your ticket off this planet."

"Ticket, sure," Kriss said. "I could sell it, maybe, or eventually earn enough playing it to buy passage . . . in a decade. If I'm lucky. But I want more than a ticket," he rushed on with sudden heat. "If you really felt what I feel, you know that. I want to *belong*—and I can't. I'm not Family or Union, and I can never be either."

Another pause. Then, "You've seen my ship," Vorlick said quietly.

Kriss stiffened. What was the offworlder about to offer?

"I can get you into the Union," Vorlick continued, and Kriss's heart skipped a beat. "All I ask is the touchlyre. Give it to me, and I'll add you to my crew as a trainee. At our next planetfall, I'll sponsor you with the Union. They will accept you without question. After that, you'll be free to take any berth you can find, on any ship going anywhere in the Commonwealth." His voice lowered seductively. "Your dream can be a reality, Kriss. You value the stars. I value your instrument. A fair exchange."

A fair exchange. Kriss swallowed, his throat tight.

He'd always seen the touchlyre as his link to his parents and the rest of the galaxy: the key to finding the world where he truly belonged, and whatever family he might still have among the stars. But thanks to Tevera, he already knew where he'd been born: Earth. And the instrument couldn't take him there.

Vorlick *could.* Such a powerful man would have easy access to Earth, could get him to the surface of the homeworld, help him find whatever relatives he might have, grandmothers and grandfathers, aunts and uncles, cousins . . .

. . . *if* he could be trusted.

Kriss suddenly felt disgusted with himself for letting Vorlick direct the conversation. "You've *already* tried to get the touchlyre, haven't you?" He hurled the accusation like a stone through a window. "Someone broke into Andru's the first night I was there. The next night he attacked me. He was your man, wasn't he?"

Vorlick did not answer at once. When he finally answered, his tone was colder than the mist shrouding them both. "I'm a businessman, making a legitimate business proposal. If I'd had anything to do with those incidents, why would I bother making this offer now?"

"You admitted you have employees here . . ."

"I do. And yes, I know you were attacked. But you were also rescued. The *rescuer* was my man."

Kriss blinked. "I didn't mention—"

"Exactly."

"Then who *did* attack me?"

"I have competitors. One of them, a minor one but active on this planet and a couple of others, is a man named Anton Salazar."

The man who tried to buy Andru's! "I've heard of him."

"Then perhaps you know what kind of man he is. He has recently suffered severe economic reversals, due in part to my business activities. I bought up certain valuable properties here in Cascata that he greatly desired. I also underbid him for some very lucrative space-station construction contracts in the Estercarth system. Possibly in relation, he recently attempted—and failed, expensively—to take over a mining operation in the Feldsparian asteroids in which I currently have controlling interest.

"Salazar knows of my interest in alien artifacts, and while he does not share my scientific curiosity about them, he fully understands their potential monetary worth. He has been known to strip-mine valuable archaeological sites, destroying their scientific value, in order to sell the artifacts to private collectors. Obviously, he, too, recognized your instrument for what it must be. He would have wanted it the moment he heard of it, not only for the price he could get for it but because by possessing it he would be able to exact a measure of revenge against me. If I had not learned of the touchlyre, he would have stolen it, and then made sure I knew he had it. Now that I *have* learned of it, and he undoubtedly knows it . . . I warn you, Kriss, he'll stop at nothing to get it."

Stop at nothing . . . in the news story about his parents' disappearance, there had been a reference to a mysterious patron. He'd been wondering if it might have been Vorlick, but if Vorlick had been his parents' patron, they surely would have reported their discovery of an emotion-projecting alien artifact to him, and he wouldn't be questioning Kriss in an attempt to ascertain its origin.

What if, instead, that patron had been Salazar? What if Salazar had used Kriss's parents to find a valuable artifact, the alien device hidden inside the touchlyre—but then they had found out what kind of man he was and fled with it?

Did he track them down and kill them to get it?

If so, he had been too late: by then, Kriss's father had crafted the touchlyre, embedding the alien artifact in it, and given it over, along with their infant son, to the care of Mella. *No wonder she raised me in the back of beyond!*

But somehow, after all those years, word had filtered back to Salazar of a strange offworld boy in a backwoods village. He had sent his men to investigate. By pure luck, Kriss hadn't been home. Protecting him to the last, Mella must have convinced Salazar's men he wasn't coming back. Otherwise, they would have been waiting for him that night, and the touchlyre would already be in Salazar's hands, while he—

He shivered. *If not for Mella, I might be dead.*

In truth, he was lucky he wasn't dead several times over, having walked right into Salazar's hands by not only coming to Cascata but playing the touchlyre in public. Zendra had said Salazar owned the police, or, at least, enough of them that he could do whatever he wanted. *Lieutenant Elcar himself might be Salazar's man. No wonder he closed Mella's case so quickly!*

"You are in great danger," Vorlick continued, as though reading Kriss's thoughts. "I'm very much afraid of what Salazar might do next, if you refuse my offer and choose to remain on Farr's World."

Kriss took a deep breath. The rush of understanding had left him with a clear decision. "No fear of that. I accept."

"Excellent!" An emotion tinged the cold voice at last: excitement. "Where is the touchlyre now?"

"Locked away in Andru's safe."

"Good. Leave it there until you bring it to my ship. How soon can you be ready to leave?"

Ready to leave. The words were music. "I'll have to give Andru a little notice . . ."

"Even Andru's is not safe from Salazar," Vorlick warned. "Don't delay any longer than absolutely necessary."

Why put it off? Kriss reasoned then. He had made Andru no promises, signed no contract. "Tomorrow morning, then?"

"Tomorrow night," Vorlick corrected. "After dark. We don't want unfriendly eyes to see you. I'll leave a port pass at the gate closest to my ship."

"All right."

"I'll see you back to Andru's." Kriss heard him move down the alley, and after a moment he followed.

All his logic told him he had made the right decision, that he was well rid of the touchlyre. *It's too powerful. It's alien. It could be dangerous. Who knows what it's doing to me as I play it . . . or what it's doing to my listeners?*

But something deeper than logic, some animal instinct, sounded a warning, sparked perhaps by the eerie, almost inhuman sound of Vorlick's cold voice in the mist.

Everything he said made sense, Kriss told himself firmly as they stepped into the street. The fog had thinned enough that he could see Vorlick in the blurred light of the streetlamps. Despite the mist, not a hair was out of place. "Until tomorrow," the offworlder said, and strode toward the port.

Kriss took two steps toward Andru's, then stopped. His misgivings wouldn't go away. He had to try to check on Vorlick some way, and the fog gave him the perfect opportunity. If Vorlick were lying, he would surely meet one of his people to tell him of his plans, and if that employee proved to be the man who had attacked Kriss . . .

Vorlick's quick, clicking footsteps were fading fast. Kriss turned from the inviting light and warmth of the inn and followed him into the misty darkness.

Chapter Thirteen

A light wind began to blow the fog in slithering tatters through the streets, enabling Kriss to keep Vorlick in sight while staying a safe distance behind him. But a moment after the offworlder crossed the ring road, a heavy transport rumbled past, preventing Kriss from following. When he could see the spaceport again, Vorlick had vanished.

Kriss dashed across the road, silently swearing at the late-working driver. A long string of lights on tall lampposts marched all around the spaceport fence, but three in a row had failed not far away. He stopped in the stretch of darkness beneath them.

The nearest gate was perhaps three hundred metres to his right, though the curve of the fence put it out of his sight behind a low building. If Vorlick were simply returning to his ship, he would have gone that way. Kriss just had to wait for him to reappear.

Kriss gripped the mesh of the fence and peered through

it at Vorlick's golden ship, glittering with the reflected lights of the spaceport and city, like a rare jewel in a box lined with black velvet. For a moment, he forgot his doubts. Within days he would ride that beautiful ship to the stars, just as he had dreamed for years. *No more dreams. This time it will be real!*

He heard footsteps out on the duracrete of the spaceport, and finally spotted Vorlick again, approaching the base of his ship. The hatch opened. A ramp extended, blue-white light streaming down it. It licked Vorlick up into the ship, the hatch closed, and all fell silent again.

Kriss leaned his forehead against the fence's cold metal links. He'd learned nothing, but he tried to put his doubts aside. He *wanted* to believe Vorlick had told the truth because otherwise his last chance of fulfilling his dream was gone, imprisoned with Tevera in *Thaylia*.

He stared across the landing field at the Family starship. The fog had thinned to little more than a haze, which cast a soft glow around *Thaylia*'s silvery skin. Kriss wished that, by some miracle, he might see Tevera coming down from the ship and crossing the field to him. He wanted to apologize, he wanted to tell her his dream was coming true after all, and he wanted, most desperately of all, to say good-bye to her.

Or rather, he wanted desperately to not *have* to say good-bye to her.

His throat felt tight, and his eyes burned. When he left with Vorlick, the whole galaxy would be between them forever, the odds of them ever crossing paths again literally astronomical. Whatever might have been—whatever could have come from that achingly sweet kiss—would be lost. At that moment, he would have chosen to stay with Tevera on

Farr's World over going into space without her—but there was no one to make the offer.

He turned and stepped away from the fence—then froze as he heard, from somewhere on the landing apron, a man's deep, rasping voice. "Fog's lifted. We could be seen now."

"Who's to see?" said a second voice, smoother and higher-pitched. "There's nothing over here but warehouses. And we took out those three fence lights."

"I don't like it. It's too easy."

"You'd rather have it hard?"

"I can't believe we got aboard."

"Boss has strings he can pull with the port maintenance crews. Our IDs were perfectly legit." The second man laughed. "The crew trusted spaceport security. They forgot they're on Farr's World."

The other man chuckled, too, and at that moment, Kriss spotted them, briefly silhouetted against the distant lights: two big men carrying a long, sagging bundle between them. Kris felt a chill. *Murder?* He stayed still in the darkness beneath the failed lights, afraid he would attract their attention if he moved . . . but they were coming straight toward him.

"Heavy," the deeper-voiced man complained.

"You're just fat and lazy. Now shut up. We're getting close to the road."

Kriss crouched, trying to make himself invisible, as they reached the fence and set their bundle on the ground, off to his left at the other end of the stretch of shadow. He heard a low moan. So, not murder—not yet, anyway. What had he stumbled on?

One of the men produced a short rod. It gleamed in the

faint light; then its tip came to glowing red life. He touched it to the fence. The mesh parted with a flash, revealing a face Kriss knew all too well: it was the man who had attacked him and Tevera in the alley.

In seconds, the man had cut an opening in the fence the size of a door. Then he and his companion picked up their victim, who groaned and doubled up as though in pain. As they came out on Kriss's side of the fence, the lead man shifted his grip and turned to get a better hold—

—and the prisoner's feet suddenly drove into his stomach.

The man's breath whooshed out. He dropped his end of the bundle and staggered back. The prisoner twisted out of the other's grip, hit the ground hard, and began to struggle, emitting muffled, wordless squeals.

There were no words, but Kriss didn't need them.

Tevera!

AS PART OF HER PUNISHMENT, Tevera had been assigned nighttime ramp watch for a week. Most of the *Thaylia*'s crew were out in Cascata on shore leave. While some had a curfew related to their duty in the morning, those who didn't could straggle in at any hour of the night . . . if they bothered coming back at all.

It wasn't unheard of for spaceport maintenance to show up at a ship in the middle of the night, either: there were workers on duty all the time. The men's badges were in order. "Just checking in with you, as ordered," one of them told Tevera. "There's a maintenance tunnel access nearby.

We wanted to make sure you knew we were authorized to be opening it up."

The second man grinned at her. "Graveyard shift," he said. "Guess you know what's that like."

"Yeah," Tevera said.

The first man was looking past her. His eyes suddenly widened. "What's that?"

Tevera turned . . . and an instant later, a hand clapped over her mouth, and a strong arm circled her, pinning her own arms to her sides. The hand pulled away, but an adhesive gag muffled her cries for help. One of the men yanked a cloth bag over her head while the other tied her wrists together behind her back. Hands spun her around, swaddling her in cloth, then she was picked up like a side of meat and carried down the ramp.

She went limp, trying to be so much dead weight. Her captors muttered to each other. One of them mentioned the fog lifting. She heard about their boss pulling strings to get them the maintenance IDs, and a complaint about how heavy she was—so that was something.

Moments later, they dumped her onto the ground. She moaned, and though it wasn't entirely acting, it mostly was. When they picked her up again, she moaned louder and doubled up, as though suffering a cramp. She felt the man at her feet shift his weight, trying to get a better grip—and she drove her legs out as hard as she could.

They plunged into something soft, and the man lost his grip. She twisted free of the hands at her shoulders and crashed to the ground, trying to call for help but only managing muffled squeals, trying to stand but thwarted by the cloth wrapping her.

She heard running footsteps. The sound of someone falling, almost on top of her. A grunt. A sickening, fleshy thud.

What was happening?

WITHOUT A SECOND THOUGHT, Kriss charged, intending to tackle the man who hadn't been winded, but his target heard him coming, sidestepped, and tripped him. He crashed heavily to the ground, not far from Tevera. He got to his hands and knees, tried to get up . . .

. . . and the man's heavy boot thudded into his stomach, lifting his whole body and hurling him back. His head cracked against the duracrete and filled with a vast, roaring pain, through which words reached him faintly.

"Who was that?"

"Just some idiot bystander who thought he'd be a hero. Let's get out of here."

"What about *him*?"

"I think he's dead. Anyway, he can't identify us."

"But Salazar—"

"I'll worry about Salazar. Come on, move it!"

Salazar! Kriss managed to roll over. He tried desperately to get to his hands and knees. *Salazar's got Tevera!* He tried to shout her name, but only a whisper came out.

On his belly, he wriggled to the fence. Clinging to the mesh, he pulled himself painfully upright. There was no sign of Tevera's captors on the ring road. Kriss clung to the fence for a long time, until some measure of strength returned to him; then, clutching his bruised gut, he began the nightmarish journey to Andru's.

Pain crashed into his skull with every step; the ring road seemed a kilometre wide. On the far side, he crept up the street, clinging to the wall for support, but it wasn't enough: he kept falling, picking himself up and staggering on a few more metres, then falling again. Twice he vomited into the shadows. The second time nothing came up but sour-tasting bile.

Finally, he lay still, spent; not unconscious, but too exhausted and pain-filled to be fully aware of his surroundings.

Chapter Fourteen

An indeterminate but interminable time later, brilliant light speared Kriss to the pavement, stabbing his head with daggers of pain. "Ya can't sleep there, boy." Strong, rough hands hauled him to his feet. "Bit young to handle yer liquor, eh?"

Kriss blinked bleary eyes at the tall, uniformed man who held him. "Police?" he mumbled.

"That's right. Constable Piltzer. Now, where do ya live?"

"Black Rock . . ."

"Come again?"

Kriss tried to think. "No . . . no, Andru's."

"Ah. That's more like it. Come on, then, let's get ya home."

Zendra answered the constable's firm knock on the door at Andru's, took one look at Kriss, and took charge. The constable was sent on his way, and Kriss was led solicitously up the stairs to his room. "Lie down," Zendra told him. "I'll be right back."

Kriss needed no encouragement. His head throbbed and, exploring his skull, he found a sizeable bump. The middle of his abdomen felt like . . . well, like someone had kicked him. The room turned slowly around him, and he swallowed hard: even though he had nothing left in his stomach, he didn't want to throw up, especially when he didn't think he could make it to the bathroom.

Zendra, true to her word, reappeared in two minutes. She had a shiny white case, about the size of a briefcase but thicker, in her right hand. She set it on the bed beside Kriss and opened it. He couldn't see inside it, but it lit Zendra's face with the white glow. Her fingers tapped on something out of his sight, then she said, "Hold still," and drew out what looked like a shiny white egg. She ran it over his head. Then she pointed it at his right eye. "Look straight ahead." A light passed over his pupil. She repeated the process with the left eye. Then, "Lift your shirt," she said. He did so. She ran the egg over his bare midriff. Then she put it back inside the case.

Something beeped. Her eyes flicked back and forth—she was clearly reading a datadisplay. Then she nodded decisively, closed the case, and set it on the floor. "AutoDoc says no concussion, no broken ribs, no internal bleeding," she said. "Just a big bump on your skull and a bruise you'll be feeling for quite a while." She got up, went into his bathroom, and returned a moment later with a cloth soaked in cold water. "Why you would take a walk in the middle of the night is beyond me," she muttered as she applied the compress to his bump. "Cascata's not safe at night. You're lucky you only got beat up."

He didn't reply. He couldn't tell Andru and Zendra or

the police what had taken him into the night or what he had witnessed at the spaceport. He certainly couldn't tell them Salazar had Tevera. He was now convinced Salazar had killed his parents and Mella. How little would it take for him to kill Tevera?

Zendra left the room again, taking the AutoDoc with her, and returned a few minutes later with a small, dark bottle and a shot glass. She poured a dollop of blue liquid. "Drink this," she said. "It will lessen the pain and help you sleep."

He downed it gratefully. It burned, but almost immediately, a pleasant warmth and lassitude filled him.

His eyes closed for a moment. They jerked open again when Andru's voice said, "You have a penchant for attracting trouble."

Kriss blinked up at the innkeeper, who was standing over him.

"Let the boy sleep, Andru," Zendra said firmly, screwing the lid back on the bottle of blue liquid.

Andru grunted. He stared down at Kriss a moment longer, then turned and went out.

"You may still have a bit of a headache tomorrow, and your tummy's going to turn all sorts of interesting colours over the next few days, but I think you'll be able to navigate," Zendra said. "It's that hard head of yours saved you." She patted him on the shoulder, then left in her turn, closing the door behind her.

An instant after that, Kriss was asleep.

TEVERA HOPED whoever had tried to rescue her—if that was what had happened—wasn't badly hurt. She'd never had any real chance of escape—she knew that now. But she'd had to try. She had to show these men hired by . . . what had the name been? Salazar? . . . that she wasn't just some helpless girl they could kidnap with impunity. She was a member of the Family. She was part of the crew of *Thaylia*. That they had *dared* to take her, right from the ship . . .

She imagined Great-Grandmother Nicora's fury. The captain would make someone pay for this outrage, of that she was certain.

But the prospect of future punishment for her captors and their employer did little to alleviate the immediate misery of her situation: taken prisoner, gagged, bound, and being carried like a trophy to an unknown destination through the streets of Cascata. She ached all over, and the men carrying her weren't worried if she occasionally drooped a little low and bounced on the ground.

She gritted her teeth and passed her time imagining shoving both of them out of an airlock. It helped . . . but only a little.

Eventually, they got where they were going. Where that was, she couldn't say. They passed from outdoors to indoors—she could tell that much. They put her on a cot, which was better than the floor. They didn't take the bag off her head or the sticky gag off her mouth. They did pull away the cloth wrapping her body, but left her wrists tied behind her, and then bound her ankles, too.

And that was it. A door opened and closed. She could tell she was alone. She couldn't hear or see.

All she could do . . . was wait.

"A BIT OF A HEADACHE" turned out to be a considerable understatement: Kriss woke in the morning with a terrible pounding inside his skull that made it hard to think. But he *had* to think, and he couldn't stay in bed—not when Salazar had Tevera. Somehow, he had to help her. Feeling as though he were moving through thick mud, his bruised midriff throbbing in counterpoint to his head, he put on fresh clothes and slowly and stiffly descended the stairs, frowning as he tried to make his shaken brain consider his options.

Tell Andru everything? Salazar might kill Tevera. And Andru had some secret of his own concerning the Family; he might take no action at all, or the wrong one.

Tell the police? Even worse—the police were on Salazar's payroll.

Tell Vorlick? No. Something inside him still didn't trust the businessman. Kriss remembered what Zendra had said about Vorlick buying and selling whole planets, with no concern for their inhabitants' homes, families, or futures. Vorlick cared nothing for him or Tevera. His sole interest was the touchlyre. He thought he had a deal with Kriss to get it—but Kriss was about to break their agreement; he had to, now that Salazar had Tevera. The touchlyre was the only bargaining chip he held.

"Well, you're walking on your own, at least," Zendra said cheerfully as he entered the common room. "That's better than last night. Sit down, and I'll bring breakfast."

Kriss sat by the window as usual, looking gloomily out at the sunlit street until Zendra brought him a tray with hot cereal and cold juice. "Here you are." She winked. "Nothing that takes much chewing. Oh, yes, and you have a couple of messages . . . dropped off this morning." She placed two sealed envelopes by the platter and went back to the kitchen, whistling a cheery tune.

Kriss stared at the envelopes as if they might bite him, then slowly reached out and picked one up. His fingers trembled as he opened it.

The message inside was short and to the point. *Give me what I want or lose what I have. The Red Horse Inn. Midnight.* S.

He squeezed his eyes briefly shut. He'd known it was coming, but . . .

The second note puzzled him. Vorlick couldn't know what had happened yet, could he? So, who . . .?

The message was written in silver ink on black paper. *My sister was taken because of you. You will help us get her back. Come to us at once. Rigel.*

Kriss let the note drop to the table. *The Family.* Salazar must have told them he had Tevera—and with that, the matter had been taken out of Kriss's hands. He really had no choice: he had to go to the Family.

They're right, he thought, his heart stabbed by a pain worse than the throbbing in his skull. *It's my fault.* If he had never met Tevera, never tried to use her for his own ends, she would be safe.

But he *had* met her, and tried to use her, and thus put her in danger. He had to help the Family get her back—and as he made that decision, the shameful thought rose inside him that maybe if he helped them, they would take him into space and . . .

Angry and disgusted with himself, Kriss pushed away

from the table without touching the breakfast Zendra had brought him.

He *would* help Tevera—no matter what it meant for him.

He found Andru in his office. He expected the innkeeper to protest, or at least ask questions, when he asked for the night off, but his employer, preoccupied, granted the request without even looking up from his computer interface.

Though he wasn't hungry, when the time came, Kriss forced himself to eat a mid-day meal. Fortunately, the inn was busy, so he didn't have to face Zendra. As much as he appreciated her concern, he didn't see how she could help, and he didn't want to get her involved. He had brought nothing but trouble to everyone close to him—his parents, Mella, Tevera. He didn't want Zendra to be the next to suffer.

The afternoon seemed to drag on for centuries. Kriss, wanting to be well-rested for whatever came that night, lay on his bed, watching the slowly creeping patch of sunlight on the wall of his room—until clouds obliterated it—but though he occasionally dozed off, he was never able to fall deeply asleep, partly due to mounting nerves, partly due to the continuing ache in his head and gut.

At last, the room grew dark, and with a tightening and twisting in his already hurting middle, Kriss sat up, wincing as his head gave a painful throb. *Time to go.*

He pulled the touchlyre case out from under the bed. He removed the instrument, pushing it out of sight under the bed, then slung the case over his back. If he didn't escape, whoever captured him would still need him alive in order to get the touchlyre—but to begin with, at least, it seemed like a good idea to make them *think* he had it.

He tucked his miniflashlight into his pants pocket, then went to the door; but before going out, he paused and looked around the room where he had lived for two weeks. It had gradually come to feel something like home. Now he wondered if he would ever see it again.

After a moment, he turned off the light and closed and locked the door behind him.

He met Zendra as she came out of the kitchen with a food-laden tray and asked her for directions to the Red Horse Inn.

She raised one eyebrow. "The Red Horse? Why do you want to go *there*?"

"Just curious. It's the only inn I haven't seen. I must have missed it that first night."

"But the Red Horse—" A customer called to her from across the room. "All right, all right!" She turned back to Kriss. "Up the street to Babus Place, left five blocks, then right onto Tailor's Lane. Eventually, you'll come to a big courtyard. The Red Horse will be on your right. And sometime, you'll have to tell me what you *really* went there for." The customer called her again, and she hurried off.

"Thanks," Kriss said to her retreating back. "And goodbye," he added under his breath.

Thunder rumbled in the west as he stepped outside, and a cold wind ruffled his hair and clothes, making him shiver. No rain had fallen yet from the overcast sky, but in the last of the twilight, he could see the clouds scudding furiously overhead, as though fleeing some onrushing threat.

It will be very dark at the Red Horse, Kriss thought. From

Zendra's directions, he knew it must be near the outskirts of the city, where the streets were mostly unlit. He checked again to make sure he had his flashlight, then jumped down from the porch and set off briskly into the teeth of the wind, dreading what was to come but anxious to get it over with.

He tried an old trick of his, putting his mind a day ahead and looking back on this night as history—but it didn't help lessen the cold lump in the pit of his sore stomach. He knew he could be dead before the next day dawned, and even if he lived, Salazar or Vorlick or the Family—or all three—would be after him.

Run, a part of his mind whispered, as his legs carried him relentlessly toward the rendezvous. *There are outlaws up in the mountains, the police said. Join them. Survive.*

If he were the only one involved in all this, he might have. But it wasn't just him. Through his own stupid selfishness, he had drawn Tevera into this mess. Mella had been killed protecting him and the touchlyre. He wouldn't let Tevera die for him, too!

He paused when he reached the last streetlight, just at the beginning of Tailor's Lane, a narrow, crooked street leading off into the dark, twisted byways that rimmed Cascata. Somewhere among those black alleys and courtyards lurked Salazar, the shadowy enemy Kriss had never seen, with Tevera in his clutches. Elsewhere, Vorlick and his men would also be making their way toward the Red Horse. Hidden from them all would be the Family, a law unto itself, determined to rescue one of its own. The three ingredients together made an explosive combination, a bomb that only he could detonate.

Stepping into the darkness, he lit the fuse.

Chapter Fifteen

Fighting the urge to keep looking over his shoulder, Kriss walked steadily along the cobblestoned lane. The last streetlight disappeared behind him. No light showed in any of the buildings he passed. "Funny place to put an inn," he muttered.

Abruptly, he emerged into a large, echoing courtyard. The lights of the city reflecting off the clouds silhouetted the hulking shapes of dark buildings, crouched like huge sleeping animals all around the open space. Several streets met in the courtyard, spots of deeper blackness like gaping mouths. But where was the inn?

Kriss pulled his tiny flashlight out of his pocket and switched it on. Its small circle of illumination showed him nothing but blank windows, sagging roofs, and peeling plaster.

Then something creaked off to his right, and he spun.

In front of a boarded-up wooden building with a toppled

chimney and swaybacked roof hung a lopsided sign, swinging from a tall pole in the strengthening wind. Kriss walked closer, reached up, and stilled it. His light shone on a red horse prancing across a green background. Faded gold letters spelled out "Red Horse Inn."

He stared at it. No wonder Zendra had been puzzled by his interest.

Suddenly, brilliant light pinned him to the pavement. He turned toward it, raising his hand to shield his eyes from the painful glare, which had reawakened the ache in his bruised head.

TEVERA SPENT several uncomfortable hours lying on the cot: uncomfortable not just because of her arms and legs being tied and the bag over her head, but because of the most prosaic of reasons—an ever-growing need to empty her bladder.

Just when she thought she would have no choice but to wet herself, the door opened and closed, footsteps came toward her—and the bag came off her head.

The man looking down at her was no one she had seen before, a heavyset, older man with the dark skin of the native Farrsians, though his hair and moustache were mostly silver. He wore an expensive-looking light-grey tailored suit. Behind him stood one of her captors from the night before, the one who had seemed to be in charge, holding a platter with a bowl of cut fruit, a chunk of black bread, and a glass of water on it. He'd exchanged his spaceport maintenance overalls for black military-style fatigues. The barrel of some kind of weapon peeked over his left shoulder.

"Good morning," the suit-clad man said. "Arnason has brought you breakfast."

"I can't eat tied up," Tevera said.

"I am aware of that."

The man leaned down and untied her. She thought about kneeing him in the face—there was a moment when she could have—but it seemed likely to end up hurting her more than it did him, so she restrained the impulse.

The man straightened again. "I am Anton Salazar."

"You've kidnapped a member of the Family," Tevera said. With a groan, she sat up, swung her legs over the side, and began massaging her ankles. "Are you crazy?"

"Not at all," Salazar said. "What I am after is worth the potential fallout."

"And what are you after?"

"No need for you to know." He glanced at Arnason. "Put the platter on the table."

For the first time, Tevera looked around the room. Aside from the cot, the only other furniture was a cheap card table (where Arnason dutifully placed the platter) with a single rickety-looking folding chair tucked beneath it. The floor was wood, and the walls and ceiling dingy plaster. The only light struggled fitfully through the dirt-covered window next to the door.

But of greatest interest to Tevera was another door, across from the cot and to the left of the table, which she hoped might lead to a toilet. She asked.

"Check it out, Arnason," Salazar said.

The black-clad man nodded, went to the door, looked in, made a face, and stepped back. "Not very clean," he said. "But, yeah, it's a toilet."

"Any way out?"

The man shook his head. "Window's too small."

"Go on, then," Salazar said.

Tevera went in and closed the door. Arnason wasn't lying about it not being very clean—or, unfortunately, about the window being too small for her to escape through—but to her surprise, the water worked. After she'd washed her hands—no soap, and no towel—she splashed more water in her face, then dried it and her hands as best she could on her crewsuit's sleeves. When she came out, Arnason was gone. Salazar stood looking out the window.

"What are you going to do with me?" she asked. She went to the table and sat down, her stomach growling at the sight of food.

"I plan to exchange you for something," Salazar said, turning to face her. "A message has been sent. If all goes well tonight, you will return to your precious Family, I will get what I want, and no one will be hurt."

"Someone already *has* been hurt," Tevera said. "Whoever tried to rescue me at the spaceport."

Salazar shrugged. "I'm assured his injuries were not serious." He nodded at the table. "Please, eat.'

Tevera ate. The fruit—some local variety, she guessed, since she didn't recognize it—was fresh and tart, the black bread so sweet it might almost have been cake. She ate both, then drained the water glass. The whole time, Salazar simply watched her. It was creepy.

"I have a question," he said at last, as she set her glass back down on the table.

She folded her arms. "So ask it."

"Before our . . . meeting . . . were you also approached by Carl Vorlick?"

"Vorlick?" Tevera blinked, surprised. "Why would one of the richest men in the Commonwealth approach *me*?"

"Is that a no?"

"Yes, it's a no! I saw his ship land. Everyone in port saw it. Everyone was talking about it. But no, he never approached me. Or anyone else in the Family, as far as I know."

"Good." Salazar went to the door, then turned back with his hand on the knob. "I'm afraid the day may drag," he said. "I will send more food later." He turned, opened the door, and went out, giving Tevera a brief, uninformative glimpse of a cobblestoned courtyard surrounded by derelict buildings.

The door closed. Tevera heard the lock click. A shadow moved across the window, and Tevera saw that Arnason stood outside it now, his back to her.

SALAZAR WAS right about the day dragging. By sunset, Tevera was ready to climb the walls. She'd taken as long as possible to eat the lunch Arnason provided—sourdough bread this time, a chunk of stinky cheese, some sliced sausage, and another glass of water—but even so, she'd had hours of nothing to do but sit and think.

Mostly, she'd thought about Kriss and how betrayed he must

have felt after Rigel ordered her away. But what could she have done? Family Law was Family Law. She had already bent it by seeing him in the first place. Once told by her brother to return to the ship, once confined to port by order of the captain, there had been nothing more she could do, no way to reach out to Kriss.

She remembered the mysterious attack in the alley. Had *that* been related to *this*? Had she been the target all along? She couldn't imagine why. Did Salazar actually think he could blackmail The Family? Great-Grandmother Nicora would not risk the safety of *Thaylia* or its crew for any single member. Her duty was to the ship as a whole, to the Family as a whole. Salazar did not have the leverage he thought he did.

Her thoughts chased each other in unproductive circles of ever-diminishing circumference until, at last, it was dark outside, and Salazar and Arnason returned. "He will be here soon," Salazar said.

"Who?" Tevera demanded.

She got no answer, of course.

Salazar took her out into the darkness of the courtyard she had glimpsed through the door and window. The city skyglow in the clouds showed her the bulk of a dark object in front of them, but she couldn't tell what it was. Arnason and Salazar pulled her around behind it.

Then, they waited. No one spoke.

Tevera heard a faint crackling sound and instantly recognized it as the sound bleeding from a communications earphone—she'd heard similar things all her life, on the ship, and in various ports. "He's in the courtyard," Arnason said, his voice barely above a whisper. "The sign is drawing him, as we intended . . . he's there. Looking around."

And then he grabbed Tevera's arm and twisted it behind her. Something cold pressed against the side of her neck . . . the barrel of a weapon. She swallowed.

Salazar straightened his shoulders and leaned forward. There was a sharp click, and the thing they'd been hiding behind revealed itself to be a giant searchlight of the kind that surrounded the port—only, rather than being pointed at a starship, this one was aimed squarely at a slim figure standing in front of a swinging inn sign, pinning him to his own shadow.

Tevera's heart leaped to her throat.

Kriss!

"NOT VERY LIVELY, IS IT?" someone called to Kriss. The deep male voice echoed back from the ring of deserted buildings.

"Who are you?" Kriss shouted back. He could see nothing except the light.

"The one you came to meet."

"Salazar?"

"Who else?"

Kriss wondered if Vorlick would reply to that, but if the other man was nearby, he wasn't yet revealing himself.

"You have the artifact?" Salazar continued.

"Do you have Tevera?" Kriss countered.

"Of course."

"Let me see her!"

The beam swung down, out of his eyes, so that he stood in a long oval pool of illumination. For the first time, he could see a shadowy group of figures standing behind the spotlight. Someone switched on a flashlight, and its beam lit Tevera, in the grip of a grim-faced, black-clad man who held a pistol to her neck. Kriss's heart kicked once, painfully, at the sight. "Tevera? Are you—"

"I'm all right," she called. "They haven't hurt me."

"And I'll have no reason to if you've brought me the artifact," Salazar interjected. "So. I've shown you your girl." The spotlight swung up, blinding Kriss once more. "Now show me the artifact."

Rigel, where are you? Slowly Kriss slipped out of the instrument case's straps and held it up. "It's in here."

"Open it."

The remembered image of Tevera at gunpoint froze Kriss in place. His stomach churned. *I've ruined everything by trying to protect myself. The Family isn't there, Vorlick isn't here, and as soon as Salazar sees I don't have the touch-lyre, he'll kill Tevera . . .*

Acid burned the back of his throat. He felt like throwing up. He didn't move . . . *couldn't* move.

"Show me!" Salazar shouted. "I'm warning you, I'm running out of patience!"

But then another voice, higher-pitched and far colder, rang out from the mouth of a dark passage between two buildings, behind Kriss and off to his right. "So am I," said Carl Vorlick. "How *interesting* to meet you here, Salazar. How *unfortunate* you have gone to all this effort for nothing. The artifact is mine."

"Vorlick? *Vorlick?*" Salazar voice rose in incredulous fury. "*I made a deal with the boy!*"

"So did I. I wonder how he intends to keep both? Well, Kriss?"

Despite the chill wind, Kriss felt a single drop of sweat roll down his face. "I'm sorry, Mr. Vorlick. Salazar kidnapped a friend of mine. He said if I didn't give him the touchlyre—"

"I'd kill her. And I will!" Salazar shouted. "Give me the artifact now, or my man blows her head off!" The spotlight angled down again. Once more, Kriss could see Tevera, Salazar's flashlight showing that the man guarding her now had his brawny forearm across her neck, and the gun pointed at her left temple.

"Kill her, and you'll never get it!" Kriss yelled. He flipped open the instrument case and upended it, showing it was empty. "I don't have it, Salazar. The touchlyre is hidden where you'll never find it!"

Salazar snorted. "You've been watched every time you set foot outside Andru's, boy. So, you left it in the inn. Do you really think that dump's second-rate locks can keep my men out? You had your chance! Now your girl dies, and you die, and then I'll take the artifact at my leisure!"

"Are you going to let him have your prize, Mr. Vorlick?" Kriss cried desperately.

"Don't look for help from *him*, boy," Salazar snarled. "He's already killed your parents!"

The words hit Kriss like a punch to the stomach. *Vorlick?* Vorlick *killed my parents? Not Salazar?*

He wanted to deny it, but it suddenly made sense . . . horrible, horrible sense. His parents' mysterious, wealthy patron was far more likely to have been Vorlick than Salazar. Zendra had said Vorlick had wealth that Salazar couldn't hope to match. If his parents had found out what kind of man Vorlick really was and tried to escape him . . .

But even if Salazar was telling the truth about Vorlick killing his parents . . . "*You* murdered Mella!" he screamed at the man he could not see.

"She had a heart attack. My men were ordered not to hurt her."

"Liar!"

"That's right, Kriss, he's lying!" Vorlick shouted from the darkness. "*He* killed your parents *and* your guardian. Promise me the artifact, and I'll get you and the girl away safely!"

"Would you trust your parents' murderer?" Salazar bellowed.

A blast of icy wind howled through the eaves of the derelict inn, and a sudden, matching blast of red-hot fury roared up in Kriss. "I hope you both rot in hell!" he screamed.

TEVERA UNDERSTOOD EVERYTHING NOW–SHE had been kidnapped to convince Kriss to hand over his mysterious musical instrument. Vorlick was after it, too—must have come to the planet specifically to get it.

It didn't do her any good to know all that, not while Arnason still had a weapon aimed at her head. But as Kriss screamed out his defiance, a bolt of flaming red energy suddenly seared the air. It ripped into the spotlight . . .

. . . which exploded.

The blast knocked her to her knees, ripping her free of

Arnason's grasp, who staggered back, swearing. Electricity arced through the wreckage of the light, and in its flicker, she glimpsed Salazar on the ground. Arnason's gun wasn't aimed at her anymore: he swung it wildly back and forth, looking for enemies. Seeing her chance, Tevera leaped up, kicked the gun from Arnason's hand, spun, and kicked him again, in the stomach. As he went down, she slammed both fists into the back of his neck. He dropped, stunned.

Salazar stumbled up and lunged at her, but she dodged past him and dashed across the dark courtyard toward Kriss. She grabbed his arm and pulled hard, barely breaking stride. "Run!"

Kriss gasped and ran with her. A beam sliced through the space where he'd been standing, so close she felt a blast of hot air, and shattered the post of the inn sign, so that it clattered to the ground. More beams zipped across the courtyard, from more than one direction. Two tore into the walls of the Red Horse, whose rotting wooden beams exploded into flame. Every searing flash left an afterimage in Tevera's eyes, until it seemed the whole night burned.

The light from the beamers and now the burning inn showed her an exit from the courtyard, a dark street she dashed for, holding Kriss's hand. Glancing back, she saw Arnason sprawled on the cobblestones near the destroyed spotlight, smoke rising from his body—one of the beams must have found him after she'd felled him. There was no sign of Salazar.

Another beam flashed and a man screamed, and then they were out of the courtyard. Hoarse shouts continued to echo behind them, and Tevera tasted smoke and burned flesh on the air. They ran toward the lights of the city's heart, but before they had gone fifty metres, people leaped out of the darkness and surrounded them.

Tevera gasped, then suddenly released Kriss's hand as the glow of the fire behind them showed her the face of one of the shadowy figures. "Corvus!" she cried, and threw her arms around the man.

KRISS BARELY HAD time to realize the strangers were Family before someone clapped a hand over his mouth and dragged him into a side street. "Listen, worldhugger," Rigel's voice growled. "You did your part. We got Tevera back. I suppose I should thank you for that. But you will *not* be permitted to see her again. Understand?"

"Yes," he said, sick at heart.

"Good. I'm going to let you go. But don't follow us. Tevera is my responsibility. If you cause her any more grief . . ." He shook Kriss once, hard, then released him and hurried back into the lane.

"LET'S GO," Corvus told Tevera. He grabbed her arm. "We have to get away from here."

Pulled along, she followed. "Where's Kriss?" she said, looking over her shoulder.

No one answered her. She tried to stop, but Corvus's grip tightened.

"Kriss?" she called. "Kriss!"

"Quiet," said a new voice. Rigel's voice. "We don't want Salazar's or Vorlick's men after us."

"But—"

"That's an order!"

Tevera fell silent. *Where is he?* she thought, sick with worry. *What have they done with him?*

With others of her Family, she stumbled through the darkness toward the spaceport.

KRISS LEANED MISERABLY against the wall as, just a few metres away, but out of his sight, Tevera called his name in a worried voice. "Kriss? Kriss!"

He heard Rigel order her to be quiet, and then the Family members were gone . . . and Tevera with them.

He stayed put until the last faint noises of battle from the courtyard ended. He hoped both Salazar and Vorlick were dead but didn't really believe it. At least one would have survived, probably both, and would be after him, with resources he couldn't hope to match and reputations to uphold—reputations more important to them than even the supposedly immense value of the touchlyre. Tonight, he had made two of the most powerful men in the Commonwealth his bitter enemies—and shattered what little remained unbroken of his dreams.

After tonight, he was cut off from the stars forever. All that was left was survival, and that meant fleeing into the wilderness—but he had to have some provisions first, or he'd just be saving his enemies the trouble of killing him.

And he had to retrieve the touchlyre. Both Salazar and

Vorlick knew where he'd left it, and that meant Andru and Zendra were in danger.

He took a deep breath, pushed himself away from the wall, and started running back toward Andru's—just the beginning, he thought bitterly, of a lifetime of running.

It consoled him very little that that lifetime would probably be short.

Chapter Sixteen

Tevera expected questions, outrage, a meeting with the captain . . . but all that happened, when they reached *Thaylia*, was that she was shown to her cabin, given food, and left in silence. The door was security-sealed, preventing her from opening it. Her attempts to use the comm went nowhere. She was a prisoner of her own Family.

She showered, put on clean clothes, sat, ate, waited . . . and worried.

What will the Family do about Salazar and Vorlick? was a part of that worry, but a very small part. Most of her worry was devoted to the one question she most desperately wanted an answer to.

Where's Kriss?

RAIN POURED down with shocking suddenness before Kriss reached the inn, soaking through his clothes in seconds and chilling him to the bone. But he was grateful for the dark cloak it drew across the city; even in the glare from the frequent bursts of lightning, the falling sheets of water would hide him from unfriendly eyes.

Andru's looked as derelict as the Red Horse Inn, not a hint of light escaping around its closed door and shuttered windows. Kriss darted across the rain-pounded street and up onto the porch, seized the latch, and pushed.

The door didn't budge.

Kriss swore under his breath. He didn't dare knock; he'd wake the whole inn and alert any watchers Salazar, Vorlick, or the Family—likely, all three—had nearby. As he stood there indecisively, the rain suddenly slackened, and at the next flash of lightning, he flinched, feeling exposed.

He backed to the edge of the porch and looked up at his window, almost directly overhead. Even if he could climb to it, he couldn't get in; he'd locked it himself. Unless he could somehow pick the—

The front door swung open. Kriss yelped, stumbled back, and fell off the porch. Stunned, bruised, and breathless, he stared up at Andru, who shone a flashlight down at him. In his other hand, he held a beamer. "Are you all right?" the innkeeper asked.

Kriss wiped rain from his eyes and picked himself up, wincing. The bruises he'd just inflicted on himself throbbed in time with the renewed ache in his head, but otherwise . . . "Yes."

Andru holstered the beamer. "You set off my alarms." He

held out his hand and helped Kriss back onto the porch. "You should have told me you'd be coming back late."

His plans for a quiet escape in ruins, Kriss followed Andru into the common room, where the sullen red glow of a few embers in the fireplace seemed to only deepen the shadows in the corners. Andru turned on a single lightglobe over the bar, then cinched his dark-blue robe tighter around his broad waist and sat on a barstool, gesturing Kriss to another. "Where were you?"

Kriss remained standing. "I just came back to get the touchlyre. Then I'm leaving for good."

Andru's only reaction was a quirk of his left eyebrow. "Why?"

"It's not safe for me to be here."

Andru's left eyebrow lowered and converged with the right in a frown. "Explain."

Kriss looked away without speaking. Too many people had already suffered because of him and the touchlyre. He wouldn't involve Andru and Zendra, too.

But then Andru rose, towering over him. He gripped Kriss's chin with one massive hand and tilted his head back, forcing him to face Andru's glare. "If you are mixed up in something that may cause trouble for me or my inn, you *will* tell me about it!"

Kriss jerked his head free. "There's no time. I have to leave *now*!"

"You're not going anywhere until you explain," Andru said, steel in his voice.

Kriss clenched his fists in frustration, then let out his breath in an explosive gust. "All right. All right! But then I'm leaving. And I won't let you stop me." Although exactly how he'd prevent it, he wasn't sure.

Andru folded his arms. "Talk."

Kriss told the tale as succinctly as he could. When he finished, he expected Andru to rage at him for involving him in a conflict between Salazar and Vorlick—but the innkeeper only looked thoughtful. "Some of this, I guessed," he said after a long pause. "I've known from the first your touchlyre must have alien technology tucked inside it. When I heard Vorlick had arrived and saw him here listening to you, I suspected he might offer to buy it. But I did not know of this girl, Tevera, or Salazar's involvement, or the way the Family treated you. I knew your dreams of leaving Farr's World, thanks to the mysterious abilities of your instrument, but not all of your reasons. Now I do." He stood abruptly and walked out of sight, through the beaded curtain into the short hallway that led to the back stairs, which creaked as he climbed them.

Kriss glanced at the front door. He could run now, leaving the touchlyre behind, and vanish into the rain before Andru returned. But if he did, Andru and Zendra would be caught in the struggle between Salazar and Vorlick, and he couldn't let that happen.

Instead, he waited. He moved to a chair by the fireplace, where a few fading, flickering flames and glowing embers still gave off welcome heat. Steaming in his wet clothes, he sat tensely, head twisting sharply toward the door with every creak of the inn or crack of the fire, expecting Salazar or Vorlick—or both—to burst in at any moment, beamers in hand, and demand he hand over the touchlyre. But the door remained shut.

The bead curtain rattled as Andru reappeared, wearing a long black weatherproof coat and matching broad-brimmed hat. "I have an errand to run," he said. "You—"

"I'll be gone when you get back."

"—will stay here," Andru finished as if Kriss hadn't spoken. "Zendra will join you. You still work for me, Kriss Lemarc, and I take care of my own." He strode to the door, opened it, and, after a final silent glance at Kriss, vanished into the rainy night.

Instantly, Kriss leaped up and dashed toward the main stairs. He almost collided with Zendra as she descended, brushing her grey-streaked hair. "Where are you going?" she asked sharply.

"Only up to my room." He slowed, though only a little, fumbling for his key as he reached the top step. A moment later, he threw open his room's door and snatched up the touchlyre. He'd lost the case in the Red Horse courtyard, so he wrapped the instrument in one of the dark-red blankets from his bed, clutched it to his chest, and ran back down the stairs, two at a time.

He found Zendra behind the bar, engulfed in a cloud of steam. "Fresh stimtea," she said as he appeared. "A mug for each of us. Sit by the fire, and let's talk. Andru won't be back for a while."

"Neither will I." Kriss headed for the door.

Zendra rounded the bar in a hurry. "Andru said to stay here!"

"I'm not safe to have around." He opened the door. Cold rain splattered his face, giving him pause.

"You could be killed!" Zendra cried.

"*You* could be killed if I stay," he shot back, but still he hesitated, staring out into the dark, rainswept street. *Once I leave Andru's, all my dreams are dead . . .*

"Please!" Zendra said. Looking back, he saw tears on her dark cheeks. Her work-roughened hands twisted the heavy fabric of her white robe. "Don't go!"

He wavered, but only for a moment. Then, "Good-bye, Zendra," he said, voice rough and choked. "Thank you for . . . for caring."

He stepped out and shut the door behind him.

Darkness and rain closed around him, a comforting, concealing curtain, as he ran through the streets, away from the spaceport, splashing through puddles, holding the blanket-wrapped touchlyre tight in both arms. After a block, he slipped into an unlit side street and then stuck to the alleys as much as possible, zigzagging, but always heading away from the city centre.

Once, in a narrow, twisting lane, he thought he heard footsteps other than his own above the noise of the wind and rain. He pressed his back to a concrete wall and looked back. For an instant, he thought he'd glimpsed a dark form ducking out of sight. But though he stared a long time, he didn't see it any more movement. Finally, he ran on, telling himself he had imagined it. Surely no one could follow him in such a storm.

He dodged across a brightly lit, but utterly deserted, thoroughfare and began picking his way along another garbage-strewn alley. *Where did Andru go?* he wondered. *Surely not the police. He must know Salazar owns them.* Well, no matter; he'd made his decision. There was no going back now.

He didn't stop moving until the first light of dawn forced

its way through the lowering overcast. Then he paused in the scanty shelter provided by the sloped metal-roofed overhang above a dwelling's back door. The rain had dwindled to a miserable drizzle, and Kriss savoured the pleasure of being free of its icy grip, if only for a few minutes.

The house that protected him seemed deserted. Peeling blue paint hung from its cracked plaster walls in long strips, and its slate roof sagged. The houses surrounding it were in no better shape. Some of their roofs had collapsed entirely, and one house had a tree twice as tall as Kriss growing in its front room.

Weeds pushed through the cracked cobblestones of the street, which gave way just a few metres farther on to a muddy trail that led into a cornfield, disappearing among stalks of green taller than Kriss.

He slumped to the ground, back against the rough wooden door, and pulled his knees to the instrument he held tight to his chest. He rested his forehead on the damp blanket protecting it, listening to the dripping of water all around him.

Thunder rumbled, and the rain intensified, clattering on the metal roof of his shelter. He pulled his feet in closer, even though they couldn't get any wetter than they already were. *I'll move on as soon as it lets up*, he told himself.

Lightning flashed. The rain poured down in sheets. His head drooped. He dozed . . .

A massive blow to his ribs knocked him sprawling, face-first, into a filthy puddle, the touchlyre beneath him. He gagged on foul water and tried to get to his hands and knees, but another blow smashed him down again. "Enough," someone growled. "Haul him up."

Salazar!

Rough hands gripped his arms and jerked him to his feet, to the accompaniment of lightning and thunder. He struggled feebly, dazed. Whoever held him shook him so hard he bit his tongue, and he swallowed blood as his captor asked, "Where to?"

Kriss tried to focus. Salazar's right arm hung in a sling, and he had a blood-stained patch of gauze taped to his left cheek. Blood and mud stained his expensive grey suit, now tattered and torn. "Not here," Salazar said. "Even out here, people will be stirring soon." He pointed across the street. "There's a courtyard behind that wall. That will do." He bent down and picked up the touchlyre one-handed, holding it by the neck, the blanket trailing as he strode across the cobblestones. The man holding Kriss, whom he had yet to get a good look at, propelled Kriss in Salazar's wake.

Shoved roughly through the archway into the courtyard, he fell, scraping his hands and knees on the sharp, wet stones. "All right, boy, now we'll have a little talk," Salazar said.

Kriss struggled to his feet and turned. The man who had held him had held him once before—the night he'd attacked Kriss and Tevera in the alley across from Andru's. Kriss looked from him to Salazar. He remembered Arnason holding a gun to Tevera's head, and rage rose in his throat like bile. "I hoped you were dead," he snarled.

"Some of my men are."

Kriss ran his sore tongue over his swelling lip. "Then why don't you just kill me and get it over with?"

"Don't tempt me." Salazar held out the touchlyre to

Kriss, and when Kriss hesitated, jammed it viciously against his ribs. Kriss gasped. "Take it!"

Kriss took it. "What do you want?"

"Unwrap it," Salazar commanded.

Reluctantly, Kriss did so, letting the blanket fall. The rain splattered against the polished wood and copper plates, forming heavy drops that ran harmlessly away.

"Play it."

That was the last thing Kriss had expected Salazar to say. He looked around the courtyard: walls on three sides, and on the fourth, the tumble-down wooden porch of an abandoned building. "Here? Why?"

"I've never heard it. I need proof it does what I've been told. Play!"

Kriss wrapped his arms around the touchlyre. "Why should I? You're going to kill me anyway."

"Not if the touchlyre works as advertised. Not if what's inside it is really alien. I'll just take it from you—and leave you for Vorlick's man."

Kriss blinked, confused. "What?"

Salazar laughed. "You weren't nearly as clever as you thought you were, boy. You were followed *twice*. We chased him off, but he could be back any minute with reinforcements. So, play *now*, or I *will* kill you and take the touchlyre on faith." He nodded to his henchman, who grinned and drew a long black knife from a sheath at his waist. Salazar turned back to Kriss. "Well?"

Kriss took a deep breath. He did not want to play the touchlyre ever again. Once his dearest possession, a link with his lost parents, he now knew it for what it truly was: a dangerous alien artifact, a bit of bloody space debris that had already led to more deaths than he wanted on his conscience. How could he let it invade his mind again after all the grief it had caused?

Let Salazar have it! he thought bitterly. *I'll be glad to be rid of it.* He glared at the black wood, the silver strings, the copper plates. He wished it wasn't impervious to the rain. He wished it would rot.

"Play!" Salazar commanded again.

For the last time, Kriss thought, and touched the plates.

Chapter Seventeen

Kriss gave no thought to what he would play, wanting only to get it over with. Perhaps because of that lack of conscious direction, in an instant, he had no control at all. The touchlyre's invisible fingers reached into his mind, found his fear, guilt, and hatred, ripped those emotions from him, funnelled them through itself—and hurled them at Salazar and his henchman.

Kriss felt every muscle in his body snap rigid, as though cast in steel, as the power of the instrument poured through him like a purge of live steam, the touchlyre's strings shrieking a single, ear-splitting discord. Salazar's man screamed and collapsed, and Salazar's face slackened, his knees buckled, and he fell to the ground like a marionette whose strings had been cut, unconscious or dead.

Only then did the instrument release its hold on Kriss, the strings quivering back down to stillness. Kriss gasped, swayed, and fell to his knees, his heart beating a ragged rhythm in his chest. He stared down at the touchlyre as though he had never seen it before.

Salazar moaned, and Kriss clambered to his feet. He had to escape. Salazar had said one of Vorlick's men had followed him, too. What would Vorlick do with the power the touchlyre had just displayed?

I should destroy it, he thought, grabbing the sodden blanket and wrapping it around the instrument again, but a surge of terror struck him like a physical blow at the thought, and he froze for a moment, feeling the touchlyre's immaterial fingers lingering in his mind. Then Salazar's hands twitched against the wet stones of the courtyard pavement, and Kriss dashed past his fallen enemies into the street.

A man scurried through the intersection down the street to Kriss's left, hunched against the steady drizzle. He didn't even look at Kriss. Otherwise, the street remained deserted, though Kriss had thought the instrument's screaming loud enough to bring the whole city running.

Around here, they've probably learned to ignore things that don't concern them, he thought. *Suits me fine. No one will tell anyone they saw me.*

Kriss turned right and hurried down to where the pavement ended. As he stepped from the worn cobblestones into the mud of the waterlogged track leading through the cornfield, he glanced back. He was afraid he would see Salazar and his henchman emerging from the courtyard, or Vorlick and a force of his men coming down the street.

Instead, he saw Rigel and three other Family crewmen rounding the corner.

Kriss spun and plunged off the track in among the cornstalks, more than tall enough to hide him, but it was too late:

he heard shouts, though the words were lost in the hiss of the rain on the corn and his own gasping breath, and knew they had seen him.

Water stood shin-deep in the ruts in the track, and the rich black dirt clung to his feet like lead shoes. He lost one boot and sock, then the other, staggered on a few more steps barefoot, and then fell, twisting awkwardly so that he splashed down on one side, touchlyre still cradled against his chest. Holding it with one arm, he managed to push himself up with the other and get to his feet once more, but now he could hear the sound of the Family men crashing through the corn in pursuit.

Gulping air, he ran on, the long leaves slicing his bare hands and face, but within a dozen steps, he fell again, and this time, he barely made it to his feet before Rigel and his cohort reached him. He spun to face them, arms wrapped around the touchlyre.

Rigel, panting, glared at him. "The captain wants to see you. Why did you run?"

Kriss replied by lowering his head and charging. He hit Rigel in the stomach with the top of his skull, sending the Family man splashing butt-first into the mud, kept his own feet, and tried to dash into the corn, but was tackled from behind and fell face-first into the muck, the hard shape of the touchlyre against his gut driving the breath from his body. Someone hauled him to his feet and took the touchlyre from him while he gaped helplessly, trying to force air back into his body. By the time he was breathing semi-normally, Rigel had seized his arms from behind and was pushing him back through the field toward the city.

Rigel released him as they reached the paved street, but

with four of the Family surrounding him, and barefoot on the cobblestones, he couldn't run. Despite his helplessness, even though his final bid for a kind of freedom had been thwarted, he kept his head up defiantly as he walked among his captors.

Suddenly Rigel grabbed his arm and pulled him to a stop. "Salazar!"

Kriss jerked around to see Salazar stumbling out of the courtyard, his once-fine clothes even muddier than before. Fresh blood ran down his face from a cut on his forehead.

Kriss's companions tensed, flicking glances at the surrounding buildings—but Kriss only watched Salazar. The man's piggish eyes blinked in bewilderment, as though he had misplaced something. His gaze met Kriss's for a moment but wandered on with no spark of recognition. He brushed past the Family group and moved uncertainly down a side street, vanishing into the rain.

Rigel stared after him, then shook his head and started forward again. "Come on, worldhugger, we're in a hurry."

Not having much choice, Kriss followed. "Why couldn't you let me go?" he said bitterly. "You said you never wanted to see me again."

"I *didn't*," Rigel snapped. "But the captain had other ideas. Now be quiet!"

Kriss subsided. It occurred to him that the touchlyre might do to his new captors what it had done to Salazar if he could grab it from the Family man holding it, but he pushed the thought away. However Rigel and his friends felt about him—however *he* felt about *them*—they were Tevera's family. If he hurt them, he would hurt her. And he still shuddered at the memory of how the touchlyre had ripped his emotions from him and forged them into a weapon.

They strode on through the rainswept streets, Kriss limping as the cobblestones bruised his unprotected feet, his boots—the boots Mella had made for him, he thought with a renewed flare of sorrow and rage—lost in the muddy cornfield. The few people they passed, cloaked and hooded against the storm, seemed more concerned with keeping as dry and warm as possible than with five offworlders, one of them a bedraggled, muddy, barefoot boy.

At a corner where they should have gone straight to reach the spaceport, they instead veered left, startling Kriss. A few minutes later, they turned another corner—onto the avenue that led to Andru's. He stared at the inn in disbelief. "What are we doing *here*?"

"I wish I knew," Rigel growled. He led the way up onto the porch and knocked. The door opened, and they entered.

Kriss looked around the dim, shuttered room. A dozen offworld men and women sat silently at the tables in the common room, shadowy figures silhouetted against the single light over the bar. He saw Zendra at the fireplace, putting fresh wood on the coals. As flames began to lick the logs, she turned, saw Kriss, and smiled at him tentatively, but he ignored her. Instead, leaving a trail of bare footprints on the hardwood floor, he pushed through his escort and went to confront Andru, who stood in front of the bar, arms folded.

"This is how you 'take care' of me?" he demanded. "Turning me over to my enemies?"

Andru, his eyes still on the door, didn't even glance at him. "Quiet."

"Let him speak!" Rigel's cry startled Kriss. He turned to

see Tevera's brother striding toward them. "I'd like to know what's going on, too. This worldhugger put my sister in danger!"

Andru's glance shifted to him. "*And* helped rescue her," he growled.

"She wouldn't have *needed* rescuing if not for him! And after that, I warned him to stay away from the Family. We even left a man here to make sure he didn't try to contact Tevera again. Then suddenly, you show up at *Thaylia*, and the next thing we know, the captain is telling us to go and get him!"

Andru's steel-grey brows drew together. "Are you questioning orders?"

Rigel stiffened and almost replied; then he dropped his gaze and muttered something too soft to hear.

"Your questions will be answered in Council," Andru said. The innkeeper swept the crowd with his stormy eyes, as though daring anyone to take exception.

But Kriss thought he already had his answers. "The temptation was just too much, wasn't it?" he snarled at Andru. "You've decided to take the touchlyre for yourself!"

Zendra gasped. Andru's face reddened. He raised his hand . . . then clenched it, let it drop, and took a deep breath. "Events will speak for themselves," he rumbled. "Be silent."

Zendra came toward Kriss from the fire. "You should get out of those wet clothes . . ."

He turned on her, voice half-choked. "Drop the charade! How much extra did Andru pay you to 'mother' me, so I'd trust you both? It worked, you know—I thought you really cared!"

Zendra paled, but he pressed on, wanting to hurt as he

had been hurt. "I'd even started to think of this place as home —but at home, you're *safe*." He looked around at the Family. "Safe," he repeated bitterly.

Zendra's hand suddenly cracked across his face, then she sobbed and ran out through the beaded curtain. Kriss stared after her, his ears ringing, and raised a hand to his burning cheek.

An iron grip seized his shoulder. Andru spun him around and shoved him hard against the bar, holding him there. "Listen, *boy*!" Andru snarled, his dark, weathered face, twisted in anger, only centimetres from Kriss's. "Everything she did for you was out of the goodness of her heart."

But Kriss refused to feel remorse. "All I see from here is betrayal."

The powerful, gnarled fingers dug deeper into his flesh. Andru's other fist clenched. Kriss waited for the blow to fall —but then cool, wet air rushed around them, and Andru spat a curse, shoved Kriss away, and turned around.

Kriss, rubbing his bruised shoulder, looked past the innkeeper to see a black-clad man and woman entering the inn, silver beamers drawn. They scanned the room with emotionless eyes, then stepped to each side of the door, crossing their deadly weapons over their hearts.

Behind them, moving slowly and with great dignity, came a white-haired woman wearing a long dress as black as space, and a silver-lined cloak, clasped at her neck by a crystal sunburst that glowed with its own deep, inner fire. The light from the broach cast the wrinkles on her face into deep relief and lit eyes a startling shade of green. Kriss stared at her, wondering who this ancient woman could be.

Andru crossed to her. Beside him, she looked almost doll-like, but Andru bowed his head with great respect. "Captain Nicora."

Kriss stiffened. *Captain?* There was only one ship she could be captain of: *Thaylia.*

And then the door opened again, and through it came two more people: another man, wearing a Family uniform . . .

. . . and Tevera.

Chapter Eighteen

No one told Tevera where they were going or why. Yverras, a taciturn, grey-haired man, one of her more distant relatives on the ship—third cousin, was it? or fourth?—simply appeared at her cabin door and told her to come with him. He would not answer her questions, looking straight ahead, stone-faced, as they descended the loading ramp, stepped onto the spaceport's blackened duracrete, walked to the main gate, and went out into the city.

It did not take her long, however, to recognize their route.

"Why are we going to Andru's?" she said. A part of her was overjoyed—surely, Kriss would be there—but another part of her had a sinking feeling that whatever was intended, it wasn't a surprise reunion for the two of them.

She knew she was right about that when she and Yverras rounded the last corner, and she saw ahead of her a slender woman with white hair, wearing a long black dress and silver-lined cloak, climbing the inn's porch and then disappearing inside.

If Great-Grandmother Nicora had left not only the ship but the *port* to come to Andru's, something extraordinary was in the offing. The captain never strayed far from *Thaylia*, even on far more civilized worlds than this.

With Yverras, Tevera entered Andru's familiar common room. The captain stood a short distance ahead of her, flanked by her bodyguards, facing Andru. All the highest-ranking members of the Family were there, too, some seated at tables, others standing around the room's perimeter. She knew at once what that meant. *It's a Council meeting!* But she couldn't imagine why *Thaylia*'s Council would have been convened in a portside inn.

Andru stood with the captain . . . but then, behind him, she at last spotted the person she wanted to see most of all: Kriss, back against the bar, face flushed, rubbing his right shoulder as though it pained him. His eyes widened when he saw her. She tried to smile at him but wasn't at all sure she succeeded.

Andru and Nicora stiffly exchanged greetings. Andru escorted Nicora to a table near the bar. Tevera's great-grandmother glided toward it in stately fashion, her cloak whispering across the floor, the silver lining reflecting red flashes of firelight. Her bodyguards, Estra and Levit, second cousins of Tevera's, moved with her and stood a step behind her, one on either side, as she sat and folded her thin hands on the table.

Yverras pushed Tevera to a table near the door. Rigel, standing nearby, gave her an angry look, then deliberately turned away.

Nicora's voice, thin and crackling, but sharp as a monomolecular-edged blade, cut through the thick silence. "I agreed to this extraordinary Council, in this extraordinary place, for your sake, Andru," she said. "I did not ask you for your reasons, but now I must. Without explanation, this Council cannot proceed."

Tevera's eyes widened. Andru had called for the Council to meet off-ship, in his inn, and Great-Grandmother Nicora had agreed? She knew Andru was an offworlder, of course—everyone knew that—but how had that given him the pull to arrange *this*? And why had he?

"My reasons will be made clear in due course," Andru countered. "But first, *I* need more information." He pointed to Kriss. "How has this boy offended the Family?"

"I'll tell you how!" Rigel cried from Tevera's left. He pushed his way through the older members of the Family and into the light. "My sister," he pointed back at Tevera, "was almost killed because of him!"

"That's not fair!" Tevera burst out.

Yverras grabbed her shoulder and squeezed hard, and she subsided.

"Quiet, both of you!" the captain snapped. "Neither of you have sufficient rank to speak at this Council unless asked to do so. Rigel, sit down."

Rigel sat at a table near the captain, his back to Tevera. Even from behind, she could see his fists were clenched.

Nicora turned her gaze back to Andru. "Though he speaks out of turn, Rigel's summary is essentially accurate."

Tevera pressed her lips together but stayed silent, the pressure of Yverras's hand a warning.

"I would prefer a little more detail," Andru said.

To Tevera's surprise, it was Kriss who answered. "You know what I did!" he shouted. "I told you myself! So, get it over with! Steal the touchlyre and do whatever it is you plan to do to me!"

Andru rounded on him. "Silence!" he roared, his voice like thunder. "Silence, or I'll gag you myself!"

Kriss folded his arms, but he still looked angry. "I'll be quiet—for now. But you'd better keep that gag handy."

Silently, Tevera cheered him on.

The innkeeper turned toward the captain again. "Pardon the interruption."

Nicora regarded him. "So, if I provide a more detailed account of this boy's offences, you will explain why you called this Council?"

"I will."

She inclined her white head. "Very well." She paused for a moment, as though gathering her thoughts, then spoke crisply and dispassionately. If Andru's voice had been thunder, hers was a sliver of jagged lightning, bright and sharp. "Kriss first contacted Tevera in this inn. Her brother, Rigel, and her cousin Corvus kept that contact appropriately brief.

"Kriss contacted her a second time the next day, near the port. Tevera, curious about the boy's musical talent, agreed to talk to him privately that night, though she knew it violated Family regulations. When they met again, he tried to enlist her help in gaining him a berth on a starship. She explained that it was impossible. He refused to accept her explanation and grew angry. She fled his presence, but before she could make good her escape, became entangled in a violent encounter between Kriss and men we now know worked for Anton Salazar and Carl Vorlick."

The bald declaration of facts filled Tevera's heart with ice. She wanted to argue . . . but Nicora's account was completely accurate. What it had meant . . . what Kriss's performance had meant to her, what they had felt for each other . . . none of that would have any influence on whatever decision this Council was going to be called on to make. And what that was, she still couldn't grasp.

She looked from face to face. Most of the gathered Family gazed at Kriss as though he were a slimy alien creature found under a stone. Rigel glared. Nowhere did she see sympathy.

"Simply by being near Kriss, Tevera was in danger," the captain continued. "Then, as near as we can gather, he compounded the offence by threatening to reveal their secret meeting if she did not use *Thaylia*'s computers to find out what she could about his parents. Because she feared punishment, she agreed. She gave him the information he requested at a second private meeting."

That wasn't the only reason I agreed, Tevera thought. She caught Kriss's eyes, then, afraid she'd see betrayal in them . . . but she didn't. He even managed a small smile. She tried her best to return it.

"Rigel saw them together, and ordered them apart, and that should have been the end of it." Nicora looked directly at Kriss for the first time, her green gaze piercing. "But Salazar had already connected Tevera with Kriss, and in an attempt to obtain the boy's peculiar musical artifact, he kidnapped her. Thus, Kriss *again* endangered her life. He redeemed himself somewhat by helping us rescue her . . ."

Somewhat? Tevera thought angrily.

"... but he was then warned most sternly by Rigel to stay away from the Family."

Rigel jumped to his feet, warning not to speak unless questioned forgotten. "And then we were sent to find him again!" he shouted. "Why? Why is he here? Why are any of us here?"

Tevera glared at him, seething with anger. Kriss had been "warned most sternly" to stay away from the Family? *Rigel threatened him! That's why he didn't come with us when we left the Red Horse Inn!*

"Although Rigel *again* speaks out of turn," Nicora said, with just enough edge to her voice that Tevera's brother subsided, and sat down once more, "his question is the one I, too, must ask. Why did you insist on bringing Kriss back to this place, and summon the Family? Why did you call this Council?"

KRISS HAD BEGUN to wonder the same thing. He'd thought Andru intended to sell the touchlyre to the Family, but none of this seemed to have anything to do with the instrument. And, come, to think of it, how did a spaceport innkeeper have the authority to summon, not just members of the Family, but the captain of one of their ships, to a gathering like this?

"One moment," Andru said. He glanced at Kriss. "Is the captain's account accurate?" he rumbled.

Now, he thought. Now he could justify himself, explain what happened. Tevera was watching him. It could serve as his apology ...

No. No, he would not whine or beg. And he would apologize to Tevera directly—if ever given the chance to speak to her again. He uncrossed his arms, stood a little straighter. "Yes," he said defiantly. "I will do whatever it takes to get into space."

Andru looked at Tevera, then back at the captain. "And what is the girl's punishment to be? Surely, she is as much to blame as the boy—perhaps more so, since she knew the rules she was breaking, and he did not."

"Aside from this appearance, she is confined to quarters for the duration of our time on this planet. Once in space, she will be assigned extra duty, and certain privileges will be temporarily suspended."

"But she is still part of the Family."

"Of course, she is," Rigel exploded. "She's my sister! She's the captain's great-granddaughter! Get to the point!"

Kriss blinked, startled. *The captain is Tevera's great-grandmother?*

"If you speak out of turn again, Rigel," Nicora said without looking at him, voice like ice, "you will share your sister's punishment."

Once more, Rigel subsided.

Andru didn't so much as glance at Tevera's brother. He kept his gaze on Nicora. "The point is this: if Kriss were Family, his punishment would be no more severe than Tevera's. Certainly, he would not be left to the mercy of enemies like Salazar and Vorlick."

"Of course not. But he is not Family."

"Once part of the Family, always part of the Family, correct?"

"You know that." Impatience had crept into Nicora's voice.

"But there is an exception, isn't there?" Andru said. "The pertinent regulation states, 'A Family member may give up his or her rights voluntarily, transferring them to an outsider, who thenceforth is recognized as Family, taking that member's place. The Family will welcome their new brother or sister as one of their own.'"

Nicora took a sharp intake of breath. "Such a thing has not happened in my lifetime, my mother's lifetime, or *her* mother's lifetime."

"You will not be able to say that after today."

Kriss stared at Andru, startled by the sudden strain in his voice.

Nicora's face paled. A murmur swept through the Family. Tevera's eyes widened. Rigel stared at the innkeeper, slack-jawed.

"You are my witnesses!" Andru shouted above the rising din. He turned toward Kriss. "Give me your hand."

Bewildered, uncertain, he stretched it out. Andru's rough fingers gripped his. The hubbub trailed away into horrified silence as the big man's voice boomed out. "I, Andru, once of the Family of the starship *Thaylia*, hereby relinquish all my rights and privileges as Family to this boy, Kriss Lemarc of Earth and Farr's World. He is my chosen replacement. I call on the Family, once mine, now his, to welcome him to the fellowship of the stars!" He squeezed Kriss's hand so hard Kriss gasped in pain, then released it, stepped back, and took a deep, shuddering breath.

Kriss stared at his tingling hand. He clenched it, then opened it again. His heart pounded, and his knees trembled.

He remembered the terrible things of which he had accused Andru and Zendra. Yet the innkeeper—*once of the Family of the starship* Thaylia!—had still done *this*. Why?

And . . . how could he ever make amends for what he had said?

The uproar in the room seemed as distant as though he and Andru stood alone in some secluded place. "Andru, I'm so sorry . . ." His throat closed on the words.

The big, work-roughened hand rested on his shoulder again, but this time gently. "No apology needed," Andru said gruffly. "You've been through hell. I've been there myself. I understand."

On impulse, Kriss flung his arms around the big man, who awkwardly returned the hug; then, he pulled back as the realization of what had just happened began to seep in. He was Family. *Family*! He *would* go into space—and on the same ship as Tevera—

He turned toward her eagerly but instead saw the captain rising from her chair, the silver-lined cloak swirling around her thin form. Her face had gone from white to red, and her eyes blazed.

"I do not accept this!" she said, voice as harsh and high as an over-tightened string. "I will *not* have this boy thrust into my Family against my will. This Council is at an end!"

She turned toward the door, her black-garbed guards turning to follow, and all Kriss's new-born hopes crashed to destruction behind her.

Chapter Nineteen

As Nicora turned to leave, Tevera leaped up, twisted free from Yverras's hand on her shoulder, and dashed to the door. She stood in front of it, blocking her great-grandmother's path. "No!" Tevera shouted. "Now, I *will* be heard!"

Her cousins Estra and Levit took a step toward her, scowling, but Nicora said, "Hold," and they stopped and stepped back. The captain studied Tevera with her cold blue eyes. "Well?"

"I wondered why Kriss disappeared after helping to rescue me," Tevera said. Her heart pounded to be facing down the captain—and some small part of her wailed in a little-girl voice, *What are you* doing?—but she didn't move from her place in front of the door. "Now, I know. My *brother—*" she saw Rigel's face flush at the scorn she poured into that word, and felt vicious satisfaction—"threatened him and told him to stay behind, even though he'd risked his life to save mine!"

"He risked *your* life from the moment he laid eyes on you!" Rigel snarled, stepping up beside Levit, the bodyguard to Nicora's right.

Tevera met his gaze squarely. "He didn't force me to meet him *or* help him! He didn't *make* me do anything, whatever he may have thought."

And then she stepped forward, brushed past Estra on Nicora's left, and crossed the common room to where Kriss stood. She took his hand. He stared at her, eyes wide. She gave him a brief, strained smile, then turned to face Nicora and Rigel and all the rest of the gathered Family. "I *chose* to help him! I heard him play, I felt what he felt, and I *chose* to do what I did. He didn't have a family, but he wanted one so badly it shames those of us who claim to hold family so dear. He deserved whatever help I could give him!"

"Enough!" the captain snapped. "Estra, Levit, escort Tevera back to the ship."

Kriss thrust Tevera behind him as the black-uniformed bodyguards stepped forward. "No!"

"Stop!" Andru's shout rattled glasses.

Nicora glared at him. "You defy me, too?"

"You are not on *Thaylia*, Captain Nicora," Andru said. "You are in my inn, and by Family *and* planetary law, *I* am master here. The boy *and* girl under my protection as guests in my house."

Estra and Levit looked to Nicora for guidance. Thin-lipped, she nodded once. The pair returned to her side, but their eyes never left Kriss.

Tevera pushed past him. She didn't need his protection, though his impulse to provide it had warmed her. She glared at her diminutive great-grandmother. "You dare lecture *me* about obeying Family law, when you refuse point-blank to accept Andru's decision to give up his place in the Family to Kriss, as the law so clearly gives him the right to do?" Tevera had had no idea until tonight that Andru had once been a part of *Thaylia*'s Family. He had clearly left the ship, and built this inn, long before she was born. But once Family, always Family, and the law was explicit: he *could* give his place to another, whomever he chose—and he had chosen Kriss.

Her heart still pounded, but now with righteous fury as well as fear.

The Family officers stiffened at the scorn in her voice. Rigel paled. Nicora's face remained calm, but Tevera heard the harsh thread of the captain's own anger in her cracked voice, making each word clipped and precise. "My concern is the well-being of the Family and the ship. This boy does not belong on *Thaylia*. And *you* are travelling a dangerous course."

"I don't care!" Lifted high by the rising heat of her anger, Tevera grabbed Kriss's hand again and held it up, fingers entwined with his. "I choose this 'worldhugger' and this world over the kind of Family you've shown yourselves to be!"

THE CAPTAIN'S bodyguards both took steps forward, eyes narrowed, hands on their beamers. Kriss tensed, dropped Tevera's hand, and clenched his fists, but once again, the captain stopped her guards with a clipped command. "Hold!" Then she stepped forward herself. She looked at him for a long moment, then at Tevera for a longer one. "I must think," she said finally. "Andru, a room to myself."

The innkeeper nodded once and escorted her through the beaded curtain, presumably to his office. He returned a moment later and stood in front of the curtain, arms folded. Nicora's guards stationed themselves on either side of him, stone-faced. He ignored them.

A low murmur of conversation swept through the gathered officers, who glanced repeatedly at Kriss and Tevera. He looked from their hostile gazes to her warm eyes. He didn't know what to say to her. Instead, driven by impulse, he pulled her to him and hugged her, hard, his cheek against her wet hair, her body warm and soft against his. Only then did the words come. "I love you," he whispered and felt her press herself more tightly against him in response.

"Let go of her, worldhugger!" Kriss's head jerked up, and he released Tevera just as Rigel slammed into him. Tevera screamed as both of them crashed into the bar and then to the floor, Kriss on the bottom.

Rigel straddled him and pulled back his fist. "If the captain won't protect my sister, I will!"

But before the blow could fall, Tevera grabbed her brother's arm and twisted it behind his back. He grimaced in pain as she hauled him upright. "Let go!" He tried to pull free and failed. Kriss, back aching where it had banged into the edge of the bar, rolled over and scrambled up. Andru strode toward them, looming like a storm cloud.

"Let him go, Tevera! Andru, stay out of this!" Kriss clenched his own fists. He owed Rigel for a lot of things. He stepped forward . . .

But at that moment, Nicora's harsh voice, cold and hard

and brooking no disobedience, cut through the room. "Tevera, release your brother. Rigel, move away. *Now!*"

Tevera released Rigel. Breathing hard, he shoved past Kriss, who bristled but obeyed the restraining hand Andru laid on his shoulder.

Nicora, now at the end of the bar, continued in that same wintry tone. Her withered face displayed no emotion. "Tevera spoke the truth. I allowed anger to influence my decision."

Tevera moved closer to Kriss, who wondered what was coming. Andru stood behind them.

"The question before me is, does this boy belong in the Family?" Nicora said. Rigel drew a sharp breath but did not speak. Nicora's green eyes flicked toward him. "His previous actions have no bearing since he acted out of ignorance." Her gaze shifted to Andru. "Yet, we cannot allow someone into the Family without knowing more of his motives. We are a special people, calling no planet home. We have no family but the Family. Deep space is the cradle of our kind. Is this boy suited to that life? That is the most important question."

"Let *him* tell you!" Tevera said.

Kriss stared at her. *How?* No matter what the captain said, he knew his past actions *would* weigh against him. Nothing he could say could possibly convince them . . .

Tevera gripped his hand. "Don't use words," she whispered fiercely. "Use the touchlyre!"

"No . . ." Kriss remembered Salazar's face going slack as the power of the touchlyre struck him, the way he had collapsed onto the wet cobblestones as though clubbed. "I can't!"

"You have to!"

"You don't understand . . ."

She spun to face the captain. "There's only one way you can understand. Have him play for you!"

"Captain, no!" Rigel shouted. "That thing is alien —dangerous!"

"Tevera, your brother's right," Kriss said, earning a startled look from Rigel. "The last time I played it—I almost killed Salazar!"

Tevera's eyes never left Nicora. "Captain, the decision is yours. But I know this instrument will tell you exactly what Kriss feels. As for being dangerous . . ." She glanced back at Andru. "He's been playing here for over two weeks. Any problems?"

"Business has never been better," the innkeeper said.

Tevera returned her gaze to Nicora. "Captain . . ." She dropped her voice. "Please?" she almost whispered.

Nicora regarded her with sharp eyes. Then she looked at Andru, and finally, at Kriss. She nodded once. "I will hear him play."

Unwillingly, Kriss turned to the bar, picking up the touchlyre from where he had left it. Already he thought he could feel its ghostly fingers in his mind, and when he unwrapped the now-filthy red blanket, the silver strings vibrated faintly, though he had yet to touch the copper plates.

Feelings warred inside him as he gazed at the mysterious device. Tevera was right: if he played it, they *would* understand him, maybe better than he understood himself. But he knew, now, that the touchlyre was far more than just a musical instrument. Hidden inside the beautiful exterior his father had made was a deadly alien artifact, with a power he didn't understand and was no longer sure he could control.

Last time, it had controlled *him*.

He imagined Nicora's ancient, lined face going blank like Salazar's; then pictured the same thing happening to Andru, or—terror scraped at his throat—Tevera. Though he knew she wouldn't understand, it was for her sake he reached out to the touchlyre—and began wrapping it again.

Tevera ran to his side and put a hand on his arm to stop him. "What are you doing?" she cried. "You have to play!"

He turned toward her, trying to make her understand. "Tevera, you weren't there when the touchlyre struck down Salazar. It was horrifying. And I can't be sure it won't happen again. I can't risk that. Not to . . ." His throat tightened, and he fell silent. He turned to Nicora as Tevera's hand fell away from his arm. "I'm sorry, Captain. I will not play."

"I commanded you." Her tone held warning.

"I'm not Family yet." *And now, never will be,* he thought miserably. "It's too dangerous. I don't know for sure what the touchlyre might do. Even if I *were* Family, and you ordered me—I would not play."

"Does my offer mean so little to you?" Andru rumbled, anger edging his voice.

Kriss turned toward him desperately. "It means everything to me! But I dare not play!"

Nicora folded her thin arms, her lips once again a tight, straight line. "So. As you say, you are not yet of the Family, so I cannot order you to play. But you admit that even if you *were* Family, you would disobey me. I must ask myself, does such a defiant worldhugger *belong* in the Family? Do I want someone who presumes to judge what risks I, the captain, choose to take?"

"Kriss, you're ruining everything!" Tevera gripped his arm again. "Please, play!"

He shook his head.

The captain glanced around at the assembled officers. Most watched her, but Tevera's eyes were on Kriss, as was Andru's glare. Rigel, too, stared at him, looking slightly bewildered but pleased.

Nicora's gaze came back to Kriss, and he waited for her verdict, sickly certain of what it would be.

But it never came. At that moment, the front door crashed open. Borne on a storm-blast of spattering rain, six men poured into the room and fanned out against the far wall, beamers ready.

In the doorway behind them, silhouetted against the grim, grey morning light, stood Carl Vorlick.

Chapter Twenty

Kriss pulled Tevera to him, but she struggled free and stood defiant. Andru, Rigel, and Nicora's guards surged forward, but the threat of the beamers stopped them.

Vorlick himself carried no weapon. A blistered streak of red flesh marked his left cheek, and his once-immaculate suit dripped muddy water onto the hardwood floor as he strode into the common room, his fists clenched. When he spoke, his voice was colder than the wind that whipped around him through the open door. "I've come for the artifact, boy."

"My parents wouldn't deal with you. Neither will I!" Kriss spat the words, and Nicora's piercing green eyes locked on him.

"Remember what happened to *them*," Vorlick said.

"Kill me, and you'll never even *find* the touchlyre. It's hidden." As he told the lie, he prayed the Family would not betray him—and that Vorlick would not recognize the misshapen, sodden, blanket-wrapped bundle on the bar as the artifact he sought.

Vorlick's blue eyes narrowed. "Killing you would almost be worth losing it." He smiled sardonically. "It's not as if I need the money."

Tevera edged closer to Kriss, and he saw Vorlick's eyes flick to her, then back. Vorlick's smile broadened, making Kriss think of a predator licking its chops after a kill. "But I have a better idea. I'll keep you alive . . . for a while. Why don't I start with the girl, instead?"

Rigel growled a curse and took a step forward, but three beamers swung to cover him, and he froze. The muscles in his neck stood out like steel rods.

Kriss's stomach knotted. "You wouldn't . . ."

Vorlick jerked his head, and the black-bearded giant to his right showed his yellow teeth in a humourless grin. He holstered his beamer, drew a knife from his belt, and started forward.

"Try it," Tevera spat. "I'll break your arm."

The bearded man only grinned wider. Tevera tensed—

"All right!" Kriss cried. He closed his eyes. "All right."

Tevera spun toward him. "Kriss, no!"

"Kelly, back in line," Vorlick ordered. The bearded man shrugged, sheathed his knife, drew his beamer again, and returned to his place.

Tevera grabbed Kriss's arm as he turned toward the bar, but he threw her off and pulled the wet red cloth aside, revealing the rich black wood of the touchlyre. A deep hush fell on the room, through which he could hear Tevera's ragged breathing . . .

. . . and the sharp crackling of the fire.

"Bring it here!" Vorlick snapped.

"All right," Kriss said. He lifted the touchlyre, turned—and then dashed to the fireplace.

A beamer ray seared the air by his cheek, dazzling him, and he heard Tevera scream. He stumbled, and another bolt shot over his head, then he was at the hearth, holding the touchlyre over the blazing logs. "Stop firing!" Vorlick yelled.

"*Now* we'll bargain, Vorlick!" Kriss shouted, his eyes fixed on the leaping flames. "Or the touchlyre burns!"

But trembling gripped his limbs at the thought of the black wood burning, the silver strings melting and breaking, the copper plates buckling, the alien device hidden inside blackening and bursting . . . the vision was so real it shocked him. He thought he felt the touchlyre's phantom tentacles in his mind, scrabbling for survival.

"I can kill you from here!" Vorlick cried.

"Instantly? Because the last thing I'll do is throw this into the fire!"

Silence. Sweat stung Kriss's eyes, but he shivered as though he stood naked in a blizzard. And all the time, horror gnawed inside him at the thought of destroying the touchlyre, horror he held at bay only by thinking of the even more horrible alternative, of Tevera in the hands of that black-bearded monster . . .

Vorlick tried again. "I can kill everyone—including your girl!"

"The touchlyre will still burn!"

More silence. Kriss gasped for air, tortured by the heat, but he would not move. He could not.

"All right!" Vorlick snapped. "What do you want?"

"Let everyone else go. Now. When they're gone—the

artifact is yours." *What's left of it.* Once the room was empty, he would throw the touchlyre into the fire anyway. He couldn't let Vorlick abuse its power. As for himself—his parents and Mella had died because of this alien monstrosity. Tevera and others had been endangered by it. It was time he faced that same risk. "Now, Vorlick!"

But it was Nicora who replied. "No."

He squeezed his eyes shut in agony. "Captain, take Tevera and go!"

"No, Kriss."

"Who are *you*?" Vorlick demanded.

"Captain—" Kriss began again, pleading.

But Nicora snapped, "Tevera, keep him quiet."

AT LAST, an order she could obey. Tevera dashed to Kriss. He started to turn toward her. She seized the touchlyre, jerked it away from him and the fire, and put it on the bar. "Tevera, no—" he whispered behind her.

She turned, threw her arms around him, and hugged him tightly.

He closed his eyes and held her. "What are you doing?" he murmured in anguish in her ear.

She pulled away, then reached up and brushed his sweat-slick hair out of his eyes. Her cheeks were wet with tears. "Trust the captain."

"But Vorlick—"

"Thank you," Vorlick said sardonically, self-assured once more. Tevera looked the length of the dark room and met the man's cold-steel eyes over Rigel's tense shoulder. "Take him," Vorlick commanded his men.

"Stay where you are!" Nicora's tone assumed obedience, so much so the armed men hesitated.

Vorlick's narrowed eyes shifted to her. "Old woman, I came for the artifact and the boy. What happens to you is of no concern—unless you get in my way."

"I am already in your way." Nicora pointed at Kriss. "To take him, you'll have to shoot me."

Kriss drew in his breath, but Tevera gripped his arm painfully tight. "Shut *up*!" she whispered fiercely.

"Old woman—"

"Captain, to you."

"Of what? A fishing boat? A garbage scow?"

There was a hissing intake of breaths from the Family scattered all around the room, but no one moved, held impotent by the threat of the beamers. Tevera held onto Kriss and watched Nicora draw herself up. Her white hair caught the firelight so that she appeared to be wearing a queenly crown of red gold, and Tevera, for all she had rebelled against the old woman just moments before, burned with pride as her great-grandmother said, slowly and distinctly, emphasizing every word, "I am Captain Nicora of the free Family trader *Thaylia*."

"Family?" Vorlick sounded incredulous. "Then why are you protecting this—this 'worldhugger?'"

"He is not a 'worldhugger.' He, too, is Family." Tevera felt a surge of relief and joy at those words. Nicora glanced at Kriss, who stared at her, mouth open. She turned to Vorlick once more. "He and his artifact are under my protection."

"I said *take him*!" Vorlick shouted to his men.

Two started forward, but Nicora interposed herself between Kriss and them and spread her thin arms. "I said you'll have to shoot me first. But if you do, you will be marked men." Nicora's voice, calm but intense, dropped to a near-whisper. "Vorlick can't protect you from the Family. No one can. The only place you might be safe is a planet where no Family ship would ever call—and there are no such planets, not in the Commonwealth. And even if you found one, you'd know we were after you, and what we'd do if we caught you. Will you risk that?"

One man stopped. "It's not worth it."

His companion took only two more steps. "You're right," he said. "I'm not shooting a Family captain."

Both strode back to their places, beamers now pointed at the floor.

Vorlick glared at them, then at the rest of his men, but they wouldn't meet his eyes. One by one, they lowered their weapons. He spun back toward the captain. "You can't keep him on-ship forever. Whenever and wherever he steps off, he's fair game."

"He's Family, Vorlick," the captain said in the tone of one explaining something to a not-very-bright child. "If anything happens to him, we're going to blame you. And the Union will back us. You harm Kriss, and you're out of business. You won't be able to buy a ship, find a crew, or unload cargo on any planet in the Commonwealth. And you'll have to have guards around you all the time . . . for all the good they'll do you. Ask your men about Family vengeance."

Vorlick's face had gone purple. "But he's just a worthless boy!" he roared.

Nicora's gaze didn't waver. "A *Family* boy."

Vorlick's mouth snapped shut. His jaw clenched, then he let out an explosive breath. "Pfah! All right! Maybe you *could* damage my business—but I own a lot of planet-based industry, too. How long can *you* last without supplies?"

"You have competitors. We don't."

Vorlick looked from face to face, as though searching for a way out. "Then sell him to me! You're traders. How much for the boy and the artifact? Any of you—name your price!"

A muted growl ran through the Family. The captain stood a little stiffer yet. "This conversation is ended." She turned her back on Vorlick, silver-lined cape swirling.

"Damn you—" Vorlick started forward, but Estra and Levit intercepted him, beamers aimed at his heart, while his own men stood motionless. Stopped by the bodyguards' unwavering weapons, Vorlick made an abortive motion toward something at his belt, then suddenly swore, spun, and strode out into the rain.

His men backed nervously out in his wake. Rigel slammed the door shut behind the last one, and the room erupted as everyone suddenly had to talk about what they had just witnessed.

Tevera let out a deep breath she hadn't realized she was holding. Kriss did the same, and they looked at each other and laughed—laughter that died as the captain approached.

STANDING WITH TEVERA, Kriss stared at the old woman with newfound respect. For a moment, as she looked at the two of them, her lined face sagged with fatigue, and she looked as old as she had to be. *Tevera's great-grandmother!* he thought. But then she took a deep breath and straightened. "He won't cause us any more trouble before we leave."

"But afterward?" Kriss said. "He won't give up."

"No," Nicora agreed. "Not anytime soon. But remember —" Her gaze locked on his. "You're not alone anymore."

Kriss met those piercing, blue-ice eyes squarely. "I am thankful, truly I am. But . . . why? I refused to play, even though you commanded it. I was sure you were going to reject me. What changed?"

"You put our safety above your own. That is the essence of the Family."

He remembered how, in turn, she had put her frail old body between him and Vorlick's guns, and his heart warmed toward her for the first time. "Thank you," he said softly. Then added, "Captain."

She nodded, then went to talk to Andru.

Tevera hugged him again. "Welcome to the Family!" she said joyfully, then looked past him, her smile fading. "Rigel . . ."

Kriss turned to see Tevera's grim-faced brother. "Rigel?" he said tentatively, and held out his hand.

Rigel made no move to take it. "The captain says you are one of our Family," he said coldly. "I must accept that. But I warn you—if you do anything to hurt my sister, anything at all, I'll make you pay. With interest. Understand?" Without waiting for an answer, he turned on his heel and strode out the door and into the storm.

Kriss silently lowered his hand.

Chapter Twenty-One

The Family officers soon followed Rigel, leaving Kriss with orders to report to *Thaylia* the next morning. Tevera, no longer confined to quarters—she'd asked, and the captain had granted her clemency—watched them go from where she sat beside Kriss near the fire, the touchlyre between them.

Kriss ran a finger over its gently curved flank. "It doesn't look dangerous, does it?"

"It's beautiful," Tevera said. She leaned over to look at it more closely. "It doesn't *look* alien."

"My father made the outside, the musical instrument, as a disguise, I guess," Kriss said. "The artifact—I don't even know what it looks like—is inside. Somehow, he connected them." His voice was soft. He paused, swallowed, then said, "It's . . . it's not the only beautiful thing in the room."

Tevera felt herself blushing and smiling at the same time.

Kriss plucked a string, and a single, crystal-clear note rang out. "Tevera . . . when you stood up for me, I . . . I couldn't find words to say how I felt. I said I loved you, and that's true, but . . . it isn't enough."

"Yes, it is."

"No. It isn't. But it's as close as I can come—in words." He took a deep breath. "I'd like to tell you another way—with this." He picked up the touchlyre. "I was afraid to play it earlier. I still think I was right. I was frustrated and angry, and the touchlyre forged those kinds of feelings into a weapon to use against Salazar. I couldn't risk that with your Family."

"*Your* Family," Tevera reminded him.

He smiled. "*Our* Family." He settled the touchlyre into playing position. "I thought I'd never dare play it again. In fact, I hated the thing. But now . . ." He paused, looking into her eyes. "There's so much I want to say, and the touchlyre is the only way I can say it. You know I can't lie with this. If I play of my feelings for you . . . it's up to you."

Tevera leaned forward, elbows on the table, head in her hands. "Play."

Kriss closed his eyes and touched the copper plates.

Music . . . crystal chords, flowing arpeggios, a warm and welcoming wave of sound . . . rose from the instrument, up to the great wooden beams of the ceiling, out, Tevera felt, into the stars. The sound became an embrace of her body and mind and soul, more intimate than any physical embrace they had yet shared. It permeated her with Kriss's love, filled her to the brim and beyond, so that she overflowed with emotion. She found herself gasping, tears running down her cheeks, as, at last, the song died away.

As Kriss gently lay the touchlyre on the table again, Tevera stumbled to her feet, came around the table, and put her arms around him. "I love you," she whispered into his ear, and then she pulled back, just a little—just enough to kiss him.

The kiss lasted a long time, or no time, she could never afterward decide. At last, she drew back. Kriss licked his lips. "Um," he said.

She laughed and hugged him again.

When she pulled away, Kriss looked down at the touch-lyre. "I don't know how I could have been afraid of playing it. It's . . . it's part of me. Not just the alien thing inside it, but the instrument itself. My last connection to my parents. My only connection to my old family." He looked up at her, smiling. "*And* it led me to my new one . . . and you."

Tevera wanted to kiss him again, but instead, she stood. "I may not be confined to quarters, but I *do* have to report to *Thaylia*," she said. "As do you . . . tomorrow. See you then?"

Kriss grinned, eyes shining in the firelight. "Tomorrow!"

Outside, the storm continued to rage, but Tevera hardly noticed. Though her feet were firmly on the ground, she felt as if she were in zero-G. She floated all the way to the ship.

AFTER TEVERA LEFT, Kriss suddenly felt unutterably tired. He went to his room and slept away most of the rest of the day and night.

The next morning, as he packed his handful of clothes and other belongings into his slingpack, he heard thunder from the spaceport. He ran to the window and leaned out in time to see Vorlick's golden ship disappearing into the clear blue sky, riding a tongue of flame and trail of vapour. Heart even lighter than before, he finished packing, picked up the touchlyre from where he had rested it on his bed, and descended to the common room, where Andru and Zendra waited. "Ready?" the innkeeper asked. Kriss nodded.

"Have everything?" Zendra said brightly.

Kriss blinked at her. "Yes . . . ?"

"Are you sure?" Andru rumbled.

Kriss stared at him. Was he . . . smothering a laugh?

And then Andru reached behind the bar and pulled out the touchlyre's case, looking a bit more battered than it had, but intact. Kriss couldn't believe it. "How . . . ?"

"Andru made a trip to the Red Horse courtyard," Zendra said. "It was still there, right where you must have dropped it."

"Thank you!" Kriss said. He lay the touchlyre lovingly into the case's red-velvet interior, closed and latched the lid, and slung the case over his shoulder, balancing the slingpack, just as he had worn it during the long walk to Cascata from Black Rock.

"You're welcome," Andru said. "Now, we should be going."

Together, they went into the street. The previous day's storm had cleansed the air, and a pleasantly cool, fresh breeze from the mountains was all that remained of the howling wind. The whole city seemed bright and sparkling to Kriss, and the silver spires of the starships gleamed like a promise of the future.

They walked without speaking to the gate nearest *Thaylia*. The guard there nodded to Kriss, clearly having been told of his arrival, but before he passed through, he turned back to Andru and Zendra. There was a moment's awkward silence. "I don't know what to say," Kriss finally admitted. "I want to leave, but . . ." He paused, then laughed. "I never thought I'd say this, but in some ways, I *don't* want to leave."

"You must." Zendra hugged him warmly. "You have a new life ahead of you."

He returned the embrace, then, as they separated, said, "Zendra, I'm so sorry for what I said yesterday. It was stupid and cruel. It's just . . . I thought . . . I didn't think anyone cared."

She smiled. "It's forgotten."

He smiled back, then turned to the innkeeper. "Andru . . ."

"The best way you can thank me is to play for me whenever you come back," the innkeeper said gruffly.

"I will," he promised. "But it doesn't seem enough." He looked into Andru's grey eyes. "I know how I feel now I have Tevera, and the Family. But I have to know—how do you feel? You're alone now . . ."

Andru shook his head. "I've still got a family." He glanced at Zendra. "Twenty years ago, they told me my heart wouldn't take another lift-off. In all that time, I've lived by Family Rule. But now . . ." He put his arm around Zendra. "I'm not Family anymore. I'm going to marry Zendra."

Kriss beamed. "That's great!"

"I thought so," Zendra put in.

"I meant what I said about coming back and playing," Andru added. "I want to hear the songs you will sing after visiting the stars." He smiled. "Besides, I'll need all the help I can get to rebuild my business. My customers weren't happy about being thrown summarily into the street when I called the Family Council."

Someone shouted Kriss's name, and he turned to see Tevera waving near *Thaylia*. He waved back. "I've got to go," he said. He kissed Zendra on the cheek, then shook hands with Andru. "Good-bye." He swallowed the sudden lump in his throat. "And thank you."

"You're welcome," Andru said quietly.

"Fare well," Zendra said.

Kriss hurried through the gate to join the Family, but it seemed to him he was leaving family behind, too. *Too much family*, he thought wryly. *That's a new problem!*

SOMETIME LATER, Kriss lay in an acceleration couch next to Tevera in what she had told him was one of *Thaylia*'s ten launch rooms, looking up at viewscreens that showed the ground below and blue sky above. There were twenty-two other Family members in the room, including Rigel, on Tevera's other side. Kriss had done his best to ignore him so far.

A voice crackled over the intercom. "Ten seconds."

I'm almost free of Farr's World, he thought; but in some ways, he knew he would never be free. His parents and Mella had died there; he had grown up there. Only now that he was leaving it did he realize how much a part of him it was.

"Five seconds."

Tevera gripped his hand, and he turned his head to see her smile—but saw Rigel glaring at him over her shoulder, too. *There's going to be more trouble with him*, a voice warned him inside, but the impending take-off blotted out all other concerns. He grinned impudently at Rigel, then turned back toward the viewscreens as the voice completed the countdown.

"Two seconds . . . one . . . engines firing."

White fire blotted out the ground, and acceleration pressed him into the couch; but with what little breath he could spare, he whooped with joy as the starship thundered skyward. Several of the other Family members laughed at his reaction, but it was good-natured laughter, and he didn't mind in the least.

Cascata dwindled and finally vanished beneath them, and in the other viewscreen, the sky darkened and stars began to appear, brilliant jewels scattered across the eternal night. *At last*, Kriss thought. *At last!*

If Kriss had been writing a song about his life, he would have ended it at that moment, with Farr's World fading behind them on the viewscreens and the universe unfolding in front of him like a spring flower. But his life wasn't a song, or if it was, he wasn't writing it. Even as he gazed hungrily at those stars, he remembered Vorlick. Somewhere out there lurked a man who wanted to kill him. And when he glanced at Tevera again and once more met Rigel's angry gaze, he wondered if maybe there wasn't someone on board who would be only too happy to help.

Absolute proof his life wasn't a song came after the viewscreens were turned off, acceleration ceased, and *Thaylia* and everything on it became weightless—because nobody in a song would ever have become as violently ill as

Kriss did. The response of the other Family members in the launch room was less good-natured, this time.

TEVERA WAITED in Kriss's cabin, listening as he threw up—again—inside the tiny head. Vomiting into a vacuum-assisted toilet was nasty, as Tevera knew personally (thanks to some fish they'd once brought aboard that hadn't been as fresh as they'd thought), but it was better than simply throwing up while still in an acceleration couch, which was where Kriss had suddenly discovered he was prone to spacesickness. She wasn't, thank goodness. She'd helped him get to his cabin. Fortunately, they'd made it without any further incidents along the way.

Kriss emerged, his face pale, except for the faintest tinge of green. "Your inner ear is confused by the lack of gravity," she told him. "It will take you a while to adjust—but it does get better. And those anti-nausea pills sickbay gave you will help in the meantime. If I'd been thinking, I'd have gotten you some *before* we launched."

Luxury passenger liners had artificial gravity, and space stations simulated it with spin, but the Family couldn't waste the energy on the former, and *Thaylia* was too small for the latter. Instead, they lived the space-borne half of their lives in zero-G. Tevera, born to it, moved through it like a fish in a lake. Kriss . . . didn't. *He looks like a puppy that's fallen into the water and is desperately dog-paddling to keep from drowning,* she thought. It wasn't an unkind thought—she found it rather endearing.

Kriss swallowed hard, his hand going to his mouth, and

she decided maybe it wasn't quite *that* endearing. "You're not going to throw up again, are you?"

"I . . . don't think so?" he said. "Mainly because there's nothing left in my stomach. And where is up, anyway?"

"There isn't one," a new voice said. Tevera turned to see Rigel in Kriss's doorway, floating upside down relative to Kriss and sideways relative to her. "You know, some people *never* get over spacesickness," he added.

"Rigel—" Tevera warned, but her brother ignored her. Grinning, he came over to Kriss and clapped him on the shoulder, setting him spinning. Kriss had to grab the bed—in zero-G just a rack you tethered yourself to inside a sleeping bag—to stop himself.

"Sometimes, when we carry passengers, they never get used to it at all, even with the pills, and we just have to dump them off at the next planet to wait for a ship with artificial gravity to come along," Rigel went on. "Be a shame if that happened to you, wouldn't it, worldhugger?"

"Rigel, go away," Tevera snapped.

"Can't," Rigel said with vicious cheer. "Crewman Lemarc, here, has been assigned to my watch, and I'm supposed to give him a guided tour of the ship. So if you'll just follow me, 'crewman' . . ."

Kriss tentatively shoved off after Rigel and promptly cracked his head on what would have been the ceiling in gravity. "Ow!" he said, rubbing the place.

Tevera turned on Rigel furiously. "You know he can't come now! He'll hardly be able to move around for at least a day."

"First day, and he's already missed a watch." Rigel gave Kriss a scornful look. "Not off to a very good start, are you, worldhugger?" He spun neatly in place. "I'm afraid I'll have to report this dereliction of duty." He arrowed through the door and disappeared.

There was nothing in Kriss's cabin for Tevera to throw, or Rigel would have felt it crack into the back of his skull. She had to settle for a murderous glare before turning to Kriss and pulling him back to the bed. "Don't mind him," she said. "I'll get you a medical leave-from-duty. You just strap yourself into your bunk and try to get some sleep. By the time you wake up, the anti-nausea medication will have kicked in and your brain will be learning to make sense of the new sensory inputs, and you'll feel a hundred percent better. Then *I'll* give you a guided tour of the ship—and teach you a few tricks for getting around in zero-G. All right?"

"Whatever you say," Kriss said miserably. He pulled himself down to the bunk and Tevera tucked him into his sleeping bag, smiling a little at the thought that that was what she was doing. She secured him with the restraining net.

"How's your head?" she asked. "I could arrange for a painkiller, too—"

"It's fine," Kriss said. "Though I think Rigel would have been happier if I'd cracked my skull open. Why does he hate me so much?"

Tevera glanced out the open door in the direction her brother had taken. "He thinks he's protecting me."

"From me? I would never hurt you. I don't think I *could*." She looked back at him and saw he was smiling. "Remember how you slammed me up against the wall in the alley outside Andru's?"

"Try to convince my brother of that. It's all because . . ." Tevera paused. The story of their parents' death was not something a spacesick boy needed to hear right then. "Well, it's a long story."

He wouldn't have heard it anyway: his eyes had closed. She leaned over and kissed his forehead. A small smile played around his lips, but he didn't wake.

She went out into the corridor, closing his cabin door behind her, then set off for her own duty assignment, which today involved a lot of scrubbing of deckplates. Everything might have worked out, but she still had to pay for her planetside infractions.

With Kriss sleeping in the cabin behind her, she found she didn't care.

Chapter Twenty-Two

When he woke, Kriss felt almost like himself again. He figured out how to use the zero-G shower, though he couldn't say he liked the way the water, drawn by the suction of a fan beneath his feet, crawled down his body. Nevertheless, he emerged from it feeling quite human. His shallow closet, he discovered, contained underwear, socks (and boots, but Tevera had told him they were only for planetside use), and three fresh, new, highly creased Family crewsuits, and he managed to struggle into his new clothes while only ricocheting off the walls twice and the floor once. He was admiring what he could see of himself in the small mirror when his door beeped.

Opening it revealed Tevera, hanging upside down (though he supposed from her point of view, he was the upside-down one) and grinning. "Feeling better?" she said.

"Yes," he said.

"Excellent. I've got official permission for both of us to take one day for your 'general orientation,'" she said. "And for me to give it to you instead of Rigel. We'll start with a tour of the ship—"

"I've got a better idea," Kriss interrupted. "Let's start with breakfast."

———

"YOU *ARE* FEELING BETTER," Tevera said twenty minutes later as she watched Kriss down his third sweetberry flatcake, chasing down a small piece that escaped before it could be whisked away by the constantly moving air to one of the air-filtering ducts encircling the mess hall.

"I feel wonderful," Kriss said as best he could with his mouth full, and meant it. His nausea had subsided, he was having breakfast with the beautiful girl he loved, and he was in space, on his way to other planets, just as he had longed for since—well, if he were honest, probably since Mella first told him his parents were offworlders. Farr's World had been a prison, and he'd just been set free. He flipped the last bite-sized piece of flatcake out of the syrup that held it in its container and gobbled it out of mid-air. "Let's go see the ship," he said, tossing the container into the recycler, which sucked it in with a sharp popping sound.

"We'll start aft and work our way forward," Tevera said.

She first led him to what had been an elevator, but was now, she explained, called a "transport pod." They made their way along the corridors using stirrup-like handholds that had extended from the walls once they were in space. "The most important rule about getting around in zero-G," Tevera said over her shoulder, "is to keep right—well, where right would be if we were in gravity. You can't get that mixed up since the lights are in what's the ceiling when we're in port."

"Got it," Kriss said, panting. Tevera seemed to sail down the corridor with just an occasional light touch of a handhold. He pulled himself laboriously after her using every single one.

The transport pod ran up one side of the cylindrical hull. They first travelled aft to the engine room, a vast space that took up four full decks, Tevera told him, though all they saw of it was the control room, sequestered behind a sealed door in a wall of glass, where half a dozen crewmembers sat unmoving at consoles, faces hidden inside silver helmets. "They're in a virtual space," Tevera said. "It translates input from slipspace into images and numbers the human brain can comprehend."

"I know ships use a slipspace drive to get from star to star," Kriss said, "but . . . how does it work?"

"Well," Tevera said, "the way it was explained to me is that there are an infinite number of universes, and while we can't get from ours to another one, we can get into the 'slipspace' between the next one over and ours, which is where we are now, and while we're in here, although we're not actually moving, we can very carefully orient ourselves . . . somehow . . . so that when we pop back into our reality, we're somewhere different than where we started from."

Kriss blinked. "Uh . . . okay, then."

Tevera laughed. "Those are just words we use to describe something you can only describe with math . . . and apparently, only a dozen people in the entire Commonwealth can even do the math, and that's with a lot of help from artificial intelligences. The important thing is, it works."

From there, they proceeded forward one deck at a time, bypassing the huge cargo holds. Tevera surprised Kriss with the information that their largest hold was currently filled with a variety of wheat, New Neepawa, which he knew was grown in abundance around his late, unlamented home village of Black Rock. "They make a unique gourmet bread on Finian's Find with it," Tevera explained. "That's the kind of cargo Family ships generally carry: low-volume—because our ships are relatively small—but high-value. It requires a lot of trading savvy to make connections between planets that may never have thought of trading before. Captain Nicora is brilliant at it—one of the best. Ordinary bulk goods almost always go on the giant Union ships, the ones so big they never land—everything is ferried up and down to them. Some of those *ferries* are larger than *Thaylia*!"

Living quarters, communications, sickbay, galley, the mess hall again, recycling, life-support, food storage, hydroponics, computer room—the complexity of the "relatively small" *Thaylia* astounded Kriss. It had all the resources of a city crammed into the space of a single high-rise building, operated by just over two hundred men and women—and children, because even the youngest had some ship-related duty, though it might only be cleaning a bit of glass on an inspection port or setting rodent traps. And everyone was related: the term "Family" was literal. Tevera and Rigel were among twenty-seven great-grandchildren of Captain Nicora currently living on *Thaylia*. Another twelve were on other Family ships.

"It's called bloodswapping," Tevera told Kriss as they

boarded the transport pod to ride to the bridge, the final stop on their tour. "We have very strict rules governing interbreeding. In bloodswapping, members of one ship's crew are adopted into another. Out of our 216 crewmembers, about one-third were bloodswapped to us. The rest were born on *Thaylia*, like me and Rigel."

"How did Andru fit in?" Kriss said curiously.

"I had to research that," Tevera said. "I had no idea he was Family until that night at the inn. It turns out he was one of my mother's first cousins—his father was my maternal grandfather!"

"So . . . Nicora is his grandmother?"

Tevera laughed. "No. His father was a bloodswap. My father was Nicora's grandson."

"Oh," Kriss said, trying to keep it all straight.

"But no one had ever told me that," Tevera went on, "and, of course, he left the ship, for medical reasons, long before I was born. I think the Family pitied him and wanted to spare him embarrassment." She shook her head. "And yet, in the end, *he* embarrassed the Family . . . embarrassed Great-Grandmother into doing the right thing."

"She came through spectacularly in the end," Kriss said. "At least, from my point of view."

"Mine, too," Tevera said, and squeezed his hand, which she'd been holding most of the time they'd been touring the ship, ignoring the occasional slightly scandalized looks from her crewmates.

The bridge, Tevera had told him, was not the foremost deck, which was reserved for the captain's quarters, but the one behind it. The transport pod stopped five decks short, while they were still in crew quarters.

To Kriss's dismay, Rigel entered.

"Hello, Rigel," Tevera said, with a notable lack of enthusiasm.

Rigel nodded to her, but he spoke to Kriss. "Well, world-hugger, I see you've gotten over your spacesickness."

"Yes," said Kriss neutrally.

"That means you'll be able to work tomorrow." He glanced at his sister. "Or have you managed to get him out of that, too?"

Tevera said nothing.

"What sort of work?" Kriss asked.

Rigel grinned. "Oh, you'll love it. You'll just *love* it." The pod stopped at the deck just aft of the bridge, and the door slid open. Rigel scooted out and turned around. "Tomorrow, we'll find out what you're really made of, worldhugger." He wriggled his fingers in farewell as the door closed again.

"What sort of work?" Kriss asked again, this time of Tevera.

"I'm not sure," Tevera said, not looking at him.

"But you have a pretty good idea."

"Well . . ."

"Well?"

"I think Rigel has been put in charge of cleaning out Hold Three," Tevera said reluctantly. "I imagine that's what he wants you for."

"Hold Three?"

"Livestock hold. It's always a problem. Herd animals don't adapt well to zero-G, and they tend to overload the automatic waste-recycling units, so . . ."

Kriss grimaced. "I get the picture."

"Anyway, that's not until tomorrow. For now—" The door slid open. "The bridge."

They floated out into a room that filled, it looked like, the entire deck. Blank, black glassy walls—darkened video screens, he thought—surrounded a sunken well where about two dozen control consoles, each with its own acceleration couch, were set in a circle around a central holographic display that, right now, was just a fuzzy ball of white fog. Only six people currently crewed the bridge, lightly strapped to their seats, so they floated a few centimetres above them, and they didn't seem particularly concerned about anything happening. In fact, one of them, Kriss was almost sure, was playing a game on his own holographic display. He asked Tevera about it in a low voice.

She laughed. "He's running a training simulation. There's not much to do up here while the ship is in slip-space: the engineers are in charge. Take-off, re-entry and landing, orbit insertion and modification, inter-ship rendezvous, and slipspace transition are the busy times on the bridge. This is just a skeleton crew, on watch in case something goes wrong."

"What happens if something goes wrong?"

"While we're in slipspace?"

Kriss nodded.

"I believe the current theory holds that our constituent subatomic particles would be randomly distributed throughout our universe. Or possibly some other universe."

"Oh." He resolved not to touch anything.

"Normally, we wouldn't be allowed on the bridge," Tevera told him as they pulled themselves back into the pod.

"The door wouldn't even open. But I cleared it ahead of time."

"Are there any other areas that are off-limits?"

"Engine control room—you saw how that was sealed off. Sickbay, if you aren't sick, injured, or visiting a patient. The galley, unless you're assigned there. Any holds with cargo in them, ditto. Other people's private quarters, obviously, and especially the captain's quarters. But off-limits or not, if an officer sees you somewhere you haven't been assigned to be, you'd better have a darn good reason for being there."

They returned to the computer deck, where Tevera guided Kriss to one of many cubicles containing a chair and a flatscreen display. "Computer, hardcopy Family Rule," Tevera said into thin air.

After a prolonged whirring sound, a small opening appeared in the wall and extruded a thick book, which floated gently into the cubicle. Tevera plucked it out of mid-air and handed it to Kriss, who read the cover out loud. "*The Rule of the Family*. As set down by the Council of Captains, Standard Date 01292765, and subsequently revised in decennial Councils. This edition that of Standard Date 03302955." He glanced at Tevera.

"Learn it," she said simply.

"Learn it?" Kriss stared down at the book. He opened it at random and read, "Family members accused of a crime while on a planetary surface are subject to the legal system of that planet or the sub-planetary politico-geographical entity in which the offence occurred, except in extraordinary circumstances as determined by the captain, who must defend his or her actions at the next Council of Captains. The Family will assume all costs incurred by the accused

Family member, with the following exceptions (see also Expenses, On-Planet, Reimbursement of) . . ." Kriss looked at Tevera again. "*All* of it?"

"From the moment you were adopted by *Thaylia*, you became subject to Family Rule. And the Rule does not permit ignorance of it as a defence, although the captain may show leniency."

"But—" Kriss looked at the thick book helplessly. "It will take years!"

Tevera laughed. "Start with the section on shipboard life. I doubt you'll need to know about the rules governing blood-swapping and market information exchange among Family ships anytime soon, and hopefully, that section on funeral rites can wait, too."

"Hopefully."

"Don't worry, you'll manage."

At that moment, carrying a book so thick he was glad they were in zero-G, so he didn't have to risk muscle strain lugging it around, Kriss doubted it. But of course, Tevera was right; he did manage. For one thing, he soon discovered that learning whom to salute and whom to call "sir" or "ma'am" was no problem, because absolutely everybody on board (except for certain small children) outranked him—but he also learned that when two Family members were off-duty, it didn't matter if one was an officer and one was the lowest of the low, rank-wise; they were officially equal.

His first test of that, however, was less than successful, since he failed to take into account the difficulty of telling the difference between an officer who was off-duty and one who was just visiting the recreation lounge on an inspection tour. Fortunately, the officer chose leniency over the prescribed Rule punishment of three days of double duty.

The scrubbing of the livestock hold that, as Tevera had predicted, was his first official duty on the ship went on for a week. Kriss, to his own surprise, found he had an advantage over his two space-born fellow workers: Mella had had a cow for a while, a couple of years ago, and had kept chickens, too. He'd been glad when she'd sold them, but while he hadn't enjoyed cleaning up after them then and he didn't enjoy this now, neither was he as disgusted and miserable as the others.

At the end of the week, he surveyed the now-spotless, disinfected hold with satisfaction Rigel did his best to dampen. "Should have known a worldhugger would feel right at home in a pigsty," Tevera's brother said. "Starting tomorrow, we'll see how you do with some *real* spacework."

"I'll do my best, sir!" Kriss said smartly.

"Then I won't expect much." Rigel shot across the empty hold, flipping gracefully at midpoint and exiting feet-first through the open hatch on the far side. Kriss resisted the impulse to throw the scrubber after him. He made his own way to the hatch by pulling himself along the walls using the ropes strung there for that very purpose.

"Your brother still hates me," he complained to Tevera later in the rec lounge, as they floated by the huge holographic display of their journey—or what that journey would have looked like if they'd had the requisite several hundred years to make it in normal space; it bore no relationship at all to however they were "manoeuvring" in slipspace. "He doesn't want me on this ship, and he doesn't want me with you, and never mind what the captain says—or this blasted Rule of yours."

Kriss had spent the previous night reading the section governing Andru's gift of Family membership to him and had gained a new appreciation for the sacrifice. But he obviously should have been reading a different section because, on his way to the lounge, he had been yelled at by an officer —one of Tevera's uncles—for failing to announce his presence at a blind curve. "Page 236, paragraph 5, section 2a, intraship movement under micro-gravity conditions, safety, curves, blind, announcing presence at," the officer had quoted.

"Are you sure he's your brother?" Kriss went on. "Maybe he's really a bloodswap."

Tevera laughed. "No, he's my brother, all right."

"Well, maybe your parents should give him a good talking-to. And when do I get to meet them, anyway? Are they on *Thaylia* or . . .?"

His voice trailed away, and he suddenly felt sick. Tevera's face had just closed up like a steel hatch.

HE DOESN'T KNOW, Tevera thought. *You haven't told him.* And that was true, but his off-hand comment—and it had been off-hand, just part of an ordinary, lighthearted conversation—had hit her like a punch in the stomach.

"Our parents are dead," she heard herself say, and heard the flatness of her own voice.

"Oh!" Kriss looked horror-stricken. "I'm so sorry—I should have—I mean, I know what that's like—"

"No. You don't." Tevera didn't want to be there anymore, didn't want to talk to Kriss anymore, didn't want to talk to anyone. She pushed away from the display. "I think I'd better go now."

"Tevera!" Kriss grabbed her arm. He released her immediately, maybe remembering what she'd done to him the first time he'd tried that, on Farr's World. But though she could have sent him spinning helplessly across the room, she just hung there instead.

It's not his fault, she told herself again. *He doesn't know. How could he?*

He knew he'd said something wrong, though. "Tevera, I'm sorry. I didn't know. But please, don't shut me out."

His pleading thawed the cold lump in her stomach, and after a long moment, she took a shuddering breath and turned toward him. "I'm sorry," she said. "You'd think I'd be over it by now, but . . ."

"You're never completely over it. I woke up crying two nights ago, calling Mella's name. I do understand, Tevera. I really do." He paused. "Do you . . . want to talk about it?"

No, she immediately thought. But she had to have this conversation with him eventually. He needed to know.

She took a deep breath. "Ten years ago, we landed on a planet called Varago, colonized at about the same time as Farr's World but even more backward." She realized what she'd said. "Sorry."

"You don't have to apologize to *me* for insulting Farr's World," Kriss said with a small smile.

Tevera managed an even smaller smile in response and felt the ice in her stomach thaw a little more. "It was a new trade venture," she went on. "Some small pieces of a beautiful gemstone called bluejade had appeared on the previous planet we'd visited. We were told it came from Varago—and that the Varagoans would be eager to trade it because their world offered little else to interest other worlds, and they needed absolutely *everything*.

"My parents specialized in trade negotiations. They wanted Rigel and me to follow in their footsteps, so they took us along. I was six and Rigel eleven—almost twelve. He was old enough to be useful, while the best I could do was practice my newest skill, sitting still, staying quiet, and trying to listen and understand."

She remembered sitting cross-legged on the carpeted floor of the ceremonial tent in which the negotiations had been conducted, its walls embroidered with strange symbols in purple and green, a floating globe giving off a bluish light that made everything look like it was underwater, the air thick with smoke from a cloying sweet incense.

"The bluejade came from a particularly primitive part of the planet, which had regressed since colonization to an almost pre-industrial state. Our hosts seemed very nervous when we arrived, but my parents thought it was just pre-negotiation jitters."

She remembered the three negotiators facing them, two men and a woman, periodically glancing over their shoulders at the armed men guarding the door to the tent.

"Unfortunately, it turned out they weren't nervous because they were worried about the negotiations; they were worried because a rival village had found out about the Family's interest and decided to take over the bluejade mines themselves. Their timing was very bad, however; they attacked *after* the Family negotiators—us—had arrived."

The negotiators had leaped to their feet as explosions sounded outside, thunder-like thumps that she'd felt in her chest. Her parents had scrambled up, too, Dad grabbing her hand, Mom grabbing Rigel's. They'd pushed out through the back of the tent, into smoke and flame and chaos.

"Our parents hurried us back to our quarters, a house near the centre of the village. I remember running—being terrified—screams, explosions, people falling down and not getting up—but that's all kind of a blur. The thing I remember very clearly—as if it just happened—" Her voice broke, and she had to swallow before she continued. "I remember my parents, looking out the window. I remember shooting and screaming in the street. I remember them sending me and Rigel into the cellar. And I remember what they said. They told me they loved me. They told me to stay close to Rigel. Their last words—their last words *ever*—were to Rigel: 'Take care of Tevera.' And then . . ."

She couldn't go on. She was back in that moment, screaming for her Mommy as Rigel led her down a ladder and pulled a trap door closed above their heads. She blinked hard, and two tears floated from her eyes, perfect glittering spheres. She forced herself to look at Kriss again. "We hid, and we heard shouting upstairs, and then shooting, and finally when everything was still, we went upstairs, and . . . and . . ."

She stopped again. She would not, could not, describe what they had found. She'd only seen them for a moment before Rigel put his hand over her eyes and turned her away from the sight, but the image burned in her mind, hard-edged, indelible, unsoftened by time: Mommy and Daddy, sprawled across the floor, blood everywhere.

"You found your parents," Kriss said softly.

"Why did they kill them?" she burst out then, though she

knew Kriss had no answer. No one had *ever* had an answer. "It made no sense. When they killed my parents, their precious bluejade became worthless—the Family placed the entire planet under a trade interdict. No Family *or* Union ship will call there again for a hundred years. They must have realized . . ."

"In a situation like that—things happen," Kriss said. "Mella . . ."

His voice trailed off, and suddenly she felt bad for telling him he didn't know what it was like, what she had gone through, because of course he did: he had found his guardian dead outside the smouldering remains of the house where he had grown up, her belongings strewn like worthless garbage around the yard. He had not only told her about that, she had felt what he felt in his music, in the strange emotional projection of the touchlyre.

"Things happen," he finished after a moment.

"Things happen," Tevera agreed bitterly. "And *that* thing changed Rigel. He blamed himself for not staying with our parents, he blamed me for being there to be taken care of—and then he felt guilty for that and tried to take care of me all the more. That's why he's so protective."

"And why he hates worldhuggers so much," Kriss said slowly.

"It's stupid. Stupid! You had nothing to do with our parents' murders, and you're certainly not going to kill me." She managed a small, crooked smile. "Are you?"

"No." Kriss took her hands and met her gaze squarely. "Rigel doesn't have to protect you anymore. I will."

"Will both of you get it through your vacuum-sealed

skulls that I don't *need* protecting?" she said, pulling her hands free.

"I'm sorry—"

She felt bad again. She tried a laugh. "That was a joke, silly." It wasn't, not really, but she kept that to herself.

He blinked, then laughed in return, a little uncertainly.

She accompanied him back to his cabin so he could get in another hour or two of study of the Family Rule before bedtime. "How's it going?" she asked as he opened the thick book.

"All right, I guess," he said. "Just one question."

"What is it?" She moved closer and looked down into the book, currently open to a section on the proper procedures for greeting planetside dignitaries.

"Where in here is the section on understanding Family girls?"

Tevera gave him a severe look. "That," she said, "is something you have to figure out for yourself."

She kissed him on the cheek and left him to his study.

Chapter Twenty-Three

"Real spacework," Rigel had promised for the next day. Kriss didn't know what he had meant, exactly, but he suspected it would be unpleasant, and felt uneasy as he floated through the corridors to the assigned rendezvous, near the holds. Most of the Family members he met—and you couldn't go ten metres on *Thaylia* without running into *somebody*—nodded neutrally, ignored him, or in the case of small children, stared at him as he passed and then giggled to each other afterward.

Only one or two people, friends of Rigel's, were ever openly hostile to him. After his talk with Tevera the day before, he could understand that hostility, but he didn't think he deserved it. In some ways, the cool neutrality of the others bothered him more—what did he have to do to *really* belong to this Family? They accepted bloodswaps easily enough—why not him?

But, of course, he knew the answer. Bloodswaps were still Family, still space-born and space-bred. He was a worldhugger, on board this ship only because a real Family man—Andru, once of this very ship—had surrendered his birthright to him. That had shaken them, and they still didn't fully accept it.

Some nights, as he struggled with the Family Rule, he wondered if they ever would. Every aspect of their lives seemed tightly controlled; everything structured and in its place, just like the layout of the ship itself. No wonder they didn't like planets, so disorderly and random. He, breaching shipboard etiquette a hundred times a day, must seem equally unpredictable.

He went through the same cycle of thoughts each night. At the beginning of the evening, he would take up the Rule with fresh resolve, determined to smooth off a few more of the rough edges that grated on the well-polished traditions of the Family. At the end of the evening, he would throw the Rule against the wall in tired frustration and float awake in the dark, his brain filled with regulation upon regulation, all blurring together until he could hardly remember the details of any of them, convinced he would always be an outsider. But finally, he would remember that to Tevera, at least, he was more than just an out-of-his-element worldhugger, and drift off to sleep.

And then in the morning . . . in the morning, there was Rigel.

He saw Tevera's brother up ahead, at the end of the corridor, floating beside a red door. Kriss frowned. Red . . . red . . . a red door meant . . .

He had it! *All doors leading into or out of airlocks shall be coloured red as an immediate visual cue for crewmembers.* Kriss's uneasiness heightened. What did Rigel have in mind?

"You're late, worldhugger," Rigel growled as Kriss reached him.

Kriss checked his chronometer. "No, sir," he said. "I'm precisely on time."

"I like my workers to be five minutes early. If you're on time, you're late."

Faced with such logic, Kriss said nothing—usually the wisest course where Rigel was concerned.

"You don't know what this red door indicates, but—"

"Airlock," Kriss said. "Are we going outside the ship, sir?"

Rigel snorted. "In slipspace? Spectacular suicide, worldhugger." He put a special emphasis on the last word, an "everybody-knows-that" kind of emphasis Kriss found increasingly irritating. "No, this airlock leads into the NLS hold. We're going to—"

Kriss hated to say it, but . . . "NLS, sir?" he interrupted.

"No Life-Support," Rigel supplied, in that same scornful tone. "Some items are best shipped in vacuum. We're going to suit up and conduct a standard cargo inspection of the high-density fuzzychips we're currently carrying in there."

"I respectfully point out that I've never worn a spacesuit, sir."

"Yeah, well, this is also a training exercise for you. Captain's orders." Rigel turned and slapped the lockpanel, not for the red door, but for one a little farther up the corridor. It slid open, revealing a small chamber with four lockers on one side and four spacesuits, red, green, yellow, and blue, attached to the other like a row of robots. "All right," Rigel said briskly, moving into the change room, motioning Kriss in after him, and closing the door behind them. "First, stick your feet in a pair of stirrups." He pointed to what would have been the floor in gravity, and Kriss saw that there were indeed stirrups there, four sets of them, set shoulder-width apart. He manoeuvred himself to them and slid his feet beneath them.

"Now," said Rigel, "strip."

Kriss blinked. "What?"

"You heard me."

"Everything?"

"Everything except your socks."

The stirrups, clearly, were intended to keep his body in place as he pulled off his clothes, though he had to slip out one foot and then the other as his jumpsuit and shorts came off. Once he was naked, Rigel explained the special underwear he had to don next, followed by a couple of layers of bulky, rubbery material, and some disturbingly intimate hoses. When Kriss finally pulled on the spacesuit itself, sweating like he'd run ten kilometres in the summer sun, Rigel simply climbed into his own *without* stripping *or* putting on the special undersuit.

Rather than swear at him like he wanted to, Kriss locked the transparent bubble down over his head, took a deep breath of air that smelled like the crowded Black Rock inn on a hot day, and heard Rigel's voice filtered through the communications system. "There's a small control panel on your left wrist. Touch the green button in the centre of that." Kriss did so, and the suit stiffened around him, and cool air filled the helmet and his lungs, thinning the smell but not doing away with it completely. Kriss wondered how many other people had worn that same suit over who-knew-how-many years.

"You'll notice I didn't bother with the undersuit and

plumbing," Rigel said. "That's because we're just working in an internal hold."

"Then why do I have to wear it?" Kriss said. "Sir."

"Because you've never been in a spacesuit before and that's what you'd wear if you left the ship in normal space. Not that you ever will. Nobody in their right mind would send a worldhugger outside the ship." Rigel snorted, as if the very idea were preposterous, before carrying on. "In the event of a hull-breach alarm, you skip the undersuit, like I just did. The outer suit will protect you against vacuum, but it won't do a thing to keep you from cooking in sunlight or freezing in shadow." Rigel droned on, explaining the various readouts Kriss saw in the helmet's heads-up display, floating an apparent fifteen centimetres in front of him.

Finally, they moved out into the corridor, and Rigel opened the red door. The chamber beyond was barely big enough for both of them in their suits (Rigel in red, Kriss in yellow). Kriss heard a hissing that rapidly attenuated to silence, and then the inner door opened soundlessly, and Rigel launched himself out into the eerie, blue-lit space beyond.

The NLS hold was a large cylinder with the lock at one end. Kriss stayed in the doorway of the lock as Rigel sailed grandly across the hold and came to rest on the far side, among the handful of hexagonal crates that were the only things that broke the otherwise perfectly smooth interior. "Come on," Rigel said, and gestured to Kriss.

Kriss hesitated—he'd never crossed that large an open expanse in zero-G before. He looked at the walls. There were no ropes or other handholds.

"Come *on*," Rigel repeated.

No help from that quarter, Kriss thought. Gathering his legs under him, he leaped.

He knew at once he was too fast. He'd jumped as though trying (impossibly) to leap that distance on a planet. He would hit the far side hard enough to break an arm or a leg or his neck, or maybe smash his helmet to shards and die with his own lungs trying to force themselves up his throat . . .

Something struck him a glancing, numbing blow on the shoulder, setting him tumbling—but also absorbing much of the energy of his leap. His stomach rebelled as the hold whirled crazily around him. *Throwing up in a spacesuit is a very bad idea*, his mind told him, *throwing up in a spacesuit is a very bad idea, throwing up in a—*

His mind lost.

He hit the wall near one of the hexagonal crates and managed to grab it and hold on, retching, his helmet filling with globules of the vile liquefied remnants of his breakfast. Miserably he closed his eyes and breathed shallowly and, in that moment, wished with all his heart he was back on Farr's World.

"Little fool! *Worldhugger*!" Rigel's voice raged in his ears. He opened one eye and saw Rigel floating beside him. "If I weren't responsible for you to Captain Nicora, I'd leave you to choke in your own vomit!" But instead, he grabbed Kriss's arm and launched both of them back across the hold. Five minutes later, they were back in air, and Kriss hurriedly yanked off the helmet, almost gagging again.

"You're going to clean that suit inside and out," Rigel snarled at him as he jerked off his own helmet. "What were you playing at? You almost killed both of us!"

"Both—"

"If we'd hit helmets when I hit you—"

"I didn't ask you to, did I?" Kriss shoved his feet into the stirrups in the floor and began stripping out of the upper part of the suit, wincing as he did so; the whole right side of his body was sore. "I'd have managed all right."

"You'd have broken your neck and smashed your helmet —and probably your skull!"

"Well, then, why didn't you let me?" Wearing only the undersuit, Kriss shoved the spacesuit away from him; it bounced against the wall and drifted back. He stopped it with his foot. "Wouldn't you be happier if I were dead?"

"Kill yourself on your own time!" Rigel finished pulling off his own suit. "On my watch, I'm responsible for you."

"Yeah, and you've got enough on your conscience already, don't you?" Kriss snarled.

Faster than he would have believed possible, Rigel leaped across the room and smashed him back against the wall, holding onto a racked suit with one hand and keeping Kriss motionless with the other. "*What do you mean, worldhugger?*"

"You blame yourself for your parents' death!" Kriss yelled into his face. "Isn't that why you hate worldhuggers? They killed your parents—and you weren't able to stop them. You didn't even try—you were hiding with Tevera!"

"They told me to look after her. I did." Rigel's eyes narrowed. "And how do you know all this anyway?"

"How do you think?"

Rigel glared at him. "Tevera."

"She doesn't need protecting anymore, Rigel. She can take care of herself."

"She needs protecting *from* herself," Rigel said. "She

doesn't know what's best for her, or she wouldn't have taken up with a miserable worldhugger like you."

"Oh, and *you* know what's best for her?" Kriss's anger and frustration boiled up in him. "You've let what happened to your parents turn you into a miserable bastard, and you resent the fact she's learned to get past it, don't you? You want her as unhappy as you are. Well, it won't happen—not while I'm around!"

"Maybe you won't be around—" Rigel began, then stopped. He closed his eyes and took a deep breath, then shoved back from Kriss. When he spoke again, his voice was calm, though his face remained flushed. "Clean out the suit you fouled, crewman," he said. "Then report to sickbay for an examination. Looks like you could have some nasty bruises. Tomorrow report back here again. This cargo hold still needs inspection."

Kriss didn't trust this sudden change any more than the rage that had preceded it. "Rigel—"

"I'm awaiting your acknowledgement of my order, crewman," Rigel said flatly.

Kriss clenched his fists. "Orders understood and accepted, sir!" he snarled.

"Good. Carry on." Rigel turned, palmed open the door, floated into the corridor, and disappeared, leaving Kriss staring after him.

Chapter Twenty-Four

That night, Kriss took up the touchlyre for the first time since leaving Farr's World.

He pulled it from its case and let it float freely, turning slowly, in the centre of his cabin, watching the light play across each surface, subtly shading the black wood, burning in the burnished copper plates, glinting and glittering across the silver strings. Finally, hesitantly, he gathered it in, tensing, ready to fling it away if the immaterial fingers from the alien device hidden inside reached into his mind and tried to turn his anger at Rigel into a weapon. He wanted—*needed*—to play it, but whatever Rigel did to him, he would not allow the touchlyre to hurt him, or anyone else in the Family. He had felt no threat of that when he had played for Tevera just before leaving Farr's World—and the memory of that warmed him even as he thought of it—but his feelings then had been considerably more benevolent than they were now.

He felt the touchlyre in his mind, as always since his

grief at Mella's death had broken whatever barrier had kept it out in the years before that, but it was firmly under his control. It still built its music from his thoughts and emotions, but this time he was able to choose which thoughts and emotions it would draw on; and rather than feed it his anger at Rigel, he gave it his memories of Mella and his childhood home, and for an hour or two lost himself in his past. When at last he set the touchlyre aside, he felt better: better about himself, and better about the touchlyre. *It's changed,* he thought. *I can control it now.* He returned it to his case, and as he closed the lid, the thought crossed his mind that maybe the change wasn't in the touchlyre, but in himself.

He thought he heard a sound in the corridor, but when he opened the door, he saw no one. He closed the door again and got ready for bed.

TEVERA FLOATED BACK into the corridor from the electronics maintenance shaft near Kriss's door into which she had pushed herself as she'd heard him approach. She'd come to his cabin intending to talk to him, having heard something from Rigel about what had happened in the NLS hold, but she'd paused outside his door when she heard the music of the touchlyre, and in the end, had simply hung there, listening.

She wasn't sure why she hadn't gone in. She hadn't wanted to interrupt, and then, as the music settled, she'd been lost in it, feeling his sadness for his lost guardian, whom she'd never known. And then it had seemed awkward to be caught by him, so she'd hidden. And now she felt bad about that, but it was *really* too late. Feeling awkward and silly and not even sure why, she returned to her own quarters.

She soon wished she'd spoken to him despite the awkwardness of the moment, because for the next several days, she barely saw him. For some reason, their personal watch schedules simply didn't coincide.

She'd have suspected Rigel of arranging things that way, except Rigel had no say in watch schedules. That left the unsettling possibility Captain Nicora herself was behind it, which did not bode well for Kriss's integration into the Family—it would mean he still wasn't trusted.

They crossed paths at last in the rec room, by coincidence, and even then, Kriss had only a couple of minutes before he was due to report to a corridor-cleaning detail, and she had only a couple more before she was due to report to the communications room, where she was currently training.

"I've done nothing but scut work since I came aboard," Kriss complained. "I want to learn more about the ship's systems, too."

"You'll get there," she said. "You're just new. Bloodswaps always start with the most basic tasks, too. Just give it time."

"It wouldn't be so bad if I could see you once in a while." Kriss took a water bottle from a storage cabinet and attached it to the zero-G coupling on the water dispenser to fill it.

Tevera didn't want to put into Kriss's head her own dark thought that perhaps the captain had taken a personal interest in keeping them apart, so instead of responding, she changed the subject. "How are things with Rigel? I heard about the . . . incident . . . in the NLS hold."

"You mean when I puked my guts out inside a spacesuit?" Kriss disconnected his water bottle from the dispenser with rather more force than was good for either of them, but she refrained from commenting on it.

"Yes," she said. "That."

Kriss frowned. "It's weird," he said. "I thought he'd be worse than ever, but he's actually been treating me courteously—well, you know, in a cold-as-a-computer, by-the-book sort of way. He's not riding me as hard for minor infractions, at least." His frown flipped to a grin. "Although that may be because I'm making fewer of them. I *can* be taught, apparently."

"I never doubted it," Tevera said.

"I've got to go, or I'll be late."

"Me, too," Tevera said. She squeezed his hand. "We'll talk again soon."

She headed for the forward exit from the rec room; he headed for the aft one.

It was weeks before they spoke again . . . *as though,* Tevera thought darkly, *someone saw us together and decided to tweak the schedules even more so we're* never *in the same place at the same time.*

She couldn't prove it, but that was definitely how it felt.

AS THE WEEKS PASSED, Kriss thought more and more about getting off the ship and exploring a bit of a new world, somewhere he wouldn't have to worry about whom to salute or which side of the corridor to travel along or how much water he could use in his shower or the proper way to scrub Type 47 residential-area decking or the correct procedure for acid-scouring the auxiliary life-support bionetic filtering system . . .

Besides, maybe on a planet, he'd have a chance to see Tevera. They were being kept apart deliberately. He was sure of it. But by whom? Rigel? Or the captain, forced to take him aboard by Andru's sacrifice, but still seeing him as a worldhugger, and definitely not good enough for one of her great-granddaughters?

He might have mentioned his fears to Tevera if he'd ever had the chance. Or he might not. She didn't seem to mind when he criticized her brother, but he wasn't at all sure how she'd take any questioning of the captain, even if she had faced down the old woman herself back in Andru's.

Six weeks out from Farr's World, and still two weeks from their first planetfall, all non-essential watches were suspended for one day to allow everyone to celebrate the captain's birthday. The livestock hold that Kriss had come to know so well in the first days of the journey was decorated in the colourful gossamer veils the captain liked, and the entire ship's company crowded into it for several hours of feasting, music, and dancing, which took on a breathtaking dimension in zero-G. To Kriss's delight, Tevera was there, and no one kept them apart. He allowed her to pull him out into the middle of the dance globe, but his best efforts to mimic the graceful moves of the others only succeeded in setting him spinning, which threatened to result in a repeat of what had happened inside the spacesuit, so he quickly retired to the netting strung along the walls and contented himself with watching Tevera, her lithe body folding and spinning and darting like a fish in an aquarium, totally at ease in the weightless environment.

When the music ended, she arrowed over to him, face aglow and eyes sparkling. "They're starting the talent show in ten minutes," she told him breathlessly. "You should play."

"The touchlyre?"

Tevera laughed. "What else?"

"But—"

"No buts. I'll go tell Third Cousin Thellis. She's the emcee." Without giving Kriss another chance to protest, Tevera leaped away.

It will be just like playing in Andru's, Kriss told himself as he headed to his cabin to retrieve the touchlyre. *A lot of them even heard me play there. There's nothing to worry about. And I've played for Tevera since Salazar, and in my cabin . . . I've got control now. There's nothing to worry about . . .*

But even that first night in Andru's, his hands hadn't shaken like they did when Thellis called his name half an hour later and he made his way to the performance space, aware of how clumsy he must still appear in zero-G to all these offworlders—

He caught himself. They weren't "offworlders" any more than he was a "worldhugger." They were Family—*his* Family. Andru had made them so.

All the same, some children giggled as he carefully manoeuvred himself into position, and whispers ran around the room. Just as had happened in Andru's that first night, when he put his hands on the copper plates, the first sound the touchlyre made was a harsh, unmusical squawk. Someone snickered. Kriss closed his eyes, shutting out the encircling Family. *It's just like Andru's,* he told himself again, and took that as his starting point.

He called on the memories and emotions he wanted to share and felt the touchlyre take hold of them and turn them into its unique mixture of music and empathy. He played of the way he had felt when Andru made his sacrifice; he played of those first glorious moments of lift-off, when he saw Farr's World receding beneath them; he played of the struggles he had had fitting into the Family Andru had given him; he played of his loneliness and uncertainty . . . and he played of Tevera. There he ended, because when he opened his eyes and saw her face, and remembered how beautiful she had been as she danced, the feelings that welled up in him were for the two of them alone.

Silence met the ending of his music, silence that stretched out for thirty seconds, almost a minute—and then erupted with applause. He looked from face to face. Though there were many he still could not put names to, for the first time, he sensed no barriers between them and him, no "off-worlder-worldhugger" distinctions. He felt their acceptance, and when Tevera came arrowing out of the crowd and hugged him exuberantly, sending them both tumbling, the Family only laughed and applauded more. Even Captain Nicora, watching from her place of honour at one end of the hold, smiled and nodded, and Kriss felt guilty for having suspected her of deliberately trying to keep Tevera apart from him.

But beyond Nicora, in the semi-darkness near the hatch, he saw Rigel watching, expressionless, his eyes glittering, reflecting the light focused on Kriss.

TWO WEEKS LATER, they made planetfall in Try-Your-Luck, capital city of a world called Fortune. There, they would unload the fuzzychips Kriss had helped inspect in the NLS hold and pick up a cargo of holographic slot machines for delivery to Gottapray, an out-of-the-way planet trying to boost tourism by promoting gambling—just like Fortune had.

Kriss had read up on Fortune once he'd learned it was their destination. Aside from near-Earth atmosphere and gravity—gravity he found surprisingly difficult to get used to, after six weeks in space; he'd already dropped things half a dozen times from absent-mindedly letting them go, thinking they'd float—Fortune had even less going for it resource-wise than Farr's World. Its only advantage was that it was within a week's travel of some of the most heavily populated worlds in the Commonwealth, and it had seized that advantage with both hands, making a fairly infamous name for itself as a pleasure planet. Reading about some of the pleasures it offered had left Kriss open-mouthed.

Although he had no intention of sampling Fortune's more unsavoury wares, Kriss still couldn't wait to get off the ship. His first new world! And he would walk the streets as Family, one of the select few who called space their home. He planned to take the touchlyre with him and find a place to play. Having done as well as he had in Andru's, with a clientele drawn from only a couple of ships, he figured he should be able to really rake in the feds on a planet like Fortune, where novelty was king. No one would ever have seen anything like a boy from a Family ship playing an instrument like the touchlyre.

He checked the time, killed the reader, and headed for what had been a transport pod in zero-G and was now once again an elevator. His watch's twenty-four-hour shore leave was about to officially begin (the planetary day was something over twenty-seven hours, but they stuck to Earth time on *Thaylia*), and in eight hours, Tevera's watch would begin *its* shore leave, which meant they'd have sixteen hours to spend together off *Thaylia* and out of sight of cousins, second cousins, uncles, aunts, and, especially, Rigel . . .

. . . who was on duty at the exit hatch, checking out the members of his watch. Kriss joined the line of a half-dozen men and women. "Looking forward to your first new planet?" the man in front of Kriss asked as he stepped into place.

"It's a dream come true, Phillis."

Phillis laughed. "Well, brace yourself for a culture shock. You can end up lying in a back alley, stark naked, flat broke, and drunker than a wobble-wing, and never know how it happened. Believe me, I know!"

"I'll be careful," Kriss promised. "No drinking, no gambling, and no—"

Phillis looked dismayed. "Hey, I didn't say you couldn't have any fun!"

"You're up, Phil," Rigel said. He handed Phillis his pass. "And please don't make me have to carry you back to the ship this time. You've put on weight."

"I promise to remain ambulatory, sir!" Phillis said, and saluted smartly before adding, "And anyway, that made up for the time before last when I had to carry *you*!"

Rigel laughed. "Get going."

Kriss, grinning at the exchange, stepped forward—and Rigel's smile disappeared. "Yes, crewman?"

"Ready for shore leave, sir!"

Rigel shook his head. "I'm afraid not, crewman."

Kriss stared at him. "What?"

"You are not authorized for shore leave."

"But I'm in this watch—"

"You are not authorized for shore leave," Rigel repeated. "Return to your quarters."

Kriss couldn't believe it. "You can't deny me shore leave just because—"

"You're approaching insubordination, crewman."

"With respect, *sir*," Kriss said, in a voice that had no respect in it at all, "I request to know why I am being denied shore leave."

"I am not required to give you reasons for my orders," Rigel said coldly. "Family Rule states it is my prerogative to withhold shore leave from anyone in my watch. That is all you need to know. Return to your quarters."

"Sir—"

"Return to your quarters, crewman!"

Kriss glared at Rigel, then spun and pushed past the two women who had come into the exit lock behind him. Once in the elevator, he banged his fist against the wall. He remembered the bit of Family Law Rigel had referenced. Tevera's brother was entirely within his rights—and had known exactly how to use those rights to get at Kriss.

Kriss stopped the elevator short of his deck. "I won't let him get away with it," he muttered. He punched new orders into the elevator's controls, and sank swiftly downward again, this time emerging on the cargo deck from which he and Rigel had accessed the NLS hold. Two men were loading the fuzzychips from the hold onto the big cargo elevator and greeted him amiably as he joined them for the ride to the base of the ship, taking at face value his explanation that he really, really wanted to see, first-hand, the cargo-unloading process. "All part of learning how the Family works," he said, and as a result, had to endure a twenty-minute explanation of the finer points of cargo handling before escaping onto the huge Try-Your-Luck landing field.

The cargo-handlers made no effort to stop him, knowing his watch's leave had just begun. "Enjoy yourself!" one of them called after him.

"I intend to!" Kriss yelled back, and with a final wave, set out toward the beckoning towers of the city.

Chapter Twenty-Five

Tevera thought her shift would never end. She'd been assigned galley duty, and not the kind-of-fun food preparation part of galley duty, either, but the scraping-and-stacking-dirty-dishes-in-the-sonic-cleanser kind of galley duty. But she also knew she had twenty-four hours of shore leave coming up, and that Kriss's shore leave had begun eight hours earlier. They'd set a meeting place—a shopping complex just on the edge of the spaceport—and she couldn't wait to show him some of the attractions Try-Your-Luck had to offer that she knew from previous visits—and discover a few more.

More than that, she couldn't wait to spend time alone with him, away from aunts and uncles and cousins and, especially, Rigel.

Shift over, she hurried to her cabin to change into planetside attire—a simple white dress that left her arms and legs bare (Try-Your-Luck was a warm, humid, seaside town), comfortable sandals, and a small shoulder bag where she carried her wallet full of feds—and put her favourite silver-and-crystal necklace around her neck. She admired herself briefly in the mirror and then made her way to the elevator.

Yverras was on duty at the exit hatch at the top of the landing ramp. No one was in line to exit—she guessed the rest of her watch had moved faster than she had. She smiled at him as she approached, but he managed only a brief smile back. She slowed. "What's wrong?"

He sighed. "It's Kriss," he said. "Rigel denied him shore leave, told him to stay on the ship."

Tevera's heart sank, certain she knew what was coming.

She was right. "He went anyway," Yverras continued. "Out through the cargo-landing hatch. If . . . when . . . you see him, tell him to get back here. He's already in serious trouble, but it will be worse the longer he stays out."

Kriss, you idiot, she thought. And then, *Rigel, you bastard*. "Why would Rigel do that?"

"He told me it wasn't his idea," Yverras said. "He said the order came from Captain Nicora. She's worried Vorlick might have gotten a message here ahead of us, by a faster ship. He might have operatives just waiting for a chance to grab Kriss."

"Did Rigel *tell* Kriss it was an order from the captain, or did he just deny him shore leave without explanation?" Tevera demanded.

"I don't know," Yverras said, putting up his hands defensively. "I'm just the messenger here. Don't put me in the middle of your brother-sister quarrels."

Tevera took a deep breath. "Sorry."

"You'll tell him?"

"I'll tell him, *if* I see him," Tevera said, already thinking ahead and giving herself at least a thin cover of plausible deniability. Then she headed out onto the hot, humid landing field. The spaceport was right at the edge of the ocean, and out over the vast blue expanse, the sun was getting low, though that didn't seem to be affecting the temperature at all.

She found Kriss exactly where they'd agreed to meet. He grinned and came toward her, clearly intending to give her a hug: she pushed him back. "What do you think you're doing?" she demanded.

His smile faded. "Exactly what we talked about. Enjoying my first shore leave."

"You don't *have* shore leave," Tevera said. "Your shore leave was cancelled by your watch commander."

"Rigel," Kriss said. "He had no right . . ."

"He had every right," Tevera said. "He's your watch commander."

"I've got twenty-four hours coming to me, and I'm going to take them," Kriss snapped. "I'm going to enjoy myself with you, and Rigel can go eat vacuum, for all I care. He's just doing it to punish me for daring to get close to you."

"It wasn't Rigel's idea," she said. "It was an order from the captain. They're worried that Vorlick could still be after you. He could have gotten a message here ahead of us. He could have people watching for you. He could be here himself. His ship is faster . . ."

"Did Rigel tell you that?"

"Yverras told me."

"But Rigel told *him*."

"Yes."

Kriss snorted. "I don't believe it, then. It's just an excuse.

Your brother wants to spoil our shore leave together, and now that he knows I've escaped, he's trying to spoil it through you. Well, it won't work! Come on!"

He turned and strode down the street without looking back.

Tevera could have gone the other way. She could have gone back to the ship.

She didn't. She followed him. She swore at him under her breath, but she followed him.

SIX HOURS LATER, well into the evening, Tevera sat at the back of a small Union-catering bar, listening to Kriss play the touchlyre.

They'd done few of the things she'd thought they'd do. When she'd caught up to Kriss, they'd argued some more. They'd done that off and on all day. The rest of the time, they'd walked around in mutually grumpy silence, while Kriss tried to find someplace that would let him perform.

Most places had turned him down. Try-Your-Luck had a musician's guild you had to belong to if you wanted to access the nicest venues. But eventually, an hour or so ago, Kriss had convinced the thin, sour-faced proprietor of this hole-in-the-wall to give him a chance. They'd eaten an extremely mediocre meal in uncomfortable silence, then he'd gone up to the front.

Some of her anger and frustration (not to mention guilt, for not having somehow forced Kriss back to the ship by now) melted as she experienced, once again, the magic of the touchlyre. She felt Kriss's fascination with the endless Void she had lived in all her life, with the far-flung stars burning within it and the fragile vessels that sailed its infinite reaches. Once more, his childhood dreams came to life in her mind, and his joy at the reality he had come to know as a member of the Family . . .

The Family whose Rule he was even now flouting. Some of her pleasure faded. She pushed back at the touchlyre's immaterial fingers of emotion, drove them out of her mind, and sat sourly in the back of the dim, blue-lit bar as Kriss's music came to an end.

She wished she'd never come ashore.

She *really* wished *he* hadn't.

CRADLING the touchlyre in his arms, Kriss looked out at the small crowd of Union spacers, feeling satisfaction at having touched his audience deeply. He glanced at the dour barkeep, who had been dubious about allowing a strange Family youth to try to entertain his hardened clientele. The man grudgingly nodded his approval.

But then Kriss looked the other way, toward the door, and saw Tevera sitting alone at a table, not looking at him, and suddenly he felt guilty. Every minute he spent in Try-Your-Luck without a pass, he dug himself deeper and deeper into a hole on board *Thaylia*. She'd tried to convince him to go back right away, but he'd refused to give her brother the satisfaction. He wouldn't let Rigel's petty tyranny spoil their shore leave together.

Except, of course, it had. He hadn't been able to fully enjoy his time with Tevera, not with the spectre of what would happen on his return to the ship hovering around them. He'd managed to put it out of his mind while he played, but now . . .

He jumped up from the hard, plastic stool and strode through the metal tables to the barkeep, who willingly paid the hundred feds Kriss had asked for "on approval." But then he had to face Tevera.

"Feel better?" she said sardonically as he came up to her.

He put the touchlyre back into its case, which he'd left on the table while he performed. "Everyone else gets shore leave when we make planetfall. Why should I stay locked up like a prisoner?"

"We've been over that. Multiple times. Everyone else doesn't have Vorlick out to kill them."

Kriss clicked shut the latches on the case. "Have you seen any assassins? I haven't." He slammed out through the swinging glass doors.

Though it was nearly midnight, the street was noon-bright in the glare of the garish light-signs of the bars, night-clubs, and gaming halls that lined it. Kriss strode toward the spaceport, slinging the touchlyre case over his neck and shoulder as he walked. Tevera had to almost run to match his long, angry strides, but he hardly noticed. "What can Rigel do to me, anyway?" He had to shout to be heard above the hubbub of the crowds of people moving both ways along the street, and the jangling, competing music from the bars. "Confine me to the ship? He already has!"

"Only to port—and not even there, not indefinitely! With a proper escort, you could have—"

"An escort. Bodyguards!" Kriss shoved his hands into the pockets of his crewsuit and walked even faster. "I thought once I got off Farr's World, I'd be free. Instead, I have rules and orders and regulations wrapped around me like baling wire!"

Tevera grabbed his left arm and jerked him to a stop, pulling him around to face her. "But you've got the Family —and me!"

He said nothing, staring over her head down the crowded street.

She let go of him. "What's wrong with you? Everything's been so good since the captain's birthday—you've been fitting in so well. But now—"

Kriss jerked his head down to meet her eyes. "Fitting in? Oh, I fit in all right. Just one of the Family. Except, all of a sudden, I find out I'm *not* one of the Family. I'm more like a prisoner of the Family! And when I get back, I'll be punished for daring to try to escape." He spun away from her and strode toward the port, yelling, "I'm sick of being told what I can and can't do every minute of the day!"

"You're Family now!" she shouted after him. "You have to live with Family discipline!"

"Then maybe I was better off alone!" He took half a dozen more steps before he realized she was no longer following him.

He glanced back to see her leaning against a building, her back to him. Remorse hit him like a punch to the stomach, and he hurried back to her. "Tevera . . ." Tentatively he touched her shoulder, but she jerked away.

He spread his hands helplessly. "You know I didn't really mean that, Tevera. It's just that . . ." He groped for words. "Sometimes I feel like . . . like I'm in a cage, a cage of rules and orders and yessirs and no ma'ams, and I've got to break some of the bars just so I can breathe. I had my hopes set on this planetfall, on shore leave, and then Rigel . . ."

Silence.

"Tevera?"

Still no reply.

Shoulders sagging, Kriss turned away. "Come on. We've got to get back." He moved away a couple of steps, heard Tevera start to follow, and walked on without looking around.

AS THEY NEARED THE SPACEPORT, the clubs and bars petered out into quiet, dark warehouses and widely spaced streetlights. Tevera's anger petered out, too. She took a deep breath. "Wait, Kriss."

Kriss stopped without turning around. She moved up close behind him, then, with a gentle hand on his arm, made him face her. "I actually *do* understand," she said. "I've hard you play the touchlyre. Of course, I understand. And the truth is . . . sometimes I feel the same way."

He blinked. "Really?"

"Really," she said. "It's my Family, but it can be a bit . . . constraining. But you have to realize the Family is more than just a group of relatives. It's also the crew of a starship. We *have* to have rigid discipline—it could save all our lives someday."

Kriss started to speak, but she hushed him, touching a finger to his lips. "Every time you break a regulation, they'll bind you with two or three more. If you keep trying to break free so you can 'breathe,' you'll end up suffocating—or you really will break free and lose the Family."

He pulled her hand from his mouth and clasped it. "And you?"

She shook her head. "No. Never. I said on Farr's World I'd choose you over the Family, and I meant it. But it doesn't have to come to that, Kriss!"

He pulled her to him and put his arms around her. She let him. He pressed his cheek against the top of her head. His body was warm against hers. "It won't," he said softly. "I promise."

AN HOUR LATER, Kriss sat glumly in his tiny cabin on board *Thaylia*. It could have been worse, he reflected; Yverras, still on duty when he returned, could have locked him in his cabin instead of just re-confirming his confinement to port, assigning him disciplinary work for the remainder of their stay on Fortune—and, worst of all, declaring Tevera off-limits until they were once more in space.

Rigel had told Yverras (who had then told Tevera) the truth, he'd learned to his shame; the order to refuse him shore leave pass *had* come from the captain. He would have had his chance, under guard, as Tevera had said—but instead, he'd acted hastily, out of his anger at Rigel.

Of course, he was quite sure Rigel had *hoped* he'd react the way he did. If Rigel had told him it was an order from the captain, instead of leaving him to think it was all Rigel's idea, he would have grumbled, but obeyed.

Would you? came an unbidden thought. He shoved it

down and resolved to be a model Family member from then on.

OVER THE NEXT FEW DAYS, he did his best to live up to that resolution, performing his duties promptly and conscientiously, even sending a formal apology to Captain Nicora via intraship communications, and receiving an equally formal acknowledgement.

He spent little time in his cramped cabin, preferring to wander around the port; boring compared to the temptations of Try-Your-Luck, but better than four blank walls. Several ships were scattered across its kilometres of landing field (easily four times the size of Cascata's), among them two other Family ships, the *Athabasca* and the *Coronach,* both somewhat smaller than *Thaylia.* Their captains had visited *Thaylia* for a banquet their first night in port.

Kriss wished he could have roamed the spaceport with Tevera, but though she wasn't with him, he gradually realized he wasn't exactly alone.

At first, he put the feeling down to imagination, but day after day, he saw the same person, never very close, but not far away, either: a wiry man with a black beard, dressed in a dirty, patched crewsuit a couple of sizes too big.

Vorlick's man? Kriss wondered. *Keeping an eye on me?* He considered reporting it but put the idea aside. After all, it could just be coincidence. There were other people he saw multiple times, and he was under enough restrictions without adding more fuel to the "we're-only-doing-this-for-your-own-good" fire. *Probably just some spaceport employee,* he thought. By the end of the week, when Captain Nicora ordered Kriss to attend her in her quarters, he had almost forgotten his shadow.

The summons, coming while he was still being disciplined, made him uneasy. He put on his best blue crewsuit, carefully brushed his blonde hair, shorter than it had been on Farr's World but still longer than most Family men wore theirs, and made his way to the elevator for the journey to the top of the ship. Estra and Levit, Nicora's black-clad bodyguards, gave him only cursory glances when he reached her door, then waved him inside.

The captain stood looking out over the spaceport via a viewscreen in the wall, but she turned as he entered. She wore a shimmering robe that rippled with colour as it swirled around her. "Good morning, Crewman."

"Good morning, ma'am."

She sat behind her desk and motioned him to sit opposite her, her clear green eyes piercing his. He sat, but only on the edge of his chair.

"You are confined to port, I understand," the captain said.

"Yes, ma'am."

"You realize the original withholding of shore leave privileges was by my order, for the safety of you and the Family?"

"Yes, ma'am. I'm sorry."

"You showed a disturbing disregard for Family discipline in this matter, crewman. I have reports of other breaches of Family Rule. Most of them have been minor, and I have put them down to your unfamiliarity with the Family—but this latest incident causes me to reevaluate them. I feel that you are not fully comfortable with our way of life. May I remind you of the sacrifice made so that you might be a part of this Family—the sacrifice, I might add, you played of so movingly at the celebration of my birthday? I trust we shall see improvement in the future."

"I'll . . ." *try*, Kriss started to say, but then thought better of it. "Yes, ma'am."

"Very well." Nicora glanced at a display on her desk. "I have changed the duty roster tonight so that you are free as of 1900. Report to the landing ramp at 2010. An escort will meet you and take you to the *Coronach*. The *Coronach's* captain is returning the hospitality I showed him on our first night here and is interested in hearing you play. The captain of the *Athabasca* will also be present. You are expected at 2030. Don't be late. Is that clear?"

Kriss's heart beat faster. Playing for three Family captains, as an official representative of *Thaylia*? "Yes, ma'am!"

"Dismissed."

He stood, bowed, and strode happily back to the elevator, even smiling at the dour guards. This would be far better than playing for a few spacers in a dingy bar, or even playing for *Thaylia*'s crew. This would be the kind of audience he'd only dreamed of!

He only wished Tevera could be there, too.

At 2000 he inspected himself for the third time in his cabin mirror, then, touchlyre under his arm, made his way to the exit hatch, which stood open, the ramp extending out into the darkness, down to the port's blackened duracrete.

There was no one there: no escort for him, and not even the sentry required by Family Rule. Kriss waited in what he thought of as the ship's "porch" for a minute, then five, then ten. No one appeared, and time was passing. If he didn't leave right away, he'd never make the *Coronach* in time—and the thought of being late to such an important performance made his stomach churn.

Maybe the escort is waiting outside and wondering where I am, he thought suddenly. He hurried down the ramp and stared around into the darkness, though since his eyes hadn't adjusted yet, there was little to see. Still, clearly, the escort wasn't out there, either.

He looked across the field to where the *Coronach* stood, maybe eight hundred metres from *Thaylia*. From his explorations of the port, he knew there was nothing between the two ships but smooth duracrete; it wasn't like he could get lost or fall into a hole.

I must have misunderstood, he thought. *And I can't be late. I* can't*!*

With sudden resolve, he set out toward the *Coronach* on his own.

He hadn't gone far when he heard footsteps behind him. *The escort!* he thought. "I'm here!" he called, stopping and turning around. "Where were you?"

No answer came from the dark figure he glimpsed against *Thaylia*'s lights—and then the figure charged toward him, and he suddenly remembered the man who had been tailing him all week and realized what an idiot he had been to come out into the darkness alone.

Gasping, he spun and bolted toward the *Coronach*. His unknown pursuer shouted something after him, but he ignored it, pounding across the hard pavement. The gleaming spire of the *Coronach* grew nearer. *I'll make it!* he thought.

Then two more men leaped out of the darkness ahead of him, silhouetted briefly against the brightly lit ship. One clamped a rough hand over his mouth and threw him to the ground; the other jerked the touchlyre case over his head and whipped plastic cord around his ankles and wrists.

Then, taking his arms and feet, they carried him across the darkened port.

Chapter Twenty-Six

Kriss's captors carried him to a dark warehouse at the edge of the field, through a creaking door and into a musty room, empty except for a few broken crates. They dumped him on the floor, then closed the door and turned on the lights.

One of the men was bald and middle-aged, the other young and bearded. Neither was the man who had been following Kriss for a week, but he assumed that was who had chased him into the trap. "Where's Vorlick?" he demanded as soon as the younger man undid his gag.

"Who's Vorlick?"

"The man you work for!"

"Never heard of him," said the bald man.

Kriss struggled upright and glared at him. "You expect me to believe that?"

The bald man shrugged. "Don't really care."

"What are you going to do with me?"

"What we're being paid to." He looked at his watch.

"Going to keep you here until an hour after midnight—then let you go."

"Let me go?"

"That's right." The bald man sat down on a crate, leaned back against the wall, and closed his eyes. "You might as well make yourself comfortable."

Kriss stared at him. He couldn't be telling the truth. What did they *really* intend to do with him? "Where's the touchlyre?"

The bald man opened one eye again. "The what?"

"I think he means this," the younger man said, holding up the instrument case.

"There you go. Now be quiet, or I'll put that gag back on you." The bald man closed his eyes again and soon began snoring.

Kriss struggled uselessly with the cords that bound his wrists. If he could get his hands on the touchlyre, maybe he could . . .

But he couldn't free himself, and finally subsided and lay still, fuming. *Maybe they don't* know *who they're working for,* he thought. *Vorlick could be trying to cover his tracks. But I'll bet he shows up in another hour or two.*

It was a bet he would have lost. Precisely an hour after midnight, the bald man's watch beeped loudly, and he opened his eyes and sat up, stretching. "Well, lad, that's that." He stood and nudged the younger man, who had also fallen asleep, with his foot. "Some guard you are!"

"Still here, ain't he?" the other man grumbled.

"No thanks to you. Cut those cords, give him that touchlyre thing, and let's get out of here."

Two minutes later, Kriss stood on the landing field

outside the warehouse again, while his captors vanished into the darkness. He stared after them, completely bewildered. Was somebody playing a joke?

Finally, he set out for *Thaylia*. *They must have been searching for me since I failed to show up for the banquet*, he thought. *Nicora will think Vorlick got me.* I *thought Vorlick had me.* He shook his head. "I don't understand," he muttered.

Analet, a recent bloodswap, stood guard at the top of the ramp. "The captain wants you," she said stiffly as he reached the hatch.

"Thank you." *They must have seen me coming*, he thought as he made his way deeper into the ship. *Nicora will be glad to see I'm still alive.*

But as he stepped out of the elevator in the captain's quarters, Nicora's guards seized his arms roughly, ignoring his angry protest, and propelled him to the captain's black desk, where she awaited him.

Rigel stood behind her, his face inscrutable.

What's he doing here? Kriss wondered.

Captain Nicora spoke without preamble. "Crewman Lemarc, you failed to appear as ordered at the *Coronach* to play for the assembled captains and their officers. This has shamed *Thaylia*."

"Captain, I—"

"Silence!" The ice in her tone froze the words in his throat. "I know what you have done. You fled Rigel, who was on sentry duty and was to serve as your escort. He followed you as far as he could and saw you leaving the port, entering the city, at the very hour when you were due on board the *Coronach*. How *dare* you go to play in some worldhugger bar when Family captains await you? And worse, while you were confined to port?"

"But I didn't! I was kidnapped!" *Rigel was on sentry duty? He was my escort? But I never . . .*

And suddenly, he felt cold as he realized what Rigel had done . . . cold, then blazing hot with fury.

"Kidnapped?" The captain raised a frosty eyebrow. "By whom?"

"Ask *him*!" Kriss shouted, thrusting a finger at Rigel.

Rigel raised his eyebrows. "Me? I know nothing about it. Are you saying you were kidnapped after you left the port? That still doesn't excuse your failure to follow your captain's order."

"You—"

"If you were kidnapped, how did you escape?" Nicora said, cutting him off.

"I didn't. They let me go." Even as he said it, Kriss realized how ridiculous it sounded.

The captain glanced at Rigel.

"I have no idea what he's talking about," he said. "My report stands. He evaded me, fled across the port, and entered the city."

Kriss lunged at him, but the guards pulled him back. "Liar!" he shouted. "You abandoned your post. You hired those men. *You set me up!*"

The captain's eyes transfixed him. "We in the Family do not lie."

"But you're saying *I'm* lying!"

"You were not raised in the Family." Nicora took a deep breath. "Crewman Lemarc, you are confined to your cabin for the duration of our stay in Try-Your-Luck, and for the duration of the next jump, except for periods of special disciplinary duty. You are also confined to the ship for the next three planetfalls. Nor are you to have any contact with Crewwoman Tevera during your sentence. Dismissed!"

"But that's *months!*"

Nicora stood, green eyes sparking. "I said, *you are dismissed!* Guards, escort him to his cabin!"

Choking on helpless rage, Kriss was dragged from the room, his last view of it a glimpse of Rigel's stony face.

Later, he sat fuming in his cabin. He knew Rigel hated him. But enough to set up this whole charade, just to get him punished? Enough to lie to the captain? Kriss shook his head. There had to be more motive than that.

He was no closer to puzzling out an answer when the intercom at the head of the bunk beeped, disrupting his thoughts.

TEVERA HAD SPENT the evening in one of the recreation lounges, drinking a sweet tea she'd discovered in Try-Your-Luck during one of her leaves after Kriss's confinement to port and reading a rather trashy historical romance novel set on Old Earth she'd downloaded on a whim in a Try-Your-Luck bookstore and printed out in hardcopy. She had the place to herself until Yverras came in. He looked around, spotted her, and came over. She smiled up at him. "Pull up a chair," she said. "I can make you a cup of this . . ." Her smile faded as she took in his grim expression. "What is it?"

"Kriss," Yverras said. "He's currently *persona non grata* in the captain's eyes. He's confined to quarters for the remainder of our stay on Fortune and for the next jump, except for disciplinary details. I've been sent to tell you you are not to contact him, or, should you encounter him by accident, to speak to him. Is that clear?"

She gaped at him. "But why . . .?

"Is that clear, Crewwoman?" Yverras snapped.

Tevera stiffened. "Aye, aye, sir."

"Good." Without another word, Yverras spun on his heel and left the rec room.

She stared after him, tea and novel forgotten. What could have happened? Kriss was supposed to have gone to the *Coronach* to play for the three Family captains . . .

The room was empty. The comm unit was close at hand. With a quick, guilty glance at the door through which Yverras had just exited, she punched in Kriss's cabin number.

He answered with a snarl. "What do you want?"

"Kriss," she whispered, even though there was no one around to hear. "It's Tevera."

"Tevera!" He lowered his own voice. "How—"

"I'm alone in Rec Four. I'm not supposed to even talk to you, but unless someone looks closely at the monitor on the bridge and knows I'm in here . . . what's going on? Why are you locked up?"

"There was no one waiting to escort me to the *Coronach*," he said, his voice flat and bitter. "Rigel was supposed to be there but wasn't. I didn't want to be late, so I started out on my own. I was jumped by two men, gagged, tied up, dragged off, and held somewhere until after midnight, then released. Rigel claims otherwise. He says he was on duty as he was supposed to be, and saw me leave the port on my own. The captain believed him. He's lying. He set the whole thing up."

Tevera listened in horrified silence. Rigel, lie to the captain? She knew he hated Kriss, but he'd never do that . . . would he?

Her silence went on too long. "Tevera?" Kriss said.

"I'm . . . still here." Then, in a rush, "Kriss, are you sure there's no way Rigel could have seen what happened and just . . . misunderstood?"

"I was bound and gagged! How could he misunderstand that? And if he saw it at all, why didn't he help? We're both supposed to be Family!"

Tevera shook her head, even though she knew Kriss couldn't see her. "There has to be an explanation," she whispered, as much to herself as to him.

"There is," Kriss said grimly. "Your brother wants me off this ship."

"But Rigel is Family. Family men don't lie!"

"You obviously think *I'm* lying!"

"No!" Tevera protested.

"But you don't believe me."

"Yes, I do! It's just . . . I believe Rigel, too."

"You can't have it both ways!"

Another silence. Tevera's stomach churned. "I need to think," she finally said.

"Think all you want to. But don't call me again until you've decided to trust me!" He cut the connection.

The rec room door opened. Shella, a young second cousin of Tevera's, came in and smiled brightly. "Hi!" she said. "I didn't expect to see anyone else in here this time of night."

"I'm just leaving," Tevera said. She managed to dredge up the smallest of smiles, then fled to her own cabin.

In bed, she clutched the pillow to her chest, mind whirling. There had to be some other explanation than the one Kriss favoured. Rigel would never lie to the captain. He wouldn't!

But Kriss wouldn't have done what Rigel accused him of, either. He *had* been kidnapped. He must have. But by whom? Vorlick's men? Vorlick's men wouldn't have let him go, not if he had the touchlyre with him. They'd have taken him straight to their boss, if he was here, or kept him locked up until their boss got to the planet.

The more she thought about it, the guiltier Rigel seemed.

I have to talk to him, she thought. *He's my brother*.

The thought of that conversation filled her with dread.

It was a long, long time before she slept.

AFTER SMASHING his hand against the intercom button, cutting off the conversation with Tevera, Kriss hurled his pillow across the room and flung himself on the bed.

After a bitter time of black thoughts, he finally drifted into sleep.

He jolted awake an indeterminate time later when his cabin door opened. He couldn't see a thing, which brought him bolt upright: he hadn't turned out the lights before he fell asleep.

No light came through the door, either, though the corridor outside should have been filled with dim blue night-glow. "Who's there?" he said into the darkness.

A hand suddenly clamped over his mouth. “An old friend,” a voice whispered, and something cold pressed against his temple. “That’s a beamer, so keep quiet. You’re leaving this ship right now—forever.”

Kriss didn’t have to see his assailant. He knew that voice.

“Get the touchlyre,” said Rigel.

Chapter Twenty-Seven

Rigel produced a hand-light, and once Kriss had retrieved the touchlyre from his closet, forced him quickly and quietly at beamer-point through the strangely blacked-out corridors. They didn't take the elevator, instead descending through the emergency tunnel, where ladders and zero-G handholds allowed access to all decks even in the event of a massive power failure or other catastrophe.

They exited through a small one-man hatch Rigel had to enter a security code to open—which, of course, he had. *Because Rigel is a good Family man whom the captain trusts implicitly*, Kriss thought bitterly, *while I'm nothing but a worldhugger to her—and always will be.*

Rigel marched him briskly away from *Thaylia* into the darkness. Once well clear of the Family ship, he turned him toward a beat-up, antique freighter near the port's perimeter. "Where are you taking me?" Kriss demanded.

"Vorlick."

Kriss stopped in shock. "What?"

Rigel jabbed him with the beamer. "Keep quiet and keep moving."

Stunned, Kriss walked on mechanically, puzzle pieces falling into place inside his mind. Rigel had hired the men to keep him from making it to the banquet on the *Coronach* and convinced Captain Nicora that Kriss had sneaked off on his own. Now, he would deliver Kriss to Vorlick—and tell Nicora that Kriss had deserted, angry at the way he had been treated. Nicora had never really believed Kriss could adjust to Family life, so she'd accept that claim without question. Vorlick would have Kriss, and the touchlyre, without having to worry about Family vengeance, and Rigel . . .

I wonder how much he sold me for?

A small hatch opened and a ladder descended as they neared the base of the freighter. Two tough-looking spacers met them. One took the touchlyre, then together they escorted Rigel and Kriss into the ship and up a series of ladders to a small, brightly lit cabin.

As they entered the room, Carl Vorlick stood up from behind a smaller version of Nicora's computerized desk. "Kriss," he almost purred. "How nice to see you again."

Kriss said nothing.

The touchlyre case thudded onto the desk as the spacer carrying it tossed it down. "Careful, you idiot!" Vorlick snapped. He unlatched the case, lifted the lid, and touched the artifact almost reverently before looking up sharply at Rigel. "You're sure no one will suspect?"

"I'm sure," Rigel said, voice tight. "I've convinced the captain that Kriss is a liar who will never fit into the Family."

"The Family never lies," Kriss said bitterly. "Except you. Why, Rigel? How many feds was your honour worth?"

Rigel didn't even look at him.

"You'd better get back to *Thaylia* now and report his desertion," Vorlick said.

Rigel jerked a single nod and went out. Kriss folded his arms over the icy lump of fear in his stomach and glared at his enemy. "Are you going to kill me now or later?"

Vorlick laughed. "My dear boy, I have no intention of killing you. I have the touchlyre. What would be the point?"

"Then what are you going to do with me?"

"As it happens, I have use for you. We're going on a trip."

"Where?"

Instead of answering directly, Vorlick touched a control on his desk. "Captain, we can take off now."

"Yes, sir," a man's voice came back. "Destination?"

Vorlick looked up at Kriss. "Earth." Then he laughed at Kriss's expression.

TEVERA FOUND Rigel in the mess hall, eating breakfast. There were half a dozen other Family members there. She didn't care.

She marched up to her brother and slammed her hands down on the table in front of him, making him look up. "Did you do it?" she snapped.

He raised an eyebrow. "Do what?"

"Make Kriss disappear."

He reached for his cup of stimtea. "You heard, did you?"

"Of course, I heard!" Tevera clenched her fists. Her

voice shook. "He told me you arranged his kidnapping last night, so he'd miss the banquet on *Coronach*."

"You weren't supposed to talk to him," Rigel said mildly. He sipped his tea and put it down again. "And he lied to you. I saw what I saw. He just took off, probably to play at some bar in Try-Your-Luck. The feds he could earn there meant more to him than his duty to the captain." He picked up his fork. "Not really surprising, for a world—"

Tevera slammed her hands down on the table again and leaned across it. "Did you lie to the captain?" she shouted. The other Family members, who had been studiously ignoring the brother-sister byplay, now all turned toward them in shock.

Rigel froze. He put the fork down. Then he stood. "I am a member of the Family," he said. "And your brother. How *dare* you accuse me of that?" He looked around the rec room. "In front of others?"

One by one, those "others" looked back down at their meals.

Tevera was still shaking, but she lowered her voice. "Did you have anything to do with his disappearing from the ship last night?" she whispered. "Look at me, Rigel."

He did. "I don't know where Kriss is," he said. "When I woke up this morning, he was gone. I'm telling the truth."

"You didn't—" *answer my question*, she intended to say, but Rigel turned and walked away before she could utter the words.

The mess-hall hatch closed behind him. She looked around at the other Family members, none of whom returned her gaze.

She had one more shore leave coming. She spent it asking people in Try-Your-Luck if anyone had seen Kriss. No one had.

When *Thaylia* left Fortune, Kriss wasn't aboard . . . and Rigel had stopped talking to her.

KRISS DIDN'T SEE Vorlick again during the month-long journey. To his surprise, he was treated like a low-ranking member of the crew rather than a prisoner. His duties included cleaning and general maintenance, pretty much the same tasks he'd been doing on board *Thaylia*—dull, but better than being locked in a cabin.

He had a lot of time to wonder what Vorlick was up to. What "use" could he possibly have for Kriss, now that he had the touchlyre? Why take Kriss to Earth? Sure, it was his birth planet, but he had no memory of it. Before he'd joined the Family, he'd dreamed of visiting Earth and trying to discover if he still had relatives, but now he tamped down any excitement he felt at that prospect. He seriously doubted Vorlick intended to arrange a family reunion.

At least I'm still alive, he thought as he swabbed a corridor, early on the day they were due to arrive at Earth. He was using a zero-G mop that cleaned the walls and floor and sucked up (with a rather disgusting sound) the grimy water, without ever letting a droplet float free. He wondered again, as he had daily, what had happened on board *Thaylia*. Had Nicora believed Rigel's lies?

She believed them once, he thought bleakly. *Even Tevera*

believed him. The thought that Tevera might believe he had deserted *Thaylia*—deserted *her*—made him feel sick.

A bell shrilled. "Prepare for docking with Earth station," said a disembodied voice, and Kriss hurriedly stowed his mop and pulled himself down the corridor to a nearby observation port. Maybe today he would finally get some answers.

He grabbed a handhold and stared out at the still-distant barrel shape of the space station, and the blue-and-white planet beyond: Earth, capital of the Commonwealth, home-world of humanity—and, almost unbelievably, his birthplace.

The slowly spinning station drew nearer. Over more than a century, micrometeorites and space junk had pitted and discoloured its hull, but the symbol of the Common-wealth, a star enclosed in three interlocking circles, burned bright blue on the central, stationary docking cylinder.

The freighter's bow rockets fired, and station and planet alike swung out of view as the ship turned its fat stern for the final approach. At the same moment, a voice crackled over the intercom. "Kriss Lemarc, report to Hatch 2."

Vorlick awaited him there. "Follow me," he said. "Stay close."

Follow you where? Kriss wondered.

The ship shuddered. There were a couple of loud clangs. "Docked and secured," the captain's voice said over the intercom.

"Acknowledged," Vorlick said. "Disembarking." He touched the lock's control pad, and the inner door slid aside. He floated into the lock, Kriss trailing him. The inner door closed, and the outer lock opened, revealing a cylindrical chamber. "I've already cleared us both through customs,"

Vorlick said as he drifted across the room and touched another control panel, opening another door. He slipped through it, and once Kriss had joined him, poked yet another panel to close the door, labelled "8A" in red letters, behind them.

Kriss looked both ways: they were in a tube-shaped corridor. "We won't be going into the spinning portion of the station," Vorlick said, leading him to the right, using a cable stretched in stanchions on the inner wall to pull himself along. "We'll board my private shuttle in one of the other docking tubes."

"*Then* will you tell me what you want with me?" Kriss demanded, pulling himself along in Vorlick's wake.

"When you need to know." Maybe a hundred metres down the corridor, they reached another door, identical except for its label, which read, logically enough, "7A." Vorlick opened it, and they floated through two more airlocks, finally emerging into a room with deep gold carpet, dark wood panelling, crystal-and-silver lighting fixtures, and chairs and couches upholstered in white. "We'll have artificial gravity as soon as we're out of the station," Vorlick said. "You'd better find a place to sit."

Kriss looked at him in astonishment. "Artificial gravity? In a *shuttle*?" Such a profligate use of energy in something so utilitarian was—well, "decadent" was the word that came to mind.

"Of course. A luxury I can well afford, which serves the dual purpose of impressing those I want impressed and making *me* more comfortable." As Kriss positioned himself above a comfortable-looking armchair, Vorlick, who remained upright but held onto the back of one of the couches, said into thin air, "Take her down."

After a moment of faint scraping and the beginnings of acceleration, the artificial gravity eased on, and Kriss sank into the cushions, gradually feeling his normal weight take hold. "That's better," Vorlick said as his feet settled into the gold carpet. "I hated travelling in that zero-G rustbucket." He released the back of the couch, crossed to a cabinet, and took out two cut-crystal goblets. (Kriss could tell from the slight resistance to his lifting them that they were magnetically affixed to the shelves, for when the artificial gravity was turned off.) He placed the goblets on the low, glass-topped table the chairs and couch all faced, then returned to the cabinet, opening a receptacle at the back and bringing out a metallic bottle. He twisted off the top, poured something blue-green and sparkling into both goblets, then replaced the bottle in its chamber.

Returning to the table, he lifted one goblet and indicated Kriss should take the other one. Kriss picked it up and sniffed it suspiciously. It had a strange, sharp scent he couldn't quite place. "Drink," Vorlick said. "It's Verilian sparkling brandy. Very expensive. Not at all poisonous . . . well, unless you drink too much of it." He laughed and sat down on the couch he'd been holding onto before the gravity came on.

Still a little cautious, Kriss took a sip. Ice-cold, it tasted both sweet and spicy—strange, but not offensive—and burned in his mouth and on the way down. On Farr's World, he wasn't old enough to legally drink alcohol. He didn't know what Earth's laws were. Vorlick clearly didn't care.

Vorlick sipped his own brandy. "Now, two months ago—even six weeks ago—I very well *might* have poisoned you," he said conversationally. "You thwarted me, with the help of the Family—temporarily, of course, but I'm not used to waiting for what I want." He took another swallow, then set the goblet down on the table's glass top. "But since then, I've realized how you can still be of use."

"What if I refuse?" Kriss said. He set his own goblet down without taking another sip. He wasn't used to alcohol, and he suddenly thought it might be a really good idea to keep a clear head.

Vorlick shrugged. "I can still kill you. But why worry about such an unpleasant possibility? You won't refuse."

"Why not?"

"You want to know more about your parents, don't you?"

Kriss's heart skipped a beat. "You know I do."

Vorlick smiled again. "I share your curiosity. In particular, I would very much like to know where they found that artifact of yours—well, mine, now, of course. And I know how we can both find answers to our questions." He lifted his goblet again, took another swallow, then set it down, stood, and went to a large viewscreen in one wall. When he activated it, it showed the view from the shuttle's bow. To Kriss's astonishment, they were already deep in the atmosphere; he hadn't felt so much as a bump. Sparkling towers glittered near the distant horizon.

"New Oxford, home of the Commonwealth Central Data Bank and Information Processing Centre—usually called the Library. That's it there." Vorlick tapped the image of the largest tower of all. "The Library is the nerve centre of the Commonwealth. The actual administrative personnel are elsewhere, but every order, every law, every public communication, every bit of information gathered in the

Commonwealth is stored and correlated here. Every planet in the Commonwealth, most ships, and many individuals maintain slipspace contact with it." He glanced at Kriss. "As did your parents."

"I don't understand." Kriss stared at the rapidly nearing city, now close enough that he could see the immense, complex system of antennae spread around it for kilometres.

"Your parents were in contact with the Library during their expedition," Vorlick said. "They may have told the Library where they were, or at least left enough hints for me to figure it out."

"Then why haven't you?"

"Because I can't get at the records. That's why I need you." Vorlick frowned at the image of the city. "The Library's security is impenetrable, even by me. It's overseen by the most advanced artificial intelligence in existence. It would never let me access your parents' privacy-locked communications. But it *will* let *you*."

"Why?"

Vorlick turned to him. "I've had your identity confirmed. You are now officially recognized in Commonwealth records as Kriss Lemarc, son of Jon and Memory Lemarc of Earth, born on this planet a little over sixteen standard years ago and therefore an Earth citizen. As sole heir of the deceased Lemarcs, you have the right to access their private records." He spread his hands. "You're going to give me what I want—and it will all be quite legal."

Kriss stared at the viewscreen. For years he had longed to find out everything he could about his parents. Now Vorlick had given him that opportunity. He supposed he should be grateful . . . but he still felt uneasy. What would

Vorlick do with the knowledge he wanted Kriss's help to uncover?

He decided another sip of brandy was in order after all.

———

THE SHUTTLE LANDED UNEVENTFULLY, and Kriss and Vorlick walked from the small spaceport into the city, a quiet place with few people in sight but a great many flowers, fountains, and trees. Birds, strange to Kriss's eyes and ears, sang in the foliage beneath a clear blue sky. The buildings, low and simple near the port, rose stair-step fashion to the towers at the city's centre, and the tallest tower of all, housing the Library.

They didn't go all the way to the Library itself, though. Instead, Vorlick led Kriss to a small, windowless white building, surrounded by flowering shrubs. A bronze door with the emblem of the Commonwealth incised on it slid silently open at their approach. The short, shiny white corridor beyond had ten black doors opening from it, five on a side. Vorlick opened the first door to the left, ushering Kriss into a cubicle containing only a chair, a desk, and a holographic display cube.

Vorlick pointed Kriss to the chair and stood behind him as he sat down. At once, a disembodied female voice said, "Please identify yourself."

"Uh . . . I'm Kriss. Kriss Lemarc."

"Insufficient response. Commonwealth Citizenship Number?"

"I don't—"

"SPX-496-241-KMQ-1129746," Vorlick put in.

Kriss glanced at him, surprised.

"Applicant must give data himself," said the Library.

With silent prompting from Vorlick, Kriss repeated the string of letters and digits.

"Place of birth?"

"Earth."

A moment's pause. "Scan complete. Identity confirmed. Second person, please identify."

"I'm not applying for information," Vorlick said.

"Immaterial. Current security programming requires that I confirm the identity of all humans within the Library. Please identify."

"Carl Vorlick, of Earth. SOC-140-770-JJC-0403998."

Kriss wondered how Vorlick could reel off such complicated ID codes. *Lots of practice, I guess.*

"Scan complete. Identity confirmed. How may I help you, Kriss Lemarc?"

Kriss looked helplessly at Vorlick. "What do I say?"

But the Library answered first. "I am capable of conversing in all known human languages, in all dialects. I have full command of slang, metaphor, and simile, and I am not confused by hesitations, speech impediments, improper grammar, or other irregularities. No special syntax is required. Simply state your area of interest, and I will request further clarification if necessary."

"You know what I want," Vorlick said. "Get on with it."

Kriss turned back toward the display cube. "I'd like to see the personal records of my parents, Jon and Memory Lemarc."

"That information is privacy-coded. As their son, you

may access it, but your companion, Carl Vorlick, may not. I cannot release it with him present."

Vorlick looked down at Kriss. "I'll wait outside. Find out what I want to know—and don't think you can lie to me about it, because you'll be coming along on the search. Understand?"

Kriss nodded, and Vorlick went out, leaving him alone with his past.

Chapter Twenty-Eight

"I sense you are now alone, Kriss Lemarc," said the Library. "Before I undertake any other business, I am legally required to inform you that, having been recently confirmed as the sole offspring of Jon and Memory Lemarc, who had no other living relatives, and who were legally declared dead ten years after their disappearance, you are sole heir to their estate."

Kriss blinked. "Their estate? You mean a house?"

"They did not leave a house, or any other physical possessions, on Earth," the Library said, "and the fate of whatever possessions they had with them at the time of their disappearance is not known. However, they did leave investments and a bank account. Would you like these to be transferred to your name? I can provide you with the necessary datarod to allow you to access the funds anywhere in the Commonwealth."

"Uh . . ." Kriss glanced at the door. Did Vorlick know about this? "Sure? I guess?"

"Done," said the Library, and a small golden rod extruded from an opening in the console. Kriss had seen people purchase things using bank datarods before. He'd never expected to have one of his own.

He took it gingerly and held it up to his eyes. "So . . . how much money do I have?"

"There are 517,044 feds in the bank account. Your investments are currently valued at 9,478,201 feds."

Kriss almost dropped the datarod. "That's . . . unbelievable."

"I assure you it's true," the Library said, and he almost thought it sounded a little miffed. "Jon and Memory Lemarc both inherited sizeable amounts from their respective parents and invested it wisely. Would you like me to provide detailed records?"

"No, no. It's not necessary." Very carefully, Kriss pocketed the datarod. He'd saved a few hundred feds from Andru's and the playing he'd done on Try-Your-Luck and thought he was doing well. Now, if he went back to Farr's World, he'd be one of the richest people on the planet. It was mind-boggling, but it didn't really change anything about his situation at the moment. He put it aside. "Now may I see my parents' personal records?"

"Of course."

"What do they include? Besides the financial stuff you just mentioned."

"Primarily, diaries and logs from archaeological expeditions."

"How long would it take to view all of those?"

"With continuous display, sixty-eight days, sixteen hours, nineteen minutes, forty-four seconds."

Kriss winced. "I think I'll want to narrow it down."

"Where would you like to begin?"

He didn't answer. Where *could* he begin? He wanted to know *everything* about his parents—but he didn't have time.

"Where would you like to begin?" the Library repeated.

A thought struck him, and he leaned forward eagerly. "Do you have pictures of them?"

"Affirmative."

The display cube filled with heavy, glowing mist, which coalesced into full-colour, three-dimensional images of a young man and woman. Kriss stared at them hungrily. Here were the parents he had never known.

Their youth startled him. He'd always pictured them middle-aged, as they would be if still alive, but of course, they had only been in their late twenties when they'd died—not that many years older than he was now. He found that thought unsettling.

The picture of his father had been taken outside. His eyes were focused on some distant horizon, and Kriss could almost feel the wind tugging at his father's hair, blond as his own, and the warmth of the sun that beat down on the tanned, lean face, the mouth quirked in a faint smile . . . an expression he found oddly familiar.

He should, he realized; he'd seen it often enough in the mirror.

After a long moment, he turned to his mother's image.

It had been recorded inside. She was laughing at something, and firelight tinged her skin gold, twinkled in her eyes, and glowed in the auburn hair that danced around her bare shoulders. Again, Kriss caught echoes of his own face in her blue eyes and high cheekbones.

He leaned back and looked at his parents side by side, their images as clear as though they were with him, instead of separated from him by sixteen years of loneliness, and fresh hatred rose in him toward the one who had taken them from him. "Thank you," he said to the Library. "I've seen enough."

The images vanished.

"I'd like to view the log from their last expedition," he went on briskly, getting down to business—but the first entry renewed the pain.

"September 30, 2947," said a young man's happy voice. "Our anonymous patron came through for us—we can finally start preparing for the expedition! I was afraid that old spacer's story about an alien city untouched by time would be too tenuous for him. Happily, looks like I was wrong!

"But that's not the best news of today. I'm a father! Memory gave birth less than an hour ago to our son. We've already decided to name him Kriss after my father. I only wish he and Mom and Memory's parents were still alive to enjoy their first grandson. I hope Kriss likes to travel because in about six months we'll be setting out . . ."

Three hours later, the last entry played in the cubicle. Kriss's father no longer sounded young or happy.

"October 6, 2948, on board our scoutship, *Seeker*. We're about to leave this site. We've discovered who our mysterious patron is, and he must not find this place. I wish we'd never told him *we'd* found it . . . as soon as he realizes we've run, he'll be after us.

"I tried to buy us some time by telling him in our last monthly report that our next report will include the planet's coordinates. But we'll never make that report. We're going to vanish.

"Even in this private record, I won't say who our patron is, give the coordinates of this planet, or tell where we are headed. He may be able to break even the Library's security. And there's no point in contacting Commonwealth authorities; he hasn't done anything yet, and his influence is such that if we were to accuse him, we would be the ones arrested, and shortly thereafter, we would be in his hands.

"We're leaving everything here except the key artifact. It and the fortress must be separated while there is the possibility he could find either one. He must not have access to the planet-shattering power we've uncovered, or he could effectively rule the entire Commonwealth.

"This may be my last entry."

It was. Silence descended in the cubicle, but Kriss knew the rest of the story: they had fled to Farr's World, but Vorlick had tracked them down. They had hidden Kriss and the "key artifact"—camouflaged by Jon Lemarc as a musical instrument—with Mella. Then they had fled again, to lead Vorlick away from their son and the artifact, and Vorlick had killed them . . .

Kriss stared at the blank grey wall above the holocube. The early log entries had been cheerful and excited like the first, describing his parents' search for the rumoured alien city, and their breathless, ecstatic excitement when they'd actually found it. It turned out not to be a city at all, but an ancient fortress, deep in a tropical forest on an unspecified planet. The diamond-shaped gate had stood open, as though inviting them in. The interior (as his father described, and as the many photographs he'd taken showed) had been scarred by some long-ago battle, buildings in ruins everywhere but in the centre. There, they'd found five white towers, four needle-sharp ones forming a quadrangle around a central, cylindrical one. They'd climbed that tower. Atop it, they'd found a globe of crystal, multi-faceted, incredibly beautiful—the photographs did not do it justice, Kriss's father said—and, in a depression atop a pedestal in the chamber just below that globe, a mysterious artifact, a flat, golden disk, set, in an intricate pattern, with crystals of the same material as the globe at the tower's pinnacle.

But not long after that initial breathless excitement, the tone of the messages had changed. Somehow, either from something in Vorlick's communication with them or through Jon's own research in the Library's records, they had begun to realize who their "patron" was—and what kind of man he was. While their suspicions were still only half-formed, they'd discovered what the "key artifact" could do—but exactly what those capabilities were, Jon had left tantalizingly unsaid, already mistrustful of recording any information where Vorlick could conceivably retrieve it.

His reference to "planet-shattering" power particularly puzzled Kriss. He knew only too well how dangerous the alien-powered touchlyre could be, but "planet-shattering" seemed a bit much. Still, his parents had clearly feared what could happen if Vorlick found the fortress and the artifact together—and so they had separated them and, later, Kriss's father had crafted the touchlyre in which to hide the golden disk.

Yet now Vorlick had the touchlyre, and Kriss had to locate its planet of origin for him if he wanted to stay alive.

Maybe it's impossible, he thought hopefully. "Library,

can you scan the log and determine on what planet my father found the alien fortress?"

"Negative."

He sighed with relief. He wouldn't have to betray his father.

But the Library continued. "However, it is apparent there are only ten possible planets."

"How can you tell that?" Kriss asked in astonishment.

"All the log entries were sent through the slipspace relay that orbits Farr's World. There are only ten planets fitting the available data that are within shipboard communication range of that relay."

That means one of the possible planets is Farr's World itself! Kriss thought. Tevera had said the touchlyre couldn't have come from there, but there was a lot of wilderness, including a large swath of tropical forest girding the equator . . . and there was nothing in the log to rule it out. That meant Farr's World would surely be Vorlick's first destination when Kriss gave him the data he had gathered.

And that decided him. He *would* pass on the information—because he would never have a better opportunity to escape than on his old homeworld.

He thought of something else and calculated mentally. *Thaylia* was due to return to Farr's World soon—so soon, she might either be on the planet or very close when Vorlick's ship arrived. But "very close" could mean light-years, and even if he gained access to a communications terminal, he couldn't contact the Family while Rigel had the upper hand . . .

Then he sat up straight as another thought struck him.

"Andru!" he said out loud. "He'd believe me. If I could contact him . . ."

"Whom do you wish to contact?" asked the Library.

He stared at the holocube. Of course! The Library could act as a communications terminal! And Vorlick had left him alone . . .

"His name's Andru," he said quickly. "I don't know if he has a surname, but he was formerly of the Family ship *Thaylia*. He currently owns an inn called Andru's in Cascata on Farr's World."

"Sufficient data . . . located. Signalling."

The display cube misted, then solidified into an image of Andru, blinking at the screen, his shaggy, iron-grey eyebrows drawn together in annoyance. "Who is it?" he growled, then his eyes suddenly widened. "Kriss!"

Kriss felt a flood of relief at the sight of his former employer. But he wasted no time in small talk; Vorlick must be getting restless. "Listen, I'm in trouble . . ." he began, and sketched out what had happened.

"I have to convince Tevera I'm innocent," he concluded. "But I can't call *Thaylia* with Rigel aboard. He's poisoned the Family against me. But *Thaylia*'s due there soon, isn't she?"

"Ten days."

"Could you somehow get word to Tevera? Maybe she could convince the captain . . ." His voice trailed off. Could *anyone* sway that stiff-necked old woman once she'd made up her mind? Andru had, once, but he had nothing left to bargain with—he was no longer Family.

But Andru didn't seem concerned. "We can do better

than that. Vorlick may bring you here, but I can promise you won't be leaving with him."

Kriss stared at him. "How?"

"Leave it to me."

Footsteps sounded outside the cubicle. "Vorlick's coming. Break contact!"

Andru's face had barely faded away when the door opened and Vorlick stormed in, his thin face dark with anger. "I've waited long enough. You're stalling . . ."

"I was about to come for you," Kriss said. "I've found what you're looking for." He turned back to the holocube. "Library, please hardcopy the coordinates of the ten possible planets where the alien fortress might be located, and the description of the structure as outlined in my father's log."

"Completed," the Library said almost at once, and a white sheet protruded from a slit in the table below the holocube. Vorlick snatched it up.

"Why ten possible planets?" he said suspiciously, looking it over.

"My father didn't trust you," Kriss said. "He didn't record the coordinates. But all his log entries came through the Farr's World slipspace relay. Those ten planets are all within shipboard communication range of Farr's World."

"Farr's World?" Vorlick showed his teeth in a savage grin. "How ironic if this search were to end right where it began!" He gripped Kriss's arm and pulled him to his feet. "We'll start with your old home, then. But that alien fortress had better be on one of these worlds, boy, or I may just decide to cut my losses and settle for the artifact alone . . . and then I won't need *you* anymore." He pushed Kriss out into the corridor.

"I trust I have been of some help," the Library said as the door closed behind them.

Chapter Twenty-Nine

They didn't return to the decrepit freighter; instead, they boarded Vorlick's luxurious golden yacht, *Gemfire*, at another space station. Within two hours of departing the Library, they were on their way back to Farr's World.

No question about having artificial gravity on *this* vessel; Vorlick led Kriss to his quarters through corridors, panelled in dark wood and lit by crystal fixtures, that would not have been out of place in a luxury hotel (not that he'd ever been in one), his feet sinking into the royal-blue carpet with every step. Dark wood also predominated in the cabin Vorlick took him to. "Roam the ship as you please," Vorlick said from the doorway as Kriss gaped around, not so much at the luxurious appointments as the amount of space, ten times (at least) as much as he'd had on *Thaylia*. "You can hardly run away."

Vorlick headed down the corridor, the door sliding shut behind him. Kriss sat gingerly on the bed, which automatically shifted beneath him to provide maximum comfort. He looked from the elaborate entertainment console in one corner of the cabin to the equally elaborate food-synthesizer in the other. Through a door to his right, he saw a gleaming bathroom.

The *Gemfire* impressed him—and not just with ostentatious luxury. He'd also been very impressed by everything else Vorlick had pointed out as they'd passed through her: the armoured hatches in each bulkhead, capable of sealing the ship into a hundred secure sections; the gas nozzles, beamers, needlers, netters, and surveillance devices that crowded every strategic location; and the high-powered beamers that seemed integral parts of the crew's spotless white uniforms.

It would take a small army—no, make that a *large* army—to break into the *Gemfire* and rescue him. Yet Andru had promised to try, and Kriss knew he would keep his word, no matter how hopeless the attempt. *He'll just get himself killed,* Kriss thought miserably. *Nothing's changed; I still endanger everyone close to me.*

TEVERA HAD ONCE TOLD Kriss that the trip from Farr's World to Earth took *Thaylia* two months. On board the *Gemfire,* it took only three weeks; but three weeks provided more than enough time for his spirits to sink close to despair.

When at last they touched down, and the room's viewscreen showed the familiar spaceport of Cascata, Kriss scowled at it blackly, remembering how jealous he had been of Tevera when he first saw her emerge from *Thaylia*. Could it really have been only three and a half months ago? He felt a century removed from—and envious of—the naive youth he had been then.

He used the viewscreen to scan the rest of the landing field, looking for *Thaylia*. But the Family ship wasn't among the four other vessels in port, so he let his hands slip from the controls. Against common sense, he had let himself believe the Family might be waiting for him, that Tevera, having received his message from Andru, would sway the captain to his side. But his fond hope shattered against cold reality. Either Andru hadn't been able to reach Tevera, or she had been unable to convince the captain—or worse, she had received the message but not believed it, choosing to trust her brother instead.

Like a starkling settling on a rotting carcass, his mind latched onto that last bleak thought. He almost relished the anger and self-pity it brought, emotions so strong that for a moment he fancied he felt the touchlyre's ghostly fingers reaching into his mind from Vorlick's cabin. "Just a world-hugger who couldn't make it in the Family, that's all I am to her now," he muttered. "All that garbage about giving up the Family for me . . . nothing but lies. Lies!" He slammed his fist against the viewscreen, hoping to smash it into darkness, but it ignored his effort, as feeble as all his efforts had been.

Andru probably lied, too. But that's all right. I don't need him. "I don't need any of them!" he shouted at the walls. He could cooperate with Vorlick, maybe make a deal . . .

He spun as the door slid open behind him. Vorlick stood in the hall alongside a heavyset, balding man in an ill-fitting dark-green Farrsian customs uniform. "Ever hear of knocking?" Kriss demanded, fury still bubbling inside him.

"People hide things from me when I do," the customs

official said without smiling. He ran sharp eyes over the room. "Nice cabin."

Vorlick smiled—or at least turned up the corners of his mouth—and put a hand on the official's shoulder. "This way, sir," he said with exaggerated politeness, indicating the corridor.

The official frowned at the hand, then at Vorlick.

Vorlick's smile dropped away. "Your pardon, sir." He withdrew his hand.

The official turned back to Kriss. "You look familiar. What's your name?"

Kriss ignored Vorlick's quick, tight-lipped headshake. "Kriss Lemarc," he snapped. "What's yours?"

"Lemarc, Lemarc . . . oh, now I remember. You were playing that peculiar instrument in Andru's a few months ago."

"You want an autograph?"

"No," the official said. Now it was his turn to smile, or at least to show his teeth. They were yellow. "I never heard you and wouldn't care to. But I've seen your picture. There's a warrant out for your arrest." The predatory smile vanished, and he jerked his head toward the door. "You're in custody as of now. Let's go."

Kriss just stared, caught off guard. Vorlick blocked the doorway. "Wait a minute—"

"Get out of my way, or I'll charge *you* with obstruction," the official said evenly.

Vorlick looked shocked, an expression Kriss had never seen from him before. "Do you know who I am?"

"Of course, I do. You're Carl Vorlick. And the law applies to you the same as anyone else."

Vorlick lowered his voice. "I'm sure we can work this out . . ."

"Mr. Vorlick, if you are thinking of offering a bribe, don't," said the official. "Despite the reputation of my world, not all officials on Farr's World are corrupt or incompetent. If you offer me a bribe, you will join this youth in custody, and you just might find yourself before a judge as unimpressed as I am by your wealth. Do I make myself clear?"

Vorlick's fists and jaw clenched. He glared at the official for a long moment. The official simply waited. Finally, Vorlick *whuffed!* out a great gust of breath and stepped aside. "All right, take him!" he snarled. "But I'll have him free again by this time tomorrow."

"Maybe. But in the meantime . . ." The official gripped Kriss's arm.

"What's the charge?" he demanded, trying to hold back, but the official, too strong to resist, only pulled him faster along the plush corridors.

Outside, a waiting automated groundcar whisked them swiftly across the landing apron to the administration building. They stopped in front of a door marked "Customs and Immigration: Detention and Impound," and the still-silent official led Kriss inside, through a maze of corridors, rooms, and fenced areas piled high with crates. They finally emerged through another door into the main lobby, as usual, nearly empty except for a handful of bored-looking workers behind a long black desk. Brilliant sunshine streamed through a tall wall of glass, beyond which Kriss could see the familiar ring road and its steady flow of transports, groundcars, and wagons.

The official stopped at one end of the desk. "Wait here,"

he said, then strode swiftly across the bright mosaic floor to an open door, climbed into another groundcar, and drove off, leaving Kriss staring after him, astonished.

He glanced around. No one was watching him, or apparently even aware of him. He took two tentative steps toward the door, and nothing happened. He walked halfway across the lobby, and still, no one shouted or even looked up.

Finally, he hurried out the door and onto the sidewalk, then glanced both ways along the ring road, wondering what to do. Vorlick would soon find out he'd escaped, and Andru's was the first place he'd look. He didn't dare go there . . . yet he had to warn Andru and tell him not to attempt any rescue.

Before he made any decision, a blue groundcar with mirrored gold windows pulled out of traffic and stopped right in front of him. The glass on his side rolled down.

"Need a ride?" asked Tevera.

Chapter Thirty

When *Thaylia* landed in Cascata on the return leg of her round-trip journey to Fortune, Tevera felt as though the near-Earth-normal gravity of the planet had somehow doubled during her time away. She knew it wasn't physical weight she felt but the drag of memory and loss and betrayal. Here she had found Kriss, felt the rush of his emotions, helped him, been kidnapped, welcomed him into the Family . . . and now she had returned without him. On *Thaylia*, his name was never mentioned. The joy of his performance at the captain's birthday celebration had been blotted out by the ineradicable stain of his desertion, first of his duties, and then of the ship.

She didn't want to believe he had done what he had done, but Rigel had never wavered from his story . . . or so she supposed, since he still wasn't talking to her. Captain Nicora had never spoken to her about it at all. Yverras, too, refused to discuss it. She sometimes felt as if there were a chill in the corridors when she passed, as if her own Family blamed her for having brought him aboard, though it was Andru who had made that possible.

On the ground in Cascata, she had foregone the opportunity to take shore leave with the rest of her watch—not that any of them tried to convince her to. Feeling lonely and bitter and unutterably sad, she was lying on her bunk when a message arrived from Andru.

What she heard had her up and out into the city within half an hour. Andru had welcomed her and then hidden her when Rigel came to the inn. The Family had searched the city for as long as they could, but in the end, *Thaylia* had lifted without her, as it had lifted without Kriss, the business of trade waiting for no one. Tevera had watched her ship—her home—burn its way into the sky from the window of the room that had been Kriss's, and felt as if her heart were being ripped from her chest and pulled off the planet in its wake.

But now, here was Kriss, staring speechless at her from the sidewalk in front of the main spaceport entrance, and it was as if her heart had returned from its abortive journey to the stars to beat normally beneath her ribs once more.

Andru leaned his head over the back of the front seat to look out the window at the gaping boy. "I suggest you accept the offer," he said dryly. "The *real* customs officials are probably boarding *Gemfire* about now."

"Uh, sorry." Kriss quickly opened the door and climbed in, Tevera scooting over to make room for him. Her heart continued to pound in her chest. Why was she so nervous?

For his part, Kriss didn't even look at her. Sudden doubt seized her. Had she misjudged how he felt? She found herself unable to speak, even though part of her wanted to pull him to her and hold him forever. Maybe he felt the same way: they sat very close, but neither reached out to the other.

Kriss finally broke the silence as Andru turned off the ring road, but only to ask, "Where's *Thaylia*?"

Tevera said nothing. Andru gave her a quick glance in the rearview mirror, then answered, "Tevera didn't dare tell the Family about your message. Rigel has convinced them you deserted. The captain has exiled you."

Now, at last, Kriss looked at Tevera, though she only saw that out of the corner of her eyes, as she continued to stare straight ahead. "Then how . . .?

She didn't want to tell him. She didn't want to say the words. To say the words would make it all too real. She stayed silent.

Andru shot her another look. "She deserted. Jumped ship. I hid her while the Family searched—not long. They had to get a cargo of perishable luxury foods to Eagle's Head."

Deserted. Jumped ship. She hadn't said the words, but Andru had, and their naked truth burned, bright and hot as a white dwarf. "Great-grandmother has probably exiled me by now, too," she whispered.

And then, at last, Kriss took her hand, and her heart leaped into her throat. She heard him swallow, hard, and then he said the words she desperately wanted to hear. "Thank you. What—whatever the Family thinks doesn't matter as long as you're on my side."

Tears suddenly sprang to her eyes and spilled down her cheeks. Unashamed of them, she turned to him, searching his blue eyes, speaking in a trembling voice. "I didn't want to believe my brother had lied. But I couldn't believe you'd done what he claimed. I told myself you were both telling the truth, that he'd simply misunderstood . . . but he wouldn't talk to me about it. He acted so strange . . . then I got your message from Andru, and I thought about everything we'd gone through together here on Farr's World . . . and here I am." And then, at last, she flung her arms around him. "Here *I* am."

He held her close, and the weeks they had spent apart melted away.

Andru politely ignored them, concentrating on negotiating the crowded, narrow streets, occasionally checking behind for pursuit. Finally, he turned sharply left into a narrow, dead-end alley and parked. "Here we are."

KRISS DIDN'T WANT to let go of Tevera. He'd known he'd missed her; he didn't know how much he'd missed her until he took her into his arms. Holding her also helped alleviate the guilt he felt for what he'd been thinking on board *Gemfire* just a short while ago. But as much as he would have liked to, he couldn't hug her forever, so he released her, looked around, and recognized the lane behind Andru's. "But the inn is the first place Vorlick will look," he protested.

"Maybe. But he won't find you. There's an attic room no one knows about except me and Zendra. It's where I hid Tevera from the Family. You'll be safe there until Vorlick gets tired of looking and lifts."

"That won't be long." Kriss met Andru's eyes in the rearview mirror. "He already has what he needs to find the site where the touchlyre was found, and he has the touchlyre itself. All he needs *me* for is revenge . . . and he knows I have no way off this planet. He can always come back for me."

"I agree," Andru said. "I think he'll be gone by this evening." He got out of the groundcar and led them into the empty kitchen. "Zendra's keeping the staff busy out front," he said over his shoulder. He opened the door to the storeroom, piled high with supplies, and moved four crates away from the opposite wall, revealing a door Kriss had never known existed. Andru unlocked it with a key hung on a chain around his neck; beyond was a rickety-looking ladder in a narrow space. But as he was about to lead them up, angry shouting broke out in the common room. Andru swore, shoved Kriss and Tevera into the little room with the ladder, and slammed the door shut behind them. Kriss heard him pushing the crates back in place. Scarcely daring to breathe, he held Tevera's hand and listened.

"I know you took him, Andru. Where is he?" said Carl Vorlick's unmistakable voice.

"Look all you like—he's not here," Andru replied coldly.

Kriss heard the door to the storeroom crash open, and Tevera's hand tightened convulsively in his. He swallowed and held his breath.

"Nothing in here, sir!" a man's voice called.

The storeroom door slammed shut again, and Kriss gulped air with relief. "Leave my inn now, or I'll call the police . . ." Andru's angry voice faded away as he apparently followed Vorlick and his men back into the common room.

After a few minutes that seemed more like hours, they heard someone enter the storeroom again. Kriss tensed and heard Tevera's small gasp as the crates were pulled aside, and gathered his legs under him, ready to leap at whoever opened the door . . .

But when it swung aside, Zendra, not Vorlick, peered in at them. Kriss still leaped at her, but only to hug her fiercely. Zendra laughed. "Welcome home!" She held him at arm's length as Tevera eased out of the stairway behind him. "You've grown some more," she said accusingly. "But you're getting skinnier. You should eat better. And you need a haircut."

He ran a hand through his shaggy hair. "I've had a few other things on my mind."

"Hmmm, yes, we know. We just had a visit from one of them."

"What did he do?" Tevera asked.

"Nothing." Zendra smiled. "Andru had made a few preparations, you see. There happened to be a half-dozen rather large spaceport stevedores drinking in the common room. Andru told Vorlick you weren't here, allowed him to search the inn to prove it . . . and then told him to get lost. Which he did."

"Where's Andru now?" Tevera asked.

"Keeping an eye on Vorlick and his men. He wants to be sure they'll stay gone. He'll be back in a few minutes."

"He's back now." Andru appeared in the storeroom door. "Come on out of there. We have a call to make."

A moment later, they stood behind him, though off to one side, as he sat down at the computer interface in his office. They could see the screen but were not in the field of view of its vid pickup. "Who are you calling?" Kriss asked.

"*Thaylia*," Andru replied shortly.

TEVERA GASPED. *Thaylia*? While she was in slipspace? She knew it was possible, but the cost . . .

Andru's fingers danced across the antique control pad, and letters flashed on the screen. "They're about a quarter of the way to Eagle's Head," Andru said. He swiped his finger across the pad.

The terminal beeped, the screen turned white, and then suddenly, a bored young man was looking out at them. Tevera wasn't sure of his name—he was a recent bloodswap from *Diefenbaker*. "Family Trader *Thaylia*," he said indifferently. "State your name and business."

"Andru of Farr's World, and my business is with your captain," Andru growled in a fair imitation of thunder. "You will relay this call to her at once!"

The crewman snapped to attention. "Yes, sir!" The screen went white again.

Andru chuckled. "I may not be Family anymore, but I haven't lost my old officer's voice."

A new face appeared on the screen: Captain Nicora. Tevera swallowed, feeling almost ill. What must her great-grandmother think of her?

She found out soon enough.

"What is it, Andru?" Nicora snapped. "Your inn must be doing better than I ever thought if you can afford in-flight slipspace communication . . ."

Andru interrupted her. "Captain, I have found your missing great-granddaughter."

Nicora's face went granite-hard, and Tevera thought her heart would break. "That is of no concern to me. Tevera jumped ship, corrupted by that worldhugger you forced on us . . ."

Blindly, Tevera grabbed Kriss's hand. He squeezed it.

"Wrong, Captain. Carl Vorlick forced her to stay behind." Not *exactly* a lie, Tevera thought, since she'd stayed behind because Vorlick had captured Kriss. "He hoped to use her to blackmail Kriss into giving him the touchlyre, just as Salazar tried to do." That *was* a lie. Family never lied to Family, supposedly, but Rigel certainly had, and hadn't even had Andru's excuse, that he wasn't Family anymore. "He knew you'd exiled Kriss and thought you would believe Tevera jumped ship because of that, allowing him to kidnap her without arousing the Family."

Silence. Then, coldly, "Is Vorlick still on Farr's World?"

"Yes, Captain, though I expect him to leave in a few hours. However, I'm quite sure he'll return. Although I succeeded in rescuing Tevera and hid her from him, he knows she can't leave this planet."

"Indeed," Nicora said. "Andru, *Thaylia* is returning. Tell Tevera we will not abandon her. Eagle's Head's lords and ladies will have to do without their candied spiderfish eggs. Expect us in three days." She paused. "Also, tell Tevera her brother has been very concerned about her safety. I will inform him at once that she is all right. Nicora out."

As the screen blanked, Andru turned to Kriss and Tevera and shrugged his broad shoulders. "Nothing to it."

"But you lied to the captain!" Tevera blurted out.

"I had to. With Rigel on board, possibly in contact with Vorlick, we couldn't tell Captain Nicora the truth."

"Will we be able to tell her the truth—and get her to believe it—even here?" Kriss said.

"I think so. You'll be here to refute Rigel's stories, and Tevera and I can back you up. I have the record of your message from Earth, and you arrived on Vorlick's ship. Rigel's story will begin to look pretty thin."

"All this, just because of his hatred for worldhuggers?" Kriss shook his head. "It's almost unbelievable."

"There's more to it than that," Tevera said fiercely. "There must be! Whatever he's done, he did it because he felt it was the right thing to do."

Kriss gave her a disbelieving look, and she felt a surge of anger. "Don't look at me like that! I'm not saying he's right—he's not! But he's *not* evil. And he's not working for Vorlick. He *can't* be . . ."

"Men often do strange things for strange reasons," Andru said softly.

"I suppose even Vorlick has his reasons," Kriss said. Tevera glanced at him, surprised by his musing tone. "Even he must have had parents, brothers, sisters . . . family who loved him. Maybe they still do. So, how did he become what he is today?"

"No, I doubt he's ever been loved by anyone," Andru said.

Tevera stared at him, surprised. "Why do you say that?"

"I believe in knowing my enemies, so I researched him thoroughly, both in the public databases, and through . . . other channels. He grew up on Earth, in the streets of Berlin Megapolis, abandoned by his parents. No siblings. Lived hand-to-mouth until his teens and not only survived but rose to the leadership of one of the toughest youth gangs in the city. Just before he legally became an adult, he dropped out of sight for a year—and re-emerged, his juvenile record having been sealed, as a clean-cut and aggressive young businessman with a tidy sum ready to invest."

If his juvenile record was sealed, Tevera thought, *how did you find out about it?* Those "other channels," she supposed.

"No record of where that money came from, of course," Andru continued. "He bought a struggling Earth-Moon shuttle company and within ten years had parlayed it into a controlling share in United Galaxy Spaceways . . . before his thirtieth birthday. And he's only gotten more powerful as the years go by. He never misses an opportunity to add to his empire.

"Since Anton Salazar suffered his 'breakdown,'" Andru glanced at Kriss, "Vorlick has absorbed most of his operations, on Farr's World and on other nearby worlds. Here in Cascata, he now owns all of Salazar's former inns—and I hear he's working on Salazar's pocket policemen, too." Andru shook his head. "He told an interviewer once that, as a boy, he swore to himself that someday, he would be able to have whatever he wanted, whenever he wanted it.

"Well, right now, while he wants revenge on you," he nodded at Kriss, "for keeping him from the touchlyre for so long, he wants that alien fortress your father found even more. I believe he'll leave you alone for now while he searches for it."

"Three days until *Thaylia* can get back," Tevera said. "Vorlick could have found the right planet by then."

"No. He'll spend at least that much time in orbit surveying Farr's World. Only if it's on this planet—highly unlikely, because I don't think Kriss's parents would have tried to hide out on the same planet where they found the alien fortress they went to such great lengths to keep out of

Vorlick's' hands—will he have a chance of finding the site before we have the Family in action."

"But what kind of action?" asked Tevera.

The innkeeper smiled grimly. "When Carl Vorlick finally finds this alien fortress he wants so much, the Family's already going to be sitting on top of it."

Chapter Thirty-One

On a cool, wet afternoon three days later, Kriss lay on his old bed, staring at the wall, remembering those times when, feeling trapped by the Family Rule and Rigel's unrelenting coldness, he had thought longingly of this room as some kind of refuge he had lost, forgetting how much of a trap it, too, had seemed.

But now he knew it was neither a trap nor a refuge. It was only a room, a very small room, on a very small planet. He didn't belong to just one planet anymore; he doubted he ever could again. He rolled over onto his back, feeling as if he had lost something, but not sure what it was.

Worse, though Farr's World wasn't for him, he wasn't sure the Family was, either. What he wanted . . .

"What I want is the best of both!" he said to the ceiling. He wanted to travel among the stars as he had with the Family, he wanted Tevera's love, he wanted the support Nicora had given him in the beginning—all without giving up any of his independence.

But I can't get there from here.

He sat up, studying the room almost fiercely. He might not belong here, but unless Andru's plan worked, this was all he could look forward to for the rest of his life—which would only last until Vorlick made a determined effort to end it. And even if Andru's scheme succeeded, would the Family really be able to accept him back after all that had happened —and would he be able to accept *them*?

Thunder crashed across the sky, interrupting his thoughts. A ship—and only one ship was due! He scrambled off the bed and dashed out into the hall, almost colliding with Tevera. "*Thaylia*!" they said in the same breath.

Andru met them at the bottom of the stairs. "We're going to meet her."

"They won't even let me on board," Kriss protested.

"I have been talking to Nicora for the past half-hour. Though I no longer have the right to call a Council, I have persuaded her to do so. She gave me permission to bring any witnesses I wish, as long as I take responsibility for their behaviour." He looked hard at Kriss. "I can vouch for your behaviour, can't I?"

"Of course!"

"I'll keep him in line," Tevera put in.

"You'd better. We'll only get one chance at this." Andru led them across the common room and out into the dripping street.

A few minutes later, they passed through the spaceport gate and strode across pavement still steaming from the heat of *Thaylia*'s braking rockets. "They'll see me—they must have seen me already!" Kriss said nervously. "Are you sure they'll let us in?"

"They'd better," Andru growled.

Nevertheless, Kriss was relieved to see the ramp down and the hatch open. At least they'd be able to board.

Nicora's bodyguards, Estra and Levit, met them just inside. "The captain expresses surprise at your choice of witnesses, Andru," Levit said, his tone emotionless. "She will allow him to board, but she orders us to guard him closely at all times."

Kriss tensed and started to protest, but Andru placed a friendly hand on his shoulder—so friendly he winced. "Perfectly all right," the big innkeeper said evenly.

"Council is convened on the bridge." Estra and Levit fell in on either side of Kriss.

Kriss hadn't been on the bridge since Tevera had taken him there on their tour of the ship his first full day on board. Aside from the fact that then they had been in zero-G and now they were in the grip of Farr's World's gravity, it mostly hadn't changed: blank, black glassy walls, various control stations, acceleration couches, and a sunken well in the middle around a holographic display.

The biggest difference was that then, there had only been a skeleton crew on duty, and now a crowd of silent, standing figures stood around the central display. Kriss remembered the first Council he had seen, in Andru's. Now he could put names and ranks to each of the men and women present. One or two of them he had even counted as friends, for a time, but he saw nothing friendly in any of their expressions now.

Now, too, he understood better how the Council worked. It was not a democratic body, where a vote would decide matters; it was only a group of advisers for the only one who could decide anything—the captain.

He looked at Nicora, who stood directly across from the elevator, wearing the same black dress she had worn when she'd come to Andru's, minus the silver-lined cape. Her green eyes met his and seemed to burn into his soul. Innocent though he was, he had to look away. He knew she felt he had betrayed her trust, and it hurt. She had saved his life and welcomed him into the Family. Making her despise him was the worst of Rigel's crimes.

His enemy sat at the captain's left. Rigel was gazing at his sister with relief, but then he glanced at Kriss. Their eyes met briefly; then, Rigel looked away. *He looks miserable*, Kriss thought in astonishment.

"You test my patience, Andru," the captain said, her thin voice even harsher than usual. "We have exiled this youth. You did not mention his presence when you contacted me."

"Captain, I dared not."

Her green eyes narrowed. "*Dared* not? Why?"

Looking straight at Rigel, whose head was bowed, Andru said, "I dared not let Vorlick's spy among you know of Kriss's whereabouts."

Only firing a beamer into the centre of the controls could have caused more consternation. Everyone began talking at once—everyone except Rigel. But Nicora held up her hand, and gradually, order returned. Only then did she speak. "This is a serious charge, Andru. Whom do you accuse—and of precisely what crime?"

The innkeeper pointed at Tevera's brother. When he spoke, his words rang like a chisel carving stone. "I accuse

Rigel mal *Thaylia* of selling one of the Family to an avowed enemy—in short, of being in the pay of Carl Vorlick!"

Pandemonium erupted again but died away as Rigel made no effort to defend himself, until everyone was simply staring at him in silence. He raised his pale, strained face then, slowly, as though Farr's World's gravity had suddenly triple.

"I have proof," Andru said softly, but Nicora shook her head.

"I do not think he is denying it," she said, pain in her voice. "Why, Rigel?"

He took a deep, shuddering breath. "For Tevera."

TEVERA FELT as if all the air had vanished from her lungs, as though, planetbound though they were, the bridge had suddenly experienced explosive decompression. Her heart laboured to beat. Out of the corner of her eye, she saw Kriss glance at her, but all her attention was on her brother, her ally and best friend for so many years, her only comfort when their parents had died, now revealed as a traitor to the Family.

"Explain."

Yes, she thought. *Please!*

Rigel swallowed. "When I left Andru's after he—did what he did—Vorlick was waiting for me. He knew I was angry, that I didn't like the idea of my sister getting involved with a worldhugger . . . he tried to convince me to help him get Kriss. He offered me money—a lot of it."

"And you accepted?" Nicora said, eyes and voice cold as space.

"No!" Rigel's shout had a strangled quality, as if he, too, were finding it hard to breathe. "I told him I would never betray the Family for money, not even for this."

"Then, why?"

"He . . . he threatened Tevera." Now he found his breath, taking a deep, shuddering intake of air, and then the words started pouring out of him, as though a dam holding them back had broken. "He said if I didn't help him get Kriss and the touchlyre, he'd find a way to get Tevera, instead—and then he told me in . . . explicit detail . . . what he'd do to her. *Another* worldhugger threatening her. Worldhuggers killed our parents, and I just let them—well, this time, I wouldn't just stand by. I *couldn't.* I wouldn't let *him* hurt her, and I wouldn't let *this* one—" he pointed at Kriss "—hurt her. So, I agreed. I agreed!"

Oh, Rigel, Tevera thought, heart breaking.

"I decided to do everything I could to make Kriss look bad, to make it appear he would never be able to fit into the Family, so that when I—handed him over—you'd think he'd deserted. I almost betrayed myself. That day, in the NLS hold—" He looked at Kriss. "I almost told you I knew you wouldn't be around much longer. But then I caught myself, and I realized I had to be more subtle." He looked back at Nicora. "After that, I treated him strictly according to the Rule. I know Tevera asked you to check up on my treatment of him . . ."

Kriss shot a startled look at Tevera. She'd never told him that.

"And I know you found I was treating him with

complete propriety. But all the time, I was pushing him in little ways, hoping he'd do something foolish when we made planetfall—and he did. He ran off without a pass. I hoped he'd stay gone, and I wouldn't have to go through with the rest of my plan, but no such luck. He came back, and I had to take more direct action. So, I had him kidnapped, and lied about seeing him leaving the field on his own—and then I kidnapped him again, in person this time, and handed him over to Vorlick." His eyes focused on Tevera for the first time: until then, he had avoided her gaze. His voice softened. "I did it for you, Tevera. Mother and Father told me to keep you safe . . . and so I did what I had to." He looked down again. "What I had to."

The unseen chains that had seemed to hold her frozen to the deck fell away, and she ran to her brother and threw her arms around him, sobbing. "I forgive you," she whispered to him. "I forgive you."

He said nothing, but his arms closed around her, and they clung together for a long moment, clung together as they had clung after their parents' death, when it had seemed they were all either one of them had left in the world.

It could not last, but she closed her eyes and willed it to last as long as it could, before what she knew had to happen next became the reality that would change her world forever.

KRISS WATCHED Tevera and Rigel embrace, and his own heart seemed squeezed in a giant fist. *Tevera's right,* he thought. *Rigel's not evil. But he's wrong. Dead wrong. You can't deal with the Devil and not get burned—and if Vorlick isn't the Devil, he'll do until the real item came along.*

Nicora looked at Estra and Levit, still standing watch on Kriss. "Release him," she said, and they stepped back. She turned to Rigel. "Rigel mal *Thaylia*."

He gently disengaged from Tevera's grasp but kept one arm around her shoulders. "Yes, Captain."

"A hundred years ago, the penalty for what you have done would have been death," she said. Her voice cut through the silence like a laser burning metal. "But we have since become merciful. I have no choice but to exile you to—"

"No."

That single word from Andru, heavy as a stone, stopped Nicora's pronouncement. She turned narrowed eyes on him. "*What?*"

He met her gaze steadily. "You *do* have a choice. Captain Nicora, you keep punishing your own people—Kriss, Tevera, Rigel—when the real villain is none of them. Who has been behind all the turmoil? Who has threatened and blackmailed your great-grandchildren and the boy I gave up my Family rights to?"

Nicora's eyes glittered. "Carl Vorlick." But then she looked back at Rigel. "Yet, I cannot simply ignore an offence of this magnitude."

"Nor should you. By all means, discipline Rigel. But exile from the Family?" Andru shook his head. "The penalty outweighs the crime. Believe me—I know. Rigel let his determination to protect his sister and his understandable hatred of worldhuggers override his obedience to Family Rule. His motives were good, however foolish and damaging his actions. Can you exile him for trying to protect Family, Captain Nicora of the Family?"

"You spend far too much time telling me how I should run my ship, Andru," Nicora said. She pressed her lips together and looked from him to Rigel, then back again. "However, your question . . . is pertinent." She faced Rigel again. "Rigel mal *Thaylia*, you are confined to quarters for a month and reduced two steps in rank."

Rigel bowed his head in acceptance, but Nicora wasn't finished.

"The reduction in rank is immediate. However, you will not be confined until we have settled a little unfinished business." She smiled grimly. "With Carl Vorlick."

And then she turned to Kriss, and said softly, "Welcome home, Crewman."

Chapter Thirty-Two

Kriss slammed his fist on the table. "Nothing!"

It was late the next day, and for several hours he, Tevera, and Andru had been sequestered in a conference room one level below *Thaylia*'s bridge, reviewing Family records for data on the planets where the Library had indicated the alien fortress might be found. Andru's plan depended on the possibility that somewhere in those records, which Vorlick could not access, they would find a clue.

But they had found nothing beyond what they already knew: all ten worlds had tropical forests, gravity, and atmosphere within the indicated limits, and were within range of the Farr's World slipspace communications relay.

"These records just aren't detailed enough," Andru said, scowling. "They're all long-range scans. Uninhabited worlds don't interest Family ships, so they never bothered to go in close. The Family is interested in trading, not exploring."

Tevera looked from him to Kriss. "Are we beaten?"

Kriss shrugged wearily, but Andru suddenly stiffened. "Not yet, we're not!" He twisted the interface sensor toward him. "Keyboard," he said, and a virtual keyboard appeared on the table before him. He began tapping, talking as he typed. "You said the Library told you it could only trace your father's communications back as far as the Farr's World slip-space relay. But it *should* have been able to ask the relay's computer exactly where the communication originated from. The reason it couldn't is that our relay is ancient, pre-dating the Library: it's so primitive the Library can't access it properly. But *we* can, with the right codes—and I spaced among these stars for years." He lifted his hands from the glowing keyboard. "I've sent the relay's computer the exact dates for the transmissions your father made to Earth. It should be able to . . . there!"

The screen that took up most of one end of the conference room had been showing images of each of the ten candidate planets. But suddenly, nine of those blue-and-white spheres vanished, and the remaining one swelled to fill the display.

"There's our planet!" Andru said with satisfaction.

Kriss stared at it, then at him. "But . . . that was easy."

Andru snorted. "It *should* have been easy. Instead, we wasted hours waiting for my old brain to finally figure it out."

"And you're sure Vorlick can't access Family records?"

"I'm sure."

Kriss felt as if an enormous weight had just fallen from his shoulders. He grinned. "Then what are we waiting for? Let's tell the captain—"

"—and lift ship!" Tevera finished triumphantly.

But Andru's rugged face, alight with excitement a moment before, suddenly sagged. "You tell the captain. You've no time to lose. I'll go back to my inn."

"Back to the inn?" Kriss stared at him. "But—oh!" Suddenly he remembered—Andru could never space again.

But the innkeeper straightened his broad shoulders, and some of the light came back into his grey eyes. "No matter. Good luck to you both." He went to the door, which slid open; he paused there to look back at Kriss. "One thing I've learned, in my years as part of the Family but separated from it, is this: though the Family's support is useful and welcome, in the end, it's what's inside of you that's important. Remember that." Then he was gone, and the door slid shut again.

"Andru . . ." Kriss took a half-step after him, but Tevera put a hand on his arm.

"Let him go. He's said his good-bye. And when this is over, we'll come back and tell him all about it."

Kriss stared at the closed door, then sighed, turned, and smiled down at her. "Let's go see the captain."

AN HOUR LATER, *Thaylia* roared up from Cascata. Kriss sat in the same acceleration couch in the same launch room as he had on that first thrilling lift-off from Farr's World—and felt strangely out of place. It made him wonder if he could ever truly belong to the Family again.

It made him wonder if he ever had.

He hadn't seen Rigel since the Council and didn't much

want to, but two days into the week-long journey, Rigel floated up to him in one of the rec lounges as he was getting a drinking-bulb of fizz-frenta from the robovendor. Kriss saw Rigel's reflection in the shiny surface of the machine and stiffened, but didn't turn around. "What do you want?" he said neutrally.

"I need to talk to you."

Kriss picked up his drink. "Some other time, maybe." He pushed away from the vendor, trying to brush past, but Rigel grabbed his arm and then grabbed one of the manoeuvring lines strung across the lounge, bringing them both to a stop.

"Sorry," Rigel said. He let go. "But I really do have to talk to you."

Kriss hesitated. "All right," he said finally. "But not here. My cabin."

In that confined space, a few minutes later, Kriss let the bulb of fizz-frenta float free, then turned to Rigel, who had closed the door behind him and oriented himself the same as Kriss, so they were face to face. "So, talk."

"I just want to tell you—I'm sorry." Sweat-beads glittered on Rigel's forehead. One drifted free, a tiny, glittering sphere.

"Sorry? *Sorry*?" Kriss couldn't keep his voice from rising, though at least he kept it under a shout . . . barely. "For driving me out of the Family? For turning me over to Vorlick? For handing the touchlyre to him? Do you really think 'sorry' is *enough*?"

Rigel looked down. "No. But it's all I can offer."

"You said you were trying to protect your sister. Do you realize how much you've hurt *her*?"

"I have some idea." Heat came into Rigel's voice now.

"Look, you don't have to accept my apology. But I had to make it." He turned to go, but Kriss grabbed his shoulder and spun him around again.

"I don't want your apology. I don't want anything from you!" All the anger and frustration of the past weeks welled up in Kriss. "There's no way you can undo the damage. Just stay away from me, you hear me? Just *stay away*!"

Rigel half-raised a clenched fist, then let it drop. He took a deep breath. "All right," he said. "All right." He went out.

Shaking, Kriss turned toward the bed—then grabbed the bulb of fizz-frenta, spun, and hurled it against the closed door. It shattered in a most satisfying manner.

Then, of course, he had to spend the next half-hour chasing down and suctioning up all the little floating globules of fluid . . . but it was totally worth it.

FOUR DAYS LATER, they came out of slipspace above a blue-green planet, shining brightly under the brilliant disk of its star. Three tiny moons spun around it.

As *Thaylia* swung into orbit, the serious work of searching for the alien fortress began. Kriss gripped a handhold on the bridge, watching the scanner console, as the viewscreens began to display details of a part of the surface far below.

Tevera joined him and touched his arm. "It's up to the ship, now," she said softly.

"Maybe the ship could use some help," he replied, and stayed where he was. Tevera laughed and stayed with him.

The hours dragged by. Together they watched the

screens, strapping themselves loosely into the chairs before the controls. Around them beat the heart of the ship; watches changed, system checks were run, repairs were carried out—but Kriss was almost oblivious, wrapped up in his thoughts and in the ever-changing views of the planet's surface, awaiting his first glimpse of the end of the quest he had, in one sense, begun the night Mella died.

One thing he wasn't oblivious to was Tevera's steady presence beside him. She didn't speak, but every now and then, her hand would reach out and find his, and he would turn at the touch of her fingers to see her gentle, reassuring smile.

Ship-day gave way to ship-night. Kriss dozed for a few hours, but long before the morning watch came on duty to replace the night-shift, his eyes were once more locked on the screens, while Tevera slept in the chair beside him, her gentle breathing a comforting sound in the silence of the almost-deserted bridge, her arms and hair floating loosely, waving gently in the currents of air.

Then, in the early hours of the new ship-day, every screen flashed and locked onto a huge, rectangular structure. Tevera grabbed his arm as his heart spasmed painfully in his chest. "That's it," he breathed, unbuckling and floating closer to the console. He stared at the image frozen on the screens. "That's it!" he shouted, and hugged Tevera so hard they both spun wildly, and every face on the bridge turned toward them. Kriss grabbed a handhold before they floated away entirely and stabbed the intercom button Tevera had previously programmed to connect him directly to the captain's quarters. "We've found it!" he said, without preamble.

"I'm coming," Nicora said calmly.

TEVERA STARED AT THE SCREEN, at the mysterious structure Kriss's parents had found, the source of the alien artifact inside the touchlyre, the source of so much trouble . . . and so much joy. She slipped her hand around Kriss's waist. "Now what?" she asked.

"Land, get inside, map it—then get back to Farr's World and lay claim to it in Commonwealth court. Even Vorlick won't dare touch it with the full force of Commonwealth law on our side." She glanced up at his face, but his eyes were locked on the screen. "Think of it, Tevera. This is where my parents found the artifact Dad hid in the touchlyre. You know what it can do. Who knows what else might be down there?"

Tevera turned her own gaze back to the screen, and a worm of doubt entered her heart. They knew nothing about the aliens who had built this place, who had made the strange device hidden inside the musical-instrument disguise crafted by Kriss's father. Kriss had told her how it had destroyed Salazar, emptying his mind, how he had felt its immaterial fingers reaching into his own. It had never been intended to power a musical instrument; his parents had called it the "key artifact." How had the aliens used it? What else might they have left behind in the ruined fortress below?

"Who knows?" she said softly.

Kriss shot her a quizzical look, but she turned away from him as the captain entered the bridge.

Nicora glanced at the screens. She swiped her hand across one, shrinking the image of the fortress so she could study the contours of the land around it. "See that?" she said, pointing to a flat area three kilometres south of the fortress. "That's artificial." She raised her voice. "Pilot!"

"Ma'am!" The pilot on duty, a woman named Scintilla—Tevera didn't know her well; she didn't even know exactly how they were related—faced the captain smartly.

"There's our landing spot. Begin de-orbiting."

"Yes, ma'am." Scintilla turned toward her controls, screens lighting up around her.

Nicora looked at Kriss. "Congratulations," she said.

"No sign of Vorlick," Tevera told her great-grandmother. "We must have beaten him!"

The captain gave her a cool glance. "Perhaps." She nodded to two of the empty acceleration couches in the bridge. "You can ride out the landing here. After that, head down to the main lock. The rest of your team will join you there."

"Yes, ma'am," Tevera said.

She and Kriss strapped themselves in. Nicora took the captain's seat, down close to the holodisplay, not far from the pilot.

"Who'll be in our landing party?" Kriss asked her.

She shrugged. "I don't know. The captain will have chosen whom she thought best."

The descent through the atmosphere was uneventful, and *Thaylia* settled smoothly onto the ancient landing field, the external cameras showing a thin green carpet of plants burning away into ash as they descended.

Tevera felt weight returning to her, a lot of weight, like someone the size of Kriss was sitting on her chest. "Ugh," she said. She waved her hand over a nearby screen, activating it, and with practised pokes, called up a display of external conditions. "Look at that. 1.3 G. Thirty-six degrees Celsius. Ninety percent relative humidity. It's going to be like marching through a sauna wearing lead boots."

"Then we'd better get going," Kriss said.

They unbuckled and made their way to the elevator, riding it down to the main lock, where the other members of the landing party had already assembled.

Yverras met them at the elevator as the door opened. "I'm in overall command," he said without preamble. "But Kriss is in charge of surveying the site." He pointed to a white backpack leaning up against the wall. Tevera knew it contained a set of mapping drones and their controller; she and Kriss had been taught how to use the equipment, carried as a matter of course by Family ships, during the trip from Farr's World. She also knew it was very heavy. So did Yverras. He grinned. "He gets to carry that."

Kriss laughed and went over to the pack. He hadn't yet looked around at the rest of the team.

Tevera had. There was one woman, a stocky, broad-shouldered second cousin of hers named Ellevar whom she'd rarely even spoken to, an older man, a—third, was it?—cousin named Dralos . . .

. . . and her brother, Rigel.

They stared at each other. Tevera waited for Rigel to say something. Perhaps he was waiting for her. In the end, they remained silent, both looking away at the same moment.

When Tevera looked away, her eyes fell on Kriss. He had the backpack on now and didn't look at all happy about the weight. "This thing weighs . . ." he began, then he looked up, at her, then past her—at Rigel.

Another silent, staring moment. Then Kriss deliberately turned away. "Let's go," he said.

"Technically, that's my line," Yverras said dryly. "And I'm not quite ready to say it." From a locker near the elevator, he retrieved what the Family called SPBs, for "strange-planet belts." Each held a beamer, a comm unit, and a canteen. Attached to each comm unit was a wireless earpiece. Tevera fastened her belt, then donned the earpiece. She helped Kriss adjust his and gave him a brief smile. He managed to return it, but it looked to her like it was a struggle.

"All right," Yverras said when everyone had their belts on. "*Now*, let's go."

He activated the lock. The inner door irised open, then the outer hatch swung wide, muggy air whistling in as the slightly higher air pressure of the planet's surface equalized with that of the ship.

The broad ramp slid down to the steaming surface of the field, and Yverras led them down it, Kriss and Tevera right behind him. By the time Rigel, Ellevar, and Dralos joined them, her crewsuit already clung to her damply. She brushed a wet strand of hair from her forehead.

"I'm afraid it's not exactly a resort planet," Kriss said to her apologetically.

She shrugged and gave him a smile. "Our next date will be better."

He grinned, then pointed off to their left. "That way," he told Yverras.

Yverras nodded and turned to the others. "Keep your

beamers ready. We're here to explore, not feed the local fauna."

Everyone laughed except Rigel. Tevera glanced at him as Kriss plunged off the hard surface of the landing field into the tangled greenery.

For some reason, her brother was searching the sky.

Chapter Thirty-Three

The high gravity, the strength-sapping heat and humidity, and the boggy ground—which did indeed cling to their feet like the lead boots Tevera had predicted, although she'd been talking about the gravity, not the mire—seemed to stretch the three kilometres from the landing field to the fortress into a light-year, but at last, the towering, vine-draped trees thinned, and the survey party stepped out into the clearing that surrounded the alien structure.

Kriss had seen his father's pictures of the fortress, but even so, he was unprepared for its astonishing bulk. He stopped dead, along with everyone else, at his first glimpse of the endless, unbroken wall of grey-green stone, flecked with white, like white-caps on the ocean. Above the wall soared the graceful, needle-tipped spires of white stone laced with blue, green, and silver, glittering even in the mist-dimmed sunlight, the central cylindrical tower—and the jewel-like crystal globe that topped it.

"I thought—" Yverras cleared his throat and tried again. "I expected a ruin."

"My father said he could see little damage out here." Kriss started forward, hitching the heavy pack higher on his back. "Let's try to get inside."

"Wait a minute." Yverras activated the transceiver on his belt and motioned for the others to do the same. Then he spoke into the microphone set in his crewsuit collar. "Communications check. Can everyone hear me?"

Kriss heard Yverras's voice in the thick air, but also through the earpiece settled a bit uncomfortably over his left ear. With the others, he nodded.

"*Thaylia*?"

"You're clear," a new voice said in Kriss's ear.

"We have the fortress in sight and are approaching it."

"Understood."

Yverras glanced around. "We'll need someone to watch our back trail. Rigel?"

Rigel nodded and set off into the forest. Kriss frowned after him. He would have preferred to keep Rigel where he could see him. He glanced at Tevera. Her eyes were on her departing brother, as well.

He faced forward again and started toward the fortress wall. Walking in the clearing proved even more difficult than pushing their way through the trees and underbrush of the jungle. The tough, waist-high grass wrapped around their legs like tentacles, leaving them with little breath for talking.

Halfway across the clearing, Yverras stationed Ellevar on a small rise; then, they pressed on in silence, their eyes on the wall looming ever-higher before them. No visible entrance marred its smooth surface. When at last they stood at its base, Kriss reached out and touched it—and snatched his hand back at once. He stared at his fingertips: they looked normal, but they tingled as if they were asleep.

Yverras touched the wall, too, but seemed to feel nothing —or if he did, he didn't react. He pulled his hand back. "How do we get in?"

Kriss wiped his fingers on his leg. "I don't know," he said. "My father said he found an open door . . ." He led the way along the wall to the right, normal feeling gradually returning to his fingers.

Then he noticed something odd and stopped. "Look!" He pointed at the base of the wall, then knelt to get a closer look.

With a groan, Tevera knelt beside him. "Is a good idea?" she said. "I'm not sure I can get up again."

"What is it?" Yverras said, bending over them with Dralos, the remaining member of the landing party.

Kriss pointed to a five-centimetre span of bare dirt between the wall and the first sparse tufts of grass. "It looks like there's some force keeping the building from being overgrown." He stood—not without some difficulty—then helped Tevera to her feet beside him.

"Is it as perfectly preserved inside?" Yverras tilted his head back, looking up at the soaring bulk of the wall.

"No . . . but it isn't exactly a ruin, either. It's . . . well, you'll see." Kriss pushed on through the thick grass. "I wish that force field projected a little further," he grunted.

Panting and sweat-soaked, they finally reached the southeast corner of the structure. Kriss's three companions drank deeply from their canteens while he examined the smooth stone. "This is where my father found the open gate," he said, frowning.

Tevera moved up beside him. "It looks just like the rest of the . . . oh!" She broke off as Kriss touched one of the white blotches in the stone. A diamond-shaped opening three metres high suddenly appeared, the stone sliding silently aside, vanishing into the wall.

Tevera gaped at him. "How did you know . . .?"

"I have no idea," Kriss said. "It was like something inside me told me to do that." He looked down at his fingers, remembering the odd tingling sensation he'd felt when he'd first touched the alien structure. *What's going on?*

"Well?" Yverras said behind him. "Aren't you going in?"

Kriss looked back at him. "You're the leader," he said.

"Maybe," Yverras said cheerfully. "But this is your moment." He grinned. "I'll stay out here with Dralos and keep watch."

Kriss returned his smile. "Thanks." He glanced at Tevera. "Ready?"

"Ready!"

"Right. *Thaylia*, Kriss here. We're going in." He stepped through the open door . . .

. . . into madness.

TEVERA GLANCED BACK over her shoulder just as Kriss entered the fortress, searching the forest, still uneasy about the way Rigel had looked up at the sky before going back along their trail to keep watch. The first she knew of something happening to Kriss was when he fell back against her, hard and heavy, limbs rigid, eyes wide open but staring at nothing, mouth agape. She toppled beneath him. He landed on her legs, pinning her. "Help!" she cried. "Yverras! Dralos!"

Her cousin pulled her out from under Kriss. Dralos dragged him back out through the fortress's open door. Tevera didn't stand, instead crawling on her hands and knees to Kriss's side. He was breathing in short, ragged gasps. His eyes had closed, but his eyelids twitched madly. His mouth worked aimlessly. His hands clenched and unclenched. "Kriss!" she shouted. She grabbed one of his hands in hers and it squeezed painfully tight, holding on to her as if for dear life. "Kriss!"

She looked up at Yverras. "What's wrong with him?" she choked out.

"I don't know," Yverras said. "We'd better get him back to the . . ."

"Ungh!" Kriss groaned. His back arched. And then, suddenly, he relaxed, and his eyes opened.

"Kriss!" Tevera flung her arms around him.

KRISS FELT his limbs snap rigid, felt himself toppling backward, but he didn't feel himself hit the ground—because he wasn't there anymore. Instead, he drifted in chaos. Unintelligible voices whispered and roared. Powerful emotions not his own tore through him—anger, hate, fear, and joy.

Light exploded, shattered into a thousand colours, faded into darkness. Thunder rumbled, became clanging bells, their horrible discords echoing away into the indistinct distance. Odours foul and fair choked him, tastes delectable and nauseating ran across his tongue, pain and ecstasy and fiery heat ripped through him in rapid succession.

He screamed, or whispered, or sang, or made no sound at all, he wasn't sure . . .

. . . and then, he fought back, struggling in the confusion that had swallowed him, pushing back the terrifying hallucinations, battling to find himself in the boiling storm of false sensation.

Suddenly, all of it was gone. He opened his eyes to see Tevera, pale-faced and teary-eyed, kneeling beside him, holding his left hand in both of hers, Yverras and Dralos behind her.

Tevera flung her arms around him and hugged him tightly. He hugged her back, then she pulled away, rubbed tears from her cheeks, and said, "Are you . . . are you all right?"

He sat up and looked around. They were just outside the wall: someone must have dragged him there. The diamond-shaped door mocked him. "I don't know. What happened?"

Yverras answered. "You took one step through the gate and went down like you'd been clubbed. We dragged you back out."

"What's going on?" demanded the voice from the ship.

"We're all right," Kriss reported. He struggled to his feet, taking deep breaths of the hot, wet air, then looked hard at Tevera. "You didn't see or hear or . . . feel . . . anything when you came in after me?"

"Nothing. You just toppled." She gave him a shaky smile. "On me."

He winced. "Sorry." He turned to Yverras and Dralos. "What about you?"

They both shook their heads.

Tevera gripped his arm almost fiercely. "What did *you* feel?"

He stared at the gate. "It felt like . . . like the touchlyre. Only a thousand—a million—times stronger. It filled my head with . . . everything. Sound. Light. Images. Sensations."

"But the touchlyre doesn't make you hallucinate," Tevera said. Then she hesitated. "Does it?"

"Not like this, but . . . when I'm playing the touchlyre, when it really takes hold of me, I do . . . experience things. Things that have happened to me, as clearly as if I'm living them again. Sometimes, things that have never happened."

Tevera looked at the door. "Then, this is definitely where your father found whatever is inside the touchlyre." She frowned. "But if it's that powerful . . . why didn't *I* feel anything? I've heard you play. I've felt the touchlyre reach into my mind, too."

"As have I," Yverras pointed out.

"I don't think . . . I don't think it's the same," Kriss said. "You've experienced what the touchlyre *projects*, but what I feel is the touchlyre reaching inside me, pulling things out of me. Only my father and I have ever played the touchlyre, ever felt that." *And maybe Vorlick*, he thought unwillingly. "My father spoke about earth-shattering power in this fortress. I didn't understand before . . ." He looked up at the towering wall. "Now, I do. My father called the touchlyre the 'key artifact.' Not 'key' as in 'central' or 'important.' The touchlyre is *literally* a key—the key to this fortress, to controlling it. And Vorlick has it! If he finds this place, he'll be able to seize its power."

"To what end?" Yverras said. "So, it's powerful. So what? It's on a little-frequented planet in a barely populated backwater of the galaxy. What threat could it be?"

"It's not this fortress that's important, it's the technology the touchlyre and the fortress represent," Kriss said. "Think about it. Literal thought control. The ability to read the thoughts and feelings in people's minds—and, vice versa, to *implant* thoughts and feelings in others. The ability to manipulate entire populations, maybe. What do you think Vorlick might do with *that*? Or, worse, whomever he might sell it to?"

From his companions' expressions, he could see they realized the implications. "What do we do?" Tevera asked, subdued.

Kriss took a deep breath. "Just what we set out to do. We go inside, map the fortress, and lay claim to it as a Family discovery . . . and hope that's enough to deter Vorlick."

"But you can't even get in the door!" Tevera protested.

"I think I can, now that I know what to expect. I learned to control the touchlyre . . ."

"You already said you can't control this fortress!"

"I don't need to. I just need to shut it out. And I think I can do that." He smiled at her crookedly. "But be ready to catch me again in case I can't."

She scowled at him.

"Kriss, it could be dangerous," Yverras said. "Are you sure . . .?"

"My parents didn't let the danger stop them."

Yverras searched his face. Kriss met his gaze squarely,

and finally, he sighed. "All right. I just hope you know what you're doing."

Kriss relaxed a little. "So do I. Let's find out."

Tevera moved up beside him and took his hand. He looked down at her. Her smile was every bit as crooked as his had been. "Let's find out together."

His heart swelled. He squeezed her hand, then, with her fingers laced in his, walked back toward the gate. Yverras and Dralos followed close behind.

This time, as he stepped through, he was prepared for what would come. The blast of mental energy struck him with the same force, but though he staggered, he kept control, focusing fiercely on his own sense of self, imagining he was playing a much larger and more powerful touchlyre. To his relief, he was able to relegate the sensory chaos to the fringes of his mind. Ghostly images danced briefly across his eyes, and there was a distant roaring and muttering in his ears, but he thought he could function.

He wrinkled his nose at an imagined scent of corruption, then took a deep breath and smiled down into Tevera's anxious face. "I'm all right. Let's get on with it."

TEVERA SEARCHED KRISS'S FACE. He seemed more or less normal at first glance—but then his nostrils flared, and his mouth twitched. He swallowed, his Adam's apple bobbing. "You're sure?"

He nodded, hard—maybe a little *too* hard. "I'm sure."

"Dralos, stand watch just outside the wall," Yverras ordered. "I'll stay inside, by the gate."

"Yes, sir." Dralos disappeared outside. Yverras stationed himself by the door, keeping a close watch on Kriss.

But Kriss, Tevera saw, had eyes only for the fantastic interior of the fortress. Still holding her hand, he started down the broad path of glassy black stone on which they found themselves.

At first glance, it seemed to Tevera that time had stood still inside the wall: every bit of glass and metal shone as clean, new, and strong as though made the day before instead of millennia in the past. But then, her eyes were drawn to the great craters pitting the black streets, the shattered domes and scarred walls, the charred, skeletal remnants of trees.

She glanced up at Kriss. "War?"

"War," he said. "Or so my father believed. But he also said . . . it's not as bad as it looks."

Doubtful at first, Tevera understood what he meant as they penetrated further into the fortress. The farther in they went, the less damage she saw. At the fortress's centre, four tall spires with needle-sharp points formed a quadrangle around a taller, thicker tower, a cylinder of white stone rising a hundred metres into the air, topped by a globe of crystal. The spires and that central tower, surely the most important buildings in the fortress—maybe its whole reason for existence—stood untouched. The outlying smaller buildings and the streets had taken the brunt of the attack, as if whatever force guarded the towers had been taxed to the limit and unable to spare any protection for anything of lesser value.

Kriss unslung his pack and thumped it on the ground. "Oof," he said. "Glad to get that off my back." He stretched, then knelt to open it. "Ah!" he yelped, jerking his hand back.

Tevera blinked at him. "What was that?"

He shook his fingers as if they stung. "Nothing," he said. "It was just . . . for a second . . . it felt red-hot. Never mind." He pulled out a metal case and opened it, revealing four small drones. From deeper in the pack, he pulled out a folded-up control console. He opened it and touched the screen, which lit into four quadrants. He touched another control, and the drones unfurled rotors and rose smoothly into the air. Then he grunted as if something had punched him. "Ungh. I'm not sure how long I can stay in here. *Thaylia*, are you ready to receive data?" The ship didn't answer. "*Thaylia*?"

Tevera tried. "*Thaylia*, come in. Do you hear me, *Thaylia*?" She had no more success than Kriss. She looked at Kriss. "The wall?"

Kriss nodded. "We'll have to record the information and beam it to them later."

He touched the controls again, activating a pre-set program. The drones rose higher and began crisscrossing the fortress, recording every detail: later, a complete model of the site could be recreated in virtual reality. *Kriss's father had this technology*, Tevera thought. *What happened to his recordings?*

She'd talked about it with Kriss during the journey here. Neither of them had had an answer, but Kriss's best bet was that his father had destroyed the detailed recordings in case they held clues to the fortress's whereabouts.

"Now let's take our own look," Kriss suggested.

They carried on down the black street, past the needle-sharp spires, to the central tower. There, they came upon something that clearly had *not* belonged to the alien builders —a bright-orange plastic drink container. "My parents',"

Kriss said. He stared around. So did Tevera. There was nothing else to indicate humans had ever been there.

"They left in a hurry," he said slowly. "They never would have contaminated a site this way if it wasn't an emergency." He looked down at the container. "Neither will I." He bent down and picked up the container, shoving it into one of the pockets of his crewsuit. Then his fist clenched, though whether from some emotional reaction or some strange sensation engendered by the alien fortress, she had no way of knowing.

"Where did they find the touchlyre?" she asked him.

Kriss pointed up the tower. "There—at the very top, in a chamber with windows all around it. My father said he felt a strong urge to climb up there the moment he saw the tower . . ." He looked down at Tevera suddenly. "I wonder if the touchlyre were somehow calling him?"

Tevera shook her head. "I'm almost glad Vorlick has that thing. The way you talk, it's like . . . like it has a mind of its own. It scares me."

"Sometimes it scares me, too," Kriss said slowly. "But it's also done so many beautiful things . . . it brought us together, remember?" He looked around the alien fortress. "If Mella had known what it was really capable of, she would never have passed it on to me."

"Kriss! Tevera! Come back! Hurry!" Yverras's frantic shouting filled Tevera's earpiece. She exchanged a startled look with Kriss, then together they dashed back along the shattered street to the gate. Yverras waved to them the moment he saw them, then plunged out through the diamond-shaped door.

"I'm . . . hearing . . . things . . . again," Kriss gasped as they pounded along the black pavement. "Roaring . . ."

"No . . . hallucination," Tevera gasped back. "I . . . hear it, too . . ."

They burst out into the clearing, where Yverras and Dralos stood staring at the sky. "What's wrong?" Kriss choked out.

"Incoming ship," Yverras said. "It won't answer our hails." He pointed into the milk-white sky, as a point of fire as bright as the mist-shrouded sun appeared. "There!"

The brilliant dot grew swiftly into a blazing tail of white flame, and the shape that rode it became clear.

With a roar that echoed from the fortress wall like baleful laughter, Vorlick's *Gemfire* settled beside *Thaylia* . . .

. . . and Tevera felt ill, remembering Rigel searching the sky.

He's betrayed us, she thought. *Again.*

Chapter Thirty-Four

At the sight of Vorlick's golden ship, Kriss knew they had lost. *Gemfire* was heavily armed; *Thaylia*, though she carried weapons, could not hope to stand against the other ship's firepower. They could do nothing to stop Vorlick from taking the fortress.

He remembered how Rigel had stared up at the sky, and anger filled him. "Rigel," he spat. "He's betrayed us." He glanced at Tevera and could tell by the look of horror on her face that she had already come to that conclusion.

"We don't know that," Yverras snapped. He touched the comm control on his belt. "Rigel!" he called. "Stay near the trail. If any of Vorlick's men come along, pick them off. Understood?"

No reply.

"Rigel?"

Still nothing.

Yverras glanced at Kriss, then turned to Dralos. "All right. Dralos, you go back along our trail. Stay under cover, but don't hesitate; if you see any of Vorlick's men, shoot. If you see Rigel . . . tell him his communicator is out."

"That's not—" Kriss began, but Yverras cut him off.

"Never mind that now. Vorlick's here. That's all that matters. We can worry about how he found us later—if we survive." He touched his comm control again. "Ellevar!"

"I hear you," the woman responded in Kriss's ear.

"Stay put and stay covered. If anybody gets past Dralos, they're your responsibility. I'll stay here by the gate as a last line of defence."

"What about us?" Tevera demanded. "I can use a beamer!"

"So can I!" Kriss said, although he never had.

"You may have to. But for now, your job is to make sure those recordings get made. That's what we're here for. If we escape, they'll be our proof to the Commonwealth that we were here first."

A new voice suddenly crackled across the communicators. "Greetings to the Family ship *Thaylia*! Greetings, Kriss Lemarc!"

Kriss reached for his communicator to reply, Tevera grabbed his arm. "No!" she said sharply. "It's the captain's place to answer. Remember, you're Family again."

Vorlick called for him again.

A familiar voice replied, cold and stern. "This is Captain Nicora of *Thaylia*. I'm surprised you had the courage to face the Family again, Vorlick."

If the jibe registered, Vorlick's sardonic voice didn't reveal it. "Ah, Captain Nicora. It's been a long time since that night on Farr's World. Things have changed."

"I fail to see how. Kriss Lemarc is still Family."

"But I don't need him anymore, Captain. I have the alien artifact, and here we both are, at the site where it was found. You are quite incapable of preventing me from taking it."

"This site is claimed by the Family. Under Commonwealth law—"

"This site isn't claimed by anybody until the proper documentation is in the hands of the nearest Commonwealth court, Captain, and no court is going to be receiving anything from you."

"The Family will—"

"The Family is not as powerful or omnipresent as you like to pretend—or as certain of my more superstitious employees believe. Its reputation protected you on Farr's World; it will not protect you from me or those with me now, on an uninhabited world with no Commonwealth presence. The Family will never know what happened here. You will simply have vanished in space, like so many other ships." He laughed. "Perhaps they'll make a song about you."

"Others know where we are."

"I assume by 'others' you mean Andru of Farr's World and that serving wench he's taken up. Neither will live an hour past the time I return there."

Kriss pulled free of Tevera's arm and slapped his comm control. "Stay away from them!" he shouted.

Instantly Vorlick's voice crackled back. "So, young Lemarc, you *are* listening?" He paused. "And not transmitting from *Thaylia*. I do believe you've started exploring without me . . ."

Another voice suddenly drowned him out. "Yverras, this is on the emergency override frequency," their shipboard monitor said. "Vorlick's sending an armed party down his ramp—five . . . no, six."

". . . trespassing on my newly acquired property," Vorlick was saying. "I'm afraid I'm out of patience."

Yverras killed his comm unit and turned to Kriss and Tevera. "Get back inside. And close the door, if you can."

"I won't—" Tevera began.

"You'll obey orders!" Yverras snapped; then his voice softened. "I'll hide in the grass just outside. They won't even know I'm there until it's too late. Now move!"

Kriss hesitated a moment longer, then said, "Good luck!", grabbed Tevera's hand, and dashed back toward the fortress. As they passed through the diamond-shaped door, the sudden impact of the fortress's mental energies smashed Kriss to his knees—but he managed to stagger back to his feet, turn, and slap a white block like that on the outside. The door closed.

He turned again and sagged back against the wall, rubbing his temples with the heels of his hands. He had to hold out—he had to keep control!

One of the drones zipped by overhead, still busily mapping.

"Let's go!" Tevera tugged at his hand.

"Where?" he said blearily. "All we can do now is wait—"

"Maybe, maybe not. But down here, we'll never know what's happening." She pointed at the central tower. "If we can get up there, we'll be able to see the ships and the clearing. Our communicators might even work."

Kriss nodded. "I should have thought of that," he muttered. He took a step, then staggered as a sharp, phantom pain stabbed his side.

"Looks to me like you've got all you can do to think at all," Tevera commented. "But then, what else is new?"

He shot her a surprised look, saw her grin, and, despite everything, had to laugh. He squeezed her hand. "All right, then," he said. "Lead me up the garden path."

"With pleasure."

Halfway to the tower, between one step and the next, he blacked out. He came to an instant later to find himself on his hands and knees, shards of shattered pavement digging painfully into his palms, Tevera tugging at his shoulders. "Kriss? Kriss, are you all right?"

"No," he said. "But what difference does it make?"

"I never thought—" Tevera looked up at the tower. "What if that happens while you're climbing?"

He staggered upright, clinging to her. "I won't let it," he said, as empty a promise as he'd ever made. He suspected she knew it. But she said nothing, and with her supporting him, they stumbled on.

To his surprise, though, the mental pressure actually seemed to ease slightly as they neared the tower, and he was able to concentrate on the task of circling the white stone wall and feeling it carefully. "Here!" he said suddenly, and pushed. A large, diamond-shaped section moved inward and slid aside.

His vision blurred as a new blast of mental energy struck him like a blow between the eyes, spinning him around. He slid to the ground, back to the tower. His stomach churned, and he twisted to the side and threw up everything he had eaten that day.

Tevera touched his shoulder. "Kriss?"

He coughed and spat, then forced himself upright,

bracing his back against the wall. His head spun for a moment, then steadied. He took his canteen from his belt, rinsed his mouth, and spat again. He replaced the canteen and wiped his mouth with the back of his sleeve. "I'm all right," he lied. "Let's go." He turned and stepped through the tall portal.

He expected darkness but instead found an eerie, greenish light. A steep, narrow-stepped stairway made of the same white stone as the outside of the tower climbed up into dimness, spiralling around the tower's central cylindrical core.

He realized something, then. The force that had hit him so hard when he'd opened the door into the tower was different from what he had felt outside. There, he'd had the sense of dozens of mental forces pushing and pulling. In here, there was only a single force prying at his mental defences, as strong as, or stronger than, all the others combined.

Phantom fingers, he thought suddenly. *Phantom fingers* . . . like the touchlyre's, but stronger, searching his mind for something and, failing to find it, setting off random sensory impressions as it rummaged around.

Tevera touched his shoulder, and he shook his head sharply, trying to clear it, then smiled at her. "I'll go first. If I fall—catch me."

"Sure," she said staunchly.

Kriss studied the stairs. They were too steep to climb normally, and each step was too narrow to place his whole foot on, even at the outside of the spiral. Whoever . . . whatever . . . had built them hadn't been human. They'd have to climb the stairway more like a ladder. "Right, then," he said, took a deep breath and, using both hands and feet, started the ascent.

They slowly spiralled up the tower. Kriss concentrated on one step at a time, not thinking about how high they had come or how much farther they might have to go. Between the awkward shape of the steps and the higher gravity, it was hard enough to just keep moving. His shins and forearms felt on fire.

Worse, as he climbed, the assault on his senses intensified. He thought he knew the cause, now, but that didn't help when his vision suddenly filled with fireworks or his hands and feet went cold and numb.

Abruptly all his senses vanished utterly, and his mind drifted free, frozen with the horrible thought that he could be falling, crashing down the steps, Tevera tangled with him, and wouldn't even know he'd lost his grip until they both lay crushed at the bottom of the tower.

But that terror passed as swiftly as it had come, and he found he was still clinging to the stone. He risked a glance behind. Tevera peered up at him, her anxious face drawn and pale in the eerie glow. He wanted to smile at her reassuringly but couldn't quite manage it. Instead, he looked up again, into the dim green murk. How much farther?

Only a few more light-years, he thought grimly, forcing his arms and legs to pull him upward again, but in fact, just thirty steps later, he emerged through another diamond-shaped opening into a circular room, and crouched trembling on his hands and knees for a moment before turning to help Tevera through the entrance.

Her hands shook as she pushed her sweat-slicked hair back from her eyes. "Are we at the top?"

"We can't be. There are windows . . ." He looked around and saw a ladder, its rungs absurdly widely spaced, climbing to another diamond-shaped opening, this one in the high ceiling. "Up there," he said, and led the way.

A single push dislodged the upper door, and brilliant sunlight streamed into the dim room, bringing with it a blast of air as hot and humid as though from a greenhouse, but as deliciously fresh to Kriss as though he were surfacing from a long underwater dive. He gulped two or three lungfuls, then climbed through the opening, Tevera close behind. He almost fell back on top of her as the mental pressure redoubled, but he managed to hold on and push back enough to remain in control. Only then did he look around.

They stood in a circular room, three metres or so in diameter. A thin pole of blue metal rose from the floor through a hole in the transparent roof, supporting the crystal globe that capped the tower. Beside the pole rose a glassy pedestal, a perfect cylinder, except that on top, instead of being flat, it had a round indentation. Kriss put his hands into that depression. "Here," he breathed. "This is where my father found the touchlyre's artifact—right here." He stared around the room, at the eight glassless windows that pierced the thin white walls. The hot breeze swept cleanly through the space, and he imagined his father standing exactly where he stood now, only a few years his senior, the breeze ruffling his hair like in the picture the Library had shown him.

TEVERA LOOKED AT KRISS, standing in the same place his father had once stood, in the very place where the alien artifact that had brought them together had been found, and felt a moment of pure happiness that his quest for family, for understanding, had brought him so far.

But then she forced her mind back to the present. "And Vorlick has it now," she said, perhaps more harshly than she meant to because his head snapped around to look at her. She managed a small smile to try to soften her words, then went to the edge of the room and looked across the bright-green forest, holding onto one of the thin pillars between the windows. Kriss joined her. Together, they gazed at the two ships glittering on the open landing field—and then Tevera's eyes were drawn to something nearer. "There!" she cried, pointing with her free hand as bright blue flashes lit a section of the forest near the clearing. She touched her comm unit. "Yverras, we see beamer fire," she said. "Is that Rigel?"

"No," Yverras said over their communicators, voice grim. "That's Dralos. No one has seen Rigel."

Tevera's hand tightened on the slim pillar. Kriss said nothing.

Another beamer flashed in the jungle, and a horrible scream, cut suddenly short, echoed over the communicators.

"Dralos," Yverras said. "Report!"

No answer.

Tevera felt sick.

"Ellevar!" Yverras snapped. "Be ready."

"Acknowledged."

Then a new voice crackled in their ears. "Vorlick, this is Rigel. Let me board."

Tevera gasped.

"I knew it!" Kriss snarled.

Yverras's only comment was a wordless growl.

The shipboard monitor spoke, his voice icy. "Vorlick is letting Rigel into his ship. And Yverras, we have a new problem. Our sensors indicate Vorlick is training his weapons on us. Stay away from the ship. Our screens will hold for a while, but there's going to be a lot of stray energy—"

Static drowned his voice as Vorlick fired.

Thick red beams leaped across the few hundred metres separating the starships, and instantly *Thaylia*'s defensive fields flared into life, radiating the energy away in sheets of blinding, blue-white flame. What vegetation *Thaylia*'s landing had left on the field burned instantly away, and the nearest jungle trees began to shrivel and char. Thick grey smoke billowed up but couldn't hide the blinding radiance surrounding the Family ship.

Four of Vorlick's men, armed with beamer rifles, entered the clearing, then flung themselves into the grass as Ellevar opened fire, her beamer ray an insubstantial blue flicker compared to the awesome firepower of the *Gemfire*. Tevera drew her own beamer, but then shoved it back in her holster. "Too far," she said bitterly. "We should have carried rifles like Vorlick's men." She raised her eyes to the pyrotechnics surrounding the two ships. "*Thaylia* can't last more than a few minutes. Her power reserves must be plummeting. And once they're gone . . ."

Her voice choked off, but her mind relentlessly provided the gruesome details. The screens would fail. The red beams would rip into the *Thaylia* sleek silver skin, which would flare and run molten. The air inside would superheat, bursting out through the sagging metal, and the people inside . . . her Family! . . . would burn alive: men, women, and children.

She pressed her face into Kriss's chest, unable to watch any longer.

KRISS TIGHTENED his arm around Tevera as she turned to him, away from the horror unfolding on the landing field.

He didn't look away, but the awful scene was blotted out momentarily by the memory of another: Nicora, ancient, tiny, but undaunted, facing down Vorlick's henchmen to protect him. In minutes, she would die, like his parents, like Mella, like everyone he had *ever* called family . . .

For the first time, he *wanted* to wield the touchlyre as a weapon rather than a musical instrument. If he had it, he could use it to hurl his rage at Vorlick as he had at Salazar. He pictured Vorlick's face going slack, his eyes dull, as the touchlyre's hidden alien artifact forged Kriss's fury into a bright, deadly sword of revenge . . .

. . . the touchlyre . . .

Was he imagining it? *No!* Unmistakably, clear but faint, he could feel the familiar mental touch, a thousand times weaker than the force pressing on him from the tower, but utterly distinct from it, like the ringing of a silver bell in the midst of a thunderstorm.

But *how . . .?* It was locked on Vorlick's ship!

He stared across the jungle at the golden vessel pouring destruction into *Thaylia*, then glanced behind him at the metal rod rising to the crystal globe above. *The tower!* he thought. *It's like an amplifier, boosting the signal from the touchlyre . . . it must sense the presence of the 'key artifact.' It's reaching out to it . . .*

But even though he could feel it, could he *control* the touchlyre at such a distance?

He strove to pour his hatred and fury into that tenuous link, to make the touchlyre strike at Vorlick, but everything seemed locked in his own head. He could sense the touchlyre, but he couldn't make use of it.

Of course not, some inner voice said. *You've raised a mental shield against the tower. It's blocking the touchlyre, too.*

But if he lowered that shield, the sensory chaos would overwhelm him. He'd be helpless, unable to control the touchlyre even if he reached it. He spat a curse.

A bright line of fire slashed past, centimetres from Tevera's turned back.

TEVERA FELT a sudden blast of heat behind her and knew at once what it was: beamer fire. She pulled free of Kriss's arm, shoved him away from the window, grabbed her own beamer, and spun back.

From here, she could see down into the clearing they had crossed as they approached the tower. Ellevar had been lying prone at the top of a small rise. She still lay prone, but her arm was outstretched and motionless now, and smoke rose from her body. A crumpled figure at the edge of the clearing, presumably the man who had just fired at the tower, bore mute testimony to Ellevar's marksmanship, but now the remaining three of Vorlick's men were using that same hill as cover from which to shoot at Yverras—and one of them was sighting on her.

"Ellevar!" Tevera cried, and even though she knew it was useless, took aim and fired.

Her lower-power beam dispersed into uselessness in the thick air before it reached the hill.

The return beam did not.

She saw a blue flash, felt the beginning of the worst agony she had ever experienced, smelled burning meat . . .

. . . and then, mercifully, her world went black.

———

BEFORE KRISS COULD PULL Tevera back or even cry out, blue fire ripped through the chamber and into Tevera's side, making a horrible, sizzling hiss. Without a sound, she crumpled to the floor and lay still, wisps of smoke rising from her body.

Time stopped. Kriss screamed, or thought he did, but heard nothing; for in the horror of that moment, his shield against the fortress crashed down, and simultaneously, his will flashed along the link with the touchlyre—and the powerful force that had been trying to break into his mind succeeded.

Though it was three kilometres away, he sensed the tortured shriek of the touchlyre as it reacted to his blazing emotion and struck out at his enemies. Instantly, the *Gemfire*'s weapons fell silent.

But Kriss hardly realized what he had accomplished. A powerful echo of his rage flashed back along the link with the touchlyre, and the fortress seized it.

Everything drained from him. All his anger, his hatred, his fear, and his grief flowed into the touchlyre and from it into the fortress, until, suddenly, he had no more to give. He collapsed limply beside Tevera, his spirit numb, while the echoes of his own emotions howled around him like a hurricane.

Light kindled in the crystal globe high above, barely visible at first but swelling until it seared his eyes. The pain stirred him to motion, and he crawled to the edge of the room to stare out over the burning jungle at the two silent ships.

Lightning flickered across the scene. He blinked, uncertain where it had come from, then saw it again.

From the four towers forming a quadrangle around the central one where he slumped, blue-white beams of energy streamed into the globe above him.

In the clearing, Vorlick's men ran for cover, Yverras's beamer lashing at their heels. They cast sharp shadows against the tall grass in the light of the crystal globe, which now outshone the sun. The pale sky seemed darkened to twilight in its glare.

Abruptly the streamers of power ended, and for a moment, a deadly stillness hung over the jungle. Then a single dart of energy from the globe of crystal shrieked through the smoky air—and *Gemfire* exploded in a ball of white flame that swept outward and vanished, leaving only empty, blackened pavement, and smoking, fallen trees.

As the shock wave shook the tower, Kriss crawled back to Tevera's side, lay his head on her breast, and let darkness claim him.

Chapter Thirty-Five

Tevera woke in a soft bed and, for a moment, gazed blankly at a white metal ceiling. Then memory rushed over her . . . and relief. She was in *Thaylia*'s sickbay, rigged in its planetside mode, which meant *Thaylia* hadn't been destroyed . . . but how? What had happened? Why wasn't she dead?

Why wasn't everyone dead?

She turned her head, and to her surprise, found her great-grandmother seated in a chair by the bed. "Captain . . .?" she croaked.

"I was told you would be waking," Nicora said, a rare smile crinkling her face.

"What happened? Where's Kriss."

Nicora's smile faded. "He's in another room," she said. "Unconscious."

"Was he shot, too?" Tevera remembered the flash of blue, the unbearable pain, the darkness. She swallowed. "How badly is he hurt?"

"We can't find anything wrong with him," Nicora said. "But we don't know what happened in his head."

"What happened in his head? When?"

"He destroyed *Gemfire*," Nicora said. "He saved us all. He activated the fortress's weapons. But he hasn't woken up since."

"I have to see him!" Tevera tried to sit up, but pain flared in her side and the room spun. She fell back again.

"Later," Nicora said. She put a hand on Tevera's arm. "We'll tell you if there's any change," she said softly. "In the meantime, worry about your own healing."

Easier said than done, Tevera thought.

And then, a new, horrible thought struck her. "Rigel," she said. "Rigel was on *Gemfire*!"

Nicora's hand tightened. "He's dead, Tevera. I'm so sorry."

The pain in her side suddenly seemed like nothing at all compared to the pain in her heart. "He betrayed us," she whispered. "He must have told Vorlick how to find this planet, gotten a message to him somehow . . ."

"No," Nicora said. "So I thought . . . so we all thought . . . but we were wrong."

Tevera turned her head to her great-grandmother, her grief undiminished, but now with a touch of hope lightening its gloom. "But . . ."

"Rigel didn't tell Vorlick which planet we were on," Nicora said. "Most likely, Vorlick connected the dots through the Farr's World slipspace relay the same way Andru did. But when Rigel saw *Gemfire* land, he saw an opportunity to make amends.

"He convinced Vorlick to let him board. I suspect he

claimed to know an important secret about the fortress, a secret he could sell.

"In a sense, it was true—he knew that the touchlyre was a controlling device, the 'key artifact,' because he'd heard you say so. But he had no intention of telling Vorlick that.

"I don't know how he reached it—no one will ever know. But while Vorlick was concentrating on destroying us, Rigel stole the touchlyre from under his nose. We saw him stagger out of the *Gemfire*. Moments later, the weapons stopped firing. And moments after that, the fortress destroyed Vorlick's ship." Nicora's own eyes filled with tears at that moment. "We found your brother just inside the jungle. He was . . . too close to the explosion to survive."

Tevera's own tears suddenly overflowed as she saw her grief echoed in the captain's eyes. For a long time, they wept together, great-granddaughter and great-grandmother, over a death in the Family.

KRISS WOKE.

He stared up at a blank metal ceiling. There was a tube in his arm. Everything was white. *What happened?*

And then he remembered. "Tevera!" he cried.

"Hi," said a voice from his right. He twisted his head, and there she was: in a wheelchair, pale, but very much alive, Captain Nicora standing beside her.

Kriss wanted to sit up, wanted to leap out of bed and run to her, but his muscles refused to countenance the suggestion. All he could do was lie there and drink in the wonderful sight of Tevera smiling at him.

She rolled the wheelchair close enough to lean forward and squeeze his hand, all the while giving him a stern look. "You're to stay put until you're fully recovered," she said. Then the smile came back. "At least now, we know you *will* recover."

"I thought you were dead," he said to her. "I was *sure* you were dead!"

"You came closer to dying than I did," she told him. She paused, then added with a wry grin, "Okay, maybe not. If the beam that hit me had been ten centimetres to the left, we wouldn't be having this conversation. But we are." She squeezed his hand again, then released it and sat back in the wheelchair. "When I came to, they said you hadn't moved since they found us, and no one seemed to know what was wrong. So . . . what happened to you?"

Kriss thought back to those final, terrible seconds. "I was trying to contact the touchlyre," he said slowly. "I could feel it, but I couldn't reach out to it without opening up to the fortress. But then you were shot, and I lost control . . . and somehow, through me, the touchlyre and the fortress . . . connected. The touchlyre struck at Vorlick and his crew just like I wanted . . . and then, through me, it must have passed along that same command to the fortress."

He swallowed. "I think . . . I think what I felt, when we first went through the wall into the fortress, was the fortress's . . . brain, I guess . . . searching for instructions, awaiting my commands. It could sense me, but I couldn't control it with my mind alone. Once I reconnected to the touchlyre, though . . . the 'key artifact' . . . well, earth-shattering, or at least ship-shattering, power, just like my father said.

But I was . . . the weak link in the circuit, I guess. So, I burned out. Like a fuse."

He shook his head. "Maybe Dad experienced something like that, too, though he didn't put anything about that into his journals. Maybe that's what made him realize he had to keep the fortress and the artifact out of Vorlick's hands. The touchlyre's ability to project my emotions when I used it as a musical instrument . . . that's nothing but a side-effect. The artifact inside the touchlyre was really the control mechanism for an alien weapons system."

"Maybe, maybe not," said Nicora, surprising him. "We know nothing about the race that built the fortress. In human history, weapons have often been objects of art as well as killing devices. Perhaps the artifact in your touchlyre was meant to facilitate the making of beauty as well as the destruction of enemies."

"Well, we'll never know now," Kriss said sadly. "The touchlyre is gone. It was on Vorlick's ship."

Tevera shook her head. "That's what I thought, too. But . . ." She glanced at the captain.

"You know Rigel went aboard the *Gemfire*," Nicora said.

Kriss nodded, anger surging in him again. "He contacted Vorlick . . ."

"No," Tevera said. "He didn't."

Kriss stared at her. "What?"

"He went on board Gemfire to retrieve something," Nicora said. "He brought it out just before the weapons stopped firing and you . . . did what you did." She bent down, and from beneath Kriss's bed, lifted a battered, scorched case.

Kriss gasped. "the touchlyre!"

Nicora put it on Tevera's lap. She unlatched the case and lifted out the instrument. Feeling suddenly stronger, he struggled into a sitting position and held out his arms. Tevera leaned forward and handed him the touchlyre.

He held it, caressed its smooth black wood, touched the silver strings . . . and very carefully did not touch the copper plates. Impossibly, it seemed undamaged. "That's how I connected to it," he said wonderingly. "When Rigel brought it into the open, it reached out for me . . ." He turned to look at Tevera. "Rigel tried to apologize to me, and I wouldn't let him. Is he . . . ?"

"He's dead," Tevera said in a small voice.

Kriss felt a curious emptiness inside. He had known Rigel only as an enemy—yet in the end, that "enemy" had saved his life—*all* their lives. *This* time, Rigel hadn't stood by helplessly while 'worldhuggers' killed his family. *This* time, he'd stopped it. "Apology accepted, Rigel," he whispered.

Nicora cleared her throat. "There is one other matter we should discuss," she said. "What are your plans, Kriss?"

He stared at her. "What?"

She spread her hands. "You know your true identity. Your enemy is gone. The Commonwealth recognizes you as an Earth citizen. You've not only inherited your parents' rather substantial financial resources, you have Finder's Rights to this site, and a Commonwealth court in possession of all the facts would undoubtedly grant you a rather enormous compensation from Vorlick's estate, should you choose to pursue it. You are, in short, enormously wealthy."

Kriss saw Tevera's eyes widen and realized she was hearing this for the first time. For a moment, he wondered how Nicora knew about his inheritance . . . and a moment later, knew, because he remembered it from one of those long nights of study, trying to familiarize himself with every aspect of the Family Rule.

Family members' individual financial accounts are open to the captain of a Family ship, he remembered reading. At the time, he hadn't thought he'd ever *have* financial accounts of his own. *The Commonwealth would have been informed I'm now of the Family, and the Library would therefore have transmitted my new financial status to the* Thaylia, *for Captain Nicora's attention.*

"All of this means that the reasons you gave on Farr's World for joining the Family no longer exist," Nicora continued. "And I cannot deny we have wronged you, severely, and more than once." She looked him in the eye. "It is your choice, Kriss Lemarc. Do you remain Family?"

Kriss looked down at the touchlyre, seemingly untouched by all the violence it had engendered. He lifted it into playing position and, for the first time, let his fingers caress the copper plates. The strings shivered to life, murmuring a faint chord, and he felt a familiar touch in his mind.

Weapon, key, musical instrument, or all three, the touchlyre, and the alien artifact at its heart, was part of him. He had loved it, and hated it; lost it, and found it again. In a most unexpected fashion, it had brought him everything he had dreamed it might, back when Mella first gave it to him: knowledge of his parents, the freedom of the stars, and . . .

Though he spoke to Nicora, it was Tevera's eyes he held with his own. "Captain, I want the same thing I've always wanted—a place to belong, with people I love." He reached out his hand, and Tevera leaned forward and took it, her fingers warm and solid and alive and wonderful. "And I've found it."

The light that came into Tevera's tear-stained face was like the dawn of a bright new day.

THE END

About the Author

EDWARD WILLETT is the author of more than sixty books of science fiction, fantasy, and nonfiction for readers of all ages. *Marseguro* (DAW Books) won Canada's Aurora Award for Best Long-Form Work in English in 2009. His young adult fantasy *Spirit Singer* (Shadowpaw Press) won the Regina Book Award for best book by a Regina author at the 2002 Saskatchewan Book Awards. Several other of his books have been shortlisted for those and other awards.

Ed's most recent novels are *Worldshaper*, *Master of the World*, and *The Moonlit World*, the first three books in the *Worldshapers* series (DAW Books). Other recent titles include *The Cityborn* and the *Masks of Aygrima* trilogy (written as E.C. Blake), also from DAW; for Bundoran Press, the *Peregrine Rising* duology (*Right to Know* and *Falcon's Egg*)' and the five-book *Shards of Excalibur* young-adult fantasy series (recently re-released by Shadowpaw Press). His non-fiction runs the gamut from science books to biographies to history. He hosts *The Worldshapers* podcast (theworldshapers.com), winner of the 2019 Aurora Award for Best Fan Related Work, in which he talks to other science fiction and fantasy authors about their creative process.

Born in Silver City, New Mexico, Ed moved to Saskatchewan from Texas at the age of eight, and grew up in Weyburn, where his father taught at Western Christian College. He earned a BA in journalism from Harding University in Searcy, Arkansas, and returned to Weyburn to begin his career at the weekly *Weyburn Review*, first as a reporter/photographer/columnist/cartoonist, and eventually as news editor. He moved to Regina in 1988 as communications officer for the then-fledgling Saskatchewan Science Centre. He began writing full-time in 1993.

For most of two decades, Ed wrote a weekly science column that appeared in the *Regina LeaderPost* and other newspapers, and talked about science weekly on CBC Saskatchewan's *Afternoon Edition* radio program.

In addition to being a writer, Ed is a professional actor and singer who has performed in numerous plays, musicals, and operas, and sung in several auditioned choirs, including the Canadian Chamber Choir. He lives in Regina, Saskatchewan, with his wife, Margaret Anne Hodges, P. Eng., a past president of the Association of Professional Engineers and Geoscientists of Saskatchewan. They have one daughter, Alice, and a black Siberian cat, Shadowpaw.

You can find Ed online at www.edwardwillett.com.

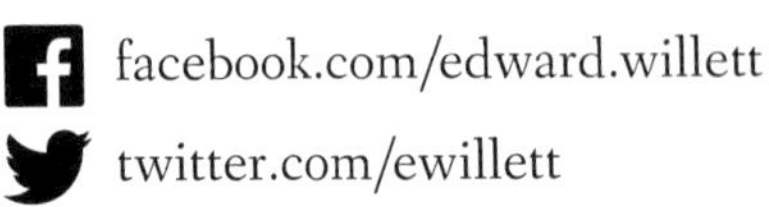

Also by Edward Willett (Selected)

From DAW Books

Lost in Translation

The Cityborn

The Tangled Stars

Magebane

(written as Lee Arthur Chane)

THE HELIX WAR

Marseguro

Terra Insegura

WORLDSHAPERS

Worldshaper

Master of the World

The Moonlit World

MASKS OF AYGRIMA

(as E.C. Blake)

Masks

Shadows

Faces

From Shadowpaw Press

Paths to the Stars

Spirit Singer

From the Street to the Stars

Blue Fire (as E.C. Blake)

PEREGRINE RISING

Right to Know

Falcon's Egg

THE SHARDS OF EXCALIBUR

Song of the Sword

Twist of the Blade

Lake in the Clouds

Cave Beneath the Sea

Door into Faerie

From Your Nickel's Worth Publishing

I Tumble through the Diamond Dust:

A Collection of Fantastical Poems